NIGHT OF ECSTASY

"A man has needs, Annabeth. A man needs a wife."

"Well, you have a wife now!" She spoke impetuously.

"Do I, Annabeth?" Eben came very close and, cupping her face in his two hands, looked deeply into her eyes. "Do I?"

His eyes seemed to mesmerize her as his thumb slowly, provocatively, traced the outline of her lips. She trembled at his touch.

"You're sure, Annabeth?" he muttered hoarsely. "You're sure it's what you want?"

In lieu of a verbal response, she found herself nibbling and delicately nipping at the fleshy part of his thumb.

Her unspoken answer told him all he needed to know. And he pulled her down onto the soft pile of pelts that constituted their bed....

Other *Leisure Books* by Sue Deobold:

THE MILITANT HEART

SAVAGE SPLENDOR

SUE DEOBOLD

LEISURE BOOKS **NEW YORK CITY**

A LEISURE BOOK®

June 1992

Published by

Dorchester Publishing Co., Inc.
276 Fifth Avenue
New York, NY 10001

Printed in the United States of America.

Prologue

"Earth to earth, ashes to ashes, dust to dust." The girl in the sunbonnet and trailworn calico gown stooped and picked up a handful of loose dirt, sprinkling it over the open grave as she intoned the phrase that had become so painfully familiar during these last weeks. Grasping a spade that was propped against the wagon-tongue in readiness, she began to fill in the grave, bending her back to the task as she whispered a heartfelt prayer, "Lord, let him lie easy." Asa, himself, had performed this last grim task for the others who had succumbed to the fever that had swept through their little wagon train. Now she was the only one left to say the words over Asa's fever-racked body and perform the last rites.

There was no one left to do it for her. No one to commend the soul of Annabeth Allan to her Maker. No one to read from Holy Writ, to dig a hole in the hard-packed earth, to shovel clods of dirt over a shallow grave and pile a cairn of stones on top, as she was doing for Asa. She shuddered. Her bones would be gnawed by wolves and coyotes and scattered over the plains to be picked clean by vultures and buzzards.

Even now they were circling overhead. How did they know? she wondered, tucking a stray lock of auburn hair back into the plain bun she wore low at the nape of her neck as she gazed up at the blue prairie sky. How did they know that she was alone and sick and helpless? How did they know that soon it would be her turn? That all they had to do was wait.

Her fingers were raw and bleeding from the rough sharp stones she had laboriously collected and she wiped them on her skirt as she knelt by the grave and tried to pray but the words wouldn't come. Her mouth was as dry as cotton wool and her head muzzy with fever. Weakly she tried to marshal her thoughts but they wouldn't be marshaled. Scraps and fragments of hymns and prayers floated through her mind, as elusive and impossible to grasp as the fleecy white clouds that floated in the sky above. Finally she groped in her pocket for the small leather-bound Bible that had been her mother's. It fell open at her favorite psalm, the Twenty-Third. The small print jumbled, dancing before her eyes as she licked her dry cracked lips and whispered, "The Lord is my Shepherd; I shall not want. He maketh me to lie down in green pastures; He leadeth me beside the still waters . . ."

Water. She must have water. She was burning up with fever though at the same time shaking with chills. Painfully she pulled herself to her feet, dropping the book at the graveside, and staggered to the water barrel that was lashed to the side of the wagon. They had made a dry camp when Asa was stricken and what liquid was left was brackish and warm but it was wet, blessedly wet on her parched lips and swollen throat. Temporarily it revived her.

There was nothing more she could do for the dead but there was something she could do for the living—the horses. She knew that she wouldn't be able to grain and water them much longer. With the fever already consuming her it was all she could do to care for herself. But if she cut the horses loose from the traces they would be able to forage for themselves. Find water if there was any in this dry and barren land.

She realized, of course, that by turning the horses loose she would be stranding herself on this lonesome prairie. But what did that matter now? Wasn't she already doomed? Even if she survived the fever, she wouldn'be be able to make her way back to civilization on her own. Still less could she go forward and cross the Rockies all by herself. And there wouldn't be any other wagon trains coming along behind. Not this late in the season. They had been the last to leave Independence.

Her head spinning, her ears buzzing, she stumbled to the team and sawed clumsily at the harness with Asa's pocketknife, blinking back tears. It had been one of her husband's most prized possessions, a gift from his father on the boy's twelfth birthday. That was the day he had carved his initials and hers, entwined in a heart, on the courting tree in the schoolyard.

Oh, what was the use of remembering? Asa was gone and she was going to die here in this lonely place, far from home and equally far from Oregon. Her bones would lie, bleached and whitened, joining others she had seen of men and animals along the lonesome trail. And there was nothing she could do to save herself. Nothing at all. Turning the horses loose to fend for themselves was the only humane thing to do, she decided regretfully.

Summoning the last of her waning strength she hacked away at the harness that connected the animals to the wagon, too weak to cope with buckles and straps, to unhitch in the normal fashion. She was sobbing with exhaustion and frustration when the wheel horse, a sturdy bay mare with a dash of Morgan blood, lifted her head and whinnied, nostrils flaring.

Annabeth dragged herself to the horses' heads and, shading her eyes from the sun's glare, looked searchingly out across the vast ocean of prairie grass that was scorched brown by the midsummer heat. There was nothing, she thought, so lonely as the prairie that unrolled itself so long and so far ahead of her. The land flowed and curved and way off to the west the sky flowed and curved down to meet the land. It was a sad, grieving, melancholy kind of land, making you feel as small and insignificant as a speck of dust. It weighed you down, pressed on you, burdened you with the weight of its loneliness, its lifelessness.

But . . . was it so lifeless after all? There was—she squinted, unable to believe her own eyes—something moving out there! Clouds of dust, like that raised by a wagon train, shimmered in the heat haze and, for a moment, a ray of hope pierced her despair. But only for a moment. No wagon train would be heading east instead of west. It could be a party of traders, though, carrying furs to exchange for trade goods in the Eastern settlements. Her heart beat faster and she strained her eyes to see through the thick veil of dust. At last she could make out tiny figures, some on horseback, others on foot. And then, smaller figures, darting here and there, running with the aimless hither-and-yon motion of children at play.

Indians!

Annabeth turned her face into the horse's mane and sobbed weakly. If she didn't die from fever she would be at the mercy of redskinned savages. The fierce and warlike Plains Indians were well-known to be hostile to whites passing through their territory. And while a few minutes ago, she had been resigned to death, to have her hopes raised only to be immediately dashed again was too much to bear!

Something, she never knew what, alerted her to imminent danger. Detaching her arms from the horse's neck, she whirled and, clutching the pocketknife in a gesture of defiance, prepared to sell her life dearly.

A lone figure, probably a scout from the tribe, had circled round and was stalking her. Dressed in fringed buckskins, he was mounted on a pinto stallion and carried a rifle, cocked and ready. She glimpsed a dark face, piercing black eyes, shaggy black hair which floated past his shoulders; one side of his hair was braided with a bright red ribbon.

He was altogether a figure of terror; a devil in buckskins!

Annabeth fainted.

1

"Who . . . who are you?" Annabeth licked cracked fever-blistered lips. Her eyes were still bright with fever and her tongue felt thick and furry but she felt reasonably clearheaded.

The man ignored her question. "Drink this," he ordered. He held a tin cup to her lips, a strong arm supporting her back as she struggled to sit up. The liquid, whatever it was, tasted terrible but it was wet and she gulped it greedily. "Easy now," the man cautioned. "You drink too much too fast and it'll all come back on you." He removed the cup from her hand and she whimpered with frustration.

Then her eyes widened as a hazy memory came back to haunt her. She tossed her head from side to side, her eyes filled with fear. "Where . . . where is he? Did you kill him?" she fretted.

"Who, ma'am?" The man spoke patiently, soothingly, wondering if she was still lost in delirium.

"Why . . . why, the Indian, of course."

He hesitated. "Ain't no Indian here," he said finally. "There ain't nothing to be afraid of," he assured her, restoring the cup to her lips. When she had drained its contents and begged for more, he said firmly, "That's enough for now. I got some rabbit stew simmering in the pot. In a little while you can have some of the broth," he promised, easing her back down on the bedding.

Annabeth gasped as the top blanket slipped away and she realized with a sense of shock that she was completely nude beneath it. "I . . . I don't have any clothes on!" she squeaked, snatching at the blanket and yanking it back over her naked body, pulling it all the way up to her neck. "You took my clothes!" she accused in outrage.

The little lines that fanned out from around the man's eyes deepened and his lips twitched. "Yes, ma'am, I surely did," he agreed equably. "I'm glad you're feeling well enough to fuss about it. That's a good sign," he said encouragingly. "There was a time or two I figgered you was gone beaver!"

"Er . . . 'gone beaver'?" she repeated, puzzled by this obscure remark.

"Mountain man lingo, ma'am. Means I didn't think you was gonna pull through. I thought you was a goner, for sure."

"Are you a . . . a mountain man? A trapper?" she asked doubtfully. "Not . . . not an Indian?" For a sudden horrifying suspicion had assailed her. The man, the stranger, didn't *sound* like an Indian. His voice was gentle and soothing, his words drawled in the soft slow cadence of the South, not harsh and guttural as she imagined an Indian's would be. But he *looked* enough like an Indian to pass as one. He had, thought Annabeth, one of the most arresting faces she had ever seen. It was strong and square-jawed, his tanned weather-beaten skin pulled taut over his high cheekbones, his eyes dark and deepset, his lips set firm and . . . and, well, *sensual*. It wasn't a word Annabeth had often had occasion to think of and her mind skittered away from it in alarm.

She was slowly beginning to put the pieces of the puzzle together and she didn't like the way they fitted. The dark face, the long black hair, now neatly tied back out of the way with a red ribbon. *A red ribbon!* With a gasp of horror, Annabeth realized that her rescuer and the demon in buckskin were one and the same.

But . . . "*Not* an Indian," he was saying firmly. Not Plains Indian, leastways. Though my old grannie back in Kentuck was part Shawnee."

"Oh," she murmured weakly. That accounted for his appearance, then, though . . .

"Bother you, does it?" His voice was suddenly scornful.

"Of course not," she denied swiftly. "But . . . that is . . . *who* are you? What are you doing here? And . . . and . . ." she swallowed hard, "Why did you undress me?"

He answered her last question first. "The way you was sweating when the fever broke I couldn't keep you in a dry nightgown. Finally figgered it wasn't worth wrestling you into one, neither."

"You . . . you changed my gowns?" Annabeth said faintly.

"Nobody else to do it, ma'am. Don't let it fret you none," he said easily.

Don't let it fret her! How could it not? Dim memories returned with his words. Of herself rambling in delirium. Of strong hands lifting and turning her, cleansing her, sponging her fevered body. She'd thought, as she drifted in and out of consciousness, that they belonged to Uncle Henry or even Aunt Anna whose big workhardened hands were as strong as a man's. She'd imagined herself back in her snug little bedroom at home with Uncle Henry and Aunt Anna nursing her through the fever as they had when she was ten years old and strikened with diptheria. At times she could have sworn she'd felt Aunt Elizabeth's gentle touch, heard her soft voice praying over her just as she had when Annabeth was so gravely ill all those years ago. They hadn't let her die then and they wouldn't let her die now, she'd thought in her delirium.

But it hadn't been her uncle and aunts who had pulled her through this. It had been this dark-faced stranger who had nursed her and cosseted her. She owed her life to him, Annabeth realized with dismay.

"I . . . you saved my life," she whispered feebly. "I—"

"Think nothing of it, ma'am," he said quickly. "Out here, we mostly help each other out. And the day may come when you'll have a chance to repay the debt."

It didn't seem likely. She couldn't visualize any circumstances in which this strong, self-sufficient man would need a helping hand from anybody, let alone her, but she let it pass. "But . . . but where did you come from?" she demanded fretfully. "You—" Her eyes widened. "You were with those Indians, weren't you?"

He had been hunkered down beside her pallet; now he stood up, the sudden lithe movement startling her. "Best you get some sleep now, ma'am. When you wake up that broth will be ready."

She half-closed her eyes obediently but she didn't sleep. Instead she watched him through slitted lids, saw him moving about the wagon, a big man accommodating himself to the cramped quarters as he performed ordinary domestic tasks, sorting clothing and blankets to be washed, though she couldn't see how. They must be almost out of water by now.

That led her to speculate on how long she had been ill. When he came to her bed a little while later, a spoon in one hand and a cup of broth in the other, she asked him.

He sat her up, bracing her back against his broad shoulder while he spooned broth into her mouth. "I didn't keep track of the days," he said briefly. "It's dirt-in-the-face moon; the moon when the dry dust blows. Fall."

"Fall!" she squeaked. "Autumn!" It couldn't be! It had been late summer when Asa died. "But that means I must have been lying here for weeks," she marveled.

"Reckon so," he admitted laconically.

"But we must be nearly out of food. And how can there be any water left?" she fretted.

"There's water close by if you know where to look for it. I've been snaring rabbits for food and a friend of mine left a haunch of buffalo for us."

"A friend?" she said, puzzled. "Another trapper?"

"Eat!" he commanded, spooning broth into her mouth like a parent bird feeding its young. He chuckled, watching her anchor the blanket more firmly about her with an elbow. "After your meal I'll sponge you down and help you into a clean nightgown," he offered.

"I'll sponge myself down, thank you just the

same!" she snapped.

But the sheer effort of sitting up, of talking, of eating, of chewing the rather stringy bits of rabbit meat in the broth exhausted her and she fell back against the bedding, utterly worn out. "Later," she pleaded when he approached her with a basin of water and a wash rag.

Seeing the dark circles that signaled exhaustion under her heavy-lidded eyes, he nodded. Almost immediately she fell into a deep sleep that lasted for hours. When she woke, later in the day, she wasn't surprised to find him sitting cross-legged beside her pallet, plaiting strips of buckskin onto a willow frame.

"What's that?" she asked suspiciously.

"A backrest," he said placidly. "The Indians use them for reclining against."

"Like a sofa . . . or divan?"

"Something like that." His skillful fingers deftly wove the buckskin plaits together as he spoke. "I figgered you'd like to try sitting up on your own."

"Oh, I would!" Annabeth was suddenly eager to try it. The first time he'd helped her to sit up she'd been too dazed, too weak, to notice that she was being supported by his arm and shoulder, but the second time when he'd fed her the broth, she'd felt the strangest sensations as his arm encircled her. She wasn't eager to feel those vaguely disturbing sensations again. If she could sit up on her own, she would be, if only marginally, more independent of him and his ministrations. She waited with growing impatience until he had fashioned the backrest to his satisfaction.

It was surprisingly comfortable. And it felt good to have her back supported by something solid. Not that the man's arm and shoulder hadn't been solid with rippling muscles, she mused, solid but . . . vaguely disturbing. She'd found the proximity of so much vibrant masculinity distinctly unnerving. The backrest, by comparison, was reassuringly impersonal.

She sipped another cup of broth, drank a mug of the noxious liquid that was, according to her rescuer, supposed to promote healing and reduce fever, and insisted on giving herself an admittedly sketchy bed-bath. Those things she could do for herself she was determined to do or die trying!

But the voluminous folds of the nightgown defeated her. By the time she had finished dabbing at her pitifully thin body with a dampened cloth, she was sweating from the exertion and her struggles with the nightie's gathers, tucks and buttons exhausted her.

He had stepped outside while she was bathing but the little whimpers of frustration she expelled in dealing with the nightgown brought him back to the wagon. "Hush now," he said sternly. "You're just hell-bent to do to much too soon, ain't you? You want to end up flat on your back again?"

"No," she said resentfully, pulling the blanket up to her neck. "I can do it myself. I *can!*" she insisted mulishly, watching him pick up the long white gown, ruffled at bodice, neckline, and wrist. It looked utterly incongruous in his strong brown hands.

"Hush your mouth and hold up your arms."

"I can't," Annabeth said with a quaver in her voice. "The blanket—"

He sighed. "All right, all *right*. I ain't gonna look at you," he promised, averting his face.

Annabeth hesitated, then held up her arms

obediently, letting the blanket fall away.

Face averted, the man pulled the opening over her head, helped her stuff her arms in the armholes, buttoned the frilled bodice by touch. Annabeth felt briefly like a tiny child again, being stuffed into a garment by an impatient Aunt Anna. Aunt Elizabeth had had infinite patience with her, she remembered, taking pleasure in dressing and undressing her like a doll. But Aunt Anna had yanked and pushed and pulled; impatient to get on to the next task she had pulled a fine-tooth comb with ruthless speed through the snarls and tangles of her niece's red-gold hair.

Her hair! Annabeth put a questing hand to her head which, now that she came to think about it, felt uncommonly light and cool. There should have been a heavy plait, as thick as a man's wrist, on either side of her head. Or a flowing molten-copper mass, hanging below her waist.

It wasn't there. Frantic, she patted her head all over. It was . . . it was . . . stubble! "My hair!" she moaned.

"It was falling out in handfuls from the fever," the man said gently. "So I cut it. Figgered it'd be cooler, too, and easier to take care of. It'll grow back again in no time," he reassured her quickly.

"Oh, no-o-o," she wailed. "It . . . I . . . oh, it must be hideous!"

"No it ain't," he said staunchly. "It looks real cute. You got little red-gold curls all over your head. It's mighty pretty."

"Pretty!" she said with loathing, remembering the glorious copper mane she had been able to sit upon. Asa had loved to watch her brush it each night and morning, one hundred strokes each time. Her hair, she was sure, had been her one claim to beauty and Aunt Anna had often chided her for being vain of it.

"Bring me a mirror," she demanded imperiously. "There's one in the top right-hand drawer of the dresser."

The man got up and moved slowly to the dresser, a massive piece of heavy oak furniture that he knew full well would never have made it across the mountains. It would have had to be abandoned somewhere along the trail. He pulled open the drawer and rummaged in it. "Ain't no mirror here," he said after a futile search.

"There must be," Annabeth insisted. Until Asa had been stricken and all her time had been taken up in caring for him, she had kept the wagon spotlessly neat and tidy. Everything had been arranged just so, in order to save space and make room—a place for everything and everything in its place as Aunt Anna had taught her. She certainly hadn't spent any time gazing into mirrors while she was nursing Asa so the mirror must still be there; she couldn't have misplaced it.

The man quit pretending to search through the drawer; he shut it with finality and stood with his back to the dresser. "Annabeth, there's something you gotta know—your name *is* Annabeth, ain't it?"

"Yes, but how did you know?" she sniffed, perilously close to tears, the weak easy tears of a pettish invalid.

He brushed the question aside as being of no importance. "Annabeth, you're damned lucky to be alive. That fever . . . it was smallpox." His voice trailed away.

She drew in her breath in a long shuddering

sob. She'd known. Of course she'd known but she hadn't admitted it even to herself. Then, remembering the horrible pustules that had disfigured Asa and the others, her voice rose to a hysterical pitch. "I'm marked, disfigured. That's what you're trying to tell me. That I'm scarred—scarred for life!"

"No!" His voice cracked like a mule skinner's bullwhip. "It ain't that bad. I tied your hands down when you was delirious so that you couldn't dig and scratch at the blisters. And what few marks you do have will fade in time." In one long stride he was beside her. "Look at me, Annabeth," he insisted. "I had the pox when I was a boy but I ain't scarred now."

She looked up at him tearfully. He hunkered down beside the pallet so that she could give him a close inspection. "You take a real good look," he ordered. "Go on, look!" He brought his face down close to her own, so close that she could feel his breath fanning her cheek. Weakly she turned her face away but he caught her chin in his palm, forcing her to look him full in the face.

Annabeth glared at him with eyes burning with resentment and frustration. Why, oh why hadn't he let her die and be done with it? But his fierce hawklike eyes caught and held her own. They were not, as she had first thought, black but a deep dark blue. The combination of blue eyes in such a dark face was arresting. Little lines fanned out from the corners of those eyes and the face itself, bronzed by sun and wind, was carved into harsh lines drawn by adversity and lean hard living in this tough exacting western land. But there were, she saw as she searched his face, no pockmarks.

"Well?" he demanded. "You see any pock-marks?"

"No . . . n-no," Annabeth admitted. "But—but there was a woman in the village back home . . . she'd had the pox when she was young and . . . and she was horribly disfigured. She never set foot out of the house unless she had to and then she wore a thick black veil . . . like a widow, you know."

"Well, maybe she was being considerate—not wanting to scare children and startle horses," he said gruffly. "Then again, maybe she just didn't have any gumption. You ever think of that, Anna-beth?"

Annabeth hadn't. "Gumption?" she said weakly.

"Guts!" His tone was fierce. "Now you're a gal with plenty of sand in your craw and every grain of it is going to be needed out here!" He sighed. "I figgered you for a gal who has what it takes. You pulled through a bout of fever that's killed many a man. And before that I reckon you nursed whoever's lying out in that grave and buried him proper. Your pa, was it?" he guessed. "Your ma? Or your man?"

"My . . . my husband," she said weakly.

"Well, now, you've had it rough, little lady, and likely to have it rougher," he said grimly. "You gonna fold up on me now, all on account of a few pockmarks?"

Annabeth caught her quivering lower lip in her small white teeth, the wildness fading from her eyes.

"No," she said, drawing a shaky breath. "No, I won't fold up on you," she promised.

"Good," he said hearteningly. "I wouldn't like to think all my efforts were wasted. You owe me anything for coming to your rescue, you owe me that." He stood up. "In a few days, when you get your strength back and some color in your cheeks you can get that mirror for yourself. It won't seem so bad then. For now, you better get some more rest." He picked up her mother's Bible and put it into her hands. "Maybe the Good Book will give you some comfort."

Annabeth lay back clutching the worn leather Bible. She didn't need to read it for comfort. She knew many of the passages by heart, thanks to long winter evenings when Uncle Henry had read aloud from it, starting at Genesis and reading straight through to Revelations (not skipping the "begats"). It was a link with home and family and she caressed the worn bindings in fond remembrance, finally opening it to the front page where her mother had inscribed her name on her wedding day and later the date of her daughter's birth. Annabeth had proudly inscribed her new name on her own wedding day and the date, March 2, 1847. She sighed. Only a few short months ago she had been a happy bride. She smiled remembering Asa in his stiff black broadcloth, herself in rustling blue bombazine, with puffed sleeves and three wide tucks around her hips. Bombazine was so practical, Aunt Anna had insisted, since it could easily be died black for funerals! Only there hadn't been any funeral for Asa, no mourners except herself.

She stared at the page through a sheen of tears, the print dancing before her eyes. Annabeth Allan! Of course—*that* was how the stranger knew her name! Well, at least he could read! He wasn't totally a savage—this wild mountain man. The thought was reassuring.

But what was going to become of her now? Would he take her back to the Eastern settlements? To Independence or St. Louis? From there she could make her way back to her family in York State.

Annabeth set her pretty round chin. It wasn't square and determined like the stranger's but she had her own share of subbornness all the same. She and Asa had set their faces to the West and she was not going to turn back just because he was gone. For she, like Asa, had received a Call to the Whitman mission in Oregon. And the Lord, she was sure, had spared her life for some purpose of His own. Doubtless it was His will that she be pockmarked and plain and shorn of her crowning glory, the better to accomplish His purpose. Now why hadn't she thought of that before? It was notorious that God tested his chosen and that the way was never quick and easy. Well, she would set her shoulder to God's work . . . do her share and Asa's too at the Waiilatput mission!

Her smile suddenly faded. The American Board of Missions insisted on married couples only. It was their policy to send out a man and a woman two by two, like Noah's Ark. Annabeth frowned. Now that she was a widow she didn't meet their qualifications. But, surely, if only she could make her way to the Waiilatput Mission, Dr. and Mrs. Whitman wouldn't turn her away. They were such extraordinary people. She remembered them well. Dr. Whitman had practiced medicine in her own home town before going west. And it was Narcissa Whitman's letters to the folks back home that had inspired her and Asa to emulate them.

No, they wouldn't send her back. They just couldn't. Not if she could make her way to Oregon and convince them of her usefulness. She would be another pair of hands to do the Lord's work and she would do it cheerfully, no matter how dirty or disagreeable it might be.

But *how* was she going to get there? There was the stranger, of course; she could pay him—not well, but enough—to serve as her guide. If he was a trapper, a mountain man, he probably knew the Rockies like the back of his own hand. So, why wouldn't he—for a fee, of course—be perfectly willing to guide her over the mountains? It didn't take long to persuade herself that he would.

Onward—to Oregon!

Buoyant with hope, convinced of the viability of her scheme, Annabeth dozed off with a smile on her face. But she didn't feel quite so optimistic when she woke at dusk. She felt miserable. Perhaps sitting up so long the first day had been a mistake. One thing was sure—drinking all those liquids her rescuer had forced down her throat that afternoon had definitely been a mistake! She squirmed uncomfortably. She hadn't given this embarrassing aspect of her illness a thought earlier in the day—well, hardly a thought. At first she had been too astonished just to find herself alive and then too upset by the loss of her hair and the disquieting possibility of being disfigured for life. At the moment, in her extreme discomfort, this seemed a surprisingly trivial complaint.

She refused her supper, pettishly shoving away the bowl of thin gruel he offered her. The last thing she needed was any more liquid—what she needed was to go outside but she was so weak she knew she would topple over if she so much as set foot on the wagonbed, let alone find the strength to clamber over the tailgate and seek privacy in the growing darkness.

What was she going to do? she wondered in desperation. Her common sense told her that this man had been tending to her physical needs all along—but that had been while she was unconscious. She shrank from confessing her need to him—Good Lord, she didn't even know his name.

As her desperation grew, she tossed and turned, squirming restlessly. Finally, the man got up from his own supper and came over to her, concern showing on his face. "Your fever coming back?" he asked, feeling her forehead with a practiced hand.

"No!" She snapped irritably.

He looked at her keenly. "Well, then, you ready to get settled for the night?"

"Yes." She said shortly, expecting him to remove the backrest so that she could lie flat.

But instead he produced a basin and deftly slipped it beneath her. "I'll be outside. Call me when you're done," he said gruffly and disappeared.

The relief was exquisite, reducing even the necessity of calling him to her assistance to manageable proportions—a minor embarrassment.

When he had Annabeth settled down, substituting a pillow for the backrest, he made his own preparations for the night. He shed his shirt, the muscles rippling under his bronze skin but, to her relief, kept his fringed buckskin trousers on. Going to a pallet on the far side of the wagonbed, he explained, "I've been sleeping in here, in case you needed me but when you're a little stronger I'll bed down under the wagon."

"I don't think I'll be needing anything more tonight," Annabeth said swiftly.

"Never can tell," he grunted, extinguishing the lantern.

"I don't even know your name," she said wonderingly.

"It's Eben." He hesitated. "Eben McDowell."

"Eben," she repeated softly. "That's a nice name." And appropriate, she mused. Asa had been a divinity student and she knew, from bits of knowledge that he had passed on to her, that "Eben" in Hebrew meant "Stone of Help". "A very nice name," she repeated sleepily. "Goodnight, Eben."

"Goodnight, Annabeth."

2

That day set the pattern for those that followed. Eben tended to her needs with impersonal efficiency, stuffed her with small amounts of nourishing food at frequent intervals, kept the wagon spotlessly tidy, looked after the stock, but refused to gratify her curiosity about himself, adroitly changing the subject whenever she turned the conversation to personal topics. Her curiosity grew as she gained strength until she could hardly contain it. She spent most of her waking hours speculating about him.

Finally, on a beautiful autumn day when he had scooped her into his arms and carried her outside, bedding and all, to bask in the waning warmth of the sun, she decided it was time for a showdown.

"Eben," she demanded his attention. "Where did you come from that day? The day you came to my rescue. One minute you weren't there. And then, the next minute, you were. And how did you manage to fight off all those savages by yourself?" Her brow wrinkled. "Or, did I only imagine them? Were they a figment of my imagination? Conjured up by a fevered brain in delirium?"

28

He evaded her with his usual skill. "You warm enough, Annabeth?" He tucked a blanket more tightly around her. "There's a bit of a breeze. Don't want you catching a chill."

"I'm plenty warm enough," she snapped. "And I want to know. Why do you insist on being a mystery man?" she demanded querulously, kicking at the confining blanket.

"Ain't no mystery about it, Annabeth." He sighed. "The savages, as you call them, weren't no figment of your imagination. And I didn't have to fight 'em off. I was with them."

"With them!" Her voice raised several octaves. It was, to be sure, no more than she had suspected all along but to have her suspicions confirmed so calmly . . .

"The Cheyenne ain't murdering bloodthirsty savages, Annabeth," he said mildly. "They're human beings, people, same as you and me. *My* people," he said with emphasis. "We didn't have no designs on you or your wagon. It was no war party. We were out on a buffalo hunt when we saw the buzzards circling and I moseyed on over to investigate. And there you were," he chuckled, "a slip of a girl, brandishing that penknife as if you expected to take a scalp with it!"

"It was my scalp I expected to get lifted!" she retorted.

"Would have made a good one!" he teased in his easy drawl. He grinned reminiscently. "But if the Cheyenne had found you they would have taken you captive. Married you to one of the bucks, most likely."

"A fate worse than death!" Annabeth said in horror.

His broad shoulders rose and fell in an indifferent shrug. "Depends on your point of view, I suppose. Myself, I figger living is preferable to dying, most times. Death comes soon enough to us all. And they wouldn't have treated you bad, except maybe just at first. Until you learned their ways. Especially if you showed courage and learned quick."

Annabeth shuddered all the same. "I'm glad it was you who found me, Eben."

"So am I. But not necessarily for the reason you're thinking of," he said cryptically.

She looked at him, puzzled. "Why, what do you mean?"

"If the Cheyenne had found you first, you would have brought death and suffering to untold numbers of them," he said flatly.

She looked at him, wide-eyed. What on earth was he talking about?" she wondered.

"The pox," he said impatiently. "Indians got little or no resistance to the diseases the white men bring."

"We also bring civilization," Annabeth said defensively.

Eben's mouth twisted in scorn. "Oh, is that what you call it? Disease and rotgut liquor and the plough that'll bury the buffalo."

"Civilization," she insisted, stung. "Law and order, the blessings of Christianity—"

"The Cheyenne got their own law and order within a highly developed society. And they have their own religion too. They don't need the white man's God!"

Annabeth reeled in shock. It was . . . it was blasphemy to compare the superstitious beliefs of heathen redskins to Christianity! An impulsive rebuke trembled on her lips but she swallowed it down. The man was ignorant and untutored, probably through no fault of his own, and it was the duty of a true Christian to enlighten ignorance, to teach by patient precept and example. So she merely said kindly, "No doubt your Indian friends do have a 'religion' of a kind but it is a savage heathen religion, full of superstition."

"No more'n any other religion, I'd say," he observed.

Annabeth ground her teeth. Was it her physical weakness that so quickly exhausted her patience with him? she wondered. "But there is only one true God, Eben," she protested, "and they are ignorant of his word as revealed in scripture. My husband and I came west to spread the Word to the heathen and—"

He drew in his breath sharply. "Missionaries!" he ejaculated.

"Yes. We were headed for Oregon, to the Whitman Mission."

"I should have known," he responded with disgust. "Only missionaries would be damn fools enough to start out with only one wagon so late in the season."

"It wasn't just one wagon to begin with," Annabeth said defensively. "We were a party of six, with three wagons. We joined up with a large wagon train at Independence. But bad luck dogged us all the way."

He looked at her enquiringly.

"Our horses strayed one night and it took the better part of a day to round them up. They were hobbled but—"

Eben grunted. "Sounds to me more like poor management than bad luck. A horse can travel miles on a hobble. They should have been staked out on a picket line. You'd have done better with oxen anyway. They last longer and fare better on the trail."

Color flared in Annabeth's face but she kept her temper. "So we were told," she said briefly. "Well, then," she resumed her story, "one of our wagons broke an axle fording the Big Blue and we had to call a halt to make repairs. The main party went on ahead. We thought we would catch up to them in a day or two but Eliza Sloane had a baby and that delayed us a while longer."

"You set out for Oregon with a woman so near her time!" Eben said incredulously. "The trail is no place for pregnant women!"

"The baby came too soon," Annabeth explained uneasily. "Eliza was in the wagon that tipped over in the river. She was thrown into the water and the fright precipitated the birth." She shrugged. "Well, we were held up for several days waiting for Eliza to get her strength back. Then, one night, a stranger, a trader, wandered into our camp. He was burning with fever." She sighed. "We didn't realize what ailed him until it was too late. By that time we'd all taken turns nursing him and all of us had been exposed to the disease. We were stricken down one by one until only Asa and I were left. We were the youngest and strongest, I suppose. When we'd buried the others, we moved on, thinking that we'd been spared. Then Asa fell ill and—" Her voice trailed off.

Her velvety brown eyes mirrored the horror of the tragedy she'd passed through and Eben said quickly, "You given any thought to what you're going to do now, Annabeth?"

As a diversionary tactic it succeeded admirably. Annabeth looked up at him, startled out of her reverie. "I . . . well, not exactly," she hedged, wondering if the time was right to mention her scheme to him. Her instincts told her that he would throw cold water on her plan to forge ahead to Oregon. He would say that the trail was no place for a lone woman, that even when she reached her destination she would have no man or kinfolk to look out for her . . . She was busy summoning all the arguments she could think of in her favor when he took the wind out of her sails by remarking thoughtfully, "I wish I could take you back to the States but I can't."

"Whyever not?" Annabeth exclaimed in surprise. She didn't really care; on the contrary, she was delighted that he wasn't insisting on her going back. But she was puzzled. It did seem the logical thing to do, to one who wasn't impelled by fervor as she was.

His rugged face darkened. "I can't. That's all there is to it," he said shortly.

She might better have left well enough alone since turning back was the last thing she wanted to do but her curiosity was piqued and she unwisely persisted. "But *why*? I could pay you well and—"

He shook his head. "It ain't a question of payment."

"Well, what is it then?"

He sighed, seeing the questions trembling on her lips. "You sure don't give up easy, do you, little lady?"

"Never!" she vowed, a rueful smile playing about her lips. She hadn't given up—not even in the teeth of her family's opposition to the Oregon scheme. And it was she who had persevered, who had overcome Asa's last-minute qualms about taking a sheltered young bride on a cross-country journey, convincing him that it would be a great and glorious adventure. Just at the moment she forgot how tragically that adventure had ended for Asa. She was convinced that she was on the verge of a discovery, that with a little probing she would learn something of the background of her mysterious rescuer.

"Well then, if you must know," he said harshly, "It's because there's a price on my head!"

"A . . . a price?" Annabeth's smile faded. "You mean you're a . . . a wanted man?" she faltered. "Wanted by the law?"

He nodded.

"But why? For what?" She had to know. Having come so far, she couldn't back down now—couldn't let it lie.

"Murder."

"Mur—" Annabeth gasped, feeling a chill shiver through her slight frame. The day that had seemed so warm and bright suddenly was dark and overcast, or so it seemed to her, as if Eben's terse announcement had cast a pall over the sun itself. Instinctively she tucked the blanket more tightly around herself as if to ward off a chill though she knew quite well that her discomfort was the effect of shock rather than that produced by wind and weather.

"Is . . . is that why you came out west?" she finally asked timorously. "To escape the law?"

He grinned mirthlessly. "Hell, no! I was no more'n a wet-behind-the-ears kid when I came out here. My paw, he was a wandering man and so was his father before him so I figger I come by it honest. Grandpaw, he follered Boone over the Cumberland Gap into Kentuck. My folks moved twice in Kentucky, once in Tennessee, then from Missouri up into Indiana. Paw died there, killed in a fall from a green-broke colt. My mama, she married again within the year. I can't fault her none for that. I was only a half-growed boy and there was five younger than me to provide for. But I didn't care for my new step-paw and he didn't take to me. I was a sight too fond of roaming the hills and woods to suit him when I should have been following behind the plow. We had words over it more'n once. Finally my mama gave me her blessings and my paw's Hawken rifle and I lit out for the shining mountains.

"Right off, I had the good luck to fall in with Old Gabe . . . Jim Bridger," he explained, seeing Annabeth's enquiring look. She nodded. Even in far-off New York State she had heard of the famed mountain man.

"Old Gabe kinda took me under his wing," Eben continued. "Showed me the way around the mountains, taught me all I know. I trapped with his brigade a number of years, until the price of beaver dropped and the bottom fell out of the fur trade."

"The . . . the man you killed . . . was he a trapper?" Annabeth couldn't help interrupting.

"No, that came later. Much later. And it wasn't murder, Annabeth. It was a fair fight." Eben's lips tightened and his dark eyes glittered like blue water over granite. "And the son-of-a-bitch needed killing!" His hand fell to the Bowie knife that hung at his belt. Withdrawing it from its beaded sheath he ran its thumb down the sharpened edge, his eyes dark with bitter memories. Suddenly, he took it by the point and flipped it end-over-end into the dirt at their feet where it stuck upright, the sun flashing on the bright blade as it quivered there between them.

Annabeth gulped. She knew she didn't need to ask how the deed had been done. She could imagine. But other questions that had been jostling around in her mind came tumbling to her lips. "But . . . who, Eben? And . . . and, *why?*" There had to be a reason . . . some compelling reason that had turned the thoughtful gentle man she knew into a wanted killer.

Eben sighed. "It happened in St. Louis. The bastard was kin to the Chouteau. They're a powerful family that made their money in the fur trade. The man I killed was a young sprig off the family tree and if I set foot in St. Louis or any of the eastern settlements, they'll have my hide."

"But you said it was a . . . a fair fight!" Annabeth protested.

"And so it was. Fair enough! I gave him a fighting chance. Better than the chance he gave my wife!"

"Your . . . your wife?" Annabeth echoed.

"My Cheyenne wife." Eben's white teeth snapped together. "The bastard killed my wife—after he'd raped her. I suppose he thought she was just another pretty little squaw to tumble. And that she wasn't willing just added to the spice of it. Well, he found out different!"

Annabeth was appalled at this bleak and bare recital. That Eben had loved his Indian "wife" devotedly and that her loss deeply grieved him was understandable. But it was no justification for taking the law into his own hands! Moreover, that he had been a "squaw man" like some of the other trappers and traders she had heard of, that he had lived with an Indian woman in an unsanctified union unblessed by the church was abhorrent to her. Almost as abhorrent as the fact that he was a man with blood on his hands. And though he had not said so in so many words, she felt sure that his wife's rapist was not the first man he had killed. How could it be otherwise when he had lived with the Cheyenne on friendly terms, when he had a Cheyenne wife? Why, he was virtually a white Indian himself!

All of this was deeply disturbing to Annabeth's eastern-bred sensibilities. She plucked nervously at the blanket while peering at him from behind the veil of her thickly fringed dark lashes. He *looked* like a man in complete control of himself but obviously appearances were deceptive. Underneath that impassive facade he must be a man of unbridled appetites—a man of passion and vengeance. She shivered. And she was at his mercy!

But he hadn't been anything but kind and gentle to her—so far—she reminded herself. And if she kept her wits about her perhaps she could turn the situation to her own advantage. It was already to her advantage that he couldn't take her back to the States—wasn't it?

She frowned. But if he couldn't take her back east what *was* he planning to do with her? He couldn't—he wouldn't—just turn her loose to fend for herself, would he? Even if she had her full strength back she would never be able to recross the prairie on her own. There were rivers to ford and a hundred other dangers that a lone woman couldn't possibly cope with. Annabeth sighed. For the first time she fully appreciated the reasoning behind the Board of Missions' refusal to send single women west. A woman needed a man out here, Annabeth had to admit to herself, albeit grudgingly. Sheer survival depended on it.

She bit her lip with vexation, gathered her courage and said, "What . . . what are you going to do with me?"

He hunkered down beside her, pulled the Bowie knife out of the earth and began whittling on a stick. "Well, now, I'm studying on that very thing. Seems to me, the best thing would be—"

"Because what I'd like you to do," she interrupted, "is guide me to Oregon."

"To Oregon!" he exclaimed. He shook his head. "Lady, I think you've been out in the sun too long! That's a crazy notion!"

Annabeth was taken aback by this blunt pronouncement. "I don't see why," she argued. "I—"

"No, I don't suppose you do." He ran a hand through his thick thatch of black hair. "Ma'am . . . Annabeth . . . you just can't cross the Rockies so late in the season. Nobody can. 'Fore you know it them passes will be blocked with snow."

"But—" Annabeth sputtered, reluctant to admit defeat, even though she could see the sense of what he was saying.

"No buts, Annabeth. I know what I'm talking about. No way in hell can you cross the Rockies this year. Now, in the spring I can take you to Fort Bridger. Old Gabe has a soft spot in his heart for white women. Even sent his little half-breed daughter out to Mrs. Whitman to be raised like a lady. He'll look out for you till a wagon train comes along that you can join up with."

"But what am I going to do in the meantime?" Annabeth wailed.

Eben doodled in the dirt with the whittled

stick. "Like I said, I been studying on that. Wasn't going to bring it up till you was a mite stronger but I s'pose we might as well hash it out now as any other time." He hesitated momentarily, wondering if it was too soon to spring the idea on her. She was still so frail and weak, her anxious face thin and far too pale, and he didn't want to upset her unnecessarily. On the other hand, she would need time to prepare herself mentally and emotionally for what lay ahead. And time was running out. His decision made, he said bluntly, "I reckon the best thing you can do is winter with me among the Cheyenne."

3

Annabeth recoiled in shock. Surely he couldn't be serious! But a quick glance at his grimly determined face convinced her that he was. White to the lips, she gasped, "Winter among the Cheyenne! I . . . I can't possibly!"

"Why not?" he said easily. "Way I see it, it's not just the best thing to do—it's the only thing. There ain't any other choices."

"There must be!" Annabeth babbled. "To spend a whole winter among Indians—it's un-thinkable!"

"Why? You were heading out to Oregon to spend your life among Indians there, weren't you? It amounts to the same thing," he said reasonably. "Different tribe is all."

"It's not at all the same thing," Annabeth sputtered. "At the mission I'd be under the Whit-man's protection and—"

"Among the Cheyenne you'd be under my protection," Eben reminded her. "We can build a lodge of our own. As my woman you'll be safe and respected. No one will harm you."

"Your woman!" Annabeth gasped. Her wide eyes were enormous in a face that had gone stark white. They looked, Eben thought absently, like the pansies his mama planted around the cabin door when he was a boy. Annabeth was as lovely and delicate as those flowers. She was right, of course, an Indian encampment was no place for a gently bred woman like herself. But there was no help for it.

"Now I understand," she cried out shrilly, looking at him with loathing. "I see why you won't take me to Oregon. You . . . you want to keep me for yourself! You . . . you want to make a squaw out of me!"

Eben scowled. "Lady, I don't like this any better than you do!" He hated to be rough with her but he knew of no other way to quell the rising tide of hysteria in her voice. "What earthly good is a pampered white woman to a man like me? What the hell do you think I'd want with a fofarraw white gal?"

"Fofarraw?" she said uncertainly.

He shrugged. "Frippery . . . no account—" he elucidated. "What good are you?" he said scornfully. "You can't make moccasins, can you? Or tan hides? Or make pemmican?" he rapped out.

Annabeth shook her head dazedly. Pemmican? She had never even heard of pemmican.

"That . . . that wasn't what I had in mind and you know it!" she said defensively. "The plain fact is—you want me for—" she gulped, "For . . . immoral purposes!"

Her face flamed at the look of scorn he gave her. "I'm not the kind of man that takes a woman to bed against her will. You oughtta know me better than that by now, Annabeth," he said reproachfully. "I wouldn't ever do anything to hurt you." He reached out to give her bright curls a reassuring pat but she flinched away, as if from a blow.

"Don't you touch me!" she hissed through her teeth. "You . . . you have blood on your hands. You're a renegade white! No better than a savage yourself! A . . . a killer!" It was on the tip of her tongue to hurl the taunt, "murderer", at him but some instinct warned her not to provoke him too far. "Don't you touch me, ever again!" she cried, her voice rising in hysteria.

His dark face was as impassive as an Indian's but a betraying muscle twitched at the corner of his jaw and a note of impatience crept into his voice as he said, "For God's sake, Annabeth, use your head. Whatever you may think of me you still need my help. Just how do you think you're going to get back into the wagon without me?"

"I'll get back the best way I can!" she retorted. "Even if I have to crawl!"

She didn't have to crawl—not quite—but she was thankful for the whittled stick Eben had left within her reach and which was thick enough to bear her weight, serving as a kind of cane to lean upon as she made her laborious way back to the wagon. By the time she had managed to boost herself up onto the tailgate she was trembling and sweating from the unaccustomed effort. No, not sweating—perspiring. A lady does not sweat, Annabeth, she perspires. She could almost hear her sharp-tongued aunt's admonition.

Poor Aunt Anna, she had tried so hard to turn her willful niece into a proper lady. What would she say if she could see her now! At the mercy of an uncouth illiterate mountain man, destined for an Indian encampment where she would be regarded as his woman—as much his property as his horse or his gun!

Tears of weakness and self-pity trickled down her cheeks. He had promised that she would come to no harm. Promised her that he would not lay a hand on her without her permission. But could she trust him?

He had tried to convince her that she could. "I'm not the kind of man that takes a woman against her will, Annabeth. The only reason we'll be sharing a tepee—living as man and wife—is because the Cheyenne won't accept you no other way. It's for your own protection. I've done a lotta things in my time but I've never forced myself on a woman yet. I leave rape to your so-called civilized city man—like the son-of-a-bitch that raped Walking Wind!"

Finally his sincerity had penetrated her hysteria. Getting a grip on herself, she'd choked out, "I'm sorry, Eben. For what happened to your wife, I mean. And . . . and for the hard things I called you . . . I—"

He shrugged. "It's natural for you to be scared of spending a winter with a man you don't really know, Annabeth," he said gently. "But you don't have nothing to fear from me. And you keep in mind what I said a while back—that the best way you can thank me for what I done for you is to trust me. Can you do that?"

A wry smile touched her lips. "I guess I don't have much choice in the matter, do I, Eben?"

Nevertheless, she had refused to let him help her back to the wagon. It wasn't only her revulsion at his bloodstained past. During their confrontation they had slipped out of the roles of nurse and patient and she had become acutely aware of him as a man. Now that she was getting her strength back, the intimacies which she had come to take for granted must cease.

True to his word, Eben did not touch her again, though his jaw hardened and his lips tightened when he saw her tottering around with her improvised cane or clutching the sides of the wagon for support. Once or twice her legs gave out from under her and she went sprawling in the dirt but she picked herself up determinedly and went on trying.

It took all of Eben's self-control not to go rushing to her aid when this occurred but he knew she wouldn't welcome his help and, dammit, even though he found her attitude exasperating, he had to admire her spunk.

Annabeth found, to her surprise, that her strength came back with astonishing rapidity, now that she was exerting herself more, but she also found that she missed the feel of Eben's strong arms around her, missed his strength to lean on more than she had thought possible. Well, she would just have to do without it, she told herself sternly. She wasn't going to let his blood-stained hands touch her again! It didn't occur to her to wonder if he hadn't already and irrevocably touched her heart.

They made plans to set out for the Cheyenne camp as soon as Annabeth was strong enough to travel. "I suppose I ought to start packing things up, battening down the hatches," she remarked idly one day.

He looked up quizzically from the bridle he was mending. "What do you mean?"

"Why, the jostling of the wagon will dislodge things that aren't screwed down or otherwise protected. I wouldn't want Aunt Anna's clock to be broken, for example." She glanced fondly at the fine mantel clock that had been her aunt's parting gift. It rested upon the dresser that Uncle Henry had built and carved into ornate designs on long winter evenings.

Eben sighed heavily. "Annabeth, I don't think you understand. We're not taking the wagon."

"Not . . . taking . . . the . . . wagon!" Annabeth's pretty mouth curved downward mutinously.

"We can't take the wagon into the Cheyenne camp. It's a rolling pesthouse. You ought to have thought of that yourself."

"But you removed the canvas and aired it out," she reminded him.

"So I did," he admitted. "But that was to make it pleasanter in here while you was bedfast."

She nodded, remembering that the interior of the wagon had been fetid and close, the air reeking of pestilence, mortal illness and death.

"We can't take the wagon or its contents with us, Annabeth," he said resolutely. "Nothing goes with us but the clothes on our backs and them I'm gonna boil the day before we set out so we can put them on fresh and clean in the morning. I think a scouring in strong lye soap will purify them. I sure hope so. I don't relish riding into the Cheyenne camp naked as a jaybird and I don't reckon you do either."

She blushed at the vivid mental image his careless words conjured up and barely heard him announce that when they left he would put the wagon to the torch. When it finally penetrated, she gasped, "Burn the wagon!"

He nodded. "It's the only thing to do, Annabeth. I wouldn't want some stray buck coming onto it and then carrying the pox back to his people. You ain't never seen what the white man's dieseases can do to Indians, Annabeth. It sweeps through a tribe like wildfire, leaving death and desolation in its wake. Why, a few years back the whole Mandan nation was wiped out by smallpox."

But Annabeth was barely listening. She was looking around her with stricken eyes. Her possessions were few but well-cherished. Aunt Anna's clock; Uncle Henry's dresser; Aunt Elizabeth's double wedding ring quilt; her mother's Bible; Asa's pocket knife; her wedding dress, the sampler she had laboriously stitched when she was seven . . .

His eyes followed hers. It wasn't hard to guess what she was thinking and feeling. "Most of this stuff wouldn't have made it over the mountains, Annabeth," he said gently. "Up ahead, the trail is lined with discarded belongings, like that dresser. Sometimes carts and broken-down wagons, too."

"But . . . but . . . not everything they owned!" she cried rebelliously.

"Not always, no," he said uncomfortably. He watched her get up and go over to the dresser, stroking the carved surfaces with a caressing hand. The smooth planed surfaces brought to mind her uncle, his kindly gray-bearded face and gentle brown eyes. Just as the clock brought back angular sharp-tongued Aunt Anna. She opened a dresser drawer and brought out Aunt Elizabeth's cherished quilt, wrapping herself in its soft folds, as if by doing so she could feel her aunt's soft plump arms wrapped around her. Dear Aunt Elizabeth who had been the closest thing to a mother the girl had ever known and upon whose capacious bosom she had sobbed out many childish woes.

Eben cleared his throat. "I'll be outside if you need me," he murmured. She looked so woebegone it was all he could do to keep himself from gathering her into his arms, urging her to cry out her heartache on his broad chest. His strong arms ached to hold her, he realized with a start of surprise, as if they were remembering how it felt to lift and hold her during her illness. She was a small woman, as light and fragile as a little bird he might hold in his two hands but spunky and spirited for all her small size and physical frailty. Wrongheaded, of course, with her crazy notions of converting the heathen and such but somehow she had twined herself around his heart, much as one of her springy red-gold curls would twine itself around his finger if he touched it. But, of course he couldn't touch it or her either. He felt an over-whelming urge to comfort and protect her but she didn't want any comfort he could offer and it wasn't likely she ever would, he acknowledged sadly. The most he could do for her was leave her alone to get used to the idea of parting with her treasured possessions, to give her the privacy to grieve over her loss. He realized dimly that it was not the possessions in themselves that she cherished but the memories they evoked.

He got up heavily, brushing past her in the confined space but he realized that she barely saw him through a mist of tears. She was far away on a rocky hillside farm in York State, a place she had mentioned often in her fever delirium as she called repeatedly for the family that most likely she would never see again.

When Annabeth called him to supper that

night she was red-nosed and puffy-eyed but composed.

"You all right?" he asked uneasily, dipping stew onto his plate.

"Why, yes. Why shouldn't I be?" she said in a steady voice, her tone forbidding him to speak of what must be done. She laid a biscuit on his plate. "I mixed up a batch of biscuits while you were hunting this afternoon," she volunteered. "Did you get anything?"

He glanced in her direction. Though she was pale, and only picking at her food, he was relieved to see that she had her emotions under control. "Not a thing," he said in disgust. "Game has learned to make itself scarce so near the trail. I guess we'll have to make do with jerky."

He frowned. If she didn't want to talk about what was bothering her that was all right with him. He figured he was lucky—most women, white or Indian, would have made more of a fuss than she had when ordered to leave everything they owned behind them. But Annabeth was special. He wished there were something he could do for her. Well, maybe there was. It wasn't much, God knew, but maybe it would ease some of the heartache she must be feeling.

When he finished eating, he got up and went to the wagon, rummaging around until he found what he was looking for. Carrying the slab of wood out to the fire, he sat down cross-legged, and, by its light, began to shape and carve the wood.

Annabeth, who was washing up the supper dishes, watched him out of the corner of her eye. He was good with a knife in more ways than one, she had to admit grudgingly. He'd whittled her out a couple of long-handled wooden spoons so she wouldn't be forever singeing her fingers as she cooked over the open fire. And a long wooden fork for turning bacon sizzling in the pan.

What was he working on now? she wondered, drying her sudsy hands on her apron and walking over unobtrusively to stand beside him. Peering over his shoulder she saw that he was carving letters into the smooth board and, as she watched, she saw that the letters spelled out a familiar name, A-S-A A-L-L-A-N.

He glanced up at her, the firelight playing across his swarthy features. "What was your husband's birthdate?" he asked.

"1823," she answered with a lump in her throat. How had Eben guessed how much she hated leaving Asa here, on the lonely prairie, buried in an unmarked grave? She watched in silence as he carved the dates 1823-1847 underneath Asa's name.

"There's room for something more, if you want it," he suggested tentatively. "A verse from the Bible, maybe?" A missionary, he figured, would set a heap of store on a text from the Good Book.

"The eighteenth psalm was Asa's favorite. Could you add a line or two from that?" she said after a moment's thought. "If it isn't too much trouble."

"No trouble at all," he assured her, waiting expectantly.

"The Lord is my rock and my fortress and my deliverer; my strength in whom I will trust," Annabeth quoted softly. "The Lord, my God, will enlighten my darkness."

"Well, now, that sounds mighty fine," Eben said hearteningly, carving the words to Annabeth's dictation. Satisfied with his handiwork he stood up, uncoiling his long legs, and side by side they walked to the cairn of stones that was Asa's final resting place. Eben pounded the marker into place at the head of the grave, tamping the earth down well around it.

"No one could ask for better," Annabeth remarked, remembering the crude crosses of twigs or boards torn from wagons, without even a name or date, that marked so many graves along the Oregon Trail. "Thank you, Eben," she said simply. To her shame, she had not credited him with so much sensitivity and impulsively she took his arm, giving it a slight squeeze. "It makes me feel better to know that his grave won't go unmarked. We weren't married for very long but we'd known each other all our lives. We grew up together. It . . . it hurts to leave him behind." Awkwardly, she added, "I . . . I guess you can understand how I feel because of your wife. This must bring back memories for you, of her death and . . . and burial."

"It does," he acknowledged. Her gentle touch had filled him with confusion. A tingling sensation had run up the full length of his arm when she had grasped it—a sensation that unaccountably spread to other parts of his body, reminding him that he'd not had a woman since his wife's death— leastways not one that he cared deeply about. And he *did* care about this spunky little redhead. It wasn't hardly decent to be thinking about her in that way, though—not right here at her husband's graveside. But maybe it was only natural, after all, a natural urge to go on with life and living in the face of death—to rejoice in being alive. Life was a chancy thing at best.

To cover his confusion he remarked, "It's not

just the same, though. For one thing the Cheyenne don't put their dead in the ground."

"No?" Annabeth had taken her hand from his arm in order to draw her shawl more tightly around her for a chill wind had sprung up. Now she looked up at him, rather shocked by the disclosure. "Why not?"

"Because they believe that the tasoom or spirit cannot begin its journey to the spirit world while it is still bound to the earth, trapped within its darkness. I buried Walking Wind according to the customs of her people, laying her out on a scaffold after I'd plaited her hair with ribbons and dressed her in her best robe. I spread her tools out beside her for her to use in the spirit world. And I sacrificed her pony so she'd have him to ride there, as she did on earth, her long black hair flying in the wind."

Annabeth was momentarily stunned into speechlessness. When she could find her voice again she said sharply, "Surely you don't believe in that . . . that superstitious nonsense!"

Eben frowned. He had temporarily forgotten that Annabeth was a missionary, obsessed with the white man's notion that his way was the only way and his religion the only way to salvation. Her conviction of superiority was not only annoying. In the Cheyenne camp it could be downright dangerous—if not fatal!

Eben sighed. He would have to set her straight about a few things, he decided.

"I can't see that it matters whether I believe it or not; Walking Wind did," he pointed out reasonably. "And it's not superstitious nonsense, Annabeth. The Cheyenne—they have their own customs and beliefs that they cherish just as you

51

do your own. They have their own kind of spirituality. It's different from the white man's in that it's part and parcel of nature; a reverence for the forces of nature. But it's just as good. As good for them as your beliefs are for you," he said hastily, seeing a mutinous expression cross her face. "You have your God; they have Heammawihio, the Wise One Above."

"But there is only one true God!" Annabeth protested. "Only one road to salvation!"

"That's kind of narrow thinking, ain't it? The Cheyenne say that all things are of Heammawihio and the spirits of the dead go to him by the Hanging Road."

"The Hanging Road?" Annabeth repeated, stupefied. She was uneasily aware that she was not getting the best of this argument.

Eben pointed to the evening star hanging in the sky. "The stars, the path that leads to Heammawihio who lives in the sky. We all go there someday, for death is forgiving and eternity belongs to all."

"To all?" Annabeth's voice rose in outrage. "You mean there's no heaven or hell? No punishment for sinners?"

"That's right." Eben shrugged. "Maybe Heammawihio is kinder than the white man's God. I reckon each of us makes his own heaven right here on earth," he added thoughtfully. "Or," his jaw tightened, "his hell."

This was so contrary to the stern doctrine in which Annabeth had been raised that she was appalled. "You can't really believe that!" she gasped.

"Don't rightly know what I believe," he admitted thoughtfully. "Seems to me though that humility is supposed to be a Christian virtue and it's one that the missionaries are sorely lacking. I can't think of anything more arrogant than a missionary charging in and telling people that their religion is wrong. Beats me how they can be so sure they're right."

"Because they . . . we," she corrected herself, remembering that she was one, "have the Bible, the Word of God revealed," she said swiftly. Now there was something she could be perfectly certain of.

"The Bible has one religion and it's a good one," Eben admitted, "though some of those Old Testament prophets were mighty bloodthirsty fellows, if I remember rightly. But there's more than one religion and each one is good for the people who believe in it and try to live up to it."

"Oh!" This was too much! "Eben McDowell, you're as savage and as heathen as any Indian!" she declared roundly. "Worse! Because you ought to know better!"

"Maybe so." he said, unruffled. "But I respect the beliefs of others and I expect you do the same. There'll be no proselytizing while you're among the Cheyenne. I want that understood here and now, Annabeth."

She stared into his stern face resentfully.

"Is that clear, Annabeth?"

"Perfectly," she snapped, flouncing away from him. Who did he think he was, accusing her of spiritual arrogance and laying down the law to her? she fumed inwardly, scrambling up into the wagon and pulling the canvas flaps shut energetically. It was as close as she could come to slamming a door in his face and that was exactly what she felt like doing at the moment!

She frowned. Ever since she had become strong enough to get out and about on her own, Eben had been making his bed underneath the wagon and, though at first she had missed the even sounds of his breathing, the reassuring rustle of the pallet as he turned over, the quiet conversations they had had on sleepless nights, she was glad—*glad*—that he was sleeping outside tonight. She sighed. Every time they seemed to get a little closer, seemed on the verge of developing a deeper friendship, something happened to remind her that in ways of thinking, in values, in everything that counted, they were worlds apart.

It was probably a good thing too, she reflected moodily as she got undressed and ready for bed. From time to time she needed the reminder that their essential differences left an unbridgeable gap between them. Because he *was* an attractive man—a strong and gentle man—and it would be only too easy to get too fond of him. She would need that reminder more than ever once they were in the Cheyenne camp—the only two whites amid a horde of howling heathen! But he was just as much a heathen as any of them, she told herself sternly. And it would never do to let herself become too fond of him. Just because he had saved her life, nursed her back to health when she'd thought she was dying didn't mean—didn't mean anything, she reminded herself for the umpteenth time. It only meant that he was a kind and compassionate individual in spite of his uncivilized ways and beliefs.

A kind and compassionate individual—yes—but also a man, presumably with a man's needs and desires! A man with whom she was going to have to live on terms of utmost intimacy through the long winter months with the Cheyenne.

Brushing out the riot of red-gold curls that clung closely to her scalp she paused thoughtfully. It wouldn't be any different than the long weeks they had already spent together during her illness and convalescence, would it? And all the time he had been the perfect gentleman. So why should she fear . . . or was it that his advances wouldn't really be unwelcome? That was such an appalling thought that Annabeth couldn't bear to pursue it further. She picked up the hairbrush again and began to wield it with punishing ferocity.

One thing she was sure of—it was bound to be different because the circumstances would be different. She was fast recovering her health and strength and a healthy man and a healthy woman couldn't live together for very long without . . .

Of course they could, she told herself firmly. After all, she and Asa had . . . well, Asa had been most considerate. He hadn't expected her to fulfill her wifely duties until they got to Oregon. Both their mothers had died in childbirth; hers when she was born and Asa's more recently. It had made a profound impression on the boy. Childbirth was a hazardous business at best, Asa had decreed, without the additional risk of Annabeth's getting pregnant and being brought to bed somewhere along the trail, as Eliza Sloane had done. So they had made a pact not to live as man and wife until they reached their destination; their marriage had never been consummated.

But this man wasn't like Asa. With Eben the veneer of civilization didn't even go skin-deep.

Well, her looks should prove a deterrent, Annabeth reflected. Eben would probably be more attracted to Indian women than to her—after all, he had already taken one for a wife, hadn't he? And some of them were very lovely, she had heard, especially when very young. Whereas she . . . she took up the once-forbidden mirror and studied her reflection in the lamplight. No—no man in his right mind would want a pockmarked woman when he could probably have his choice of lovely Indian maidens.

In truth, the few pockmarks she had were not nearly as unsightly or as protuberant as they appeared to Annabeth. Nearly all were scattered along her hairline and could readily be concealed when her hair grew out a bit more. But to Annabeth they seemed like ugly craters marring her small heart-shaped face, twice as numerous and a hundred times more repulsive than they really were. Experimentally she pulled a few curls forward to see if they could be hidden but her hair was still too short to do anything with and she gave up the attempt with a sigh when the hair bounced back into her curly crop. No, a man who admired long black hair flying in the wind would find nothing appealing in a crophaired redhead who was disfigured. The thought, which should have been reassuring to a woman who feared for her virtue, was curiously depressing, she mused as she trailed off to her bed and extinguished the lantern light.

The storm woke her long before dawn, violent as prairie thunderstorms tend to be, with brilliant jags of lightning and great rolling billows of thunder. Rain plummeted down on the canvas-topped wagon, sounding like tiny beating drums whenever the greater tympanies of thunder did not drown it out altogether. Then the wind came up, hard and fast and tearing.

Annabeth pulled the covers up to her chin and lay awake listening to the storm rage. From the roaring of the wind and the flapping of the canvas she knew that underneath the wagon Eben must be getting drenched.

Well, let him. That was her first thought. It wouldn't be the first time, she was sure of that. He was a man in tune with the elements, at home with the forces of nature. He must have gotten soaked to the skin scores of times. He was as tough as old boots; he could take it! Rolling over, she pulled the blanket over her head to shut out the noise of the storm and tried to go back to sleep.

But she couldn't. Thunder boomed, rain and wind dashed the canvas and Annabeth couldn't keep her mind off Eben. She visualized puddles of rainwater forming underneath the wagon and Eben lying in them, shivering with each blast of rain and wind. Annabeth tossed and turned. What was the matter with her? Back home she wouldn't have left a dog outside on a night like this. Why, it wasn't Christian!

With that, she leaped out of bed and padded barefoot towards the back of the wagon. Pulling back the fluttering canvas flap she peered out. The darkness was lit by one forked tongue of lightning after another. There was crackling and booming and rattling and rolling and when the thunder clapped loudly it reverberated away into the distance even as the lightning lit up the sky with an unearthly brilliance that was light enough to read by.

"Eben!" Annabeth shrieked into the storm. "Eben!" But her voice was lost in the wailing of the wind so she stuck her head out, the rain pelting down on her face as she screamed again, "Eben! Eb-en!"

And then she saw him illuminated in the next

flash of lightning—a bolt that sizzled to the ground, burned and seemed to leap upward, crackling and dangerous. He was scrambling out from under the wagon, the rain pasting his hair back against his skull and streaming down his body.

"Eb-en!" she yelled, giving it her all.

With a bound he was beside her in the wagon, the rain pouring off his buckskins and puddling at their feet.

"You all right?" he enquired anxiously. "Did the storm scare you, Annabeth?"

"Of course not!" she snapped. The very idea—that she, Annabeth Allan, would be scared by a little thunderstorm, or even a big one! "It *woke* me up, that's all, and I was worried about you. Don't you have sense enough to come in out of the rain!" she scolded, in a manner reminiscent of crotchety Aunt Anna. "Look at you—soaked to the skin! You'll catch your death!"

He shrugged, thereby causing rainwater to pour from him in a stream. "I've been wetter." His white teeth flashed in a rueful grin. "Well, just as wet," he amended.

Annabeth pursed her lips. Pattering over to the dresser, she fished out two towels and a long flannel nightshirt. Handing him the garment and one of the towels, she said, "You'll have to shuck off those wet clothes and toss them outside. When you've dried off, you can put this shirt on." Turning her back to him, she knelt and, with the other towel, began soaking up the puddle of water that had formed at his feet, her eyes glued firmly to the damp floorboards. Presently she heard the rustle of clothing being removed and then his low rumbling chuckle.

"Reckon you're gonna wear a hole in that towel if you swish it around that rough wagonbed any more," he observed. "You can get up now; I'm decent." Automatically he reached down to give her a hand up and just as automatically she took it.

Her hand was immediately engulfed in his large one. It was warm and rough—a man's hand—Annabeth thought dizzily. The hand of a killer, she told herself wildly but still she clung to it, pressing her small soft palm against his large callused one. Then he opened his fingers and pressed hers gently against his and breathlessly Annabeth permitted this small liberty, her heart fluttering wildly in her chest. Presently her fingers began to tremble in his grip like the heart of a small trapped bird.

He dropped her hand and said gruffly, "Best you get back to bed, Annabeth, 'fore you take a chill. You ain't got your full strength back yet and you don't want to get sick again," he reminded her.

"No, no, of course not," she mumbled, retreating to her pallet. "But where will you sleep?"

"Oh, I'll make a nest of blankets like I did when you was ailin'," he said cheerfully. "I'll be snug as a bug in a rug."

Annabeth didn't doubt it. The man was tough as old boots, seemingly impervious to the ravages of wind and weather. It was *she* who was chilled, for her feet, she now realized, felt like ice from padding around barefoot. She pulled them up under her, trying to warm them with her body. She shivered. The warm spot in her bedding where she had snuggled had cooled off while she had been absent from it and the blankets felt clammy with damp. She could feel goose-pimples rising on her body and before long her teeth began to chatter.

She clenched her jaws together tightly in an attempt to silence their rattle, mindful of the man occupying the next pallet. It was, she thought, perfectly exasperating that the storm, so noisy in its effects a few minutes ago had apparently moved off across the prairie, leaving only the faint thrumming noise of rain on the canvas roof, over which the chattering of her teeth must be clearly audible to Eben.

It was. She heard a rustle from his pallet, a sigh, and then—"You *did* take a chill," he said almost accusingly.

"It's . . . it's just my feet. I can't seem to get them warm," she admitted, trying to control the little jumps and jerks that had taken possession of her limbs.

In the dim light, she saw him uncoil his long frame from the nest of blankets and move towards her. His dark face reflected only kindness and concern as he bent over her. He only just fit into Asa's nightshirt, she noted, seeing how his massive shoulders strained its seams. In order to squeeze into it he had had to leave the top buttons open so that a vast expanse of chest was bare. If you could call a chest bare that was covered with a wiry pelt of thick dark hair. More bearlike than bare, Annabeth thought tartly, trying to conceal the effect the sight of his muscular physique had on her pulses.

"We've got to do something about those feet," he muttered, stripping back the clammy blankets and gently chafing her lower limbs, restoring warmth and circulation to them. "Better?" he said, after a few minutes.

Annabeth nodded. Oh, she felt better, she guessed. At least her feet were no longer solid lumps of ice attached to her ankles. In fact, she felt a tingling in her toes that went went all the way up to her fingertips—fingers that yearned to reach out and caress him. It was exhilarating and frightening all at the same time—this strange sensation that went coursing through her body, making it feel heavy and languorous. It was as if her veins were not filled with blood at all but with the hot sweet sap that Uncle Henry boiled down from their sugar maples every spring.

She had never experienced such feelings before and they made her quiver with a strange wild wanting that she couldn't understand. She had an almost irresistible urge to reach out her arms, twine them about his neck, and pull him down beside her.

Eben felt her shiver and frowned, coming to quite the the wrong conclusion as to its cause. "You're still cold," he said flatly.

Annabeth was powerless to deny it because how could she explain what was happening to her? He mustn't know—and, anyway, she didn't understand it herself.

"Damn!" he swore in frustration. He sat back on his heels, still frowning. "There's no way I can build a fire to get you warm tonight. But we can't have you coming down with lung fever either." He got up and dragged his nest of blankets over to her pallet. "Only thing I can do is lie down against you and warm up your spine," he explained. "That ought to do the trick."

Annabeth drew in her breath sharply, her eyes widening in alarm.

Taking her inhalation for an expression of fear, Eben said, with as much patience as he could muster, "I told you once, little lady, that you don't have nothing to fear from me and, whatever else I am, I'm a man of my word. I've never yet harmed a helpless woman or forced one that wasn't willin' and I'm not about to start now. You can rest easy," he assured her as he lay down beside her, his back rigidly turned to her.

But though they kept warm, neither of them rested very easy that night.

Eben had learned self-control in a hard school; he had known years of hardship and deprivation in the mountains; he was inured to discomfort and loneliness; he was accustomed to disciplining himself until he could get by on only those things necessary for sheer survival. But never had his self-control been so sorely tested as it was now. He was only flesh and blood, after all, and the soft female form pressed so closely against his own was an almost irresistible temptation. He could feel the soft swell of her gently rounded buttocks tucked against the small of his back, feel the soft almost imperceptible rhythm of her breathing. Visualizing her even more rounded bosom gently rising and falling was almost unbearable. Gritting his teeth, he fought the instinctive urge to roll over and take her in his arms.

Well, why not? he asked himself moodily. She was a widow lady, after all. She knew what it was all about. He wouldn't be violating a virgin. And would she really be all that unwilling? Even though she was repelled by what she called his heathen ways, she was, at the same time, attracted to him—he could sense it! With that thought, he half-turned towards her and then, with a smothered groan, rolled back.

No, he couldn't do it. Dammit, she was too vulnerable. He had promised her that she could trust him. He couldn't turn around and betray that trust for a momentary physical gratification—for the release he was sorely in need of. He was a man, not an animal. Self-control and self-respect went hand in hand. Besides, if he took advantage of their situation now, she might well hate him for it. And the last thing he wanted was for her to hate him. It would, he told himself, make the winter in the Cheyenne camp intolerable. As it was, the winter was going to be a whole lot more difficult than he had foreseen, feeling the way he did about her.

Annabeth felt Eben half-turn towards her and her heart pounded in her chest. Despite her inexperience, instincts as old as time told her that Eben would be a passionate, yet gentle and considerate lover. And if he took her now, she could still pretend that it was against her will. She could have the sweet pleasure of his caresses (and somehow she knew that they would be inexpressibly sweet) and yet maintain the illusion of her superiority—she could, in a manner of speaking, have her cake and eat it too.

But he didn't, of course. And when he rolled over and turned his back to her again, Annabeth didn't know whether she was relieved or disappointed. Perhaps a little of both.

Eventually the strange wild yearning that had taken possession of her ebbed and she dozed off.

When she woke up, he was gone. If it weren't for the imprint of his big body in the tangled blankets, she might have imagined that she had dreamed the events of last night. She wished it *had* been a dream for she felt distinctly self-conscious

Sue Deobold

about coming face to face with him.

But she forgot her self-consciousness the moment she set foot outside. The storm had moved off before dawn, the sky had cleared, the air was brisk, nipping at fingers and toes, and the world was covered with a frosty mantel of white flecks that sparkled in the sunlight.

At her exclamation of delight, Eben glanced up from the fire by which he was squatting, cooking breakfast. "Pretty, ain't it?" he remarked. "The Cheyenne have a mighty nice name for it—they call it 'the bones of the rain.'"

"It's like a fairyland," Annabeth marvelled, looking around her in wonder. The prairie stretched as far as the eye could see, each blade of grass glimmering, bejeweled, in the morning light.

"It won't last the morning," Eben volunteered. "Bright as the sun is, it'll be burned off long before noon. and I'm glad it's not snow, so soon. All the signs point to an early winter. One good snowstorm and the horses will be belly-deep." He handed Annabeth a tin plate and a mug of coffee. "You figger you're strong enough to travel yet?"

Annabeth hesitated. She hated to relinquish the relative security of the wagon—it had been her rolling home for weeks—for the dubious comforts of the Cheyenne camp. Moreover, she had the feeling that she was placing her life squarely in his hands. She might as well be his captive—in essence that's exactly what she was, she thought gloomily. Still, there was nothing she could do about it. Certainly they couldn't winter on the open prairie.

Squaring her shoulders she said sturdily, "I'm ready whenever you are. When do you want to leave?"

Eben squinted at the sun. There was virtually nothing to pack except coffee, cornmeal, and strips of dried meat. They could be underway in an hour or so and far from here by sundown. There was a long way to go and now that the last spell of warm weather had broken, he had the feeling they'd lingered too long already.

"Sooner the better," he said briskly. "You get some food together for the trail and I'll saddle the horses and break up some bits and pieces for kindling."

Annabeth made one last appeal. "*Must* we burn the wagon, Eben?"

His face set in a stern line. "You know we must, Annabeth. I wouldn't ask it of you if it wasn't necessary."

"But isn't it too wet to burn?" she protested. "Last night's rain—"

"By the time we're ready to travel the sun and wind will dry it out enough. And with the ground still damp we won't be starting any prairie fires. It couldn't be better." He drained his mug of coffee and rose to his feet. "You get the provisions packed up. I'll see to the horses."

But when he brought the horses around, Annabeth balked. "I want my sidesaddle on the bay mare," she insisted.

"Ain't you ever ridden astride?" Eben enquired.

"Well, yes, when I was a little girl, riding the farm horses bareback. But that was years ago. A Lady shouldn't ride astride."

"Annabeth, you can't ride for hours with your leg crooked around the horn of a lady's saddle. It'll go numb on you within the hour," he warned her patiently.

Annabeth tilted her chin. "Ladies do not have

legs—they have limbs! And you're no gentleman to mention such a thing," she declared roundly. Heavens! Next he would be expecting her to dress like a man!

"Never pretended to be a gentleman," Eben said quietly. "I'm only telling you what makes sense. This ain't no pleasure jaunt. You've got several days of hard riding ahead of you. You won't be able to keep up riding sidesaddle. Indian women ride astride all the time," he added encouragingly.

"I'm no squaw!" Annabeth flared.

Eben was beginning to lose patience. "Maybe not, but you're built the same as them, I reckon!"

Ooh! How could he be so crude? Annabeth straightened her spine and clenched her hands into fists. "If . . . if you don't put the sidesaddle on Dolly, I . . . I won't go with you!" Her lower lip quivered and she bit down on it hard to stop its trembling.

Eben sighed. "Now, Annabeth—"

"I mean it!" She was being childish and she knew it but she just didn't care. More was at stake here than the issue of riding sidesaddle versus riding astride. Eben was asking her—no, he was telling her—to give up all the appurtenances of civilization and go off and live with him among the Indians. There was no other choice, he'd said, and she didn't question his judgment. But on this small point she would not give way. She would take a stand. She would *not* lower her standards; she would leave here in a civilized fashion and she would enter the Cheyenne camp riding like a lady—or not at all!

Her obduracy obviously baffled him. "Annabeth, you're not making sense," he protested.

She scowled up at him, repeating, "Sidesaddle or not at all!"

Eben was exasperated. He felt like pulling her across his knee and paddling her behind. It was no more than what she deserved for throwing such a temper tantrum, he thought sourly. The prospect was enticing but he regretfully abandoned it and considered simply throwing her up onto the saddle willy-nilly. Likely she'd carry a grudge, though, and it wasn't worthwhile getting her riled. Might as well humor her whim, he decided, she'd be the one to suffer for it but that was her choice, not his.

Annoyed at getting bested by this slim girl with the flame-red curls and the determined chin, he growled, "All right, suit yourself. I'll switch the saddles for you."

It was done all too soon to suit Annabeth. Perched on Dolly's broad back, she watched tight-lipped as he set a brand from the cookfire to the wagon and its contents. When it became a flaming pyre, he swung into the saddle.

"I thought you'd want to wait around until everything is destroyed," she commented.

"It'll burn," he said tersely. "And the fire will be a beacon for miles around. We better make tracks."

"I thought the Indians were your friends," she snapped, gathering up the reins.

"Not all of 'em. The Pawnees or the Kiowas would lift my hair as quick as any other white man's."

Annabeth made no comment. She had craned her head around for one last look back, blinking back tears. Seeing her eyes fill, he said gently, "You can look at this as the end of everything,

Annabeth. Or, you can look at it as a new beginning. Now, let's make tracks.''

And putting their heels to their mounts' flanks, they turned their faces to the West.

4

For as long as she lived Annabeth knew that she would never forget her first sight of the Cheyenne camp. They came upon it just at dusk after several days of hard riding. Her small store of strength was almost spent and she was so tired that even the tall cone-shaped dwellings and strange copper-skinned people seemed welcoming. Whatever else was lacking, she reflected, at least she would have a roof, of sorts, over her head and some protection from the elements.

Their arrival created a flurry of excitement in the camp and men and women left their cook fires to form ranks between which the newcomers passed in silence. Annabeth was too weary to do more than follow where Eben led and she kept her eyes on his broad back, half-mesmerized by the swaying fringes of his buckskins as they fluttered with the easy motion of his supple frame. She hardly dared to glance left or right, where, it seemed, hundreds of dark impassive eyes were staring holes in her. Only vaguely was she conscious of the half-naked children who darted back and forth, winding around the adults and between the tepees, until two small boys, a pack of dogs yapping at their heels, ran up and tugged at Eben's ankles. He checked his mount, said something in Cheyenne that Annabeth could not understand and let down his arm so that the smallest boy might swing himself into the saddle. The other boy grinned as he was boosted up behind, one arm wound tightly around Eben's mid-section. Both boys were obviously proud and happy to be part of the little procession. They looked enough alike to be twins, to Annabeth's undiscriminating eye, and she wondered if their father were the friend who had kept Eben supplied with meat while he was nursing her back to health.

Eben seemed to know exactly where he was going and his people seemed to know as well for they drew back to line a path for him—a path that led to a tall grayish-tan tepee that was decorated with the sunburst emblem, one which Annabeth was to learn was a favorite among the Cheyenne. A man, a pregnant woman, and a half-grown girl-child were standing in front of it.

Eben drew rein and dismounted, clasping the Indian's hand in a firm shake. The two boys slithered to the ground and took the horses' reins. Annabeth stayed where she was, sitting quietly, proudly straight in the saddle, resisting the almost overwhelming temptation to droop in exhaustion.

The two men held a brief colloquy in Cheyenne of which she was able to pick out a few words for Eben had been teaching her the Indian tongue. Then he turned to her and lifted her out of the saddle, saying, "Annabeth, this is my brother, Gray Bull. His wife is Silent Moon and their daughter is Little Deer. And these two imps of mischief," he ruffled the boys' hair impartially, "are Turtle Boy and Little Lance."

She nodded and mumbled a greeting, clutching Eben for support for her legs were shaky and she would have crumpled up and fallen on her face if Eben's strong arms had not steadied her.

He spoke rapidly in Cheyenne and explained to Annabeth, "I told them you are weak because you have not fully recovered from illness—not from fear. Isn't that so, Annabeth?"

"Of course," she said staunchly. She forced a smile to her lips, trying to hide her trepidation from the darkly impassive faces surrounding her. To her relief, the woman's round moon face smiled back in response and she chattered something in Cheyenne which Annabeth was not able to follow.

"Moon, here, welcomes you to her lodge," Eben interpreted. "She'll show you where you can rest, get you something to eat. Go along with her, Annabeth." And he gave her a gentle shove towards the other woman.

Reluctantly she followed the other woman into the tepee, assisted by the little girl who giggled and pulled one of Annabeth's bright curls wonderingly. A softly worded rebuke from her mother sent the child scurrying to the cook fire, presumably to tend whatever was simmering there. Annabeth's stomach growled. It smelled like buffalo stew and it smelled delicious.

The interior of the tepee was also pleasanter than Annabeth had visualized. The air, it was true, was hazy with smoke from the fire which burned a little back of center and which made her eyes smart a bit but the walls had been lined with hides that were cleaner and creamier than the skins that lined the outside. They were decorated with geometric designs, Indian corn, and bits of red trader's cloth. Buffalo robes formed sleeping pallets which had been made into makeshift couches by the addition of willow backrests similar to the one Eben had made for her. Buckskin pillows, embroidered with porcupine quills and red and blue trader's beads added comfort and color.

Silent Moon, chattering softly all the while, led her to one of these couches and Annabeth sank down gratefully, almost too tired to sample the bowl of stew that Little Deer brought her. Silent Moon—a misnomer if ever there was one, Annabeth had already decided, clucked encouragingly and spoke softly, partly to her and partly to her daughter while Annabeth dug in with a spoon carved out of buffalo horn. She wondered, as she ate, if the fall hunt had been a success. Eben had already told her that the life of the Cheyenne, like that of all the Plains Indians, depended on the buffalo, and she didn't want to be a burden to these people during the long winter. When she had expressed her concern to Eben, he had misinterpreted her motive. "You may go slack-bellied," he told her bluntly, "but you won't be any hungrier than anybody else. It's share and share alike among the Cheyenne. They're generous to a fault. Give you the shirt off your back if you need it."

She thought with some compunction that if that were true, the Indians might well have something to teach the whites. She remembered that two of her fellow missionaries, Caleb and Harriet Paterson were so tight they squeaked, as Aunt Anna would have said. Annabeth knew for a fact that they had hoarded food and medicines along the trail.

She had cleaned her bowl of stew when the men came in and their womenfolk went off to serve them. She hoped that Eben would come over and sit down beside her and she tried to catch his eye but he studiously ignored her. The Cheyenne world, he had told her previously, was a man's world, by and large, and she saw ample evidence of that now, for mother and daughter waited until the men were done eating before eating their own meal, in the woman's place, the south side of the tepee. Annabeth took a dim view of this sexual segregation. She found herself wondering if Eben had insisted on his own wife conforming to these traditions. She sniffed. He certainly need not expect it of *her* when they had a lodge of their own!

Her strength had been restored by the food and she was tempted to get up and go join the men—just to show them that *she* wasn't going to be treated like a squaw but some little inner voice counselled prudence and, for once, she listened to it. Now was not the time to assert herself. Eben would be angered by her rashness, she knew, and while she certainly wasn't afraid of him, his Indian "Brother" was something else again. Stern-faced and massively built, Gray Bull looked like he was capable of swatting an impertinent woman with no more trouble than if he were swatting a fly or a mosquito.

So she huddled down amidst the buffalo robes and listening to the low-voiced, only half-under-stood conversation of the men, fell asleep.

She woke up some time during the middle of the night and lay there in the darkness wondering dazedly where she was and why she was still fully clothed. The fire had died down to a bed of glowing coals. As her eyes adjusted to the dimness she could make out silent forms, stretched out on buffalo-skin pallets, all to the left of the door. By straining her eyes she could detect Eben's sleeping form among them. So he was considered a member of the family, she mused. Her own pallet was to the right of the door which was an area reserved for guests.

He seemed so far away! On the trail they had necessarily bedded down together for warmth and for her protection. But nothing that could remotely be considered an impropriety had taken place. He had lain down very correctly with his back to her and she had snuggled up to him (purely for the warmth his body provided, or so she told herself).

Well, she certainly didn't need his bodily warmth now. The fire, banked for the night, was giving off plenty of heat still. The tepee was, if anything, too hot to be comfortable. So why was she so restless? She supposed she must have grown used to sleeping out of doors, under the stars, in the cool crisp autumn air, and used, too, she admitted honestly, to Eben's hard muscular body stretched out alongside her own. She missed him. Though they had always started the night back to back, somehow they had become intertwined during the course of it, and more than once she had awakened to find her head pillowed in the hollow of his shoulder. It had made a good pillow, too, she thought, pummeling her buckskin substitute a little angrily. Of course, whenever this happened, she had sprung up with profuse apologies—apologies which he had accepted a little angrily. He always seemed to wake up as grouchy as a bear with a sore head, she recalled. Probably he was one of those people who never seemed to fully wake up until the sun was high, she thought innocently. No doubt that was why he was so tight-lipped and irritable every morning!

She had learned more about the man he was while they were on the trail, she reflected. Back at the wagon he had been kind to her and considerate, gentle as a woman with her weakness, sympathetic to her loss. On the trail she had glimpsed another side to his character—that he was tough and strong and tireless, impervious to the fatigue that had gripped her. Yes, she mused, he was a man made for the wilderness. She had looked at the rolling prairie stretching out ahead of them, unknown and unknowable in its vastness, and had feared it, seeing herself as a small, unimportant speck of humanity, lost in its seemingly limitless expanse.

But Eben, on the other hand, had seemed to come into his own. She could sense that he felt released and free, that he knew it and loved it . . . it was a big land fit for a big man, she had thought at the time. The men she had known on the wagon train—Asa and the others—they had been as awed by it as she was. They saw its vastness as an obstacle to be overcome, something to be endured as best they could, something to be got through, as the Rockies, when they came to them, were to be got over, traversed, conquered. But Eben accepted it, was a part of it, could meet every challenge that the wild country threw at him and would not only survive but actually flourish.

It wasn't quite fair, she supposed, to compare men like Eben to men fresh from the East, men like Asa. Her late husband had been a good and decent man, earnest and learned and devout. But compared to Eben he had been no more than a boy, immature, untried, inexperienced. She knew now, rather sadly, that if it had not been for her Asa would never have tried to pit himself against the West. He would have been content back East in a quiet village parish. It was she who had burned with missionary fervor and as she lay wakeful, she began for the first time, to explore her own motivations. Had they been as unmixed as she had thought at the time? Or had her zeal for converting the heathen been, in truth, nothing more than a thinly disguised zest for adventure, born not of Christian convictions but of a yearning for the strange and unknown and unfamiliar? For the wild, unmapped places of the earth and . . . and for wilder, uncivilized men?

Oh, it was true that the prairie frightened her but it fascinated her at the same time, in much the same way that wild Eben McDowell exerted a fatal fascination over her. Not that she was *afraid* of him. Not exactly. Why should she be? After all, he had been nothing but gentle and kind to her. And yet . . . there was some spark or spirit within him that called out to her—attracting and repelling her at the same time. She knew, some primitive instinct warned her, that if ever there were a clash of wills between them, it would be his will and not hers that would prevail. Underneath that seemingly gentle exterior of his lurked a core of solid strength—he was, by far, stronger than the strongest man she had ever known. Too strong, really. Too uncivilized without a doubt. Too uncouth. Too untutored. Too . . . Bah! She pummeled the buckskin pillow which exuded a wild piney scent. Why she should be pining for him when she should be getting her much-needed rest she couldn't, for the life of her, understand. She forced herself to breathe deeply and evenly, tucked her hand under her cheek, and closed her eyes.

When she opened them again a shaft of sunlight was pouring through the open flaps of the tepee, which like all Cheyenne lodges faced east towards the rising sun. Everyone appeared to be outside. She could hear the voices of women calling back and forth to each other, children shrieking in play, dogs barking.

She got up and straightened her clothing as best she could. Her riding habit was stained and travel-worn, the skirt ripped in several places. She wondered if she could borrow a needle and thread from Silent Moon to mend it. But first she would take advantage of the emptiness of the lodge to wash off some of the stains of travel. Thinking to rinse her mouth out first she lifted the gourd dipper to her lips, astonished and indignant when it was struck aside. A rapid-fire volley of Cheyenne from Silent Moon left her baffled.

Eben, who had followed the Indian woman into the lodge, chuckled. "Moon is trying to tell you that water is unfit to drink," he explained.

"But I saw you drinking from this same clay pot just last night," Annabeth protested.

"The Cheyenne consider water that's stood overnight 'dead water,' " he translated. "She's just brought some fresh from the river."

Annabeth watched the Indian woman toss the contents of the pot outside and replenish it from a full bucket. "I could have used it to wash in," she remarked, thinking of the daily labor of lugging buckets of water from the river.

"Moon'll take you down to the river bank to

wash later on. After we've eaten." He spoke to the woman in Cheyenne. She nodded, smiled, and went off to rummage in a large buckskin bag, withdrawing from it a cream-colored doeskin tunic which she shook out and handed to Anna-beth. It was fringed and beautifully decorated with dyed porcupine quills and beads.

"This is her best dress," Eben translated again. "One that she keeps for ceremonies and special occasions. She wants you to have it, Anna-beth. For you to change into after your bath."

"Oh, but I couldn't—" Annabeth demurred.

"Take it. You need it. That riding habit is in bad shape, girl."

Silent Moon grinned, chattered something again, and patted her bulging belly.

Eben chuckled. "She can't fit into it now. Not until the child is born. By that time she will have made another. I promised her a doeskin from the first deer I get."

Annabeth was blushing furiously. No decent white woman would have referred so frankly to her pregnancy in front of a man. Indeed, most women that she knew draped themselves in shapeless sacques and shawls as soon as they began to show and, if possible, confined them-selves to the privacy of their homes for the duration. None carried themselves with such frank and obvious pride as Silent Moon.

Eben, who could remember his own mother so concealing herself throughout numerous pregnancies, accurately guessed the reason for Annabeth's flaming face and, with a provocative grin, muttered in her ear, "You're gonna have more shocks than this but you'll get used to it."

Annabeth tore her eyes from Silent Moon's

protuberant midsection and stared at her feet intently. "Please tell Silent Moon that I will be very pleased to accept her offer of a dress," she said stiffly. Remembering one of the first Cheyenne phrases Eben had taught her she added weakly, "Ha-ho," meaning thank-you.

"So that's all settled," Eben said heartily. "Good. Come on out to the cook-fire, Annabeth, and get some fry bread and meat. The village crier has called all the men to council and since I figger the subject of the big pow-wow is us, I better make tracks." He lifted the tent flap and went out, leaving Annabeth to tag along behind Silent Moon.

It was her first sight of the Indian village in the bright light of day and its clean orderliness surprised her. She had expected it to be dirty and stinking with piles of refuse and ordure lying about. But it was not. Such women as were present also appeared to be clean and well-groomed. In fact they made Annabeth acutely conscious of her own grubby state and she was glad when Silent Moon, chattering softly all the while, as if she could make Annabeth understand if only she repeated herself often enough, led her down to the river.

The day was warm and sunny, more like summer than late fall but all the same the water was *cold*. It didn't seem to bother the Indian women, though, and Annabeth decided that she would show herself to be at least as hardy as they were. After all, hadn't she often had to skim the ice from her washbowl and pitcher back home?

What bothered her more was shedding her clothing in front of all these strange women, who, away from the restraining presence of their menfolk, gathered around her, laughing and chattering, exclaiming, she supposed, at the whiteness of her skin and redness of her hair. Some, bolder than the rest, reached out to stroke her body or tug at her curls. She supposed that, compared to themselves, she must look rather underdone, and tried to take it philosophically. At least they weren't unfriendly.

At last a toothless old crone spoke to them sharply and they melted away, leaving Annabeth to wash and dress in relative peace. Even Silent Moon, who had completed her own ablutions, wandered away to talk to the old woman. From their gestures Annabeth guessed herself to be the subject of their conversation.

Shivering with cold, she hastily scrubbed her body and her hair and slipped into the doeskin dress. Beautiful it might be, she thought to herself, but it was so *skimpy!* How in the name of decency could she appear in front of the men in such a guise? She felt as if she were wearing no more than her shift. The garment came only halfway down her calves leaving her bare white legs and ankles exposed. Silent Moon had thoughtfully provided her with a spare pair of moccasins but she had no leggings that fit Annabeth.

Well, it would have to do. That was all there was. She was kneeling on the river bank washing out her riding skirt and petticoats, rubbing them on a stone to get them clean, when a feminine titter made her look up.

A strikingly beautiful Indian girl was wading onto the bank. She was tall, taller than Annabeth, and slender, with firm high breasts and long black hair that hung straight to her waist. It was a magnificent body, unashamedly naked, and Anna-beth, who was by now becoming inured to nudity, at least in her own sex, paid tribute to her statuesque beauty, looking at her with undis-guised admiration. She was startled when the girl spoke to her in an unmistakably jeering tone, spouting words that undoubtedly consisted of verbal abuse.

Unexpectedly, the old crone again came to Annabeth's rescue, sharply reproving the girl who gave the old woman a sullen answer and with a toss of her glossy black hair, a toss that sprinkled chilly water over Annabeth, grabbed her clothing and flounced away with that grace peculiar to Indian women.

"Pay no attention to Shooting Star," she advised Annabeth in broken English. "For many moons now, she has had her eye on Straight Arrow. He has courted her, folding her in his blanket outside her mother's lodge but he had not yet offered ponies for her. She believed that he would do so after the hunt. But now he brings a white woman with flaming hair to his brother's lodge and the heart of Shooting Star burns with jealousy and rage."

There was much that was bewildering in this speech but at least the old woman could speak English, and Annabeth could have fallen on her neck and hugged her, so delighted was she to find another woman with whom she could communi-cate. "You speak English!" she exclaimed thankfully.

"I speak the white man's tongue well," the old woman proclaimed proudly if not quite accurately. "When Owl Woman young girl—younger than Shooting Star—younger than you,

Flame-Hair Woman," Annabeth started at this new appellation but let it pass in silence, "I captured by the Crows. They take me north with them and there a white trapper traded whisky and beads for me and take me for his woman. We go to mountains where he trap beaver, take many fine plews to Green River rendezvous. I give him two fine sons. He plenty happy, you betcha. He teach me English—want sons to grow up white. But he killed by grizzly bear one winter. When spring comes I take sons and go back to own people. Father of Gray Bull, he take me for second wife. I have fine sons, he think I give him more. But we have only daughters and they die of spotted sickness many moons ago."

"And your sons?" asked Annabeth curiously, fascinated by the old woman's recital. There was a wealth of wisdom and suffering in the old crone's wrinkled face.

The old woman shrugged. "Who knows? Not Owl Woman. They go to mountains to trap beaver for white man. I hear one, he scout for wagon train. They grow up, they go own way." Her wise old eyes rested thoughtfully on Annabeth. "But I know what it like to be alone among strange peoples, strange ways. I help you. I be friend to Flame-Hair Woman."

Annabeth smiled. "Ha-ho, Owl Woman. Thank you. I need friends. Will you help me to learn Cheyenne?"

"I help you. Silent Moon help too. Teach you Cheyenne tongue—Cheyenne ways," the old woman promised. "Make Straight Arrow proud he take you for his woman." She chuckled lasciviously. "White men good in bed. Plenty good. I remember. Straight Arrow plenty good too, you betcha. By the time the moon of green grass comes, Flame-Hair woman have big belly like Silent Moon," she prophesied.

Annabeth didn't turn a hair. She was too busy sorting out the bit and pieces of information gleaned from the old woman's lengthy narrative. Straight Arrow, she presumed, must be a name that the Cheyenne had bestowed upon Eben. She wondered if it had any special significance, as her own new appellation obviously had. She also wondered about his relationship to Shooting Star. He had courted her, the old woman had said, and "folded her into his blanket." Annabeth wasn't well-versed in Cheyenne customs and she didn't know precisely what this might signify. Had Eben been sleeping with the girl? A sharp pain ripped through her at the thought. Had he made her promises that he could not fulfill now that he was taking her, Annabeth, as his wife?—for the winter, that is, she reminded herself hastily.

The three women had started strolling back to the camp, Annabeth lost in her own thoughts, when Eben appeared and grabbed her arm, saying grouchily, "Where the *hell* you been at? I've scoured the camp for you."

She was surprised at his irritation. "Down at the river, bathing."

"All this time? Well, never mind that now. The chiefs have called a council. Some of 'em don't take it kindly that I've brought a white woman to live amongst 'em. They want to take a good look at you before they make a decision."

Her heart sank. "You mean they might not let me stay the winter?"

"Damn right," he said tersely. "You and I have gotta convince them that you're willing to abide by Cheyenne ways. Turn into a good little squaw."

"But . . . but what do I do? What do I say?"

Annabeth gasped as Eben grasped her arm again and hustled her along to the council lodge.

"You don't say nothing. It's a woman place to keep silent in council. They only want to get a good look at you. I'll do the talking for both of us. You just sit tight . . . look modest and virtuous as befits a Cheyenne woman. And don't let on you're scared. The Cheyenne respect courage in a woman as much as in a man."

The chiefs of the tribe were seated cross-legged in a circle within the council lodge. Among them were the leaders of the six soldier societies, each dressed in the colorful regalia peculiar to each soldier band. The Red Shield Society was represented by Eben's blood brother, Gray Bull. He looked particularly impressive in the society headdress made of a buffalo bull's head with its horns still attached and dyed red at the tips. He also bore the emblem of the Red Shields, which was, not surprisingly, a unique buffalo hide shield painted red.

Other chiefs wore complete headdresses of eagle feathers. Every warrior present had at least two or three of these feathers dangling from his long black braids or tucked into his hair. Annabeth knew that only a man who had counted coup on his enemies was entitled to wear the eagle feather in his hair, one for each coup, and she wondered what feats of daring were represented by the three feathers wound into Eben's shoulder-length hair. Dressed in full fig as a Cheyenne warrior, he was also adorned with a necklace of bear's claws and teeth and his earlobes hung heavy with silver rings. He looked as barbarically splendid as any of the savages who sat so impassively in front of her, each performing the ritual of Nivstanivoo, that is, of passing the pipe in four directions, then hoisting it to the sky and dipping it to the earth before taking a puff and passing it to the next man. When it finally made its way to Eben, she knew the time had come for him to speak his piece. Before beginning he passed his hand over the pipestem, as an assurance that he would not speak with a forked tongue.

Eben's words were unintelligible to Annabeth, of course, but Owl Woman, who was permitted to sit beside her, provided her with a running translation.

He began by describing how he had found her at the grave of her husband whom she had nursed through a fatal illness and buried with all honor and ceremony, though burning with fever herself . . . how she had mistaken him for an enemy and tried valiantly to defend herself with a knife. Here a murmur of approval ran around the assembly. Finally, he told how he had nursed her through the dreaded spotted fever and—here Annabeth started—how he had lost his heart to her! She watched in disbelief as he made a a fist and struck his breast with it. His love for the Fire-Hair Woman was strong and true, Eben continued, and if she was not permitted to live among them as his wife he would leave the lodges of the Tsistsistas—the Cheyenne's own name for themselves—and go far away. It would grieve him to leave the lodges of the People who had been his own people for many winters but without the Flame-Hair Woman in his lodge it would be as empty and barren as his heart and he could not live, for life without her would be meaningless. It would be tasteless and senseless, like meat without salt.

Annabeth's heart gave a tremendous thump as Eben's words were related to her. Hastily she reminded herself that she must *not* put too much stock in them. Eben obviously felt a sense of responsibility towards her but as for *loving* her—why, that was so ludicrous it was laughable. She, for one, couldn't see what he hoped to accomplish by professing his love for her. Surely these fierce and savage warriors knew nothing of the tender emotions, of love between a man and a woman. Their own women were regarded as nothing more than chattels and beasts of burden, or so she had always heard.

But no, the hard-faced warriors were nodding and grinning rather ruefully, just as if they knew what Eben was talking about. All except one—a fierce young buck who jumped to his feet and, interrupting Eben, began an impassioned harangue of his own.

The chief's faces darkened for this was an unprecedented turn of events. For a youngster who had counted few coup to express an opinion without waiting for the permission of his elders and without the ceremony of the pipe was an unheard-of temerity. Nevertheless, Annabeth could see that he was making points for the elders began to nod and mutter among themselves. "What is he saying?" she whispered frantically to Owl Woman.

"Two Ponies hates the whites," the old woman whispered back. "He says that they are all treacherous and double-dealing. Only last summer his cousin, Old Tobacco, a highly respected chief of the Southern Cheyenne, was gunned down by a white soldier at the mouth of Pawnee Forks. No one of the whites can speak with a straight tongue," she whispered in translation. As proof of

86

this he insists that the "White Indian" Straight Arrow courted his sister, Shooting Star, promising to wed her after the fall hunt. Now he forgets his promise and spurns his sister for a white woman. He says Straight Arrow may be blood brother to Gray Bull but he is white in his heart and capable of great duplicity. He claims that Straight Arrow should be banished from the tribe and take the white woman with him. She bears the marks of the spotted fever on her face and carries the disease to the People."

The young man who had been pacing back and forth before the assembled chiefs, suddenly whirled and advanced menacingly on Annabeth. She desperately wanted to pick herself up and run out of the lodge but her limbs were frozen with terror and she was riveted to the spot.

But not for long. The young buck snaked out an arm and yanked her to her feet. Oh, God, she whimpered, was he going to whip out a knife or tomahawk and scalp her right on the spot?

Dragging her before the elders, he slammed her onto her hands and knees into the dirt at their feet. Then, yanking her by her curly red hair, he pulled her face up so that she was eye to eye with the most venerable chief whose wrinkled face was surmounted by the full eagle head-dress and who, like Eben, sported the bear-claw necklace, which, although Annabeth didn't know it, was the supreme token of bravery and courage.

Her heart fluttering with fear, unable to understand the Indian's impassioned words, Annabeth groveled before the chiefs for only a moment before Eben went into action.

Springing at the Indian, he snarled, "Get outta the way, Annabeth. I'm gonna teach this young buck some manners!''

The Indian's hand was still entangled in Annabeth's red curls. Eben seized his other arm in a hammerlock, twisting his arm backwards and upwards and snarling, ''Let go of her, Two Ponies, or I'll break your arm!''

The young Indian, whose face was suffused with rage and pain released his grip on Annabeth's hair and she scrambled out of the way. With his hand thus freed he reached for his knife.

But Eben was quicker. So fast were his reflexes that Annabeth never saw his hand move. One moment it was empty and then, in the blink of an eye, the sharp-edged Bowie knife was out of its sheath and glittering menacingly in his hand.

The two men crouched, circling each other, darting and feinting, thrusting and parrying, each looking for an opening. But the old chief barked a command and two Dog Soldiers, the peace keepers of the tribe moved between the opponents. Reluctantly, each sheathed his weapon.

Eben leaned down and helped Annabeth to her feet. ''You okay?''

She gulped and nodded. ''Good girl,'' he said tersely, giving her shoulder an encouraging squeeze.

''Wh-what are they going to do with us, Eben?'' she asked fearfully.

''Well, Two Ponies had a valid objection. He noticed your pockmarks and fears that you carry the disease. I'm gonna try to convince them otherwise. You go on back and take your place among the women and keep your chin up. Don't let them see your fear,'' he ordered.

She sank gratefully down beside Owl Woman who obligingly muttered a translation as Eben again took center stage.

"Straight Arrow appreciates the concern of his Cheyenne brothers. There are many among us who have died of the spotted fever of the whites. True, Flame-Hair Woman had the disease and bears the scars of it on her face. But she is fully recovered and cannot pass it to others. Before we left her wagon, Straight Arrow burned it and all her possessions so that there would be nothing left to spread disease among the People. It is I, Straight Arrow, who tell you this. I, who was given this name by my Cheyenne brothers because, unlike other whites who speak with forked tongues, my words speed straight as an arrow to its target!"

There were approving grunts. Sensing he had won them again, Eben went on. "The Flame-Hair Woman comes among you with empty hands to seek refuge. Would you turn her away? Her, whom I would make my woman, according to the Customs of the Peoples." He paused and took a deep breath. "Or is it that the Cheyenne chieftains have become old women themselves that they are afraid of one small woman?"

Mutterings ran around the council lodge. Annabeth gasped, realizing that Eben had thrown a challenge to them. How, she wondered, looking around her at the savage convocation, could he be so daring?

"Straight Arrow will await the decision of the Council in the lodge of his brother, Gray Bull." Turning on his heel he strode to Annabeth, saying shortly, "Come!" Without a word she scrambled to her feet and followed him.

"What's going to happen?" she asked wide-eyed, when they had reached the privacy of Gray Bull's lodge.

He shrugged. "Your guess is as good as mine.

They'll take a vote in Council. We should know pretty soon, one way or another."

"And if they drive us away? What then?" she fretted.

"We'll just have to try to make it to the fort before snow flies. It *can* be done, if you can stand the pace. They'd give us food and blankets and a packhorse. We wouldn't go hungry, at any rate, or be dependent on such game as I could bring down."

"And if they let us stay?" She was almost as afraid to stay as she was to go.

"Then we dig in for the winter."

"As man and wife—"

"As man and wife. It'll give you status in the tribe. It's for your own protection, Annabeth," he reminded her.

And just who was going to protect her from *him*? Annabeth wondered. She had seen yet another side to him in the council lodge. A hard-bitten man, ruthless and dangerous, as a man who could hold his own among these savage people must be, she supposed. In fact, ever since they had arrived at the Indian camp Eben had seemed to slough off his white skin and become as much of an Indian as any of the full-blooded Cheyenne warriors.

"Ah—what does a Cheyenne wedding ceremony consist of?" she asked nervously.

"Well, there ain't no ceremony to speak of," Eben admitted. "Young buck courtin' a maiden—he ties up his ponies at the girl's tepee. If she accepts them, she accepts him."

"And then?" Annabeth prompted.

"And then her mama and sisters, if she has any, build 'em a tepee and they set up house-keeping."

"And that's all there is to it?" Annabeth gasped in shock.

"That's about it," he confirmed. "Course a lotta marriages take place right after the hunt. There's plenty of food for feasting and new buffalo hides for lodges." He chuckled. "And with winter coming on a young man gets to thinking about a pretty little gal to warm his bed." Ignoring her blush he went on, "Likely, if we're given permission to wed, there'll be a feast tonight. The Cheyenne love celebrations and seize on any excuse to get together for music and dancing and laughing. I aim to sponsor one; it'll keep everybody happy and will insure that everybody knows you've been accepted by the elders and are a part of the tribe."

Annabeth plucked nervously at the fringes of her tunic. "You . . . you do realize that . . . that without God's blessing this . . . this so-called marriage is no marriage at all," she blustered.

"As far as I'm concerned it's every bit as valid as my marriage to Walking Wind," Eben said flatly.

"Oh!" Annabeth sank down on a buffalo-skin pallet feeling that her legs would no longer support her.

"Best you get some rest and quit your fretting," Eben said kindly. "Nothing's been decided yet." He went over to a buckskin parfleche and pulled out a battered pipe which he lit with a glowing coal from the fire, then sat down cross-legged beside it, taking deep reflective puffs.

Annabeth glared at him. Relax? How could she relax? Oh why, why had she let him talk her into coming here in the first place? Because there was nothing else she could do, her reason told her. She was trapped!

"And what about your other woman?" she asked spitefully. "The one that you were promised to—Shooting Star."

Eben blew out a stream of smoke. "Never promised her nothin' and her brother and the others know it as well as I do." He studied the puff of smoke and said carefully, "I have been paying court to her, I admit that. A man needs a woman and it's been a long time since I lost my wife. She's a mighty pretty gal, though, and there's been plenty of young bucks swarming around her, same as me."

"Owl Woman said you had folded her into your blanket," Annabeth blurted.

"It's the custom," Eben said patiently. "Man takes a notion to court a girl, he stands outside her tepee and waits for her to come out. Then he throws his robe around her shoulders and they snuggle down in its folds to cuddle and canoodle. Try each other out, you might say. But the rule is—everybody concerned keeps his or her feet firmly planted on the ground. What's more, her mama stands at the doorway of the tepee, peering out from under the tent flap so she can keep an eye on what's going on. But there ain't no promises made or nothing official, till he ties his ponies up at her lodge and she accepts them."

Eben's eyes began to twinkle and he kept his face carefully averted from Annabeth. " 'Course I could always take her as a second wife if you don't come up to snuff," he meditated out loud. "Ain't no law against it. Fact is, most men of position have two or three wives. One to do the heavy work, one to mind the young-uns, and the youngest and prettiest to pleasure him in bed."

He got the expected rise out of Annabeth.

"Oooh!" she sputtered, jumping up, her fists clenched. Anger sparked in her eyes but outrage rendered her speechless.

Eben chuckled. "I can see you don't cotton to the idea," he said, his lips twitching. "Well, never mind. Dunno as I'm up to it anyway. Takes quite a man to keep more'n one woman satisfied—what with having to provide food and finery and foofaraw. Not to mention," he added wickedly, "between the blankets!"

She was on the point of belaboring him with her tiny fists when he lifted his head, caught her by the wrist and drew her over to the tent flap which he tied back. "Listen!" he commanded. "It's the village crier."

Evidently the news was good for a broad grin spread across his face. "Whoopee!" he exulted, grabbing her around the waist and whirling her around. "You'll be a bride come nightfall, Annabeth!"

"Eben! Eben!" she gasped. "Put me down!" The strength of the large hands clasping her waist filled her with confusion, the more so as her small breasts were being crushed against his chest in a voluminous bear-hug.

"We did it, Annabeth!" he exulted. "We pulled it off!

"*Will* you put me down!" she gasped, pummeling his broad buckskin-clad chest. "There is absolutely . . . no . . . . need . . . to . . . to . . . to   go all primitive!" she panted.

"ah, but we're among primitive people, Annabeth and you're goin' to be my wife," he countered.

"I'm . . . I'm going to *pretend* to be your wife.

93

For the winter," she corrected him. "It doesn't mean that . . . that—"

But what it didn't mean was lost in a welter of feminine laughter and giggles as Silent Moon, followed by a number of her friends, streamed into the lodge. Laughing and chattering they surrounded Annabeth and, seizing her hand, tugged her out of the lodge.

"Eben!" she wailed, seeking protection from her erstwhile tormentor.

But Eben was no help at all. Laughing, he advised her to go along peacefully. "They're taking you to build our wedding lodge," he shouted after her.

5

Old Owl Woman took Annabeth under her wing and described the technique of raising a tepee while Annabeth kept out of the way and watched. The tops of three lodge-poles were lashed together and set up as a tripod. The lashing secured, each succeeding pole was separately passed around all three, ending in a long line that was made fast to a ground stake in order to anchor the structure. The dozen or so poles leaning against the tripod made an irregular circle about fifteen feet across. The last pole to be placed carried the center of the cover up with it. When the cover had been raised it was spread over the frame and capped six inches down the front. Annabeth could see that this maneuver lined up the holes in both edges and the women placed long wooden pins through them horizontally. She was filled with amazement at the speed with which the tepee went up. Several women, working together, had set it up in approximately three minutes.

Eben who had wandered out to watch, grinned down at her. "Think you can do it, next time?" he teased gently.

Annabeth lifted her chin. "I can try." There

wasn't anything these Indian women could do that she couldn't learn—if she had to.

"How many skins does it take to make a lodge covering?" she asked idly.

"Depends on the size of the lodge, of course. "Twenty is usual." He grinned again. "I'm gonna be in debt for these till the spring hunt. Keeping a woman sure is an expensive business," he chuckled.

"The spring hunt!" Annabeth frowned. "Surely by that time we'll be long gone," she protested.

He looked at her oddly. "Not likely," he said finally. "Heavy snow lingers in them passes a long time. 'Sides, I missed the fall hunt, you remember, so I feel obliged to lend a hand come spring. We're two extra mouths to feed," he reminded her.

The tepee erected to everyone's satisfaction, the women laughingly drew her away to be decked out in bridal gear.

Eben had been right about Cheyenne generosity, she reflected. The women had delighted in adorning her with their own cherished baubles and bangles. Earbobs made of blue beads strung on sinew dangled from her ears. Rings and bracelets of beaten brass wire, silver and copper were slipped on her fingers and around her wrists. Her hair was brushed with a buffalo tongue brush until it gleamed with a coppery sheen that put the jewelry to shame. Its color and curly texture had occasioned much mirth.

Remembering Aunt Anna's vitriolic comments on women who painted their faces, Annabeth reared back in alarm when Silent Moon began dabbing her pale cheeks with vermilion paint. But the older woman was insistent and Annabeth gave in with a mental shrug. After all, the context was not the same, was it? Here, in this situation it was expected of her. It was the thing to do. She began to wonder for the first time if right and wrong could be measured and determined by the situation in which you found yourself. It was contrary to the rigid code in which she had been reared—in which moral conduct was either black or white with no puzzling shades of gray. She bit her lip. Was she, then, losing her faith? It could not, she thought with a sigh, have been so very strong—not nearly as strong as she had thought —if new circumstances could shake it to its foundations so easily.

The same applied to the dance, in which she knew she would have to participate. Dancing was frowned upon by the members of her church and strictly prohibited by stern Aunt Anna. There had been a time when Annabeth's toes had tapped to the music of a fiddle and she had longed to practice the intricate steps of the caller when the music and voices had drifted from the town hall on a fine summer's night. But when she had felt The Call and married Asa, she had, she thought, put her desires for such worldly pleasures behind her.

"But I won't know the steps," she protested when Owl Woman warned her that she would be expected to lead the Courtship Dance with Eben.

The old woman cackled. "You watch. You learn fast."

Drums summoned the People to a large circle around a blazing fire. Torches of folded birch bark wedged into the forks of split green sticks had been set around this circle. Women lined themselves up on the south side of the fire; men positioned themselves in a line opposite. Older men and women who were tardier in arriving filed into the east side of the square. Opposite them were the drummers and singers—all of them middle-aged married men—Owl Woman muttered to her. Annabeth nodded, noting Gray Bull among them.

Two men who appeared in the center of the circle caught Annabeth's curiosity. They were, she thought puzzled, apparently men but they were garbed in women's clothing and wore strange beaded headdresses. Owl Woman saw her staring at them in bewilderment and explained, "They the Hemaneh. The Half-man, Half-woman of the Cheyenne. They very important. Have supernatural powers. Very strong medicine." The old woman cackled lasciviously. "They also make powerful potions for lovers."

The men began to move first, the torchlight gleaming on their coppery faces, and gradually the women began to move to the beat of the drums, matching the rhythms of each other's bodies. The beating of the drums and the pattering of moccasined feet on the earth had a strange, wild, barbaric charm.

When the singers stopped their chanting the dance was over, though the drumbeats continued.

Well, that didn't look too hard, Annabeth thought in relief, as the singers altered their chant somewhat and the drums beat to a faster tempo. The dancing seemed to be quite formal. There didn't seem to be any partners, as such, no swinging of the maidens by the young men—hardly any physical contact between the sexes. Even stern Aunt Anna would be hard put to find this type of dancing sinful, she thought. She was innocent of the more provocative aspects of the dance, unaware that the slow sensuous swing of the maidens' hips and their beckoning teasing smiles were an erotic invitation.

Experimentally she began to swing her own hips, mimicking the graceful steps of the other women. As she gave herself up to the spell of the music, the beating of the drums and the chanting seemed to vibrate through her body.

She spied Eben among the snakelike line of men and she began to make her way towards him, moving rhythmically, hoping that he would be proud of her efforts to shed her shyness and join in the revelry.

Many of the dancers were pairing off now, the maidens casting their blankets around the men of their choice, and Annabeth unfurled her own, preparing to do the same. She had almost reached Eben when sh saw Shooting Star Woman advancing towards him from the other direction. It suddenly became painfully apparent to Annabeth that if she did not reach him before the Indian girl, Shooting Star would cast her own blanket over him, thus claiming him as her own—if only for the dance.

What a humiliation that would be! On her wedding night, no less! Well, she wasn't going to let it happen. Not if she could help it!

The drums were beating faster now, almost as if they were hurrying towards a climax. Annabeth altered her tempo accordingly, determined to reach Eben in advance of the Indian girl. Suddenly she realized that, except for the throbbing of the drums, a hush had fallen and that she was the cynosure of all eyes. She became acutely aware that a challenge had been thrown down—a challenge which, with a toss of her red head, she accepted.

She reached Eben a fraction of a second before the Indian girl and, stepping boldly out of the line of dancers, she tossed her blanket around Eben. "He will be . . . he *is* my husband, Shooting Star," she said defiantly. Though perhaps she need have said nothing at all. Eben's actions spoke louder than any words could have done as he opened his arms to her and enfolded them both in the blanket.

A stream of vituperation poured from the Indian girl as, black eyes flashing fire, she threw her own blanket down on the ground and trod on it, as if she wished it were Annabeth she was grinding into the dirt.

"What is she saying, Eben?" Annabeth demanded from the shelter of his arms.

"Aw, Annabeth, you don't really want to know."

"I know enough to know when I'm being insulted," she said sharply. "Translate for me, please."

With that, Owl Woman pushed her way through the line of dancers and, with a little titter, obliged. "Shooting Star says that the paleface woman is not a fit wife for Straight Arrow. That she is of little stature and as scrawny as a starving cur. How can such a one warm his bed or bear him strong sons? What's more, she is ugly and pock-marked, with the fires of evil in her hair!"

Annabeth took a deep breath and lifted her chin, eyes blazing. All the ardor of her pre-dominantly Celtic heritage which had long been damped down by the stern precepts of a partic-ularly harsh brand of Calvinism suddenly burst into flame.

"Tell her . . . tell her—" she spat out, "that she is as big and ugly as a buffalo cow. That her hair is as black as a pot that has been to the fire too many times while mine is the color of the sunset! Tell her that she is a cawing black crow while I am the flame on the hearth. And," she added, carried away by her own eloquence, "that I am as capable as she is of warming a man's bed. That *this* man," turning to Eben, "Is *my* man and that I am his woman and will bear him many strong sons!"

The Indian girl let out her breath with a hiss and fingered the knife at her belt.

It was the old chief who stepped between them and held up a restraining hand. "The Flame-Hair Woman has a temper as fiery as her hair," he observed. "Straight Arrow, it is best that you take her to your tepee now. As for you," he turned to Shooting Star and spoke harshly. "You bring shame upon yourself and your people running after a man who does not want you. Your brothers should lay a lodgepole across your back."

When they got back to the privacy of their own lodge, Eben let out his breath in a long sigh. "Didn't figger you'd be one to engage in a slanging match, Annabeth."

Annabeth was beginning to feel slightly ashamed of herself. Her behavior had certainly not displayed the decorum and propriety that was the hallmark of a lady. "She started it," she said grimly.

Eben's eyes twinkled. "She sure did. Reckon she got more than she bargained for at that. But—" he shook his head, "I reckon you've made an enemy, Annabeth."

She gulped, remembering the way the Indian girl had fingered her knife. If only she had kept her wretched temper! "And what about the others?" she half-whispered. "Will they all hate me now?"

"The others?" He looked surprised. "Hell, no. they'll respect you for standing up for yourself. All but a few. Her special friends will take her part, but she doesn't have too many. She's admired for her beauty but she's proud, touchy and not well-liked."

"But you courted her," she reminded him.

"Sure. She's beautiful—on the outside, leastways. And she's a wealthy woman in her own right. Her father and brothers have given her a horse herd of her own," he explained, "and among the Cheyenne wealth is reckoned in horses. It wouldda been a good match. I never figgered I'd find anybody to love like I loved Walking Wind. But a man . . . a man has needs, Annabeth. A man needs a wife."

"Well, you have a wife now!" She spoke impetuously.

"Do I, Annabeth?" He came very close and, cupping her face in his two hands, looked deeply into her eyes. "Do I?"

His eyes seemed to mesmerize her as his thumb slowly, provocatively, traced the outline of her lips. She trembled at his touch. Instinctively her lips parted at the gentle pressure he exerted and her little pink tongue snaked out to flick over it tentatively.

With a deep-throated growl he inserted his thumb deeper into her mouth, the pressure of her tongue and teeth around it producing a warm sweet suction that was unbelievably erotic. He wondered if she had any idea what she was doing to him.

"You're sure, Annabeth?" he muttered hoarsely. "You're sure it's what you want?"

How could she answer that? She couldn't. Not in words. She didn't have the vocabulary. All she could think of was, "And the Lord God said unto the woman . . . thy desire shall be to thy husband and he shall rule over thee." But somehow this didn't seem the proper time for quoting scripture! In lieu of a verbal response, she found herself nibbling and delicately nipping at the fleshy part of his thumb.

Her unspoken answer told him all he needed to know. "A little wildcat with teeth!" he exulted. "Let's find out if she also has claws!" And he pulled her down onto the soft pile of pelts that constituted their bed.

Annabeth moaned and writhed beneath him, whimpering, possessed of a strange wild yearning. "Easy, gal, easy," he murmured softly as if he were gentling a frisky filly. "It's been a hell of a long time since I've had a woman and I want this to be as good for you as it is for me. The sweetest pleasure is prolonged." With that, he pulled off his fringed buckskin hunting shirt, so that he was naked to the waist. Annabeth lay silent, letting her eyes feast on the rugged masculinity of his body, on the strong rippling muscles of his chest and shoulders crisscrossed by old scars. The tangled black hair matting his chest accentuated his virility and her eyes followed it to a thin line running down his belly toward . . . Her eyes darted away from the all too obvious bulge straining his trousers.

Eben laughed softly. "You can look *and* touch if you've a mind to," he invited. She shook her head, blushing and averting her face from that fearful yet fascinating area.

He was a little puzzled by her shy fascination. After all, she *was* a widow lady. But then her husband had been a preacher and they, Eben had always thought, were queer cattle—ashamed to admit they had the same needs as any other man. Most likely the feller had just pulled up his own nightshirt and her nightdress in the darkness and got right down to business, probably thinking he was committing a mortal sin and needing to get it over with as soon as possible.

But that wasn't *his* way. He had always made sure that Walking Wind had got as much pleasure from the act of love as he had done and, by God, he wasn't gonna let Annabeth go wanting either. Grasping her hand he gently guided it to his bulging maleness. The butterfly touch of her fingers as she shyly explored the hard, hot, cloth-covering bulge, made him draw his breath in sharply. But his sigh was muffled by a gasp from Annabeth as her exploring hand encountered a damp spot, a dampness corresponding to the strange dampness she could feel between her own thighs.

That the same thing was happening to Eben was reassuring. That puzzling wetness must be normal then, and right.

What Annabeth knew of physiology, either masculine or feminine, could have been written on the head of a very small pin. She was almost as ignorant of her own bodily functions as she was of Eben's. Even when she had experienced her first monthly flow, her aunts had dealt with her brusquely, warning her that each month from now on she must endure "The Curse of Eve" and the less said about it the better!

Eben groaned, repositioning himself. "I'm

gonna have to get these pants off or split 'em," he said frankly. "The sight of a naked man in a state of arousal going to shock you, Annabeth?"

She caught her breath sharply, her heart pounding. Biting her lip, she admitted shyly, "I'd like to see you, all of you, if you don't mind, that is."

"Mind!" Laughter bubbled in his throat but he choked it back . . . he didn't want her to think that he was mocking her naivety. "Sugar, he said fondly, "there ain't a part of me that I don't want you to see or know, just as there ain't a part of you that I don't want to see and touch and taste." His hands went to his waist, unbuckling his belt and she, emboldened by his remark, helped him tug the waistband down below his hips, baring the ultimate proof of his maleness. Her eyes went round. "You're so . . . so big!" she whispered, awestricken.

This artless remark puzzled Eben. He didn't think he was any better built than the next man but maybe that husband of hers had been less well-endowed and it was obvious that she had never seen him in the light.

She raised her hand tentatively, daring to stroke and fondle him. A quick responsive catch of breath told her that the light touch of her fingers had a powerful effect upon his throbbing member. To her surprise he took her hand and gently drew it away, muttering hoarsely, "Any more of that just now and I can't be responsible for the consequences, Annabeth."

This speech was incomprehensible to Annabeth. "Wh-what happens next?" she whispered shyly.

He looked at her pityingly. It was just as he had thought. That man of hers must not have been any prize. Gently, he tugged at the thongs that held her dress together, saying, "Now it's my turn. 'Sides, this is the only dress you got. You don't want to get it crushed or rumpled, do you?"

The logic of this was unarguable. Trembling, she held up her arms and let Eben pull the garment over her head. His quick inhalation of breath told her how much the sight of her pleased him.

She was petite and flowerlike rather than voluptuous. Her small but shapely pink-tipped breasts were swollen and sharp-peaked with arousal. The jutting breasts tapered to a narrow waist and flat belly, below which a moist coppery triangle peeked forth between her slender thighs.

The hunger in his eyes exhilarated yet frightened her and instinctively she crossed her hands over her telltale breasts.

"Don't try to hide yourself from me, sugar," he said gently. "I want to feast on your loveliness." And he pulled her hands away, substituting his own, brushing and rubbing his rough palms against the pebble hardness of her rosy peaks.

It sent an exquisite thrill tingling through her and she whispered a protest when he slid his hands down her slender body to her buttocks. His mouth latched on to a satiny breast. Tentatively he slipped an exploring hand downwards, teasing and tantalizing the cleft between her thighs. His touch produced a melting sweetness within her as he sought and unerringly found the most sensitive spot of all. "No!" she cried, squirming half in fright and half in pleasure, momentarily shamed by the wild wanton feelings that rippled through her, feelings that were unutterably sweet in themselves but which strangely made her yearn for more, much more, for something wonderful just beyond her grasp.

"N-no!" she gasped again. "It . . . it must be a sin!"

His chest rumbled with tender laughter. "Sweetheart, just because it feels good don't mean it's sinful. I want to pleasure you, sugar. Just let yourself go. Ride the waves," he urged her.

And she did. Unable to resist the swirls of feeling that ebbed and flowed from his skillful fingers, she squirmed and writhed against him, sinking her teeth into his shoulder, her clutching fingers raking his back in red striations that matched the fever in her brain. There was a brief sweet easing of her craving and then it rose again to build to a new crescendo. Her legs spread wide in an open invitation and he was atop her, the heaviness of his body feeling good, feeling right as the tension built higher and higher. Positioning himself over her, gone beyond control, beyond stopping, he drove himself into her.

Pain ripped through her like a knife. It was enough to bring her back to reality, to freeze her mind and body and she lay suddenly still and stiff, as lifeless as a corpse.

Eben was aware that something had gone terribly wrong. Their bodies no longer were attuned to the sweet rhythm of love. But he was far beyond the point of no return. Letting himself go, he released himself within her with a strangled cry and collapsed beside her.

"It was . . . it was so beautiful . . . and then the pain—" she whispered.

"Christ Almighty!" he swore under his breath. She had been a virgin! But how could he have known?

There were tears seeping out of her eyes and when he drew her head down onto his shoulder they trickled onto his bare skin. Tenderly he flicked them off her cheeks with his thumb.

"It always hurts the first time, honey. But it'll be different next time. You'll have all of the glory and none of the pain, I promise you."

"I'm not sure I want there to be any next time," she muttered rebelliously.

Eben smiled to himself. Judging by her uninhibited response to his lovemaking prior to the moment he had pierced that vital membrane, he took her assertions with a grain of salt.

"Likely it hurt all the worse because you weren't prepared for it," he said shrewdly. "Didn't your mama or your aunts ever tell you what to expect?"

"My mother died when I was born," Annabeth said drearily, "and Aunt Anna and Aunt Beth were spinsters. If they knew about such things they never discussed them with me."

Eben snorted. To his way of thinking it was just another instance of the superiority of Indian culture over white. No Indian family would send a young girl to her marriage bed ignorant and unprepared. On the day a girl passed from childhood into puberty, her older friends and female relatives took her off to the Moon Lodge and there instructed her in the pleasures and pains of womanhood, with prayers and rites of purification and likely as not a feast or celebration afterwards.

Eben scowled. But what about Annabeth's former husband? The man whose grave lay back along the Oregon Trail? Had she been married off to some old codger?

"But your husband?" he persisted. "Was he

an old man who—" he bit off a crude phrase and substituted, "an old man who couldn't be a real husband to you?"

She looked at him in surprise. "Oh, no, Asa was only twenty-four," she reminded him. "But his mother died in childbirth, too, you see, and not so very long ago. She suffered terribly and Asa and I . . . well, we agreed to live as brother and sister until we got to Oregon where there are proper medical facilities . . . Dr. Whitman—" Her voice trailed off. "Asa was most considerate," she said flatly.

Which implied that he, Eben, was an inconsiderate brute, he thought glumly. Well, what was done was done and couldn't be undone and he, for one, didn't regret it. A lazy reminiscent smile played about his lips—no sir, he did not regret for a minute of it, except for the momentary pain and shock that Annabeth had experienced when she lost her virginity and that couldn't be helped. It was a woman's lot, he figured. If he'd known he could've been a mite gentler but . . .

"You still hurtin', Annabeth?" he asked after a minute.

"N-no," she sniffed. "Just a little sore and sticky." She grimaced.

"You may bleed a little but it's nothing to worry about," he reassured her. "I'll get you some water and cloths to wash with," he offered.

Eben gave her privacy to cleanse herself, turning his back to rummage through a parfleche for a small pot of ointment. He grunted with satisfaction when he found it and began dabbing it over his shoulders and back. Having performed her own ablutions, Annabeth watched in curiosity.

"Dab a little of this on my back, will you?" he said casually, handing her the little pot of pungent medication.

"What is it?" she asked curiously, dabbing at a long red welt on his back.

"An ointment for the scars of love, honey-bunch," he chuckled.

Annabeth was aghast. "Oh, Eben, I . . . I didn't—"

He chuckled again. "You sure did. Bit," he gestured to a small set of teethmarks on his shoulders, "and scratched. Just like a little wild-cat," he said contentedly.

Annabeth hung her head. She had never in her life felt so embarrassed and humiliated. How could she have forgotten herself so completely?

Eben tipped up her chin, forcing her to look him in the face. "Hey, now, sugar, don't you go looking like that. You're all woman. Just what a man wants in his bed." He bent over and planted a light teasing kiss on her soft lips. "And speaking of bed," he said practically, "it's getting a mite chilly out here and you're hogging all the blankets!"

Annabeth obligingly shoved over, lifting the robes so that he could slide in beside her. He twined himself around her and tucked her head onto his shoulder with a sigh of contentment. "Ah, this is the life," he grinned. "A cold night, a warm fire, and a warm and willin' woman in your bed."

Annabeth was still troubled about the scars, not the lovemarks she had left on his body, though she still blushed to think of it, but the puckered and whitened scars of old wounds. Timidly she traced one that ran down his shoulder and across his chest, ending just above his right nipple. "These other scars, Eben, how did you get them?" she asked, shy but curious.

He quirked an eyebrow at her. "Jealous?" he

teased. "Well, you needn't be, sugar. I got these scars in an embrace, sure enough, but it was the embrace of a grizzly bear."

"Ooh," she breathed. "Tell me about it."

"Ain't much to tell." He yawned luxuriantly. "And I'm too tired to go into it just now. You done plumb wore me out, woman!" He chuckled at her blush, liking to see the quick color flare into her face. "If you really want to hear about it, we'll save it for some long winter evening before the fire." He chuckled meaningfully, "That is, if we can't think of any more pleasurable way to spend the time."

Annabeth snuggled up to him, reveling in the warmth and hardness of the body pressed so tightly against her own. She was a woman, now, she thought, and he had made her so, and it somehow seemed supremely right. Maybe, she thought, as she drifted off to sleep, maybe it was meant to be. Maybe God had meant for them to be together. Would he have sent Eben McDowell, that wild mountain man, into her life, if it were otherwise? Suddenly she felt supremely sure that, even though no preacher had spoken the words over them, their union was blessed in His sight.

6

It was as Eben had thought. The pain Annabeth had experienced in losing her virginity was soon forgotten and the two settled down to a rapturous honeymoon period in which Eben, as tutor, introduced her gently into new and as yet unexplored paths of love. Annabeth proved to be an apt and avid pupil, surprising herself, as well as Eben, by her uninhibited response to his lovemaking. It was as if she had shed her inhibitions along with her corsets, stays, and petticoats, and become an entirely new woman. Well, almost.

Life was not, however, unalloyed bliss. For in the back of her mind a tiny worry niggled away, like a worm in an otherwise delicious apple.

The original plan had been for herself and Eben to pose as man and wife for the winter, in order to give her protection and status among the Indians.

So, *what* was going to happen in the spring? Would Eben take her on to Oregon as planned, and leave her there, with the Whitmans? Was this just an interlude in their lives—and when it was over, would they ever see each other again?

He had told her that he regarded their pseudo-marriage—their Indian wedding—as valid and binding as his marriage to Walking Wind. But white men often took Indian "wives" and discarded them quite casually at their own convenience. She was sure that she meant more than a convenience to Eben. But how much more? True, he had proclaimed his love for her in the Indian Council. But he hadn't really meant it, had he? It was just a tactic he had used to impress the chiefs and elders of the tribe. Since then, he had not breathed a word of love to her.

And a word of love was what she was waiting for to make her happiness complete. For she had fallen hopelessly, utterly, and completely in love with him. It had begun, she suspected, back when they were camped at the wagon. His strength and manly vigor coupled with so much gentleness and sensitivity had won her heart without her realizing it and, ever since the night he had initiated her into womanhood, she had been his, body, heart, and soul.

"Take therefore no thought for the morrow: for the morrow shall take thought for the things of itself. Sufficient unto the day is the evil thereof," she told herself. She would worry about spring when spring came.

A more immediate concern was the animosity of the Indian girl, Shooting Star. Her eyes shot daggers at Annabeth whenever they encountered each other about the camp. "Avoid her," Eben had advised. "Stay out of her way and likely she'll stay outta yours." But this wasn't always possible and Annabeth, who had heard many bloodcurdling tales of Indian vengeance, found that a shiver ran down her spine whenever the girl pinned her with a black basilisk stare. The way the girl's hungry

eyes followed after Eben alarmed her, too. She
was so very beautiful—tall, clean-limbed, her long
black hair framing a copper-tinted face, her body
moving with the easy grace of a sinuous black
panther. How could a man who was all man—a
man like Eben—spurn her?

"Count your blessings, Annabeth," gentle
Aunt Elizabeth had often warned her. "There's a
silver lining behind every cloud, if you look hard
enough to find it." And Annabeth did. Eben might
not love her the way she wanted to be loved—the
way she loved him—but he *did* find her desirable.
He gave her ample proof of that night after night.
Might not true love spring from the great physical
pleasure they took in each other? she wondered
wistfully.

She counted it as another blessing that she
was warmly accepted by the women of the
tribe—with the sole exception being Shooting
Star, of course. The others were all friendly to her
and Silent Moon and Owl Woman especially took
particular pleasure in teaching her the Cheyenne
language and customs. Annabeth was a quick
learner and a hard worker. Aunt Anna had seen to
that, her favorite maxim being, "The devil finds
work for idle hands!"

It was not unlike the fall harvest back home
on the farm, Annabeth discovered. The women,
young and old, were busy squirreling away food to
feed hungry families during the winter and
making warm clothing to keep them comfortable
in the long cold months that lay ahead. The aims
were the same; only the methods differed, she discovered. Instead of knitting woolen mufflers and
mittens and socks, as white women did, the Indian
women prepared warm robes of fur and made

winter moccasins with the buffalo hair left on and turned inside for additional warmth. And instead of putting food by in root cellars, pickle barrels, and attics, the women went out with digging sticks to gather wild roots and tubers, prairie turnips, cow parsnips, and sweet camas, rather than harvesting garden produce.

But nothing was more vital for survival through the winter, Annabeth learned, than an ample supply of pemmican. It was made from jerky—thin strips of dried meat—pulverized with a stone hammer and mixed with buffalo fat and dried chokecherries or huckleberries. Stored in a rawhide parfleche it would keep for several months. In a hard winter when game might be scarce and the earth frozen hard, too hard to yield to the digging stick, or covered with drifts of snow, pemmican might be the only food available for days or weeks on end, Owl Woman warned her.

So Annabeth learned to make pemmican. She would show Eben that she was more than a bed-warmer, that she could hold her own with any of the Indian women, including Shooting Star! The memory of his contemptuous remark back at the wagon still rankled—"What earthly good is a pampered white woman to a man like me? What the hell do you think I'd want with a foofaraw white gal?" Well, she would show him what a foofaraw white gal could do when she put her mind to it!

She also learned to tan the fresh hides the men brought in daily on their far-ranging hunt for game to eke out the supply of buffalo meat. And, when she found that the Cheyenne women were forbidden, by tribal taboo, to dress the hides of the bear, wolf, or coyote, she offered to take on these

Sue Deobold

extra responsibilities, proud to be an asset to the
tribe, rather than an extra mouth to feed.

So the women, who had at first accepted her
as one of themselves because she was Straight
Arrow's woman, soon came to like her for herself
alone, because she was eager to learn, eager to
prove herself and willing to do more than her
share. And Annabeth, who had never had much
chance to mingle with other girls her own age
except at church-related functions or missionary
meetings, found herself enjoying their companionship, sharing laughter and jokes and teasing the
young maidens about their beaux.

Just as Indians were not as solemn and stolid
as she had thought, neither were their women the
downtrodden slaves she had been led to believe
they were. Some, like Shooting Star were inde-
pendently wealthy in their own right, by means of
the horses indulgent fathers and brothers
presented to them after a raid. When they
married, the horses did not automatically become
the property of their husbands but remained their
own, to do with as they pleased.

Women, in fact, had great power in the camp,
Annabeth learned to her surprise. Even though
they were not allowed to speak in council they
found ways to make their views known and their
voices heard. If all else failed, Annabeth observed,
cajolery usually did the trick!

No, Indian women were not spiritless beasts
of burden, at least not among the Tsistsistas.
There was a roughly fair division of labor—the
women looking after the children and the needs of
the family while the men provided them with the
means to do it—meat and hides—and with protection. Hunting was not considered a diversion
and a sport as it was among white men, but as a

man's duty. It was *work* and fairly arduous work at that, especially when game was scarce. And since a man's hands must at all times be free to snatch up a bow, a lance, or a gun to defend his wife and children or the tribe in general, most of the heavy work naturally fell to the women.

So, Annabeth's days were busy and full but they were growing shorter as Hikomini, the Freezing Moon—November—drew to a close, and she was never too tired, at day's end, to revel in the lessons of love that Eben was imparting to her. In fact, the happiest part of the day was when the tent flap was tied down, the fire banked for the night, and the two of them were isolated in their own little world—to explore and to take and give pleasure in each other's bodies. Annabeth had never in her life felt so close to another human being and she couldn't, for the life of her, understand why sexuality was regarded as so sinful by preachers who had roared hellfire and damnation from the pulpit every Sunday. It seemed so natural—so right—to be Eben's woman and she found herself deeply pitying maiden ladies, like Aunt Anna and Aunt Beth, who had never known the joys of bedding with a man. It was, she thought, like a little bit of heaven right here on earth. And it made you feel so *good*, so kindly disposed towards everyone and everything! For Annabeth it was not so much a case of, "All the world loves a lover," as it was, "A lover loves all the world!"

And, indeed, it did seem that in the Indian world, at least, lovers were regarded with fond amusement. She knew that Eben was the butt of many broad jokes among the men for she herself had overheard Gray Bull grumbling good-naturedly, "No longer does Straight Arrow visit the Society lodges in the evening, to boast of his prowess in the hunt and smoke the pipe and play games of chance with his brothers. No, he hurries to his own tepee to consume himself in the fires the Flame-Hair One lights within him!" She herself suffered similar teasing from the women who twitted her about Eben's size and sexual prowess until her face flamed as red as her hair. But it was done so good-naturedly, in such a spirit of tolerant and fond amusement that she could not take offense.

"Do not mind them, Flame-Hair Woman," said Silent Moon to her wisely on one such occasion when the women were tittering over Annabeth's evident discomfiture. "It is a time of much happiness and joy when a man and a woman are newly-wed. It is as if, for a time, they own the sun and the moon and the stars. Is it not so?"

Annabeth nodded, trying to conceal her blushes at the other women's frank remarks.

"Well, then," Silent Moon said kindly, "Is it so strange that we wish to share in your joy, for life is hard and full of burdens and your happiness reminds many of us of the days when we, too, were young and went as brides to our husbands' tepees."

It penetrated Annabeth's consciousness only very slowly that there was one small person, other than Shooting Star, who frankly resented their all-too-evident absorption in each other—the Indian boy, Little Lance.

Their tepee was close to that of Gray Bull and Silent Moon and she naturally saw a good deal of the family. She was charmed with the coppery-skinned Indian children, especially with the potbellied little boys. She quickly made friends with Turtle Boy but Little Lance was standoffish and reserved. Sullen and withdrawn, he rejected all of her overtures scornfully; in fact he positively seemed to hate her, Annabeth realized regretfully. She couldn't understand why this should be so, for she usually got on well with children and, had the future been less uncertain, would have prayed for a small replica of Eben to cherish and raise.

One evening, when they had snuggled down in the blankets together and were lazily discussing the events of the day, she mentioned the boy's puzzling animosity to Eben. She had been out digging roots with Silent Moon and her daughter that day, and the two little boys had been "protecting" them, running about with miniature bows and arrows, fighting off imaginary enemies. At noon, the women had sat down to rest from their labors and eat a handful of pemmican and the boys had drawn near for a snack from their mother's parfleche. Both of them spoke a little English, picked up from Eben, she presumed, and Annabeth who sometimes felt a little missionary zeal overwhelm her, decided that this would be a fine time to teach them the letters of the white man's alphabet. She picked up the digging stick and began to trace letters in the dirt.

Turtle Boy thought this a fine new game. After all, how many imaginary foes can a small boy slay in the course of a morning? He found himself a stick lying on the ground and began to imitate her, his small pink tongue protruding between his little white teeth with utmost concentration. Lance watched warily out of the corner of his eye. She had caught his interest, Annabeth could see, though he was pretending otherwise.

"Wouldn't you like to learn the letters that make up *your* name, Little Lance?" she asked hopefully. "See how well Turtle Boy has done," she added artfully.

He scowled at her, took the digging stick she handed to him, and then, suddenly changing his mind, threw it back at her, making her jump in surprise.

"No!" he shouted. "Little Lance does not want to learn the stupid symbols of the white man. Little Lance is Cheyenne. He will be a Cheyenne warrior and take the white man's scalps!" He glared at Annabeth as if he would like to take *her* scalp as his first trophy and then ran off.

When she described this incident to Eben, he sighed. "He's jealous, I reckon."

"Jealous! Why on earth should he be jealous?" She propped herself up on an elbow and looked at him in bewilderment. "Of what? Of whom?"

"Of you," Eben said simply. "Reckon he figgers his paw's too taken up with his new wife to pay him any mind."

"His paw!" Annabeth gasped. "But . . . but isn't he Gray Bull's son? Turtle Boy's brother?" she demanded though she already had a sinking feeling that she knew what his answer would be.

Eben looked at her oddly. "I thought you knew. He's my son, Annabeth. Mine and Walking Wind's."

Annabeth's bright bubble burst. The tender dreams she had been cherishing of presenting Eben with a firstborn son evaporated, dried up quicker than the dew on a hot summer's day. Moreover, along with them went the hope that her love would be strong enough to lure Eben away from the wild nomadic life he preferred, a hope that had been tucked away in the farthest recesses of her mind.

Oh, she liked the Indians and their way of life well enough herself. It was all right for a season or two. She could even bring herself to admit that in some particulars their civilization was superior to that of the whites. But that wasn't to say she wanted to spend her whole life among them either, the only white woman within hundreds of miles as far as she knew. There were things about civilization—the white man's civilization—that she missed very badly indeed. Books and music other than Indian flutes and drums, genteel conversation, *food*—milk, butter, cream, sugar and spices. Thick rich cakes and dried apple pies. Her mouth watered at the very thought!

So, while she couldn't quite see Eben following behind the plow or escorting her to church on a Sunday in black broadcloth and a boiled collar, she had hoped . . . *hoped* that some way could be found for them to enjoy together the best of both worlds. Just how that was to be done, she hadn't yet figured out!

But—her chin quivered—now it was all spoiled, that ephemeral little dream of hers. Nothing like that could ever happen if Eben was tied to the Cheyenne by a half-Indian son. No, Lance was more than half-Indian at that, for Eben himself bore a trace of the blood. Thinking back on the boy's dark enigmatic little face and opaque black eyes she could hardly believe that he was Eben's son. He seemed wholly Indian without even a trace of white blood.

"You thought I knew?" she said in a hard, tight little voice, drawing away from him ever so slightly, "How could I have known? You didn't see fit to tell me," she said accusingly. "And he's been living with Gray Bull and Silent Moon all this time. If he's your son, why isn't he here with us?" she added coldly.

Eben tried to explain. "If you'll look back on it, you'll remember I was living in their tepee too, till we got hitched up," he reminded her. "Gray Bull is ... was ... my brother-in-law. Walking Wind was his younger sister. Ever since she was killed Silent Moon has been a mother to the boy. Among the Cheyenne family ties are strong."

And confusing, Annabeth thought grimly. She already knew that a man often referred to his nieces and nephews as *Nats*—daughters—and *Na*—son. And cousins usually thought of themselves and spoke of themselves as brothers and sisters. She herself had often heard Little Lance address Gray Bull and Silent Moon as, *Nihu* father—and *Nago*—mother. But he addressed Eben as "Straight Arrow" just as the others did. It was all very puzzling and she chewed her lip over it, trying to sort it out in her own mind.

One thing however was clear. "He should be living with us, shouldn't he? Since he is your son." Her heart sank at the thought of giving up their treasured privacy but she knew her duty!

Eben stirred restlessly. "I dunno. It's a complicated situation, Annabeth."

Now there was an understatement if ever she had heard one, she thought ironically.

"One thing is—he's all mixed up on account of his white blood. Him and me—we was as close as a father and son can be till he lost his ma. He knows it was whites that killed her, you see." Eben's voice hardened. "He knows that I avenged her but—" he shrugged. "Things ain't never been quite the same between us since. And, living with Gray Bull and Moon the way we were, he tends to think of himself—*wants* to think of himself, I reckon, as all Cheyenne. But we was getting closer, though, more like it was between us before his ma got killed—and then—"

"And then I came into the picture," Annabeth guessed.

"He don't cotton to the idea of having a white stepma and that's a fact," Eben admitted. "But he'll come round," he added optimistically, "given time." He frowned thoughtfully. "Might be better to let well enough alone for the time being, though. He *is* my boy and I'd like to have him with us but him and Turtle Boy are close as brothers—play together all day and curl up like pups outta the same litter at night. There's less'n a year between 'em in age." Eben meditated. "I can speak to him 'bout moving in with us, though, if that's what you want. Sound him out."

It wasn't what she wanted at all, thought Annabeth rebelliously. But her conscience told her it was the right thing to do. A son belonged with his father and that was all there was to it.

"Maybe you'd better. I don't want him to think he isn't wanted." Even if he wasn't! she thought, rolling over and turning her back to Eben, as if to dismiss the subject.

But his arm snaked around her and he pulled her tight against him. "This ain't gonna make trouble between us. Is it, Annabeth?"

She didn't know what to say to that—she couldn't see how it could help but change things between them.

What a tangle her love for Eben had led her into. But it was worth it—it had to be. Restlessly, she rolled over again and buried her face in his broad chest, its matted hairs tickling her cheeks and the tip of her nose, so that she sneezed, a soft little a-choo like a kitten's.

He chuckled, a deep contented chuckle that rumbled in his throat and his hands began to roam over her body in the way that had already become so familiar to her. Presently she heard him groan, "Lord, woman, what you do to me!" His hands were on her now, kneading and squeezing, and Annabeth, lifting herself slightly, found herself opening to him like flower petals opening to the sun. He moaned again, a pleasurable groaning, as he eased himself into her, murmuring, "I love it, Annabeth. That first moment I fit myself inside you. It's like comin' home."

She exhaled sharply, even now sometimes a little shocked by his frankness. "Hush, Eben, you shouldn't talk like that," she reproved him. "It . . . it isn't decent."

He chuckled, sure that she was blushing, though he couldn't see her face in the darkness. "Well, that's what happens, ain't it?" he argued. "I'm right inside your body, ain't I?" And he proved it, moving with deep slow strokes that sent her shivering to the brink of ecstasy, and then, with a quivering gasp, over the brink.

He achieved his own release quickly and collapsed beside her, breathing deeply as he cuddled her close in the sweet aftermath of love. He fell asleep almost immediately, but, for the first time, Annabeth lay awake, troubled. She was dimly aware that a new element had entered into their lovemaking. There was a new urgency, as if each were trying to convince the other that there were no stormclouds looming over their horizon.

7

Eben had a word with Lance but the boy flatly refused to leave his uncle's lodge and move in with his father and his father's white wife. Indian children were much indulged—sometimes too much so, Annabeth privately thought—and the four adults involved agreed that it would be best not to force the boy against his will or insist that he acknowledge her as his stepmother. Annabeth felt a sense of guilty relief at the decision to leave well enough alone for the time being.

It was just a day or two after that that a party of white trappers appeared at the Indian camp. There were five in all—four white men and a half-breed Cheyenne called Slays-a-Pony who had led them to camp to trade whisky and foofaraw for horses and women.

They did not come into camp unannounced. A camp guard had signaled the approach of strangers and a party of young braves, whooping and hollering, had gone out to encircle them and, forming a tight ring around the trappers, had brought them in under guard.

Annabeth heard the commotion and, like the other women, ran out to investigate. Strangers in camp, particularly at this time of year, were an event, Silent Moon chattered to her.

Watching the newcomers file in, she was vividly reminded of a similar procession—the one in which she and Eben had featured. Was it only a few weeks ago? How much had changed since then! How much *she* had changed! she mused. Then she had been a frightened girl, trying desperately not to show her fear. Now she was fully a woman, with a man of her own, and she had carved a small niche out for herself among an alien people. She could be justly proud of that, she considered.

If the strangers were scared, they didn't show their fear either, she noticed. Except maybe the final member of the little procession, a tow-headed boy of seventeen or eighteen who glanced nervously from left to right and who, from the vantage point of her new maturity, seemed very young, indeed. He also seemed not to fit in with his companions, for a more villainous looking bunch would be hard to find, she thought. The half-breed, unlike every other Cheyenne she had encountered, looked dirty and unkempt, as did the two shambling red-bearded giants who rode ahead of him. They were big hulking brutes, one with a full set of whiskers; the other just looked as if he hadn't bothered to shave for a week or so. Neither of the pair appeared over-bright, she thought critically.

But it was the leader of the party who she found most objectionable. A cocky little bantam rooster of a man with little piggy eyes and no chin to speak of. He spat out a cud of chewing tobacco as he rode past and Annabeth had to skip nimbly out of the way to dodge it. She sniffed, having always considered it a filthy habit.

Then she shivered, struck by a sudden thought. But for the grace of God it might have been those very men or others like them who had run across her back at the wagon when she was alone and ailing and helpless. What would have become of her then? It didn't bear thinking of.

Eben came up behind her and put a hand on her shoulder. "Well, Annabeth, what do you think?"

She half-turned around and looked relieved to see him. "Of them? They're not a very prepossessing bunch," she said doubtfully.

He squeezed her shoulder, proud of her acuity. It had occurred to him that she might be so overjoyed to see another white face that she would lose all sense of perspective. "Good girl," he said tersely. "I'm going to the council lodge to see what's what. I'll probably be needed to interpret."

"What about Slays-a-Pony? Won't he be doing the interpreting?" she protested.

Eben snorted. "That's one no-good Indian! I wouldn't trust him to tell me the time of day!" He grunted. "And you stick close to the other women while this bunch is in camp, you hear!"

Annabeth nodded. She could see the sense of that. She wouldn't like to be caught alone by any of them—especially the shifty-eyed leader of the gang.

She trailed along to the council lodge with the other women to watch the proceedings. After the ceremonial smoke the men settled down to serious trading. Their horses had been ridden hard and needed to be replaced. They also wanted women.

Eben's face darkened. "The Cheyennes don't trade their women."

The leader of the group, whose name was Bixby Crocker, and who had a particularly braying laugh, laughed now, with incredulity.

"I mean it, Crocker," Eben said tersely. "We will trade horses but no women." He turned toward the old chief, repeating himself in Cheyenne and waiting for confirmation. The old man nodded, his lined face impassive. "No sell women," he warned, in halting English.

The white man scowled, muttering a curse under his breath but one of the men, the full-bearded one, said, "Aw, what the hell, Bix, we can get along without women till we get to Crow country. Them Crows squaws is some punkins, I heerd tell."

"You headed for Crow country?" Eben interjected.

"Yeah," said squinty-eyes. "I figger we'll winter up in the Absarokas. Slays-a-Pony, here, he knows of some beaver streams back in them mountains that ain't been all trapped out yet."

Eben wondered what a renegade Cheyenne half-breed could be expected to know of Crow country but he shrugged it off. Crocker, he had decided within minutes of making the man's acquaintance, was a loudmouthed braying jackass of a man who thought he knew it all. Well, he would discover that the country he was heading for had some tricks up its sleeve that he had never thought of. But that was his lookout—his and that of the men who were fool enough to follow him. It was his, Eben's, job to dicker with the white men for the Cheyenne, to make sure they weren't cheated. And he would do the job and otherwise keep his mouth shut. He felt kinda sorry for the kid, though. Likely he didn't know what he was getting himself into trailing along with this bunch of hard-cases, who would probably end up getting their hair lifted by the Crow or the Blackfeet.

"What you got for trade?" he said practically.

"Whisky. The very best." Crocker gestured to the boy who took a bottle of liquor out of a saddle pack and handed it to Eben who uncorked it with his teeth, spat out the cork, and took a swallow.

Annabeth's eyes widened. She hadn't known that Eben *drank!*

Eben rolled the liquor around on his tongue and then spit it out onto the ground. "Horse piss!" he enunciated clearly.

"Whatddya mean? That's the best Taos Lightning!" Crocker protested.

"Rotgut liquor flavored with tobacco and hot pepper. If that's all you got to trade you'll wear out your moccasins 'fore you get where you're going, Crocker," Eben rapped out.

"All right, all right. You got me by the short hairs," the other grumbled. "Hey, Lenny, go get me that John Barley-corn we was saving for the Crow," he ordered the tow-headed boy.

Eben repeated his performance, but this time he nodded his approval after a sample taste. "You got a trade," he announced, first in English, then in Cheyenne, and a murmur went up from the waiting crowd.

They took so long dickering over the ratio of liquor to horses that Annabeth got bored and was thinking of going back to her tepee when Crocker motioned the boy to bring out a bundle of trade goods. "We need food, too. Run outta supplies and game was scarce," he announced. "We'll trade foofaraw for pemmican."

Eben nodded and gestured for everyone to crowd around to inspect the goods and pick out what they wanted. Annabeth hung back, feeling shy, and Eben called her over to him. "Take a look and see if there's anything you want there, Annabeth," he suggested. "A ribbon or some such." Most of it was cheap trade goods but there might be something in the plunder that would catch her eye. Lord knew, she didn't have many pretties.

Hesitantly she moved closer to take a look at the goods the boy was putting on display, the firelight glinting on her hair as she moved towards them. Suddenly, the seedy-looking individual with the week's growth of beard, yelled out, "Hey, willya look at that, Bix. The white Injun's got him a white whore!"

Annabeth froze in her tracks, feeling the eyes of the men focusing on her, feeling as if they were undressing her with their eyes.

And then Eben brushed past her and, Lord, his Bowie knife was in his hand and one arm was crooked around the speaker's scruffy neck. "You look like you need a shave, mister, a real *close* shave," he snarled. "Which you're gonna get pronto unless the lady gets an apology real quick. She's no no whore, mister, she's my *wife!*"

The man gulped and gagged, his Adam's apple moving up and down convulsively. Eben loosened his hold enough to permit speech, at the same time pricking the scruffy neck with his knife so that a red trickle dribbled down it. "I...I... apologize," he gasped out.

Eben kneed the man in the back and he fell on his face in the dirt and scrabbled away on his hands and knees, gagging and choking. Eben crouched, waving the knife menacingly. "Anybody else got anything to say about my wife?"

A flash of anger glinted in those shifty close-set eyes but Bixby Crocker said appeasingly,

"Naw. We don't want no trouble. Rufe didn't mean no harm. He just ain't none too bright."

Eben nodded, satisfied, wiped the reddened tip of his knife on his buckskins and sheathed it. "Just so you understand—if trouble is what you want, trouble is what you're gonna get." He took Annabeth by the elbow and led her over to the pile of trade goods that were heaped up on a blanket. "You see anything you want, Annabeth?"

She shook her head dazedly for she was still in a state of shock. She could never quite reconcile the Eben she knew, the gentle sensitive lover, with the powerful fighting man of lightning-quick reflexes who appeared in times of crisis.

"Nothin' at all?" Eben sounded disappointed.

"No, I . . .ah—" Taking courage from Eben's strength and protectiveness, which seemed to flow from his hand into her whole body, she addressed Bixby Crocker timidly. "I . . . I don't suppose you have anything to read?"

The man's piggy little eyes bugged out. "To *read*!" he ejaculated.

"A . . . a book or even an old newspaper? Maybe you might have an old newspaper used as wrapping paper?" she suggested hesitantly.

Astonishingly, the tow-headed boy, called Lenny, pushed his way to the fore. "I do, ma'am. A Bible and a book of plays by a feller name of Shakespeare. Ain't likely I'll ever read 'em. My maw, she sets a heap of store on book-learnin' and she tucked 'em into my saddle pack." He flushed. "I'd be right proud for you to have 'em, ma'am. And I don't want nothin' in trade neither. I'm sure sorry that Rufe called you a . . . a bad name. And . . . and they just make extra weight in my saddle bags anyways."

"Th-thank you," said Annabeth faintly, although Eben insisted on trading for the books. When she had them cradled in her arm she hurried away, back to her own tepee. She had seen enough, more than enough, of the white trappers.

There was a feast and a dance that night but Annabeth stayed well out of the way. She wanted to provoke no more insults or incidents. Instead she curled up by the fire to pore over her new acquisitions until her eyes grew tired of straining over the small print and she went to bed alone, for the first time since her wedding night. It was lonesome and she was still half-awake when she heard him come in, his step unsteady.

Annabeth's small, slightly tip-tilted nose quivered delicately. Fumes of whisky clung to him. "Eben, you've been drinking!" she said accusingly. "You . . . you're intoxicated," she said, horror in her voice.

Eben belched, loudly and satisfactorily. "Not sho very much," he assured her.

"Oh, how could you?" she cried reproachfully. "And with those awful men!"

"Bad men . . . good whishky," he said thickly. He belched again. " 'Sides, I ain't been drinking with them. I been in the Red Shield lodge with Gray Bull and the others. Good fellers," he assured her solemnly. "My brothers." He fumbled with his belt, appearing to have trouble unhooking it.

Annabeth sat up, her lips pursed tightly together. "Oh, for goodness sake, come here!" Whipping a blanket around herself, she got up and went to his assistance, unhooking the belt and helping him tug his buckskins off. "There, now get in bed before you catch your death!" she shoved at his chest and, to her surprise, he toppled over onto the pile of robes and blankets. Right into *her* spot—her own little nest that was nicely warm from her body. Ruthlessly, she elbowed him out of the way, hissing, "Shove over!" and crawled back beneath the blankets.

He lay like a log, sodden with liquor, she fumed to herself, but presently he threw a heavy leg and arm over her and his hand began to fumble at her breast, thumbing the nipple awkwardly. In spite of herself, the nipple puckered and tautened and Annabeth, as angry at her own instinctive reaction as at him, shoved his hand away, exclaiming, "No! You're reeking of rum and smelling like a brewery!"

"Ish whishky, Anniebeth, not rum." He chuckled drunkenly. "And whishky ish dishtilled."

"It's all the same to me!" Her nose wrinkled in disgust as Eben's whisky-laden breath fanned her cheek, and she slapped at the fumbling hand.

"Aw, goddamn it, don't be so goddamn starchy," he grumbled. "A man's gotta cut loose now and then or he ain't a man."

Tears trembled on her lashes. "Starchy" was she! She who had so quickly learned to respond to his overtures, to revel in his lovemaking. But *not*, she resolved, when he came to her bed the worse for drink!

His mouth was on her neck, nibbled the lobe of her ear and then trailed kisses up her cheek, breathing whisky fumes. "If you kiss me on the mouth," she warned him tensely, "I . . . I shall throw up!"

That settled it. Muttering something unflattering about "prissy misshunaries" Eben rolled over and promptly fell asleep. She turned over herself and, grabbing a blanket, rolled it up and wadded it between them. She didn't want *his* body touching *her* body. Not tonight!

But she couldn't sleep. She lay awake, missing the comforting warmth of his body cuddled close to hers, and disturbed by his snores. He had never snored before, she thought resentfully. It was all the fault of Demon Rum!

Someone else who should have been asleep at that hour was not. Little Lance had been warned by his father to keep away from the strange white men. This warning naturally piqued his curiosity—a curiosity that might otherwise have lain dormant. He had slipped out of his uncle's tepee and was skulking among the shadows watching the white men stuff themselves on Indian food that might better—in his opinion —have been saved for the long winter ahead. Lance was not generously disposed to whites! Some of the white men were dancing with Indian women and he was particularly interested in seeing if any of them would try to kiss an Indian girl. He had seen his father kiss his new white wife on the mouth. It was a sight which disgusted Lance and set him to wondering if it was a filthy habit peculiar to whites.

Lance was struggling with a whole host of ambivalent feelings towards his father. In the old days when he was a very little boy and his real mother was alive he had thought his father a wonderful godlike being. He had played with Lance and tossed him high into the air and taken him riding on his own mighty war horse which was very different from Lance's own little pony. But then *Nago* and *Nihu*, his own mother and father, had gone away to far-off St. Louis, leaving

Lance with his uncle and aunt, and he had never seen his own mother again. Bad white men had killed her, he knew that much, and he also knew that his father had avenged her. But the father who came back from St. Louis was not the father Lance remembered. He was a bitter, withdrawn sort of man who was too preoccupied with his own sorrow to pay much attention to his small son, who, in any case, had surrogate parents in the persons of his uncle and aunt. But in the last year or so his father had seemed more like himself again, taking a renewed interest in Lance, taking him on hunting and fishing expeditions, and telling storys in the evening to himself and Turtle Boy.

But then everything had changed again and for the worse! His father had brought home a new woman to live among them—a *white* woman—which Lance considered the ultimate betrayal of his mother! If his father had had to marry again—and Lance himself didn't see any necessity for this since his aunt Silent Moon had made the two of them very comfortable in her lodge—then why had he not taken an Indian woman to wife? Someone like Shooting Star whom he had been courting before the Flame-Hair One had appeared on the scene. To be sure, Lance didn't particularly *like* Shooting Star who was proud and haughty and had never paid any attention to him even when his father was courting her. But at least she was Indian, of the People, the Tsistsistas, and that would have made up for many deficiencies in Lance's eyes.

As if the very thought of her had conjured her up, Shooting Star slipped out of the shadows and grasped at his arm, at the same time putting a finger to her lips in the universal gesture for silence. "Come with me, son of Straight Arrow," she hissed. "I have much to say to you."

He was puzzled but followed her farther into the shadows behind her father's tepee, wondering what she could want with him.

"I wish to talk alone with the leader of the white men, the one with the squinty eyes, called Bixby Crocker," she elaborated. "And you will help do it."

"Why should I do that?" Lance countered. He knew that the women had been warned to keep their distance from the white men and not to let themselves be caught alone with them.

"Because you, too, hate the Flame-Hair One," she replied. "I know you do. I have seen it in your eyes. Now listen to me," she said urgently. "I have a scheme in mind that will rid us both of the Flame-Hair Woman. I will get the white men to take her far away from here—back to her own people where she belongs," she said cleverly. "Then, small one, you will have your father back again."

"Why should you do this for me?" Lance asked suspiciously.

"I do it for myself, as well as for you. Your father spurned me for her—the woman with the flaming hair. And she," Shooting Star grated her teeth with rage at the memory, "mocked me at the dance. I hate her and I will have my revenge for this!"

"My father will be very angry," Lance observed thoughtfully.

"Only at first. Soon he will forget all about the woman with the flaming hair. Just as he forgot your mother," she insinuated.

While Lance was thinking this over, she said artfully, "You know the pinto pony that runs in my herd?"

Did he not? Lance had had his eye on that pony for a long time, ever since one of her brothers had given it to Shooting Star after a raid. It was small but perfectly formed, spirited but with just the right amount of spirit for a young boy to handle. He had hoped, before the Flame-Hair Woman came on the scene, that when his father married Shooting Star, he might be given the pony for his own, as presents were customarily exchanged among family members at that time. But the Flame-Hair Woman had spoiled that dream.

"If you do this thing for me, I will give you the pinto pony."

Lance's eyes lit up. He didn't know that he was being bribed. He thought it over carefully. It would be a good thing if the Flame-Hair Woman were to go away, he considered. Then he would have his father back again and everything would be as it was before. And it would be an even better thing for him to have the beautiful pony for his very own!

"What do you want me to do?" he said again.

"All you have to do is carry a message to the white leader. It should be easy. He has been drinking heavily all evening. Sooner or later he will step outside to relieve himself. When he goes into the shadows or the bushes, tell him that a woman waits for him here, for you to bring him to me."

"What if he doesn't want to come?" said Lance doubtfully.

Shooting Star Woman smiled, remembering the woman-hunger in Bixby Crocker's eyes. "He will come," she assured the boy.

"You won't forget about the pony?" he said
cautiously for he knew that Shooting Star would
not be able to give it to him as soon as the red-
haired woman went away, lest his father become
suspicious.

"I won't forget," she reassured him.

The plan was not without its dangers, she
knew. White men were hasty and violent and this
one was particularly so, she considered. And she
had seen the greed in his eyes as he watched one
woman after another move about the camp. But,
in a way, that was all to the good—he would be all
the more eager to carry off the Flame-Hair
Woman. As for herself, she had the knife that all
Cheyenne women wore at their waists, with which
to protect herself. The worst that could happen
would be that he might be too drunk to understand what she wanted of him. If he tried to over-
power her, which was, she thought, a distinct
possibility, she had her knife and could always
claim that he had stumbled across her in the darkness and had tried to violate her.

Shooting Star tossed back her long black hair.
It was, she thought, worth any amount of risk to
get revenge on the Flame-Hair Woman who had
shamed her in the eyes of all and on Straight
Arrow who had courted her and then spurned her.
That it was his son who was helping her take her
revenge made it all the sweeter.

The plan worked to perfection. It was well
that Shooting Star Woman was prepared, however, for Bixby Crocker had totally mistaken the
nature of her invitation. When timidly approached
by Little Lance, he had grinned, finished his
business, buttoned his fly, and docilely followed

after the boy, his eyes greedy with lust. He licked his lips in anticipation. The way he'd heard it, an Indian squaw would do *anything* a man wanted for a handful of foofaraw!

He was to be speedily disillusioned. The Indian woman, Shooting Star, was ready for him, waiting with her knife unsheathed. When he had approached as close as she deemed safe, she poked it into his paunch. "Keep your filthy hands off me, white man," she hissed in Cheyenne. "I wish to have words with you and that is all you will get from Shooting Star."

Bixby Crocker felt justly aggrieved. This was not part of the deal, as he understood it. He'd thought the Indian kid was acting as pander for some squaw who desired him. What was she doing pulling a knife on him? He began to bluster.

"What does he say?" Shooting Star demanded.

"I don't know," Lance answered truthfully. The foul language emanating from the white man's tobacco-stained mouth was not part of the vocabulary he had learned from his father.

"Why did you not also bring Slays-a-Pony to interpret for us?" she said irritably.

"You didn't tell me to," Lance defended himself. It was *her* plan. Did he have to think of everything? "Besides, Slays-a-Pony was nowhere around," he added in justification.

The exasperated Shooting Star Woman grabbed him by the ear. "You! Your father has taught you some of the white man's tongue, has he not? You should be able to make him understand."

Lance scuffed his moccasined toe in the dirt. He was getting in deeper than he had originally foreseen. "It was not part of the bargain—for me to interpret," he said sullenly.

"Do you want the pony or don't you?" Shooting Star retorted.

Bixby Crocker looked from one to the other, baffled. But gradually it penetrated his slow brain that he had been led into a trap—this knife-wielding wildcat was no warm and willing squaw. He made a sudden grab for Lance who skipped nimbly out of harm's way. "C'mere you little brat," he bawled. "I'm gonna tan your hide for you."

Lance had a sudden inspiration. "You make mistake," he said laboriously in his limited English. "This woman," he pointed at Shooting Star, "not for you. But she have plan how to get a woman take with you to Crow country."

The man's ears pricked up. "A woman who's willin' to go to the Crow country?" He was interested in spite of himself.

Lance shook his head. "She not willing but she go if you make her. She bad white woman. My father's woman," he added as if that explained it all. Seeing the man's confusion, he tried again. "Straight Arrow—my father. He interpret for you today. His wife is the fire-hair white woman."

Light began to dawn. "The redhead," Bixby Crocker said incredulously. He meditated. Well, now, this put a different complexion on things. "I dunno," he said doubtfully, "that white Injun—yer paw. Dunno as I care to tangle with him."

Shooting Star understood his tone of voice if not the content of his words. She burst into a volley of speech which Lance was hard put to interpret. Finally he put together the essence of her words. "She say, if you take even one Cheyenne woman, whole tribe track you down. If you take white woman, nobody care."

Bixby Crocker thought this over. It was a tempting prospect. The little redhead had caught his eye right from the first. Of course the white Injun—what'd the kid call him? Straight Arrow?—wasn't a man to tangle with. But what the hell! It was one against five, wasn't it? Those were the kind of odds old Bix Crocker liked to have on his side. And the men would go along with him. He wasn't a selfish man—hell no! He'd let 'em all have a turn with her. After he'd broke her in good, of course, himself. Afterwards, the others could take their turns, share and share alike. Hell, it'd be a long cold winter without at least one woman between the five of them and there was no guarantee that the Crow wouldn't be as touchy about their women as the Cheyenne were.

"What're you two getting out of the deal?" he asked suspiciously. It was his experience that you didn't get something for nothing—not in this world.

"My stepmother bad woman," Lance explained gravely, unaware of the connotation Crocker put on his words. "My father court Shooting Star and then spurn her for white woman. Shame Shooting Star in front of our people. Shooting Star hate her." He hesitated. He didn't feel up to explaining why *he* hated the white woman so much. It was too long and involved an explanation and he didn't fully understand it himself. "I hate her too," he added lamely. "I be glad when she gone. Shooting Star be glad too."

"Well, now, you don't say!" Bixby Crocker stroked his bewhiskered jaw reflectively, while he

141

thought it over. Sounded to him like he'd be doing these poor Indians a good turn by making off with the little redhead. Sounded like she'd stirred up a whole heap of trouble for all concerned. It was, he thought virtuously, no more than what she deserved for turning a boy against his pa that way. Not to mention making fun of the gal his pa had been courting before she came along.

What's more, as the gal had pointed out, it wasn't like he was stealing one of their own women, in which case, he knew full well he'd have the whole tribe out for his scalp. No, likely they'd all be glad to see the back of her. And if the white Indian came after him—well, the odds were five to one in his, Bixby's, favor.

He threw back his head and laughed his peculiar braying laugh, revealing yellow tobacco-stained teeth. "By God, I'll do it!" he vowed. He made a mocking bow to Shooting Star who looked at him in surprise. "Never let it be said," he laughed, "that Bixby Crocker ain't willin' to oblige a lady!"

8

Eben woke up that morning with an aching head, a queasy stomach and a monumental thirst. The tent flap was open and bright sunlight and air cold enough to set your teeth on edge was pouring into the tepee.

He got up and stumbled over to the water bucket to quench his raging thirst.

"That's dead water," Annabeth warned him calmly.

He gulped it anyway. "Why haven't you been down to the river to get fresh?" he grumbled. That was her job; it was always the woman's job and she did it every morning, usually first thing.

"I've been busy preparing your breakfast. I hope you're hungry this morning," she said sweetly. "I fixed all your favorite things."

He looked at her suspiciously. A smug and superior smile played about her lips. She knew how he felt, dammit. Must've heard him as he stumbled outside retching in the early hours of the morning, barely making it outdoors before heaving his guts up! Goddammit, he must be getting old. Time was, he could hold his liquor better than that. Old! At thirty-two! But the West aged a man before his time, not so much by the living of years as years of living.

"Why the hell is it so cold in here?" he grabbed his buckskins and shivered himself into them. "You tryin' to heat the outdoors?"

"I'm just trying to let fresh air in and stale air out," Annabeth justified herself with a toss of her red head. "If anybody was so foolish as to light a match in here, the place just might explode—go up in whisky fumes!"

Well, there it was, out in the open. Her resentment over his little spree last night. He glared at her, not knowing what to say and she stared defiantly back at him, and then, deliberately, he thought, rattled a metal spoon against a pot she was stirring. He winced, the clatter ringing through his head like the knell of doom. Goddamn! A woman had ways to get her knife into a man's vitals and then twist it good!

He turned his back on her, strapped on his knife and picked up his gun. "I'm going out," he said curtly.

Her lips tightened. "If you hadn't traded food for liquor you wouldn't need to go hunting on such a cold day," she taunted him.

"Never traded no food for liquor," he snapped back. "Traded food for fofarraw. And the hunt was already planned yesterday 'fore them white trappers even showed up."

For answer, she clanged another pot.

"Speaking of them white trappers, I want you to stay close to the lodge till they're gone. Don't venture out unless some of the other women are with you, you hear!"

"I hear," she said without expression. Inwardly she was fuming. Who did he think he was giving her orders!

SAVAGE SPLENDOR

"Likely they'll move on out today. They got what they come for and there's plenty of men on guard in camp, should they try any funny business."

He felt uneasy about leaving her though. She looked so little and so woebegone all of a sudden.

"I'll be all right," she said flatly. "You needn't worry about me. I can take care of myself." Was he actually going to leave without kissing her goodbye? she wondered forlornly. He had never left the lodge before, even for a day's hunting, without doing so. But evidently he wasn't. His mouth tightened into a thin line and he ducked out of the door flap with a curt, "See you later."

Eben had wanted to kiss her, thought about it, but didn't dare! If his breath smelled anything like his mouth tasted right now, he figured it would be the last straw! He squared his shoulders and set off for the Red Shield Society lodge where he was to meet Gray Bull and the others, taking deep breaths of the cold frosty air to clear his aching head. He'd have to take a firm hand with Anna-beth, he mused, or before he knew what happened to him, she'd have him singing hymns and mouthing prayers and he wouldn't be able to call his soul his own. If she wasn't out of her hoity-toity mood by tonight, by God, he'd take her across his knee and show her who was boss!

Annabeth spent a large part of the morning wishing that Eben had kissed her goodbye. He'd looked as if he wanted to. If only she hadn't been so sassy to him about his drinking! Maybe she *had* been hasty and over-zealous, she mused. It was relatively easy for her to overcome her sexual inhibitions, she realized suddenly. Probably because Eben was such a skilled and thoughtful lover. But to overcome the prejudices and habits

145

of a lifetime—albeit a short one—was something else again.

But who had Eben really hurt by his . . . his debauchery last night? No one. Her lips twitched in a wicked little grin, remembering his heaving and retching last night and his obvious anguish when she had clanged those pots together this morning—he had been right in his assumption that she had done it deliberately. No, she decided, he had hurt no one except himself! And she *had* been prissy and priggish. But she would make it up to him tonight! In full measure.

The morning dragged on and Annabeth, feeling lonesome, decided to go to Silent Moon's lodge for a visit. When she poked her head out of her own tepee the village seemed strangely silent; usually it was a beehive of communal activity but perhaps the cold weather was keeping everyone indoors. Most of the men had gone hunting, except for the old ones, young boys and camp guards, but it seemed odd not to see more women about. She didn't know that Owl Woman, Silent Moon and her daughter, and a number of women in adjacent tepees had been lured away by Little Lance by prearranged agreement with Shooting Star Woman and Bixby Crocker.

But the white men seemed to be nowhere around and she judged it safe to venture out. She went to Moon's lodge, found it empty and went on to Owl Woman's which was also vacant. Puzzled, she went from lodge to lodge. Where on earth was everyone?

She only realized how wrong her judgment had been when she went back to her own tepee and found that Bixby Crocker had taken possession of it!

"What are you doing here?" she squealed in

surprise when she lifted the tent flap and went inside. She was more indignant than frightened at first. This was her home, even if there was no door to lock and he had no right to be in here without ana invitation! It was just as Eben had said, she fumed, whites had the attitude that they could just walk right in and take over. "I . . . I thought you'd gone already," she added.

Bixby Crocker grinned, displaying his scummy yellowed teeth, a sight that made her stomach turn over. "That's what I wanted you to think, little lady. Didn't figger you'd invite me in if I come scratchin' on your door so I bided my time."

Annabeth groaned inwardly. If only she had stayed in her own lodge as Eben had warned her to do, she might have had the upper hand. Eben's old rifle, the one that had belonged to his father and which he was saving against the day that Little Lance was old enough to use it, was among his plunder. But Bixby Crocker stood between her and it. It was loaded and she knew how to use it; Eben had taught her. But maybe a show of force wouldn't be necessary; she hoped not.

"Well, I don't want you here," she said frostily. "Please leave." When he ignored her polite but firm request, she added more sharply, "Get out!"

"Now's that any way for a lady to treat a gentleman caller?" he mocked her.

Gentleman! thought Annabeth, inwardly fuming.

He shook his head, his sly little eyes sparkling with malevolent amusement, and his tongue clicking against his unspeakable teeth. "Course, living here the way you do with a renegade white man it ain't no wonder you lost yer manners!" His beady little eyes roamed around the tepee. "It's right comfortable in here, I gotta admit, but an Injun lodge ain't no place for a lady. No place at all. But I got plans for you," he announced casually.

"P-plans?" A shiver of fear ran down Annabeth's spine. He was playing with her like a cat with a mouse, she realized suddenly. Her indignation drained away and, for the first time, she felt really and truly afraid. She wondered if she should scream for help. But there was no one around to hear her, Moon and the other women having mysteriously disappeared. No, she could scream her lungs out and no one would hear or come to her rescue. She would have to depend on herself alone. But could she hold her own against Bixby Crocker? she wondered desperately. He was a cocky little bantam rooster of a man, not tall and well-built like Eben, but she was a small woman and she doubted that she would be any match for him—not without a gun. She must somehow stall for time—try to get her hands on the rifle.

"Plans?" she said carefully, trying to keep a rising note of hysteria out of her voice. "What plans?"

"Gonna take you home. Back to the eastern settlements where a lady like you belongs. Now get your gear together. We ain't got all day."

"H-home," Annabeth stammered. It was the last thing she expected . . . and the last thing she could believe. "But . . . but I don't want to go back home," she protested, playing for time.

"Is that a fact?" Tiring of playing games with her, he moved closer and, leering obscenely, said, "That big white Injun musta got you buffaloed all right. Sounds to me like he's got you broke in real good. Wal, that's all right by ol' Bix. Never did like no virgins, nohow. Give me a woman who knows what it's all about any ol' time." A hand reached out to fondle her breasts, squeezing and painfully pinching a nipple through its doeskin covering. "You and me is gonna have real good times wherever we go," he promised her. "But your man is gonna think I'm takin' you back home 'cause you're gonna write him a note tellin' him so."

"Eben won't believe that. He'll follow us. He'll follow you into hell!" she cried, flinching away from him.

"Mebbe he will, mebbe he won't. Leastways, we'll give it a try. I want him to think you're comin' with us willingly." The thought of the white Injun on his tail made him pause. With a scowl he moved to the tent flap, lifted it and peered out. What he saw reassured him. "It's startin' in to snow," he told her. "By the time we move out the fresh snow will cover our tracks." He glanced back at her impatiently. "G'wan, get your gear together. And bring along some extra sacks of pemmican if you expect to eat."

She crept round the tepee gathering her possessions, extra winter moccasins lined with fur, robes and blankets, sacks of pemmican, inching her way towards the rifle. She dillydallied all she dared, hoping for a miracle, a rescuer, but none came.

If only she could get to that rifle maybe she could rescue herself from her predicament. Could she, she wondered, bring herself to use it, even if she could get to it? Could she bring herself to shoot a man? Looking at this particularly unsavory specimen of humanity—dirty, unshaven, his bewhiskered cheek bulging with a cud of tobacco, his squinty little eyes hot with lust as he mentally undressed her, Annabeth thought that she could. She might even—God forgive her—enjoy it!

Her fingers had just reached out to brush the rifle stock when the man's hand clamped down on her wrist, his dirty fingernails scraping her flesh. He chuckled evilly. "I knowed you was gonna try a trick like that," he crowed. "You can't fool ol' Bix. Figgered you was a gal with a lotta spunk. Wal, that's what I like— a gal with spirit. And just so's I don't wake up some mornin' with a knife between my ribs, you can hand it over, hilt foremost."

Annabeth started. She had totally forgotten the knife that hung at her belt. It might have proved a surer weapon than the gun but, she thought with a sigh, she would probably have been able to use it even less effectively.

The man at her side cackled again, correctly assessing the thoughts that were racing through her mind. "Been wondering if you'd think of that. Didn't figger you'd think of using a knife like an Injun would." He shifted the cud of tobacco in his jaw and spat a stream of amber fluid onto the hard-packed dirt floor. "You're too civilized." Since she made no move to hand him the knife, he helped himself to it, taking the opportunity to fondle her hip and run a groping hand down between her legs. "But you ain't too civilized to give ol' Bix a good time once we get where we're going. Yessiree, you an' me's gonna have some good times."

Annabeth stood, frozen with fear, quivering like a frightened doe, all her hopes crushed.

"Time's a-wasting," he said abruptly. "I wantcha to write that note to your white Injun lover so's we can make tracks outta here." He picked up her Bible and tore out the flyleaf, handed her an improvised pencil, a stick of wood dipped in charcoal and began to dictate. "Mind you put down just what I tell you to," he ordered with a frown, "I can read and write as good as you."

"Dear Eben—" He leered. "That's a nice touch, ain't it?—Dear Eben—The white trappers have changed their minds about going on into Crow country so late in the season. They are going back East and I am going with them. I am tired, sick and tired," he improvised, "of living like an Injun squaw. Don't try to follow us 'cause I don't want to see you again." He breathed a sigh, relieved of the effort of composition. "Oh, yeah, sign it, your lovin' Annabeth."

He spelled out the words, nodded his satisfaction, and crammed his own broad-brimmed hat down onto her head. "Tuck in them red curls," he ordered. "Now, when you get outside don't try to yell or give us away 'cause I'll be tight behind you with your own knife pointed at your back."

She went gingerly ahead of him. He was right about the snow, she observed. It was coming down fast and would, she thought with a sinking heart, totally obscure their tracks in a very short time. It would be almost impossible for Eben to follow them. And, judging by the terms on which they had parted that morning, maybe he wouldn't even want to. Maybe he would think himself well rid of a foofaraw white girl—a prissy little missionary. Tears pricked at her eyes and she brushed them away angrily. This was no time to give way to tears. She must keep her wits about her and try to find some way to escape.

The fire was out and the lodge was cold. Eben scowled. He'd grown used to a hot meal and a smiling woman welcoming him at the end of the trail.

So she was still on her high horse, was she? He wondered where she was—probably over to Moon's lodge, sulking. He stamped the snow from his feet, threw down his rifle, and sat down to peel off his wet outer moccasins.

The note caught his attention almost immediately, pinned as it was to a bead-decorated buckskin cushion on the backrest. He heard the paper crinkle as he leaned back to kick off his moccasins. He reached for it and read it with utter disbelief and incomprehension.

It didn't make any sense at all to him. Annabeth wouldn't up and run off on him on account of a silly little spat—would she? And, if she did, she surely wouldn't go with the trappers who were the purveyors of the hated whisky! But how could a man tell how a woman's mind worked?

The color drained from his face. My God, if she *had* gone with them, they'd use her like the worst drab out of a St. Louis whorehouse! His funny prim little Annabeth!

The paper crinkled as his hand shook with rage. By God, if they hurt a hair on her head he'd make 'em pay! They'd die screaming and they'd die slow—real slow. His lips twisted into a hard grim line. He had a few Indian tricks up his sleeve—tricks that would make a brave man crawl, begging for death as a merciful relief. Tricks he hadn't even used on Walking Wind's killer who at least had had the doubtful privilege of dying quick and clean.

But first he had to make sure she had gone with them. Maybe—hope rose in his breast—maybe she had written the note as a kind of prank, to make him pay for his drinking spree last night. Mebbe she was over at Moon's lodge right now, laughing at him. By God, if that were the case, he'd blister her backside for her. He'd take a lodgepole to her, for sure. But in his heart he knew he wouldn't do any such thing—he'd be so glad she was safe and sound he'd take her in his arms and cover her with kisses.

She wasn't at Moon's lodge. Silent Moon hadn't seen her all day. And, not realizing the situation, at first she was full of her own troubles, grumbling about Little Lance, who'd lured the women away from camp on a wild goose chase. He'd run from lodge to lodge, telling the women that the hunters had made a big kill—much meat for all—and that they were needed to cut up the meat and transport it back to camp by travois. Even some of the older men and camp guards had gone out to lend a hand. And it was all a hoax, Silent Moon grumbled. When they got to the place Lance had described, there was no meat, no big kill, no hunting party and they had had to turn around and trudge home through the snow, for it was just starting to snow then and . . .

Eben didn't pay much attention to this tale of woe. Boys would be boys. Only a few weeks ago a couple of older boys had roused the whole camp in the middle of the night, whooping and hollering, "Crow! Crow in the camp!" The men, himself included, had grabbed their weapons and rushed out into the cold, buck-naked. Dogs had barked, women had screamed, little children cowered in the tepees—and it had all been a big hoax. Lance had probably got the idea from that little escapade. Indians, by and large, had a rough and ready sense of humor and usually appreciated a good joke, even if it was on themselves.

He interrupted Moon impatiently, reading her Annabeth's letter. She listened in silence, her round moon-face growing troubled. Even though she hadn't seen Annabeth all day, she was sure she hadn't willingly run off with the white trappers. "The words on the paper tell big lie, Straight Arrow," she told him. "I know Flame-Hair Woman not choose to go with them. Her world revolves around you. She love you," she said simply, "just as you love her."

The words hit Eben right in the gut. He did love Annabeth, he realized suddenly, even though he hadn't acknowledged it, even to himself.

Oh, he'd loved Walking Wind and he'd thought nobody could ever take her place. Not that Annabeth had—she'd simply carved out a niche of her own in his heart. Walking Wind had been the bride of his carefree youth and he'd think of her always when the wind whispered in the pine trees or blew, wild and free, across the wild prairie skies.

But now it was time to settle down and the redhaired little missionary had captured his heart—in a way far different from Walking Wind but the love was there, just as strong and true. He hadn't realized at the time how truly he had spoken when he told the chiefs and tribal elders in council that without the flame-haired woman his lodge and his heart would be empty. But he realized it now—now when it might be too late.

Silent Moon was chittering softly to herself as was her habit. "I thought it strange at the time that Flame-Hair Woman did not come out of her lodge to help us bring in the meat," Eben came out of his abstraction to hear her say. "She is always ready to help." She frowned thoughtfully, "Do you suppose?" Her eyes met Eben's and then they both turned to look at Lance who was huddled by the fire.

If it hadn't been so cold and miserable outside Lance would have kept his distance but the fire's warmth lured him indoors even though his instincts told him it might be wiser to make himself scarce.

He had not meant to get himself so deeply involved in Shooting Star's scheme but, once involved, he had found it well-nigh impossible to extricate himself. It was, he thought, like a toboggan run—once you were on, it was downhill all the way . . . you couldn't jump off . . . it was less risky to ride it out to the bottom.

Nothing much had been done to the boys who had pulled the first prank. The women had scolded, the men had grumbled, and that had been that. He didn't think there was any reason for his father and his aunt, Silent Moon, to connect the prank he had pulled today with the Flame-Hair Woman's disappearance. He thought he would be safe enough in the lodge, particularly if he kept quiet and out of the way. . . .

Until he heard his father's voice, summoning him. There was a new and terrible note in it that Lance had never heard before.

He got up slowly and reluctantly, dragging his feet.

"Are you Turtle Boy that you move so slowly?" his mother/aunt chided him.

"Who was it gave you the idea for this prank today?" his father said harshly, in a voice the boy barely recognized.

"It was my idea," Lance said sullenly. "Whose else would it be?"

"Kinda had the notion one of the white men mighta put you up to it. No one put it into your head?" his father persisted.

Lance dug his moccasined toe into the hard-packed dirt of the lodge. "No one," he denied flatly.

"You lured the other women outta camp on a cold frosty day. Why not Annabeth? I know you don't like her. If there's anybody you'd wanta play a mean trick on, I figger it's be her. So why not Annabeth? Why not the Flame-Hair Woman?" Eben insisted.

Lance stood silent, breathing guilty defiance.

His father grabbed him by the shoulders and gave him a little shake. "Answer me, boy! Why not Annabeth?"

"I not to blame if the Flame-Hair Woman run away from you!" he said sullenly. His tone told them more plainly than any words could have done that Lance did, indeed, know more about Annabeth's mysterious disappearance than he was willing to admit.

Eben reached out and grasped his chin, tilting the boy's face upwards so that Lance was forced to look his father in the eye. "You tell me all you know about this or I'll take the hide off your backside," his father threatened.

Silent Moon made a quick protective gesture towards Lance but Eben growled, "Stay outta this, Moon. This is between my boy and me!" He pierced Lance with a look that was half-angry, half-sorrowful. "I never whipped you yet, boy, not once in all these years. I raised you the Indian way, the way yer ma wouldda wanted, though I was well-whipped as a boy by my paw and my step-paw both. They had a notion that it was a case of 'spare the rod and spoil the child'," he muttered, half to himself. "And maybe they were right and I been wrong. Whatever . . . I promise you this—you'll talk or I'll beat the truth outta you."

Thus threatened, Lance told everything he knew. About Shooting Star and her promise of the pony, and the strange white man.

Eben listened, his face growing darker and darker. "Where they takin' her?" he broke in finally. "Back East or to Crow country?"

"They say, Absarokas," the boy admitted.

Eben affixed him with a look that he never forgot—a look compounded of hurt and pain and sorrow, anger held well in check, despair, and other emotions the boy could not comprehend—a look that Lance would forever carry with him down the years, to the Little Bighorn and beyond.

But when Eben spoke again it was to Silent Moon. "Fix me up some trail food, will you, Moon. I'm gonna go get my gun."

Silent Moon pulled the boy close and held him tightly to her breasts and distended belly. "Oh, my son," she whispered, tears in her eyes, "for what you have done this day you will suffer. Suffer as much or more than the Flame-Hair Woman." For she knew, if the boy did not, that his father would never feel quite the same towards him again and that, for all practical purposes, Lance was now fatherless as well as motherless.

9

Gray Bull had gone directly from the hunt to the lodge of the Red Shields. When he came back to his own tepee and Silent Moon told him what had transpired, he said instantly, "Woman, prepare food for the trail. It may be that my brother will need my help. I will follow him." And with that, he sat down cross-legged before the fire and began to chant his prayers and to mix his paints for war.

It was dusk when Gray Bull caught up with Eben who was slowed down trying to follow a trail that was almost eradicated, while his own was easy to trace for the snow had stopped some time late in the afternoon.

Gray Bull was impressive in the full regalia of the Red Shield warrior. He had taken time to dye his body red. He wore the buffalo headdress with its horn tips dipped in vermilion and, of course, he carried the red shield. Even his horse was painted but it was his face that was the most striking of all. He had drawn a blue-black circle around it, filling it in with yellow pigment. Fine dots under his left eye meant that he had been born near water—in his case, the Cheyenne River. The bold red lines that were drawn from the eyes to the lobes of the ears and then dabbed across the chin meant that he was painted for war.

Eben scowled when he saw him. "Go back, Gray Bull," he said to him. "This ain't your fight."

"If it is my brother's fight, it is my fight, also," the Red Shield warrior said calmly. "Only the mountains live forever. A warrior, such as I, is born for his season and he fights as the Great Spirit directs him. If he is blessed by the Great Spirit he will be permitted to make many coups before his time comes, and if he dies in battle, fighting against the enemy, he will gain the greatest coup of all, death in victory. You know this my brother, would you have Gray Bull turn his back on a fight like a frightened old woman instead of living in honor as befits a Cheyenne warrior?"

"Honor ain't gonna fill no empty bellies and you got a pregnant woman and children depending on you," said Eben bluntly. "I ain't got no one to think of but Annabeth."

"And Little Lance," Gray Bull said slyly.

Eben shook his head.

"So my sister's son is wholly my son, now?" said Gray Bull sadly. "He is young, my brother, and the young make mistakes."

Eben's face hardened. "This mistake may cost Annabeth her life," he said grimly.

When it got too dark to see, Eben had to concede that Gray Bull was right—it was time to make camp. As it was, he had nearly lost the trail several times. He was, Eben figured, as good a tracker as the average Indian but Gray Bull had an exceptional talent for it. He was extraordinarily patient and tireless and he had a kind of sixth sense that allowed him somehow to pick up the trail again, even when, for a time at least, it seemed lost. When Eben commented on this, Gray bull said gravely, "It is the Great Spirit, Heammawihio, who directs me, my brother." The implication, Eben supposed, was that if only he, Straight Arrow, would have faith, he could do the same.

Well, Eben thought to himself, Heammawihio hadn't helped Walking Wind any. And he, personally, didn't have much faith that Annabeth's God would help her now. In their own way, he mused, the Plains Indians were as fanatically religious as the Christian missionaries. The wild and lonesome prairies did that to a man, he reflected, made him feel a closeness to God. He'd felt like that a time or two himself but, his face hardened, not since he'd lost Walking Wind.

A low groan which he tried to suppress and could not burst from him at the thought of his first wife's fate. Oh, God, he prayed, though he didn't actually think of it as such—it wasn't verbal, just a lot of feelings bubbling around inside him—Oh, God, please don't let Annabeth suffer the same as Walking Wind did. She had died fighting for her honor, and lost. Annabeth had a lot of spunk in her own way but he didn't think she could take that kind of punishment and live—even if they didn't actually kill her, as his first wife's rapist had done, something inside her would die a little. She was too fine-drawn, too delicate, to be subjected to such treatment. All that kind of thing, all that went on between a man and a woman was, in her eyes, so private; she was so sensitive on the subject. He was sure that her sense of shame and degradation would kill her spirit, if their brutality did not actually—physically—put an end to her existence.

He bit down on his lip till the blood came to stifle another groan but Gray Bull, who was squatting by their small camp fire eating a handful of pemmican, must have heard him or sensed something for he looked up quickly.

"Let us smoke, my brother," he said gravely, standing up and taking out the pipe. "For the smoke will travel up to Heammawihio and will be a prayer to him. It might also help if you made a sacrifice," he added.

"A sacrifice," Eben repeated numbly.

"You know that among our people it is believed that personal suffering is acceptable to the powers above and is likely to secure their favor," Gray Bull reminded him.

God! Wasn't he suffering enough as it was? Eben thought resentfully. But he was willing to do anything—anything that might appease the powers that be, or God, or whatever you might wish to call it. He would do anything that might predispose them or Him in her favor!

"By the sacrifice of yourself it may be that you will gain the favor of the Maiyun, the powers that control the affairs of men and bring good fortune or bad," Gray Bull thus encouraged him.

Eben wondered what Annabeth would think of the procedure he was about to undergo. Would she call it a primitive barbaric superstition? But, after all, her God-made-flesh had sacrificed himself upon the cross for all mankind. Wasn't it only fitting that he, who loved her, sacrifice a little bit of his flesh and his blood for her well-being?

"Will you help me perform the sacrifice, Gray Bull?" he asked. "Will you do the cutting?"

"This I will do for my brother and his woman," Gray Bull said solemnly.

Eben, who knew what was coming, rolled up his sleeves, revealing forearms that were hard, muscular, and covered with wiry black hair.

Gray Bull unsheathed his knife, chanted a prayer to the spirits, and punctured his friend's skin, carefully drawing a design in the skin, through the blood that was oozing from the wound. He made a picture of a horse's hoof print on each arm, then washed the wounds with cold white snow, muttering his approval for Eben had not flinched. Indeed, he felt hardly any pain, not nearly so much as his heartache for Annabeth brought to him. In fact, in some mysterious way, the physical pain seemed to diminish the mental anguish he was suffering.

Next, Gray Bull worked his knife back and forth in a scraping slicing fashion and removed two long strips of skin from each arm. Then he washed the wounds thus produced in clean snow again to staunch the freely flowing blood. Eben knew that the two long strips of his flesh would be offered up to Heammawihio to bring good fortune. Tonight, and for three successive nights,—four in all—Gray Bull would burn those strips of flesh and the smoke from his burning flesh would be scattered on the wind so that his prayers would travel on it up to Heammawihio.

He, Eben, didn't believe any of it, of course, but he was never one to mock another's beliefs and it was, moreover, a case of any port in a storm. Nevertheless, he lay down to wait for dawn and to snatch a few hours of rest, feeling strangely comforted.

Up ahead on the trail, Annabeth was trying to find what comfort she could in her situation and finding precious little. It seemed to her that God himself had abandoned her. She had never in her sheltered life—and she knew now just how sheltered it had been—experienced such degradation. Her only consolation was that she hadn't been violated—yet. And desperately, she was clinging to the faint hope that Eben was somewhere back on the trail behind them.

He wouldn't believe that . . . that damnable note that she had been forced to leave him, would he? Surely not. He wouldn't be deceived! He would surely know better, know that she wouldn't voluntarily run off with this bunch of hooligans and desperadoes. He would know that she wouldn't be fool enough to believe Bixby Crocker's lies. And in any case, she didn't *want* to go home—she wanted to be with Eben. Wherever he might be, *that* was home to her!

But he didn't know that, did he? He didn't know how she felt about him. She had been very careful not to tell him that she loved him. It had been on the tip of her tongue, more often than not, especially when they were in bed together. Sometimes it was all she could do to bite the words back, but she had somehow managed not to let herself blurt them out. She was waiting for some word from him—she didn't want her love to be a burden on him. She was too proud for that.

And maybe now, after her rejection of him last night, he would think that she despised him. Worse yet, maybe considering her disdainful, holier-than-thou attitude towards him last night and this morning, maybe *he* now despised *her*!

What had he called her? A prissy missionary!

Starchy! Goddamn starchy! Maybe he wouldn't want to get her back, maybe he would think himself well rid of her, despite the bravely defiant words she had flung at Crocker that, "Eben will follow you into hell!" Maybe Eben would think that he had already gone to enough trouble with her, nursing her back to health the way he had, that she had repaid her debt by freely giving him the use of her body and that now they were quits. Maybe he was only too ready to wash his hands of her!

No! She couldn't let herself think that.... That kind of thinking would drive her mad. She had to cling to the belief that Eben was back there on the trail. She didn't know how he could find it in this blinding white world but she knew that he would, if he wanted to. Eben could do anything he set his mind to!

Her hopes of effecting a rescue for herself had faded almost immediately. She was sure she wouldn't be able to get away from her persecutors on her own. For one thing, she was terrified of losing herself in this wild white wilderness. For another, the men never took their eyes off her, not even to let her go behind a bush or a rock to answer a call of nature. When sheer physical misery finally forced her to do so in front of them—what choice did she have?—they derived the utmost amusement from her wretched embarrassment. Their brutally frank and filthy comments were almost unendurable. It was so different from Eben's gentle and matter-of-fact approach when she was so ill and weak and utterly dependent upon him, that she wondered that these men could be of the same species.

Some human beings, she decided, didn't

deserve to be considered as human—they were lower than the lowest species of animal life, whatever the lowest species of animal life might be. Whatever it was, they were far below it, she decided long before that day was over.

For not only could they not keep their eyes off her, they couldn't keep their filthy hands off her either, especially now that they were camped for the night. Their leader, Bix Crocker, didn't seem to mind, even though he had her earmarked for himself.

Short of actually raping her, he let them do as they pleased. Indeed, he seemed to get a perverted pleasure out of seeing her mauled and man-handled, pinched, prodded, poked, and fondled. It aroused him, she realized with horror, to see her thus degraded, to force her to run her hands over a man's genitals until he was feverish with lust and then cut him off with a curt, "None o' that, boys. You don't get any o' that good stuff till ol' Bix has had his share. Yessiree, when ol' Bix is plumb wore out—he used a blunt expression that made Annabeth wince—then and only then can you take your turn on her. And the sight of you boys taking yore pleasure in her is gonna turn me on all over again!"

Only gradually did it occur to her that her shock and horror and hatred so openly expressed gave them, in itself, a perverted thrill. After she realized that, she tried her best to preserve a stoic countenance, trying to control her blushes and close her ears to their filthy language and insinuations.

But it wasn't easy to ignore, especially when Crocker chose to amuse himself by riding beside her and describing in lurid detail just exactly what he was going to do to her and how he was going to do it. Some of the things he described sounded so outlandish to her that she wondered if they could actually be done by two human beings. It didn't, she thought, sound physically possible.

She was unutterably thankful when they got into the foothills and the trail narrowed so that they had to ride single file.

She tried dropping behind, hoping to slow them up and wondering if she dared leave something behind to mark the trail for Eben—a bead off her doeskin tunic, perhaps? But one or another of them was always behind her, chivvying her along and she didn't dare be too obvious.

As the torturous and seemingly endless day progressed, she alternately longed for and dreaded the moment when the time came to call a halt for the night and set up camp. Longed for it because she was so thoroughly exhausted. Dreaded it because she was sure they would not let her rest. They would be on her, she thought, like a bunch of rutting animals. Except perhaps for the boy . . .

The boy, Lenny, seemed shamefaced and embarrassed by the harsh treatment the others were subjecting her to. Oh, he was keeping up a big front before the other men—if you could call them men, this scum of the earth—even, occasionally, directing some gibes at her himself. But she could sense that his heart wasn't in it. And when they halted to make camp, it was he who brought food—her own pemmican—to her.

She was too tired to eat and when she shook her head and turned her face away, he said with unexpected kindness, "Ain't no sense in starving yourself, ma'am. You gotta keep your strength up."

Keep her strength up for what? she wondered. More humiliation and degradation? But she began to pick at her food, if only to show him that she was thankful for his little bit of kindness.

The boy cast a wary look around and, satisfied that nobody was watching him, hunkered down beside her.

No one was paying any attention to them. The half-breed had been sent or had gone off on some errand of his own. The two big bruisers were busily engaged in trying to get a fire going and Bixby Crocker was supervising them. They seemed curiously inept and she wondered how they had managed to survive out here as long as they had. Probably the half-breed had been doing all of the work, she thought critically. The fire was giving off more smoke than flame or heat and she thought detachedly that its signal smoke would probably bring the whole Crow nation down upon them. She could have done a far better job of it herself. Didn't they know that pine and wet pine, at that, would give off smoke and sparks. What they should have done was look for willow and peeled the bark away, or for a stand of choke-cherries or aspen. Even scrub oak would burn better than pine, she thought scornfully.

The boy startled her, saying apropos of nothing at all, "What's a lady like you doing way out here anyways? How'd ya come to marry up with that white Injun? First time I set eyes on him I took him for an Injun hisself."

"So did I." She managed a faint smile. "Among the mountain men, to be told 'I took you for an Injun,' is a compliment."

"He a mountain man?"

"He was."

"Knows Bridger and Broken Hand Fitzpatrick, an' Kit Carson, I suppose."

"Yes," said Annabeth shortly. She was almost too tired to talk.

The boy chewed pemmican thoughtfully. "So how'd ya come to marry up with him?" he persisted.

Annabeth hesitated. It really wasn't any of his business but if she could make a friend of him . . . or alternately impress him with Eben's prowess and powerful friends . . . He was too frail a reed to depend on, of course, but it was better to have a friend than an enemy. So she told him briefly of the circumstances in which she had first met Eben. Just talking about him made her feel better. It made her even surer that he would come for her.

"Then you ain't really married to him, like he said back at the Injun camp," the boy remarked when she had come to the end of her tale.

"Well, n-no." Annabeth admitted. Seeing the sudden gleam of excitement in his eye, she saw her mistake at once and said quickly, "But we are married in the Indian way. I'm his wife in the sight of God and . . . and next spring we're going across the mountains so we can find a preacher and be married in the white man's way." This was her own private little fantasy and she saw no harm in sharing it with the boy, if it would give her added status in his eyes.

"That Injun kid said you was a Bad Woman," the boy confided.

"Injun kid?" Annabeth was puzzled.

"Yer man's Injun son," he explained, telling her what he knew of Bixby Crocker's run-in with Shooting Star and Little Lance, ending by repeating what the boy had said of her.

"Well, I'm not a . . . a Bad Woman," Annabeth said indignantly. "In fact, I'm a missionary. I was heading out to the Whitman mission in Oregon when . . . when I met Eben." She strongly suspected that to young Lenny women were divided into two categories, the Bad and the Good, according to whether they enjoyed sexual relations or endured them and she wanted to impress upon him that she belonged to the latter category.

His eyes bugged out. "You . . . you was a missionary," he gulped.

"Indeed I was," Annabeth reeled off some impressive-sounding credentials from the American Board of Missions.

"Gosh!" Lenny breathed, sounding suddenly very boyish and as impressed as Annabeth could wish. "Maybe I oughtta tell Bix and the others."

He half-rose but Annabeth caught at his sleeve. "No, don't!" she said urgently. She could imagine what capital Bixby Crocker and hulking companions would make of this information. They would, she thought grimly, derive even greater enjoyment out of humiliating her!

"You . . . you mustn't tell," she hissed. "The Lord . . . the Lord will smite them down in his own good time," she said with proper missionary fervor, "as he did the . . . the Philistine and the . . . the Amelekites and the—" There were any number of smitings in the Old Testament but in the stress of the moment she couldn't remember them in detail. "Just wait. You'll see!" she assured him with zeal.

Lenny looked around him nervously, not wishing, she presumed, to be among those smitten.

Sue Deobold

"You don't look like you belong with the rest of them?" It was part question and part reassurance. Lenny was obviously quite credulous and given time she thought she might be able to work on his credulity. Maybe, she thought hopefully, he could be persuaded to let her escape or help her in some way—she couldn't think how, she would have to wait and see.

"Don't neither," he said sullenly. Suddenly he burst out resentfully, "They think I don't know what to do with a woman. You heard 'em today."

Annabeth nodded. Part of their fun had been directed towards the hapless Lenny as well as herself. They had ragged him mercilessly, assuring him that they would show him what to do with her when his turn came. Her face burned at the memory of their graphic descriptions.

"Well, I do," he said, still resentful. "It was a gal, a woman, that got me into this fix in the first place. If it wasn't for her, I'd be back home on the farm right now."

Which was exactly where he belonged, thought Annabeth. She could almost have felt sorry for him if she hadn't felt even sorrier for herself. "She was a Bad Woman?" she guessed.

"Damn right. Sally Benson, on the farm next to my folks'." His pale blue eyes darkened with anger. "She was free with all the boys roundabout and then when she got caught and needed a father for her bas—for her brat, she named me. It couldda been a half dozen other fellers but her paw come after me with a shotgun so I lit out. Dunno why she picked me," he said sullenly.

Annabeth thought she knew. Lenny was obviously malleable as well as credulous. "And then you got mixed up by Bix Crocker?" she prompted.

"Met him in a tavern in St. Lou. He was talkin' big about the fortune he was gonna make trapping beaver—him and Rufe and Wesley. Well, it sounded good to me and he made it sound like a favor, him letting me tag along."

Annabeth frowned. "But the bottom has fallen out of the fur trade," she protested, quoting Eben. "Everybody knows that."

He looked at her doubtfully. "My husband says so and he ought to know," she said firmly. "He trapped with Bridger. And he gave up trapping, you know, to build a fort to trade with emigrants on the Oregon Trail."

"Bix says the market is bound to pick up again," Lenny said uncertainly but Annabeth could see that she had shaken his confidence in his companions.

"Hey, watcha whisperin' about?" Bixby Crocker abandoned the dubious comfort of the smoldering fire and wandered over to where Annabeth crouched, the boy hunkered down beside her. "You whisperin' sweet nothings into her ear, kid? Figger she'll spread her legs faster for you?" He threw back his head and uttered that peculiar braying laugh of his that so irritated Annabeth's nerves.

He had been chewing a mouthful of pemmican as he talked. Now he picked his teeth with his thumbnail, removed a morsel of meat from between his teeth, inspected it, and wiped it on his pants' leg. "You ready to bed down for the night, girlie?" he leered down at her. " 'Cause ol' Bix is ready and more'n ready. See if he ain't." He grabbed her by the arm and yanked her to her feeet, grinding the lower half of his body lasciviously into hers. She swayed, half-fainting with fear and instinctively clutched at him for support.

"Will ya look at that boys!" Bixby grinned. "This lil gal can't wait to get her arms round ol' Bix." The two men called Rufe and Wesley had gathered round, grinning themselves and cracking coarse jokes. The redbearded one had actually exposed himself, Annabeth saw with horror. She cast a wild look around her but no help was at hand. Even Lenny had melted away into the darkness.

Bixby hauled her over to the fire, near which he had spread his bedroll. "All the comforts of home," he announced. "Much as you got from yore white Injun lover, anyways. Hey, do Injuns do it any different'n white men?" He leered at her. "Maybe you can teach old Bix a trick or two, to-night!"

Annabeth looked at him imploringly, a look that would have melted a heart of stone, if only Bixby Crocker had had a heart. Oh, God, she thought wildly, what should she do? Should she put up a fight? Bite and scratch and claw? Or should she lie limp and grit her teeth and, hopefully, get it over with as soon as possible? Maybe that would be best, for her instincts warned her that men like these would derive even more enjoyment from watching her struggle futilely. And she knew resistance would be futile for it was three men against one small woman. She didn't count Lenny who had run off into the night. She also knew that if she did put up a fight the two hulking brutes called Rufe and Wesley would, no doubt, take a hand, holding her down until their own turns came.

She shuddered. No, better to just lie back and endure it patiently, pretend that it wasn't happening to her. But how could she bear it? She squeezed up her eyes in prayer. "Oh, God, please please help me!" she prayed.

He did. In a most unexpected fashion.

The half-breed suddenly materalized out of the darkness and, running to the fire, kicked it out.

"Hey, watcha doin'!" Bixby Crocker protested.

The half-breed grunted. "Two men back on the trail. The white man and one other. No want them see smoke."

Annabeth's heart leaped in her throat. Eben! Eben was on the trail!

Despite the cold, little beads of sweat broke out on Crocker's forehead. "The hell you say!" he swore.

Among the men a hubbub broke out. "Hey, Bix, I thought you said that white Injun wouldn't foller us," Rufe complained. He glanced around him nervously as if he expected to see Eben materalize out of the shadows, Bowie knife in hand.

"Whaddya gonna do now, Bix?" the red-bearded one demanded.

Bixby Crocker rubbed his scruffy unshaven jaw. "How far back?"

The half-breed shrugged. "Many miles. I climb up ridge," he pointed. "They far below."

"I say we leave the woman here and go on," Rufe broke in. "That's what he's after—the woman."

Bixby Crocker cursed. "The hell with that. The woman goes with us. It's five against two. Them's still good odds. We get farther up in the mountains, mebbe we can lay an ambush."

"An' they can't follow us in the dark; they'll

have to make camp soon," Wesley said practically. "We got all night with the woman, leastways. I say we take her down and have our fun with her here and now."

Annabeth turned pale.

"Who's boss here, you or me?" Crocker demanded. He stood irresolute, however, undecided as to the best course. Beneath all of his bluster, he was a coward, Annabeth thought with contempt. She could sense, could smell the fear in him. She decided to try running a bluff. Really give him something to think about.

Wrenching herself out of his grip she spat at him, "Touch me if you dare! If you . . . you take me, Eben will hunt you down. Just like the man who killed his first wife! He won't rest till he's made you pay! He'll cut out your heart and feed it to the vultures! He'll—" she cast around in her mind for Indian tortures she had heard of but never seen practiced among the Cheyenne. "He'll take a sharpened stick and poke out your eyes." He'll tie you up and build a fire between your legs. You'll burn with a fire hotter than you burn for me!" she cried, half-hysterical. "And . . . and after that, he'll take a knife and . . . and cut off your privates, piece by piece by little piece—" She could hear her own voice going on and on as if someone else were talking; she could hardly believe such words were coming out of her own mouth!

"Shuddup!" Crocker backhanded her across the face, a blow that sent her staggering backwards almost into the remains of the fire. She shook her head dizzily, her knees buckling, half-dazed by the blow that made her head ring.

"We'll hold up here for the night," he decided.

"It's too dark for us to move on but it's also too dark for him to foller us. At first light, we'll move out and look for a good place to lay an ambush."

"An' the woman?" Wesley asked eagerly.

"Nobody touches the woman. First man who brings down the white Injun, he gets first grabs on her," he decided. "Lenny," he bawled. "Lenny! Goddamit, where is that kid?"

When the boy came hesitantly into the light, Crocker hauled Annabeth to her feet and almost threw her at the boy. "You, kid, you're gonna take charge of the bitch. An' if I catch you sniffing round her 'fore I give you leave, I'll have yer hide!" he blustered. "Likewise if you let her get away. Tie her up to you with buckskin thongs and don't let her outta yer sight. You hear?"

"I hear," the boy said sullenly.

So, Annabeth was safe, for that night, at least. The half-breed set quietly about building a new smokeless fire of chokecherry and scrub oak. Bixby Crocker conferred, low-voiced, with his confederates, setting plans to lay a trap for Eben, she presumed wearily. The boy, Lenny, got her own buffalo robes out of a saddle pack and she huddled into them for warmth for it was bitterly cold in the higher elevations.

In the morning they went on as soon as it grew light enough to follow the winding trail that was drifted in with snow, though not so badly as to totally impede their progress. Annabeth thought longingly of escape; now that she knew Eben was somewhere behind her the prospect grew more and more alluring. But she didn't know how far behind he might be and she was terrified of wandering off the trail only to freeze to death, lost and alone, in this snow-covered mountain fastness. Besides, during the daylight hours she was always hemmed in by a horse and rider immediately before and behind her and when they stopped to camp for the night she was bound to Lenny, who proved to be a gentle and considerate keeper—at least when the others weren't looking. She never neglected an opportunity to sound Lenny out on the possibility of letting her escape or escaping with her, for she could see that he was almost as afraid of his companions as she was but she didn't dare press him too hard lest he turn on her in his frustration with the situation.

Their journey, which had begun with a clearly defined purpose—that of going into the mountains to trap in beaver streams, with Annabeth along to provide "entertainment"—now savored more of flight with a grimly determined pursuer ever gaining on them. Driven by the need to put distance between themselves and their nemesis, they forged ahead, too exhausted to take pleasure in taunting and tormenting Annabeth as they had in the beginning, and for that small blessing she was thankful. Their tempers grew shorter and shorter, with arguments round the camp fire every night. Rufe argued that she should be left behind for she was only slowing them down; Wesley demanded that he be allowed to have his way with her first, and Bixby Crocker swayed first one way and then another. His hold over the others had lessened with every day that passed and he began to look more and more like a cornered rat. No more was said about laying a trap for Eben. Annabeth shrewdly suspected that none of them, except perhaps the half-breed, would have the faintest idea how to outwit the experienced mountain man.

On the third day of their journey, the sky grew more and more threatening. Over the mountains black masses of clouds piled up swiftly from the north and the wind roared through the pines, deafening them all. The horses were rimed with white frost and icicles formed on their noses and hung down from their matted tails. Annabeth followed blindly where she was led, bending low over her mount's neck and huddling down into her buffalo robes as best she could.

By early afternoon, the light was already fading and Bixby Crocker called a halt, sending the half-breed back down the trail, whether on a scouting expedition or to lay an ambush, Annabeth didn't know.

The three men grumbled and groused among themselves while Lenny, with Annabeth's help, was left to gather wood and build a fire. She was almost exhausted but she peeled willow bark for Lenny willingly for she knew they must have a fire's warmth or die of exposure. While she worked, she tried to coax the befuddled boy into cutting loose from his companions and making a run for it with her.

"I dunno," he said, low-voiced. "I'm scairt of Bix and Rufe and Wes but I'm scairt of yore man, too. I never figgered on getting caught in the middle of something like this," he muttered resentfully. She tried fervently to persuade him that his best interests lay in helping her escape but he hemmed and hawed and could not be convinced.

And then, a scream rang out, ending on a long gurgling note followed by a loud triumphant war cry—"*Henahaanehe!*" The eerie cry echoed all round the mountains.

"What the hell was that?" Bixby Crocker yelled in fear.

The hair on the back of Annabeth's neck prickled. Eben was near; he had come for her! She knew it!

Crocker grabbed Annabeth by the arm and shook her until her teeth rattled. "You—" he snarled. "You've lived among the Injuns. What does it mean?"

"It means a Cheyenne warrior has counted coup!" she cried. She could not conceal the triumph in her voice.

Crocker's wind-reddened face turned pale. "Slays-a-Pony or yore man?" he wondered out loud.

A small smile hovered around her lips. "Who do you think?" she taunted him. She was sure, in her heart, of the answer.

They waited but Slays-a-Pony did not come back to camp.

"I'm not gonna wait around here to get picked off," Rufe cried out suddenly. "I say we send the gal back down the trail or we're all gonna die. We give her up, he'll let us be!" He jumped up and made a grab for Annabeth. "Put her on her horse and send her packin'!"

Hope leaped in Annabeth's heart.

"By God, you'll not! Not 'fore I've had a chance to get between her legs!" Wesley roared. "Shouldda done it long afore now!" He wrenched Annabeth away from Rufe and threw her down onto the hard-packed snow, well-trampled by the men's feet.

Annabeth tried to scramble to her feet but she was too weak and exhausted to get up on her own and no one was disposed to help her. Not even the shamefaced Lenny.

Oh, God, don't let this happen, she prayed. Not now, not when help was so close at hand! She tried weakly to crawl away on her hands and knees for Wesley was advancing upon her, a hulking red-bearded brute, easily aroused to anger or lust. His hands were busy undoing his britches.

"Come back here, girlie, and see what I got for you," he taunted her.

Annabeth looked up at him, her eyes half-crazy with fear. Wesley had one hand between his legs, rubbing and stroking himself, while the other clutched at the pants he was ready to let drop. The other two men, Bixby Crocker and Rufe, circled her like a pair of dogs from a wolf pack, ready to pounce. The erstwhile leader of the gang of ruffians seemed not to mind that one of his henchmen would be first with her. He was the type, she realized, who would derive as much pleasure from seeing her humiliation as he would from actually raping and brutalizing her himself. It would make him even more ready to take his turn with her. In fact, he was saying as much, egging Wesley on with a foul mouth. Even Rufe, who had wanted to let her go unharmed only a few minutes ago, responded to the excitement of the moment, his eyes burning with lust, his mouth slack and wet-lipped, his fear forgotten. Only Lenny was not there; he had dived behind a rock where she could hear him being violently sick.

She tried to scrabble away but the men had her surrounded, their mocking laughter rising on the cold frosty air. "You're gonna freeze it off, boy, lessen you get it in her and drive it home," Bixby taunted.

Wesley growled, reached out and grabbed her by the ankle, thus halting what little progress she had made. He dragged her to him over the hard-packed snow and frozen ground until he was almost straddling her. As he half squatted to pry her legs apart and get into position, Annabeth screamed.

Simultaneously, a shot rang out.

10

The slug hit Wesley square in the back, its force knocking him over and down so that he fell directly on top of Annabeth, pinning her beneath his dead weight. His blood spurted over her face and neck and she heard the death rattle in his throat. She screamed again and struggled feebly to free herself but to no avail.

It was, perhaps, as well that, pinned down as she was, she could not see what was transpiring at the campsite. Eben had come bounding down from a snow-covered rocky ledge, his rifle at his hip, reloading as he ran. Gray Bull followed close at his heels, a little to the left.

As the rifle shot reverberated round the mountains, Bix Crocker whirled and ran for his own weapon, grabbed it and turned, trying to draw a bead on Eben who ran light and fleet of foot, weaving back and forth to present less of a target.

Crocker raised his gun and took careful aim but it was Eben who shot first, from the hip. Crocker screamed and staggered, sprawling to the ground, clutching his belly.

Gray Bull had a rifle of his own but saw no

need to waste powder and lead on such as these. He threw the lance that was part of the Red Shield regalia. It caught Rufe in the throat.

Annabeth heard the second shot, a scream, gurgles and moans and the triumphant Cheyenne war cry—then the blessed sound of Eben's voice calling her name. "Annabeth, Annabeth, you all right?" he cried urgently.

"Y-e-s, oh, yes," she sobbed weakly. "Eben, oh, Eben, please get him off me."

Reassured as to her well-being Eben paused momentarily by the still-thrashing body of Bixby Crocker. A man could live gut-shot a long time and while that would only prolong his agony, which Eben thought was all to the good, he knew his Annabeth. She'd probably insist on hanging around till the man was dead, trying to make him comfortable and easing his last moments and praying over him! A tomfool notion that he, Eben, would nip in the bud. Slipping his knife from its sheath, he quickly and quietly slit Bix Crocker's throat from ear to ear. The knife hovered over his scalp, it wouldn't take no time at all, Eben mused, noting that Gray Bull was already claiming his trophy. But a bloody scalp lock hanging from a Cheyenne belt was one thing. He didn't figger Annabeth would take kindly to one hanging from his own. So he quickly cleansed his knife on the snow and raising himself from his crouching position, went to her rescue.

She had partially managed to extricate herself from her predicament, propping herself up on her elbows and dragging her shoulders and torso out from under the dead man, but the lower half of her body and legs were still clasped in the grotesque parody of an embrace.

"Jesus!" cried Eben, who had not heretofore realized the full extent of her plight. He grabbed Wesley's body by an arm and leg and hauled the corpse off Annabeth, flinging it down on its back. She winced, seeing the sightless staring eyes roll back in its head.

Tenderly Eben helped her to sit up. "You sure you're all right, Annabeth?" he asked anxiously. She didn't look all right. Her face was white as a ghost's except where her cheek and chin and neck were smeared with blood and the front of her doeskin tunic was damp with great spreading stains of crimson. He put his hand to her face and it came away wet with tears and blood.

"The . . . the blood . . . it's all his," she said painfully. "Oh, Eben, hold me!" She clung to him, shaking as great shuddering sobs wracked her slight body.

His broad hand rubbed her back comfortingly as his arms engulfed her. "Easy, honey, it's all over now," he murmured soothingly. "Ain't nobody gonna hurt you any more." He caught his breath. "*Did* they hurt you? Down there, I mean. They been usin' you nights?"

"N-no," she gasped between sobs. "They hurt me in little ways and they shamed and humiliated me but . . . but they didn't . . . rape me or . . . or violate me. Bixby Crocker was too afraid of you, I think." She sniffled, wiping her nose on the back of her hand for lack of a handkerchief. "And the others . . . they were too afraid of him, except towards the end." She sniffled again. "Does it matter so much to you?"

"Matter! Course it matters!" he said roughly. "Don't you know I suffered all the tortures of hell, knowin' that you were in the hands of men like them . . . thinkin' they was usin' you . . . hurtin' you . . . abusin' you."

Her eyes widened. "Really, Eben?" she whispered in wonderment.

"God, yes. It almost drove me crazy thinkin' of you at their mercy." His face hardened. "I swore I'd get you back or die tryin' 'cause . . . 'cause without you my life ain't worth livin'," he said simply.

This was wonderful to hear! But she still had lingering doubts. "Eben, if . . . if those men *had* raped and violated me, would . . . would you still feel the same? Wouldn't you feel that I'd been soiled . . . dirtied . . . degraded?"

"Oh, Annie, don't you know I love you? Ain't nothin' on God's green earth gonna change that. Nothin' they couldda done to you or forced you to do could ever make me love you any the less. I was just awful scared that they might break your heart or your spirit, with what they put you through."

But she hadn't heard anything beyond those three magic words. "You . . . you love me!" she gasped. "But you never said so before." It was, she thought, worth going through such an ordeal just to hear those sweet words fall from his lips.

He looked at her with tender amusement. "Not in so many words, mebbe. Didn't figger you needed tellin' in words. Ain't I been tellin' you I love you every way I know how almost ever since we met?"

"A woman likes to hear it in words," she said shyly. "She never gets tired of hearing it."

"That so?" he said softly, teasingly. "Well, I reckon I'm gonna have to say it every day for the rest of our lives if that's what it takes to put the shine back in your eyes."

"Oh, Eben," she whispered, taking his hand and laying it against her cheek. He thumbed tears from her eyes and tears mixed with blood from her face. "Reckon we better get you cleaned up," he chucked her under the chin, "You look like you're wearing more war paint than Gray Bull. And I gotta feed that fire or you're gonna freeze to death."

He found a buffalo robe and wrapped her in it and threw some more peeled willow onto the fire. It was starting in to snow at last, having threatened to all day. Big white soft flakes drifted down out of the sky and he frowned, thinking that he would have to rig up some kind of shelter for Annabeth. She was too weak to travel, almost too weak to stand unaided. And, he'd have to get rid of these bodies lying around cluttering up the scenery. He decided to do that first off in order to spare Annabeth's delicate eastern-bred sensibilities. She'd already been through enough and more than enough, he figured, and the grisly remains would only serve to remind her of what she'd gone through. Indian women, of course, were hardened to such sights, often having to go to a scene of battle to bring back the wounded on travois and lay out the dead. But Annabeth wasn't no Indian.

He made sure she was comfortable by the fire and then, throwing the bodies facedown over a couple of packhorses, preparatory to hauling them up the ledge and throwing them over, paused. "You wanta say a few words—a prayer—over 'em? he asked awkwardly.

"No," she answered shortly, her lips tightly pressed together.

He looked at her in surprise and then, with a

Sue Deobold

sigh, understood. She'd learned how to hate, then. Well, that was probably all to the good. It was a hard world out here and you had to be tough to take it. Only the strong survived. And it looked like his Annabeth was gonna be a survivor.

He was in the process of cleaning up the clutter, when Gray Bull, who had disappeared —tactfully, Eben had supposed, in order not to intrude on his reunion with his woman—reappeared, driving the boy, Lenny, ahead of him, his rifle barrel pointing towards the boy's kidneys.

"Well, well, what we got here?" Eben said with deceptive softness. In his absorption with Annabeth he'd forgotten all about the fifth member of the hunting party. A damnfool thing to do. The kid could have blown his head off from behind a bush or a rock and he'd not have known a thing about it. He shook his head, annoyed with his own carelessness. It could have cost them their lives! What love for a woman could do to a man! he thought ruefully. A good thing Gray Bull had been along to see to these little details.

His hand went to the knife at his belt, his eyes glittering. "You ready to meet your Maker, kid?" he said gruffly.

Annabeth who was huddled by the fire, trying to get warm, looked up at the tone in his voice. Her eyes widened as she saw Eben go for his knife.

"Eben—no!" she cried, launching herself at him and clutching his arm with both her little hands. "Lenny was good to me; he couldn't help what those men did. We even talked of his trying to help me escape. We tried to figure out ways to escape together but those men never took their eyes off us. Eben—please—listen to me!" she said frantically, throwing herself in front of Lenny and tugging in desperation at Eben's arm, the knife glittering dangerously in his hand. "Lenny wasn't like the rest of them! He wasn't cruel to me. Tell him yourself, Lenny!" she commanded over his shoulder but Lenny appeared to be tongue-tied with fright.

"Eben, please, you can't kill him in cold blood . . . you mustn't have this boy's blood on your hands!" She clung to him ferociously with all the strength she possessed. "You must listen to me," she panted. "He's just a boy—hardly any older than you were when you came West. And he had the misfortune to fall in with a bad lot . . . it could have happened to you, if you hadn't met up with Jim Bridger!"

Eben snorted. He didn't think he'd ever been that green or callow—to blindly follow after such riffraff. But Annabeth had been through a hell of a lot and he supposed he ought to humor her.

"Eben, please. Lenny wasn't to blame for what happened. And he treated me kindly and tried to help me—" This was stretching it a bit but if it served to convince Eben to be merciful . . .

"That true, boy?" he snarled.

Lenny gulped audibly, trying to find his voice. "Yeah, uh, I mean, yes . . . yessir," he said weakly.

"Well, then, where the hell were you when she needed help?" Eben demanded a little unfairly for he couldn't really suppose this callow youth would have the guts to stand up to the likes of Bix Crocker and his henchmen.

"I . . . I ran away," the boy admitted, shame-faced. "I . . . I was so scared I . . . ran behind a rock and puked," he muttered.

Well, he was honest enough, anyway, Eben decided. He sheathed his knife. "All right," he said reluctantly. "We'll take you back to the Cheyenne village and turn you loose with food, weapons, and a horse. What happens after that is your lookout. It'll make a man of you or it'll kill you—all accordin' to the way your stick floats." He said, reverting to one of his mountain man expressions.

"I take him back with me," Gray Bull volunteered, without expressing an opinion pro or con. It made no difference to him whether the white boy lived or died. "My woman is near her time and my brother no longer needs me. It is better I start back before the sun goes behind the mountains. And," a faint smile played around his full heavy lips, "my brother will want to be alone for a time with his woman."

So nightfall found Eben and Annabeth alone. Eben had erected a crude but warm shelter of pine boughs and saplings, put a large supply of wood inside, dug a fire pit and built a large fire. The horses huddled near the makeshift lodge, as if to share a bit of the warmth that was within.

All night the pellets of snow and sleet plummeted onto the crude shelter but inside it was surprisingly warm and comfortable, providing more comfort, indeed, than Annabeth had experienced in days.

But she felt strangely uneasy now that she and Eben were on their own again, which surprised her because it was what she had been longing for all those hard and dreary days of her captivity. It seemed so long since the two of them had been together—and so much had happened in the interim. It was ridiculous that she should feel shy with him—but she did.

They had shared a meal and he was sitting cross-legged before the fire puffing on his pipe.

Not the long-stemmed, highly ornamented calumet pipe of the Indians but a short-stemmed clay pipe which he smoked sometimes when he had a supply of tobacco. The air was blue with smoke and thick with a sudden inexplicable tension.

She got up suddenly and wandered over to the entrance to peer moodily out at the fast-falling snow. The way it was coming down, all signs of the battle fought that afternoon in the clearing would be soon hidden. The great splotches of scarlet staining the hard-packed snow would be hidden by the fresh fall. A generous and omnipotent nature would repair the ravages wrought by the hand of man.

Eben knocked out his pipe and came to stand beside her, looking out over her shoulder. "It's really coming down now," he remarked, seemingly casual. But there was an undertone of stress in his voice—a tension that Annabeth picked up on.

"Yes," she agreed carefully. "Yes, it is. I . . . I wonder if Gray Bull and Lenny will . . . will be all right."

"Oh, sure. Likely they'll hole up somewhere down below. An Injun knows how to sit and wait out a storm and make himself comfortable while he's waiting." His words were easy and casual but his voice sounded hard, tight with strain.

"Yes," she murmured. "I suppose so. Indians are so much a part of nature, so at one with it. More so than any people I ever saw." There didn't seem to be any more to say—she had, she felt, said it all. She turned away nervously, making for the pile of pine boughs over which their bedrolls were spread. "I . . . I guess we should get some sleep."

"Reckon so," Eben replied, his voice curiously flat. He stayed where he was, looking out into the snow-lit darkness while she disrobed.

He wanted her—God, how he wanted her! With desperate urgency he wanted to stroke her smooth belly and silken flanks until they opened for him and he could reclaim her for his own. But he stayed where he was, digging his nails into his palms and forcing himself to keep his distance.

It was only too likely, he thought dismally, that she'd had enough of men and their lusts. If he took her now, he'd be no better than that riffraff who'd held her captive. He had to give her time—time for her emotional wounds to heal— time to forget all she'd been through. And he remembered their last night back at the Indian encampment when she'd rejected him just because he'd had a little too much to drink. And now, after all she'd been through with those bastards—her near-rape which he had so narrowly averted only a little while ago—he couldn't blame her if she never wanted to feel a man's touch again. He only hoped she'd get over it in time and become her old responsive self again some day.

He heard the rustle of the pine boughs as she made herself comfortable and then her voice, plaintive, "Aren't you coming to bed?"

"In a minute." Maybe he could stand it—crawling in beside her—if he waited till she fell asleep and didn't get too close to her tempting softness.

He didn't want her! He didn't love her! In spite of his fine words about her near-rape not making any difference to him, it was only too obvious that it did. Men, in general, she thought, couldn't endure the notion of another man having their woman, taking by force what was theirs. She remembered that back at the wagon train there had been some discussion about what the women should do in case of an Indian attack. The general consensus of opinion had been that a woman should take her own life rather than suffer a fate worse than death.

Well, she had very nearly suffered such a fate only a little while ago when that horrible Wesley had taken her down and spread her legs in readiness to receive him. And Eben had seen it all! Had rescued her in the nick of time. The sight had probably repulsed him so much that he didn't want her any more.

But she wanted him—desperately. What should she do? She needed him . . . she needed his comfort . . . she wanted his tender caresses to wipe out those shameful memories that she might carry with her always. It had been Eben who had introduced her to the joy—the glory—that physical love could be between a man and his woman. She knew that only in his arms could she forget the vileness of those horrible men.

"Eben?" she said softly, tentatively, a little desperately, "Don't you want . . . *want* . . . to come to bed?" Don't you want me? was what she wanted to say but she couldn't quite bring herself to it.

He heard the desperation in her voice and turned, a little puzzled. Then he caught his breath in his throat. She was sitting up in bed, bare-breasted in the firelight, and when he turned towards her, she held out her arms to him, a little imploringly.

"Annie!" he breathed. "Annabeth!" Acting on instinct, he covered the space between them in two giant strides and gathered her into his arms.

She was so small, so frail, but she had a heart and a spirit as big as all outdoors—his woman, his Annabeth.

She clung to him, whimpering with urgency, "Eben, take me," she begged. "Take me now. Please! Wipe out those awful memories for me!"

It was more than he dared to hope for and he was more than willing to accommodate her! Her hands were busy at the thongs that laced his buckskin shirt together, tugging at them with feverish haste and impatient little whimpers, for she yearned to have the feel of his flesh against her bare breasts. His big hands helped her with the last of the fastenings and then he enfolded her tightly, pressing her to him, rocking her and crooning little love words deep in his throat as his lips brushed her hair, her closed eyelids, her face, and then her mouth.

Her blood raced at the touch of his lips on her skin and she tilted her head back against his shoulder to allow him freer access to her mouth. He teased her lips apart with a gentle insistence and Annabeth, who had kept her lips tightly clenched against a similar but unwanted invasion, now found her lips parting eagerly to welcome his teasing tongue as it probed the soft, sweet recesses of her mouth. As his kiss deepened, her arms crept up around his neck and she found herself lifted nearly out of the bedding by his strong embrace. A dizzying swirl of need made her burrow into his chest as waves of desire swept over her, making her bones melt and her body tremble in the circle of his arms.

They tumbled together over onto the pile of bedding, Eben hastily shedding the remainder of his clothing so that they would be equal in their nakedness. As naked and unashamed as Adam and Eve in the garden of Eden, Annabeth thought hazily. And then, all thought left her mind as Eben trailed heady kisses over her body, tantalizing her breasts and belly, his magic touch sending her into swirling spirals of ecstasy.

But when he moved over her, to bring their lovemaking to fruition, the weight of his heavy body seemed to press her down so that she felt as if she were suffocating as the horrid memory of another body pressing her down flashed into her mind. Oh, God, would she carry that memory with her always? she wondered, gasping in a sudden breathless panic.

She began to struggle against him, whimpering. "Eben, I . . . I can't—" she cried in frustration and anger as the black fears that she couldn't control overwhelmed her. "You . . . you're so heavy . . . you're suffocating me . . . it's like . . . like . . ."

He seemed to understand her half-frantic communication but didn't let it phase him. "That's easily remedied, sweetheart," he assured her soothingly, and grasping her by the hips rolled them both over so that she no longer had to bear the burden of his punishing weight pressing her down. She discovered to her amazement that this maneuver had unexpected benefits as, her momentary fright forgotten, she delighted in the freedom it gave her to tease and torment him with her body, alternately brushing the tips of her breasts against his broad chest, and then crushing them against it; flicking her tongue tantalizingly in and out of his mouth; grasping his aroused manhood with muscles she hadn't known she possessed. It was a sweet torment that eventually

brought them both to new and hitherto un-
experienced heights of ecstasy and a shuddering
mutually attained consummation of life and love.

It was splendor, she thought afterwards, lying
in the curve of his arm, a sweet and savage
splendor. A splendor that they were destined to
relive again and again in the blissful days that
followed, a splendor that, Annabeth thought
contentedly, bore aspects of spirituality as well as
carnality for it was blessed by their deep and
abiding love for each other as they joined together
to become one flesh.

The winter storm that had kept them confined
to the lodge broke on the third day and was
followed by a spell of warmer weather during
which much of the new-fallen snow obligingly
melted. Eben knew they ought to break camp.
Take advantage of the good weather while it held
and move on out of the high country—Crow
country. But he was loath to leave the spot where
he and Annabeth had found so much happiness.
While the storm raged and the wind whistled
outside, inside their little shelter it had been snug
and warm. They had eaten and slept and made lazy
languorous love and slept again, and roused only
to turn to each other with renewed hunger.

Her wild, sweet abandon never ceased to
amaze and gratify him. In this wilderness paradise
they had found she had shed all of her inhibitions.
Her need for him was as great as his for her and
she was, by turns, playful and frolicsome,
passionate, as generous in her giving as any lover
could wish, frank and eager to show or tell him
which of his caresses pleased her the most. And
since he was as eager for her to find fulfillment in
their lovemaking as he was to find his own, they

suited each other right well, he mused happily. It was sweeter than any birdsong he had ever heard, for him to hear—now that they were utterly and completely alone—her cries of rapture at the moment of release—cries which, back at the Cheyenne camp, she had tried to stifle, mindful that ears other than his might overhear. That she felt the same about his own rapturous utterances, he knew, for she had told him so, one night when they lay clasped in each other's arms, all passion, for the moment, spent.

And so he lingered, knowing full well that if they lingered too long they risked being cut off should the mountain passes fill with snow. But would that be such a bad thing? he wondered. They had plenty of food, more than enough for the two of them now that they had the trappers' supplies. And he had his weapons with which to hunt for game if it became necessary. Why not winter right here, where they were? The wilderness held no terrors for him. There was a beaver stream not too far away. He could rig up a trap line—do a little trapping maybe. Prime plews didn't bring anywhere near the price they had once commanded but he could make enough to buy Annabeth some pretties at the nearest trading post.

They were, of course, in Crow country but that didn't worry him overmuch. They hadn't seen any Crow sniffing around so far and if the halla-baloo and gunshots of a few days ago hadn't already brought them around to investigate, he figured nothing would. And the Crows of all the tribes, were generally well-disposed to whites. He'd thought of himself as Cheyenne for so long—and the Crows were their hereditary enemies—but he was, after all, white, and so was Annabeth.

But could she stand a wilderness winter—alone, except for himself? How would she survive if something happened to him? And there was always that possibility—an accident, an injury. A broken leg, maybe, or an encounter with a grizzly, come out of hiberation to sun itself on a fine winter's day.

No, he shook his head regretfully, he was willing to take risks himself—they were part and parcel of a mountain man's life—but he didn't want to take any risks with Annabeth. Her safety and security lay with others, among the Cheyenne. He'd have to get her back to their encampment soon. Tomorrow maybe or the next day.

But it was so sweet, just the two of them, enclosed in their own private world and he told himself that she needed more time to get her strength back before they hit the trail again.

And so they lingered several more days.

They lingered too long.

11

It was a clear bright day, not at all dark and gloomy as December is so apt to be, and Eben had taken Annabeth to the beaver stream to watch a family of young otters disporting themselves in the icy water. He had planned on leaving today but while he had been mulling over in his mind his rejected plan of wintering in the vicinity he had scouted the beaver stream for likely prospects. There he saw the otters and unwisely told her about them. She had demanded to be taken to see them for herself and he could deny her nothing so their departure had been postponed for one more day.

She had been thrilled by the sight of the frolicsome otter pups at play, exhilarated by the cold frosty air, elated by the bright sunshine, and was in the lighthearted, laughing mood that he loved. When he bent to examine the fresh tracks of a deer that had come to the stream to drink, wondering if it would be worth the trouble to hunt it down for fresh meat, she had scooped up a handful of snow and stuffed it down his back, then fled from him laughing and shrieking with glee. He caught up with her easily enough, of course, for a lifetime spent in the wilds had taught him to be fleet of foot, and when he did, he turned her over his knee and pretended to give her a spanking. And, somehow, for she was floundering around trying to get away, they ended up in a snowbank and his pretended anger and her feigned fright turned to very real passion. It wasn't lazy and languorous love this time—not in a snowbank—it was quick and hard and brief but utterly satisfying for both of them. She ran her snow-cold hands up under his shirt to warm them and cling to him at the same time, uttering wild cries of ecstasy that sent the jays overhead screaming raucous warnings as they took flight.

At least that was what he thought caused the jays' flight, but his natural caution, honed to a fine edge by years of wilderness living so that it now seemed inborn, made him get up and straighten his clothing sooner than he might otherwise have done. He reached down and helped Annabeth to her feet, brushing the loose snow off her hair and body and shaking out her buffalo robe. "We better get back to camp; the fire'll be dying down," he reminded her.

They walked back arm in arm. She felt preternaturally aware of the blueness of the winter sky, of the brightness of the sunshine on the snow, of the snow itself, crunching delightfully underfoot. She was about to comment on this heightened sensual perception when Eben suddenly stopped short, drawing her closer and a little behind him, as if to protect her with his body. His eyes narrowed, his nostrils quivered; she could see that all of his senses were alert to danger. "Somethin's wrong," he hissed, unslinging the rifle from which he was never parted.

Something twanged through the air as almost

simultaneously Eben hissed, "Get down!" He hit the ground himself, dragging Annabeth down with him, and the arrow whizzed harmlessly over their heads and embedded itself, quivering, in the trunk of a tree.

"Crow!" he muttered. "Either he only wanted to scare us or he's a damned poor shot. Young bucks, most likely, out on a fine day looking for mischief. Stay down, Annabeth, stay down," he muttered, as she cautiously raised her head a trifle in order to look about her.

Annabeth scrabbled deeper into the snow and Eben, flat on his belly, inched his way back until he could shield her with his body, muttering in her ear, "They'll be comin' at us pretty soon. When I tell you to run, you head out like you never run before. I'll try to keep you covered—keep 'em busy."

"I . . . won't leave you," she protested.

"You'll run when I tell you," he snapped, squeezing her arm painfully to remind her that he meant to be obeyed. "When you get back to the shelter, mebbe you can give me cover."

The Crow broke from ambush, whooping and hollering, bloodcurdling screeches that made her shiver. "*Now*! Git!" Eben shouted. "*Run!*" he yelled, emptying his rifle at the advancing horde of screeching warriors. Out of the corner of her eye, she saw the foremost one drop.

Annabeth did her best. She ran as if all the devils let loose from hell were at her heels. Fear lent wings to her feet, though running was not one of her accomplishments. How many times had she heard Aunt Anna rebuke her with a long-suffering sigh and a tart, "Young ladies do not run, Annabeth!"

She gained the shelter, which was about a

hundred yards away, in time to see Eben surrounded by a yelling screeching horde of redskins. Snatching up a rifle she took hasty aim and fired. Its kick sent her tumbling backwards but, much to her surprise, she saw one of the Indians go down. "My God, I've killed a man," she gasped in a dazed fashion.

The weapon felt hot in her hands. There was the stink of black powder in the air as she laid it down and snatched up another of the trappers' rifles.,

Her next shot was not as well-aimed or not as lucky. She missed. She could have wept, as she grabbed another and took more careful aim.

Eben was still on his feet. His gun long empty he was using it as a club, swinging it freely, catching one man in the knees, another in the groin. One went down, clutching his throat; another's arm appeared to have been dislocated.

And then, Eben himself was on his knees but still fighting. But even as she let off another shot which went wild, she saw him go down completely, struck from behind.

"Eben!" she screamed, the cry ripping from her throat. "Eben!"

Her screams attracted the attention of the Indians who charged her shelter with ear-splitting whoops.

She stood panting, irresolute. What should she do? She couldn't possibly hold out against so many. There must have been at least two dozen originally, of which a fair proportion still remained. And what was there to hold out for, now that Eben was . . . was dead? She might as well turn the gun on herself and be done with it.

But *was* he dead? The Indian she thought she

had killed had struggled to his feet, blood streaming down his arm.

She had seen at least three of the Indian strike Eben but had they been blows to kill or were the young Crow merely counting coup? Among the Cheyenne, she knew, three men were permitted to count coup on an enemy, with the highest honor naturally going to the man who had struck the first blow. Killing an enemy was not nearly so important as counting coup on him, to the Indian mind—a concept that was difficult for Annabeth to grasp, particularly as a coup strike did not necessarily represent a dangerous feat. But however it was accomplished, it brought more honor to a warrior than a whole fistful of scalps.

She hesitated, chewing her lip in thought. None of the Crow had made any move to take Eben's scalp. Might that not mean that he was still alive? Injured and unconscious, but, please God, still alive! And if that were true she must go to him! It wouldn't do her any good to skulk here in the shelter anyway. They would only come and drag her out by the hair of her head.

Mindful of the many times that Eben had told her of the Indian respect for bravery and courage, she took a deep breath and stepped boldly out of the shelter, still holding a loaded gun. Depending on the circumstances, she would, she hoped, know best how to utilize it. But first, she must, if possible, find out whether Eben still lived.

The Crow, most of whom she saw at a glance were young boys on the verge of manhood, gathered around her in amazement at her bravado, jabbering among themselves. But even a young boy can be dangerous, she reminded herself, when he wields a knife or a gun or a tomahawk.

One young brave who seemed a little older than the rest and who wore the coup feather in his hair, barred her way to Eben but she, greatly daring, nudged him with the muzzle of her rifle and he, much to her surprise, stepped aside and allowed her to pass. There had been a time when she would never have dared such presumption but her life among the Cheyenne had taught her that Indians were not, by and large, the murdering bloodthirsty savages she had once believed them to be. In fact this band of primarily teen-age boys—now that she saw them up close—reminded her forcibly of certain hell-raising youths back home who would get together to play pranks, like tipping over a neighbor's outhouse. Only the pranks of these boys, bred to fighting from their childhood, were likely to be deadly. Nevertheless, she clung to the analogy for all it was worth. It gave her courage.

None of these handsome youths was painted for war, she noticed suddenly. That gave her courage too.

But what really made her take heart was the sight that met her eyes as she drew nearer to where Eben lay—the slight but regular rise and fall of his chest. He was alive! There was a nasty gash on his forehead and his hair was matted with blood but he still lived and while there was life, there was hope, she reminded herself.

She caught a long quivering breath that was almost a sob. She longed to run to him, to cradle his head in her lap, to staunch the flow of blood and cleanse his wounds, but she had to step carefully, doing nothing to excite or offend her captors who seemed not to know quite what to do with their prize.

She looked around her at the assembled faces, again reassured by the absence of paint. This was not, then, a war party, she decided. More likely a hunting expedition, or a band of high-spirited youths, ripe for deviltry and mischief-making who had unfortunately stumbled across her and Eben.

What, if anything, could she do to save herself and him? She racked her brains trying to remember all she had ever heard about the Crow, trying to think of some little tidbit of information that might be helpful, that would enable to her cope with the situation in which she found herself. The Crow were notable horse-thieves, that she recollected, and honored as such by all the Plains Indians, among whom horse thievery was an art. That this was true was borne out by the leader who suddenly barked a command to a couple of the younger boys who detached themselves from the grinning horde in order to round up the horses, not only her mount and Eben's but the extra horses that had belonged to Bixby Crocker's gang of ruffians.

The Crows were also supposed to be notably friendly to whites. Some said that they had never taken a white scalp. She was doubtful of the veracity of this claim herself and Eben, who from years of living among the Cheyenne, their hereditary enemies, had imbibed some of their prejudices, was more than skeptical of it. He had admitted, though, that many mountain men had worked in Crow country confident of their safety, Broken Hand Fitzpatrick having paid a sort of toll for the privilege of trespassing on Crow land.

She didn't like the idea of putting this theory to the test but it gave her an idea. Remembering how impressed the Cheyenne had been with her flame-colored hair, as dramatically as possible she whisked the buffalo-robe mantle from her head. The sun caught her hair and framed her face in a nimbus, an aureole of red-golden light.

There was a collective gasp. "You . . . white!" the leader exclaimed in consternation.

Annabeth was equally amazed and gratified that the young man spoke at least a few words of English. "Yes . . . white—" she repeated, nodding vigorously.

"Why you with Cheyenne warrior?" he asked suspiciously.

"Oh, but he's not Cheyenne; he is white!" she insisted hurriedly, anxious to establish this point.

The young brave looked skeptical. Glancing at Eben, she could see his point. Swarthy of skin, black of hair, with the high prominent cheekbones that proclaimed Indian ancestry, clad in buckskins and Cheyenne moccasins, he looked every inch an Indian, as much so as any of the young bucks.

"He is white," she insisted, her voice rising a little hysterically. "His name is Eben McDowell and he is my husband, my man."

The leader shrugged. "He is brave," he admitted ungrudgingly. "He has much courage and fights like a madman." There was respect and perhaps a little awe in his voice.

"What . . . what are you going to do with us?" Annabeth asked trying to keep the fear from her voice and assuming an impassivity she was far from feeling.

For answer he barked another command to his fellows who bound Eben hand and foot, like Lilliputians binding Gulliver, Annabeth thought a trifle hysterically, and slung him, none too gently, face down over the back of a horse. She winced, seeing him so roughly handled but she knew that no protests of hers would have the slightest effect. She must put her faith in the Lord and in Eben's own strong constitution to see him through this.

Her own horse was brought forward and the leader, taking the gun she had almost forgotten from her unresisting hands, threw her into the saddle. It was a good thing she had learned to ride astride like Indian women, she thought grimly, watching the young braves vault onto their own horses which had been led out from a place of concealment; she had certainly had had plenty of practice in the art during the last few days.

They rode hard and fast, faster even than the white trappers, who, of course, had not had the advantage of knowing the terrain as these young warriors did. The wind had come up to crust the snow again and it crunched beneath the horses' hooves at every step, as they arched their necks and blew in the brisk air.

It was the longest and hardest ride of Annabeth's life. She was naturally apprehensive about what her own fate might be but she was sick with fear for Eben. Glancing behind her from time to time, she could see that a bright trail of blood dripped onto the snow from his head wound. When they crossed the water farther upstream, the icy water apparently splashed his face and partially, at least, revived him for after that, from time to time, she could hear him groan, even over the sound of hoofbeats. Her heart ached for him but the groans at least served to reassure her that he was among the living.

Just before dusk they reached the Crow camp. It didn't, to a tired and heartsick Annabeth, look all that different from the Cheyenne camp with which she had become so familiar. There was the usual smell of wood smoke and roasting meat, the same shrieking mob of children with packs of camp dogs at their heels, the same lineup of curious adults who watched the little procession with black impassive eyes.

But this was no stately procession. The youths swept into camp, driving the herd of captured horses before them with wild yells, yips and whoops, and startled adults, children, and dogs scattered before them! They drew up with a flourish before what Annabeth presumed must be a chief's lodge. It was larger than the rest, more elaborately decorated, and bore, at the apex of the tripod, a full dangling scalp, still adorned with its former owner's ears.

Nausea welled in her throat and she had to swallow hard.

Her captor dismounted with one fluid leap, hauled her out of the saddle and dragged her to the doorway of the lodge. He spoke in his own language to someone who was within and a man came to the entrance, muttering something in the Crow tongue. The youth jabbered a reply and whipped the buffalo robe from Annabeth's head. Her red-gold hair gleamed in the last rays of the setting sun.

"Wal, damn my eyes, if'n it ain't a white gal!" the man exclaimed. He lifted the door flap that he had been holding back with one hand and stepped out.

Annabeth gasped, hearing English instead of the expected Crow tongue, and lifting her downcast eyes, gaped at him in bewilderment. The chief, if he *was* the chief, was no Indian. Nor was he a white man. He was . . . Annabeth's eyes were nearly popping out of her head with amazement . . . *black!*

12

The old man—he was about fifty, Annabeth judged which was old by western standards—chuckled and bowed ironically. "James Pierson Beckwourth, at your service, ma'am!" he said.

"But ... but you're a ... a—" she burst out, on the verge of committing an indiscretion, "a gentleman of color," she finished lamely.

The old man chuckled at her obvious confusion. "That's a nice ladylike way of putting it," he said cheerfully. "But nigger'll do. It ain't no put-down out here where a man's worth ain't measured by the color of his skin. I'm mulatto, actually," he said garrulously. "My paw, he was a Virginny planter what liked to take his comfort in the quarters."

"Oh," said Annabeth weakly.

"What are you doing out here all alone, a white woman dressed in Cheyenne doeskin and mokersins?" he asked curiously.

"I ... I'm not alone," she stammered. "My husband is with me. He's been hurt and ... and ... oh, please, help us!" She looked imploringly at the big black man who, though old, still had a strong and powerful physique.

He glanced from her to the horse across which Eben's body was flung. "Yer husband, huh?" He went over to the horse and grasping Eben's hair, yanked up his face. "Son-of-a-b—" He looked back at Annabeth and substituted, "Son-of-gun. It's Eb McDowell!" he said in astonishment. He gave an order in the Crow tongue and two of the young braves lifted Eben from his horse a good deal more gently than they had thrown him there, slinging an arm around either of their necks, preparatory to carrying him into the tepee. Eben groaned, his head lolling, and Annabeth flew to him, saying over her shoulder to the old man, "You know him, then?"

"Know him!" the black man snorted. " 'Course I know Eb. Knowed him ever since he was a snot-nosed kid. Let's get him into the lodge and take a look at that wound."

Eben moaned again, a sound that wrung Annabeth's heart. He lifted his head, swaying between the two Crow warriors and scowling with the effort, focused his eyes blearily on the old man. "Jim?" He licked dry lips and blinked a couple of times. "Jim Beckwourth!" His lips grinned crookedly, "This is a . . . a hell of a welcome for an old friend!" Exhausted by the effort he had made, his head fell forward on his chest. "Take care . . . my wife . . . take care Anniebeth," he muttered before lapsing again into unconsciousness.

"I'll take care of you first, boy," the old man said grimly, beckoning a messenger to go for the medicine man.

The Crow, Annabeth discovered during her stay amongst them, were a fiercely proud and handsome people, perhaps even more so than the Cheyenne. The men were tall and clean-limbed with handsome hawklike profiles. They were inordinately vain of their personal appearance, she noticed with amusement, wearing beautiful elaborately decorated garments and letting their hair grow to an unprecedented length so that, unbound, it might well sweep the ground.

The women also had a glossy profusion of hair but were obliged to keep it on the short side in order not to compete with their menfolk! A notion Annabeth found quite extraordinary. They were even more skilled at tanning hides to a soft suppleness almost as white as linen than were the Cheyenne women and their beadwork, quillwork, and picturesque painted decorations were also superior. But they restricted most of their decorative arts to the clothing of their men, who refused to allow them to compete with themselves in barbaric splendor!

They were not, however, as friendly towards her as the Cheyenne women had been, which was understandable, she supposed, for she was a white woman who dressed in the garb of their traditional enemies! She was glad that she did not have to spend a portion of her stay among them immured in the Moon Lodge, the companion of women who were antagonistic towards her. She supposed that the rigors she had undergone had disturbed the regularity of her woman's cycle and thought no more about it.

Eben's head wound did not heal as rapidly as she could wish. He drifted in and out of consciousness for several days, causing her much concern. "Don't you fret none 'bout that man o' yourn," Jim Beckwourth told her kindly. "He's

'Some'—is Eben. He's Ha'r of the b'ar, all right. He'll pull through."

Annabeth knew that "Some" meant remarkable or praiseworthy in the mountain men's peculiar and colorful dialect but she had to ask for a translation of "Hair of the Bear" which meant, she discovered, about the same thing, only more so. It was a supreme form of praise. It came, Jim told her, from the Indian superstition that a man could become immensely brave by ingesting the hair of the grizzly bear, and to say that a man was possessed of "Hair of the Bear" was as far as one could go.

She suspected that kindly old Jim was trying to take her mind off her troubles by his colorful use of mountain men slang and his tall tales for she discovered, quite by accident, that he was, in reality, a literate and educated man who visualized writing a book in his old age relating his exploits. By his own exaggerated account, he was a kind of Paul Bunyan of the mountains and he told her many wild stories, some of which featured Eben as well as himself.

She took these stories with a grain of salt for she couldn't visualize her Eben plunging a knife into a man "up to the Green River" that is, shoving it in up to the trademark on the hilt and then disemboweling his enemy. She acknowledged that Eben was a fighting man but not one of such primitive barbaric savagery as all that! Old Jim took a positive relish in embellishing his own hair-raising exploits, likely he did the same by Eben's, she thought with a shrug.

Still she listened with wide-eyed fascination, learning things about Eben that she would never have suspected, things that he had never told her, some of which, she thought shrewdly, he would have much preferred not coming to her ears at all!

One night he was delirious with fever for infection had set in and Annabeth sat up with him, calling Jim to her aid only when Eben threatened to throw off his buffalo robes and run out into the snow to cool off. It took both of them to hold him down. And then in his delirium he began rambling, talking to her and about her, using their little private love words and endearments with a frankness that made her face burn. The old man divined her embarrassment and said gently, "Eb ain't responsible for what he's sayin', ma'am; he don't even know I'm here. Don't let it bother you none; it's only nature." And, when a little while later Eben ceased his violent thrashing about, Jim suggested, "Whyn't you lay down with him, ma'am? Likely it'll ease his mind and keep him quieter. As for me, I'm turning in myself."

She did as old Jim suggested and miraculously Eben did quieten, turning his hot face into her breasts like a tired child. It was her first experience of Eben, her lover and protector, as a helpless child and it stirred her profoundly. That Eben, who had seemed to her the epitome of strength, was not always strong, that he too could be vulnerable was a revelation to her. She puzzled about the complexity and infinite varieties of love—that her passion for this man could, at times, be transmuted into the kind of love one feels for a kindly protective father figure, or, at the other extreme, the tenderness of a mother for her child, was astonishing to her. Holding him in her arms she mused over this while he nuzzled her breasts and finally fell into a deep and peaceful sleep. Love was, she decided at last, before she fell asleep herself, a precious jewel with many facets.

There was one more night of fever and delirium and anxiety for Annabeth and then the fever broke and Eben was on the mend. The Crow shaman who had been called upon to minister to him from time to time with healing herbs and potions attributed Eben's recovery to his own semi-mystical ministrations. Jim Beckwourth attributed it to his vigor and iron constitution. Annabeth attributed it to the Lord, for hadn't her fervent prayers been answered? Eben himself attributed it to Annabeth's devoted nursing, for she would let no one else do for him what she could do herself, jealously guarding her prerogatives as sickroom nurse even from old Jim who would willingly have taken the heavier burdens and more distasteful tasks from her slim hands or, in his capacity as chief, ordered them done by others. "T'ain't fitten fer a lady," he protested, vaguely recalling pampered white ladies in the big house in old Virginia, as Annabeth swept past him carrying a bowl of slops.

"I'm no lady, I'm his woman!" she retorted proudly over her shoulder to a scandalized Jim. She lavished all the devotion on Eben that he had shown to her, in her own illness, almost happy to have the tables turned.

But she was happier still to have Eben on the mend, well enough to sit by the evening fire swapping tall tales and reminiscences with Jim Beckwourth and arguing amiably over the relative merits of their respective adopted tribes, the Cheyenne versus the Crow.

On their last night at the Crow camp, Jim produced a long-hoarded bottle of whisky for the two men to split. Under its benign influence, the black man waxed eloquent about the land of the

Crow, the Sparrow-Hawk People, the Absarokas. It was, he said, the best land in the world. "It is in the exact right place," he proclaimed windily. "When you are in it you fare well, whichever way you travel you fare worse . . . to the south you have to wander over great barren plains, the water is warm and bad . . . to the north it is cold; the winters are long and bitter with no grass, you cannot keep horses there . . . what is a country without horses?" he said contemptuously, pausing to take a breath and a swig from the bottle. "To the east . . . they live well but they drink the muddy water of the Missouri—that is bad. A Crow's dog would not drink such water," he snorted. "But the Crow country has snowy mountains and sunny plains; all kinds of climates and good things for every season. When the summer heats scorch the prairies, you can draw up under the mountains, where the air is sweet and cool, the grass fresh, and the bright streams come tumbling out of the snowbanks. There you can hunt the elk, the deer, and the antelope . . . in the autumn when your horses are strong and fat from the mountain pastures, you can go down into the plains and hunt the buffalo . . . the Crow country is in the right place. Everything good is to be found there. There is no country like the Crow country."

His alcohol-produced eloquence was such that even Annabeth felt a momentary pang, as if, in leaving the Absarokas she was being cast out of Paradise and even Eben seemed at a loss for words. After a while he said, "You've knocked around all over, Jim. You never seen better country than this?"

"Never!" the old man averred. "Mind *you*, over the mountains, in California, there's some

213

mighty nice country. Near as good as this." He took another swig of whisky, wiped his mouth on his sleeve and passed the bottle to Eben. "Last time I was out thataway I found me a pass through the Sierra Nevadas leading right into the Sacramento Valley."

"Is that so!" Eben looked suitably impressed. "Beckwourth's Pass, huh. Next thing you know, they'll be callin' you the Pathfinder, Jim," he chaffed.

The old man cleared his throat and spat. "Naw—that's what they're a-callin' that hotshot army lootenant, Fremont. Why, that greenhorn couldn't find his—" The old man's eye fell on Annabeth who was listening with rapt attention. "Ah . . . find his way home less'n Kit Carson had him by the hand a-guidin' him every step of the way. It's us mountain men what knows the country," he said querulously. "You know that, Eb. Why, if Jed Smith hadn't gone under down on the Cimmaron, he'd have published his own maps, a hunnerd times better'n Fremont's."

"Sure, Jim, sure," Eben agreed pacifically. "Whereabouts is this pass?" he asked.

"Lemme show ya." Jim grabbed a piece of well-tanned and whitened doeskin and began drawing a map with a stick blackened in the fire. The two men bent over the map, leaving her to drowse in the fire's warmth. When she roused again, the level of liquid in the bottle was much lower and Jim was lewdly describing the charms of certain sloe-eyed Spanish senoritas to be found in California.

She judged it was past time for her to leave the men to their whisky.

Eben came stumbling to bed much later but this time Annabeth was wiser than on the previous occasion, quietly shoving over to make room for him without a word of complaint. He undressed rapidly and slid in beside her, pulling her into his arms. "God, I'll be glad when we're on our own again," he muttered, nuzzling her neck.

"So will I," Annabeth whispered truely, unmindful of the whisky fumes that came wafting to her nostrils.

Eben sighed. Old Jim was out cold, still in his buckskins, stretched out by the fire snoring loud enough to wake the dead. But Eben knew that Annabeth would not be satisfied with less than complete privacy. So he contented himself with running his hands over her slender body as if to reassure himself of her nearness and his possession of her. Then, tucking her head into the hollow of his shoulder, he pulled her tight against him, his heart warmed by her murmured chuckle of contentment, and fell asleep.

Jim Beckwourth himself escorted them safely out of Crow territory. "Wouldn't want them young bucks of mine to get any ideas in their heads while my back was turned," he said genially. "Ain't a one of 'em but what wants to count coup on you, Eb." He sighed. "I'd like it fine to have the company of you young-uns fer the winter but it ain't wise fer you to linger, I calkilate."

The two men clasped each other's hands in farewell and Annabeth was moved to stand up in her stirrups and press her lips to the old man's cheek. "Thank you for all your help, Mr. Beckwourth," she murmured. "And may God be with you."

The old man blinked. "More'n likely he'll be with you than with this old sinner, ma'am." He cleared his throat noisily. "Take care of her Eb," he warned. "She's Some!"

Annabeth wistfully watched him turn and ride away, in the direction from which they had come.

Eben watched her, a quizzical smile playing about his full lips. "You liked him, didn't you?" he asked when Jim was out of earshot.

"Why yes," she said slowly. "Why shouldn't I? He was very good to us . . . and even if he is a bit, well, rough-hewn anyone can see that underneath he has a heart of gold. A real old sweetheart," she pronounced.

Eben burst out laughing. He bent over his horse's neck, choking, unable to contain his mirth.

"I don't see what's so funny!" Annabeth said sharply.

Eben gasped and choked down his laughter. When he had gotten his breath back, he said, "Honey, that old coot is the biggest liar and the worst old reprobate these mountains have ever seen. There's some that say his heart is as black as his hide. If he *has* a heart, which I take leave to doubt."

"I don't believe it!" Annabeth was indignant. "And besides, I thought you and he were old friends. Didn't he take you in hand and teach you all you know about the mountains, when you were just a boy? And didn't he save your life at the battle of Pierre's Hole? And didn't you save *his* at—?"

Eben shook his head, grinning. "It was Jim *Bridger*, not Jim Beckwourth, who taught me all I know. To the best of my recollection, he never saved my life or my scalp, except on this present occasion. And I'm damn sure I never saved his!"

"Then it was all a pack of lies?" Annabeth felt bitterly disappointed. She had listened to the old trapper's tales with a grain of salt; evidently what she had needed was a whole boxful!

"*Nothing* of what he said about you was the truth?" she said, aggrieved.

"Depends on what was said," he remarked cautiously.

Annabeth repeated some of the old trapper's tall tales as they rode along, to which Eben listened with an occasional chuckle, disclaiming ninety percent of them.

"And you never outfought a whole tribe of Blackfeet?" she persisted.

"There were only three," Eben said modestly.

"And . . . and you never plunged your knife into a man 'up to the Green River' and . . . and gutted him out?" she inquired.

Eben frowned. The way she put it made him think she was kind of hoping he had done that very thing! Well, he had—but he wasn't exactly proud of it. It was just something that had had to be done and he did it. He had done it more than that one time, if the truth were known.

He shook his head. For a gal who hadn't wanted him to touch her with blood-stained hands a few months back, Annabeth had come a very long way. But you never could tell with women and he figured what she didn't know, she couldn't hold against him.

"Haven't I just told you not to put any stock in Jim Beckwourth's stories?" he said impatiently. "We've got a long ways to go." He leaned over and swatted her horse on the rump. "Come on, let's *ride!*"

They came to a good campsite well before dark. It was sheltered under a stand of pines, the boughs of which they could use to build their temporary quarters. Underneath the pines, the horses could easily forage for the snow did not lie heavy there. Farther on, past a burbling brook there was a stand of willow they could use for firewood. Annabeth could take in all its advantages at a glance but . . . "Isn't it a bit early to set up camp?" she protested. "There must be more than an hour of daylight left."

Eben swung her out of the saddle with a grin. "Can't wait another whole hour to get between the blankets with you," he teased her, sensuously sliding her down the length of his hard muscular body before setting her on her feet.

The Annabeth who even a month ago might have blushed and bridled now merely laughed and said teasingly, "Well, you'll have to wait, won't you, because we have to set up camp and eat supper first. I'm absolutely *starving*!"

Eben grinned. "So am I! For you!" he said huskily. And since his need proved greater than her own, they crawled into the blankets together before their meal and Annabeth forgot all about her own amazingly enlarged appetite for food in the greater delight of satisfying a more compelling hunger.

And her hunger for Eben was as real a hunger as her more mundane appetites and as strong as his for her. Since they had last been together in that very special way he had been wounded in battle and had nearly died of his wound. And when he was past the crisis and on the mend so that they could have found comfort and reassurance in each other's bodies, they had lacked the privacy to do so. That lack of privacy had become so irksome to Eben—and to her as well—that he had insisted on their taking the trail before, she suspected, he was fully recuperated. He still suffered from severe headaches from time to time and she wondered if there wasn't more to his desire to make an early camp than he was willing to admit. She had noticed, when they were setting up the pine bough shelter, that he was looking sallow with lines of pain carved into his face.

"Eben, are you quite sure you're all right?" she asked him rather anxiously when he coaxed her into the blankets. "Your head—" she eyed him worriedly, paying particular attention to his temple and the ugly, jagged scar it bore, "—your head looks rather swollen."

His lips touched her lightly with tantalizing persuasiveness. "Woman, it ain't my head that's swollen," he muttered huskily into the hollow of her throat even as his hands began a lust-arousing exploration of her soft and yielding flesh.

"Oh, Eben!" She recoiled away from him, pretending to be shocked though she was fast becoming shock-proof and he knew it.

He held her fast with a deep low-voiced chuckle. "Since you're hell-bent on playing nursemaid, mebbe you better check it out," he invited between kisses that aroused every inch of her flesh.

When she hesitated, he took her hand and guided her to him. "You do agree it needs some attention?" he muttered between little gasps as her slender fingers set forth on an exploration of their own.

"Oh, there's no doubt about that," she whispered, her own voice husky with longing. "No . . . doubt . . . at . . . all." And then his mouth came down on hers, covering it hungrily, his tongue darting in and out and sending shivers of desire through her.

"Well, what do you suggest we do about it?" he asked, lifting his head at last.

"Do?" Annabeth murmured dreamily. She felt as if she were floating away on a sea of sensual bliss.

"Yes. Do." Eben's voice held love and laughter. "What remedy do you propose for reducing the swelling?" he teased.

"Hmmm." Annabeth hesitated, gathering her scattered thoughts and and running her tongue over her own kiss-swollen lips. "Well . . . we could . . . we could—"

"Yes?" he said encouragingly.

"Pack it in ice!" she said demurely. "That's a sovereign remedy for swellings and congestions."

Eben's bare broad shoulders shook. "Sounds kinda drastic," he chuckled. "Can't you think of anything else?"

"Hmm. Maybe. With your help."

"Ah . . . how 'bout tryin' something like . . . this!" His hands had begun to caress her body as he spoke, the palms sliding down her back to cradle her buttocks and pull her closer to him so that she could feel his hardness pressed between her thighs. She caught her breath with a gasp and her thighs seemed to spread of their own accord, issuing him an open invitation, leading him on with love and longing.

With a moan of relief he eased himself between them, feeling, as he always did, the wonder stealing over him—the wonder that they could fit together so perfectly—as if they were made for each other. It never ceased to amaze him for she was such a little bit of a thing, like a little bird, and he was such a big heavy man.

For Annabeth the sense of wonder was, actually, less. They loved each other; she was sure now that they had been meant for each other all along; how, then, could their lovemaking be anything less than perfection? That their bodies were in the most exquisite harmony with each other she almost took for granted. How could it be otherwise, given their love for each other?

She abandoned herself to the dizzying whirl of sensations he was creating within her, her breath coming in long shuddering moans, timed to the rhythm of his thrusts. Waves of ecstasy throbbed through her as he burrowed inside her, his body fitting to hers easily.

Her arms crept up to wrap around his neck and she clung to him as her body began to hum and vibrate with a molten liquid fire as she reached the shimmering peak of ecstasy. The pleasure was pure and explosive, its fiery flames licking within her and as her mouth opened in a cry of release and fulfillment, Eben fused his mouth to hers, grinding his lips into her lips and mating his tongue with hers until he finally lost his superb control and, with a burst of fire from his loins, groaned his release.

She felt as if she were encompassed in a golden wave of passion and love that flowed between them and enveloped them. How, she wondered, could it be so good, each time better and more fully satisfying? Filled with an amazing sense of completeness, she wrapped her arms around him, as if by holding on to him she could also hold on to this wonderful sense of contentment and peace that flooded her being.

Eben succumbed to the mind-drugging sleep of the satisifed lover, sliding downwards so that he could pillow his head on her breasts. His head did ache, damnably, though he wouldn't have admitted it to anyone, least of all of her. Her breasts were a soft and soothing pillow and, curling his hand around one possessively, he fell into a deeper sleep.

Annabeth, amazingly, did not feel the least bit sleepy. She found an enormous sense of satisfaction in cradling him against her thus. Perhaps it was a way of prolonging this blissful sense of fulfillment, she thought, tenderly brushing the hair back from his forehead which felt a little hot to the touch. She frowned, taking the opportunity to look more closely at his wound which seemed to have healed cleanly with scar tissue forming but . . .

Her eyes traveled downwards to where his arm lay heavily across her body, his hand cupping her breast. The arms that would forever bear the marks of the sacrifice he had made for her.

She remembered the first time she had noticed those scars back at their camp in the Crow country. She had wondered aloud how he had come by them and when he explained, she looked at him wide-eyed. "You . . . you mean you . . . you mutilated yourself for me?" she whispered, with something like horror.

"Aw, Annabeth, don't look at it like that," he said uneasily. "It ain't no big thing. You know damn well this tough old hide of mine is covered with scars anyways." He shrugged. "What's a few more?"

She looked unconvinced. It seemed to her so . . . so immoderate, so barbaric and savage an act.

Eben tried to explain. "It wasn't my idea," he admitted. "Gray Bull suggested it. It's the

Cheyenne way. They believe you can . . . can—" he fumbled for words, "get the gods on your side—"

"Propitiate?" Annabeth suggested.

"Yeah, somethin' like that. Propitiate," he stumbled over the unfamiliar word, testing it on his tongue. "Propitiate them by making a personal sacrifice. It's the same principle as the sun dance—to sacrifice the flesh in order to have success in battle, to take many horses or count many coups. And it ain't limited to men, neither. Ain't you ever noticed that some of the Cheyenne women are missing the tips of their little fingers?"

Annabeth hadn't.

"Well, they are. A woman cuts off the little finger joint to insure the safe return of her man from battle. Or sometimes she does it out of gratitude for a prayer being answered—out of thankfulness that her child has recovered from a serious illness, for example."

"I thought you didn't believe in Indian superstition," she protested.

He shifted his feet, uncomfortable with this conversation. "I told you once before I don't rightly know what I do believe," he reminded her. "I only know," he said simply, "that there ain't anything I wouldn't do for you."

Annabeth sighed, as, lost in thought, she gently traced with her finger the scars that ran along his arms. Love, she thought a trifle uneasily, could be a source of pain as well as pleasure. Well, she had had the pleasure in full measure—her cup ran over with it. What, she wondered, would be the price she would have to pay—the pain she would have to bear—and could she bear it cheerfully and uncomplainingly and with courage when her time came?

13

Annabeth and Eben made the journey home in slow and easy stages. There was no need for haste or excessive caution now that they were back in Cheyenne territory.

It was as well that they had this brief period of peace, privacy and tranquility for the rest of the winter proved long and hard, full of anxiety and even tragedy.

The weather, which had been exceptionally mild, suddenly took a turn for the worse. Snow plummeted down, covering the earth with deep drifts of white; the wind howled and the temperature dropped to thirty below zero. Annabeth had no way of measuring it, of course, but she was sure it must be at least that cold, if not more so.

But the weather was the least of it. Only two days after their return to camp, Silent Moon, who was, by her own calculations, long overdue, went into labor. It was unusually prolonged and painful and resulted in the birth of a stillborn son. Moon was heartbroken. She was no longer in first youth and had already suffered several miscarriages. It was likely that this pregnancy would be her last.

She was ill for a long time after the birth and

to give her peace and quiet during her prolonged convalescence, Eben and Annabeth took the two boys, Little Lance and Turtle Boy, to live with them.

Enforced intimacy only increased the hard feelings between father and son. Immediately after their return to the Cheyenne camp, Eben had sought out Lance and punished him severely for the part he had played in Annabeth's kidnapping.

Annabeth was against it and said so. "It's been so long," she fretted. "Lance may not understand why he's being punished now for an offense he committed months ago. Besides, it was Shooting Star Woman who engineered it," she pointed out. In their absence Shooting Star had married a visiting brave from another branch of the Cheyenne nation and had prudently taken herself off to her new husband's camp on the Arkansas. She was beyond Eben's wrath.

But Lance was not. Ignoring Annabeth's reminders that whipping a child was not a Cheyenne custom, Eben took down the boy's britches and gave him half-a-dozen licks with his leather belt.

The boy was too proud and stubborn to shed a tear even though several angry red welts were raised on his tender young buttocks. What hurt even more was the shame he endured for even though the punishment was conducted in privacy, the other children got wind of it and taunted him unmercifully.

Lance tightened his lips and blamed his pain and humiliation on the red-haired woman for, before *she* came his father had never laid a hand on him, had scarcely spoken a harsh word to him, in fact.

The atmosphere inside the tepee was electrically charged with tension and Annabeth felt she couldn't have stood it if she hadn't been able to escape to Moon's lodge to nurse her, leaving Eben to cope with a sulky, stubborn, and totally uncooperative Lance. She felt ashamed of herself for preferring the sunny-tempered Turtle Boy to Eben's own natural son but there it was and she couldn't help it.

In one of his more willful moods Lance threw a snowball packed around a stone through the lodge of the shaman, ripping it open. Lance had a grudge against that medicine man, for his herbs and potions had not cured Silent Moon and until she was well again, he could not go back to what he considered his rightful home. He was stuck with his father and his white stepmother. Oh, why couldn't he have been born of Indian parents like every other boy he knew?

The stone/snowball incident was a village scandal. In order to avert bad luck it was necessary that Lance be purified by the medicine man who unwrapped his sacred bundle of medicine arrows and with long ceremony and much passing of hands over the offender, wiped him all over with powdered white sagebrush praying that he might be forgiven his impiety. If the ceremony were omitted, who knew what might happen? Bad luck might come, not only to the culprit but to everyone in the village.

Eben had his own method of punishment and purification. He whipped Lance again.

Annabeth was beginning to feel increasingly unwell, especially in the mornings. She was not so naive or so ignorant as not to know perfectly well what this signified and was distraught to discover that she had ambivalent feelings about it. Oh, she wanted to bear Eben's child—it was the natural culmination of their love. But ... not just now ... not while Lance was being so difficult. She feared the boy would resent the advent of a little brother or sister and would resent her even more than he already did for having the temerity to produce one! No, she didn't want to have a baby while they were having so much trouble with the child they already had. It would only complicate matters. Parenthood was not an unalloyed joy, she was beginning to discover!

And the future was still so uncertain. Loving Eben as she did, she still didn't want to spend the rest of her life in an Indian village, did she? No, she didn't. But, as Eben never spoke about the future, she assumed that he planned to stay on there indefinitely.

Her physical misery increased her mental perturbation. When she wasn't throwing up, she was starving, though not for meat which was still plentiful—meat, the stuff of life of the mountains and prairies. No, what she was hungry for was real civilized food. Sweets and sours mainly. Her mouth watered at the thought of mince and apple and pumpkin pies. Cinnamon buns with a sugary glaze. Thick, rich, chewy molasses cookies, served with a tall glass of sweet, fresh milk. The cookie jar back home was always filled with cookies of some description, she thought wistfully.

And *pickles!* Red pickled beets and yellow pickled squash and green pickled cucumbers. A crock of sour pickles always stood in the pantry of the old farm kitchen. You lifted them dripping from the brine. They were so sour they made your mouth pucker up and they crunched so satisfyingly between your teeth. Her mouth watered at the very thought.

Now that her appetite was so chancy the monotony of the Indians' winter diet irked her unbearably. Meat, meat, and again meat—and when that became scarce they would have to subsist on pemmican. She never wanted to eat another piece of meat again—not wild meat, anyway. What she craved was a fine slice of fried ham served with a side dish of carrots or squash and a heaping mound of mashed potatoes smothered in cream gravy; or pork chops with spiced apple sauce; or leg of lamb served with mint sauce and tiny fresh green peas!

Her common sense told her that she wouldn't be indulging in spring lamb and fresh green peas back home in York State in the middle of winter, any more than she could in Cheyenne country. But reminding herself of that didn't help lessen the cravings that overwhelmed her.

Worst of all was the secret fear that she did her best to keep hidden in the deepest corner of her soul. The fear of childbirth, which had been revived by Moon's sufferings. The squalor of childbirth appalled her anew, unrelieved, as it was in Moon's case by the joy of bringing a new life into the world.

What if *her* baby died at birth? In the harsh creed in which Annabeth had been raised, unbaptized infants went straight to hell. And there were no preachers to baptize a baby within hundreds of miles. None closer than Independence or St. Louis on the one hand, or Oregon on the other.

When she expressed this particular fear to Eben, he was angry. "If that's what your religion

preaches, I don't think much of it," he said
bluntly. "The ways of the Lord may be inscrutable
but I don't think He could be so mean or so petty!
And I don't want you to think so either. Anyways,"
he said bracingly, "our baby ain't gonna die." It
was said so convincingly that Annabeth almost
believed him. "You're young and strong and
healthy," he said encouragingly. "No reason you
shouldn't be just fine. Moon's always been
unlucky in her bearing—only raised two younguns
out of half-a-dozen pregnancies."

Eben had been as jubilant about the news as
any prospective mother could wish. She had
wanted to keep it from him for a little while—just
until she had resolved some of the conflicts and
ambivalent feelings in her own mind. But her
morning sickness told the tale, betraying her
secret. Eben was tender and sympathetic to her
plight, insisting that she stay in bed until the
queasiness ebbed and trying to come up with
delicacies to tempt her appetite—no small feat in
midwinter!

As well as being exhilarated, he was also
surprised, though he didn't have any right to be,
he thought ruefully, mindful of the way they had
been going on. The truth was, after Lance's birth,
Walking Wind, to her sorrow, had been unable to
conceive again. So, he'd almost forgotten his
mama's old saying—"First the bed and then the
cradle." She ought to have known, having borne
six to his father and two—that he knew of—to his
stepfather. He told Annabeth this—holding his
mother up to her as an example of a woman who'd
been blessed in childbearing, hoping to calm her
fears.

It helped more than he knew to be reminded

that not all women died in childbirth. For this was her deepest, darkest fear of all, one she hardly acknowledged herself and would not have dreamed of confiding in Eben—that she would die in childbirth as her mother had done. Eben's timely reminder helped banish her fear, pushing it to the farthest corner of her mind.

The winter dragged on but it wasn't all unrelieved misery. There were bright spots amid the gloom.

Silent Moon was still too weak to do more than drag herself around and Annabeth got the idea of reading to her to while away the time that hung heavy on her hands. She had only two books to choose from—the Bible and Shakespeare. The Bible was her first choice but Eben put his foot down hard! "Told you once before I won't have no proselytizin' hereabouts," he said sternly.

Annabeth pouted but he stood firm. "They got their own religion. You got no call to be messing with their minds and their beliefs," he insisted.

"Oh, but I do have a Call!" she retorted. "A Call to bring the Word of God to the heathen." She felt a deep sense of shame that she had so far forgotten her mission . . . her primary purpose in coming West. She had been living among the Indians for months now and she hadn't converted a single soul. She hadn't even tried to!

"Mebbe you got a call and mebbe you don't but I'm telling you to leave these particular 'heathens' be!" Eben got up and strode to the doorway of the lodge. Unfastening the tent flap he paused before ducking out into the cold. "That's my final word on the subject, Annabeth," he said darkly.

She glared after him in anger, resisting the

impulse to throw something at him. Eben was so . . . so implacable when he spoke in that tone of voice that she didn't dare defy him. Not just now anyway.

Oh, well, if she was forbidden to bring the Word of the Lord to the ignorant savages . . . no, not savages . . . She hadn't thought of the Cheyenne in those terms for a long time, she realized suddenly . . . heathen, maybe but not savages . . . she could, at least, bring them the words of Shakespeare. Eben had not placed an interdict on that. She tossed her red head, a plan forming in her mind. She would introduce them gradually to the white man's higher culture and superior civilization and then, when they were hungry for more and ripe to learn . . . well, Eben couldn't object to her answering their questions about the white man's ways and, hopefully, the white man's God, could he? She wouldn't be ramming her religion down their throats . . . she would just be . . . broadening their horizons!

A warm fire burned brightly in Moon's tepee and the family was clustered around it, except for the two boys who were scuffling at the rear. She had already primed them for a story from the white man's book and she opened it at *Macbeth*. She had decided that this was an exciting, adventurous tale guaranteed to catch the primitive imagination and which would, at the same time, impart a moral lesson.

She had barely begun when Eben drifted in and sat down cross-legged by the fire, lighting his pipe with a hot coal. She held up the book ostentatiously and said, "Shakespeare—not the Bible."

He nodded, satisfied.

It wasn't easy, translating Shakespeare's English into Cheyenne but she made tolerable progress and noticed with satisfaction that even the boys had crept closer to listen.

When she finished, Gray Bull spoke first. "The man, Macbeth, he has no honor," he observed with disapproval. "No Cheyenne would do such a thing—to betray a friend for gain! Wagh!" He got up and strode from the lodge.

Silent Moon looked troubled. "The woman, Ladee Macbeth," she said, twisting her tongue around the unfamiliar name. "She was evil. She was not a wise counselor to her husband. She led him into evil ways." Moon shook her head, equally disapproving. "Do many white women behave so?" she asked curiously.

"Well—" Annabeth struggled for an explanation. Somehow, this wasn't going according to plan. She glanced toward Eben, sending him a signal for help with her eyes.

Eben snickered and, knocking out his pipe, uncoiled his long legs and stood up. "You got yourself into this, sugar," he said with a chuckle. "I'll leave you to get yourself out of it!"

When his father had left the tepee, Lance spoke up. "This white man, this Macbeth, is a bad man," he pronounced severely. "He calls on the spirits to help him do murder—the murder of a man who is his friend. That is not right. A man calls on the spirits to make him strong and brave, to help him raid an enemy's camp and to count coup. A woman calls on the spirits to protect her husband or her child. It is wrong to call on them to help you do bad things like murdering a friend. But what else can be expected of a white man or—" his black eyes pierced Annabeth with a basilisk glare, "A white woman." He grunted, in imitation of his uncle, Gray Bull, and strode out of the lodge, a small warrior unimpressed by the white man's culture.

Annabeth sighed, all the wind taken out of her sails. Perhaps something was lost in translation? The conclusion the Indians drew from her story was not what she had had in mind.

When Moon was finally up and around again, Turtle Boy went back to his family and Lance elected to go with him, to Annabeth's relief. She had tried hard to like Eben's son but she just couldn't. She'd tried to be nice to him, she'd tried to draw him out but, whereas Turtle Boy was cheerfully communicative, Lance was silent and glum, his scornful black eyes seeming to pierce right through to her very soul, making her blood run cold. She was sure he would do her more mischief if he dared. One day she had come into the lodge with an armload of wood and Lance had stuck out his foot so that she tripped and fell, sprawling heavily on the ground. She was sure that it had been no accident, sure that Lance had deliberately and maliciously tripped her up but she couldn't prove it. Fortunately she had come to no harm but, from that time on she was on her guard. She wanted no harm to come to the precious new life she carried within her.

It was a relief, when the boys left, to have her husband and her home to herself again—to be free of Lance's obsessive dislike and resentment. She and Eben were as snug as two bugs in a rug while the winds whistled around the tepee and the blizzards raged outside. They rejoiced in their newly regained privacy making gentle, tender love in the long winter evenings. And now that Lance's watchful black eyes were no longer there to zero in on them they were free during the day to display their affection openly, to exchange teasing endearments and tender caresses and kisses which were but a prelude to more passionate interludes at night.

That Eben took particular pleasure in teasing her until the quick color flared in her cheeks she had long since discovered. Now his teasing took the form of gentle remarks—and sometimes broad and not-so-gentle ones about her changing shape. Already her once-slender body had begun to show signs of pregnancy. She strove to conceal her condition even inside their tepee with doeskin wraps in lieu of a shawl but Eben teased her out of her shyness, calling her his little punkin and caressing the gently rounded mound of her belly with a possessive pride. "It ain't nothing to be ashamed of—to keep hidden like white women do," he told her. "You oughtta be proud! To my way of thinking there ain't nothing more beautiful than a female carrying new life within her."

He must truly be seeing her with the eyes of love, Annabeth thought glumly, only partially appeased, and still pining for her once trim figure. At this rate, by the time the baby came she would be as big as a cow. She probably wouldn't be able to waddle.

She thought she had become almost shock-proof about sexual matters but an event that occurred at the tag end of winter demonstrated that she was not as immune to shock as she had supposed.

Little Deer, the pretty daughter of Silent Moon and Gray Bull, came of age. This, in itself, was only to be expected; the girl had turned fourteen that winter. It was the way in which she heard of this event that left Annabeth reeling in shock.

Since she and Moon were such good friends, she wouldn't have been at all surprised if the girl's mother had taken her aside and whispered the news into her ear, but it didn't happen that way.

What did happen was that the town crier came around one morning and announced the event to everyone in the camp! Annabeth was flabbergasted. There was such a thing as modesty, decorum, decency, after all—or there should be! she sputtered to Eben.

He laughed at her horrified indignation. "It's customary," he told her. "When a young girl comes of age her mama tells her paw and then he relays the information to the town crier. When Little Deer emerges from the Moon Lodge, Gray Bull will sponsor a feast for her and give away a pony or two in honor of his daughter becoming a woman."

"Feast—" said Annabeth faintly. "Give away ponies?" she shook her head in bewilderment.

"Why, sure," said Eben easily. "It's the biggest event in a young girl's life and deserves to be celebrated and commemorated. The Cheyennes always make a big deal out of it. I reckon Owl Woman and Silent Moon have already taken her to the Moon Lodge by now. All the female relatives and family friends will rally round so you better get along over there 'fore you're missed."

Annabeth went, partly out of curiosity and partly because she was genuinely fond of Moon and her family. When she arrived, Owl Woman, as the oldest female relative in her father's family was painting the girl's body red. She then presented Little Deer with the chastity belt which was tied around her waist and wound securely between her thighs. As she did so, she warned Little Deer of the proper way to conduct herself henceforth, "You must not smile too much or too often at the young men of the tribe, my daughter. And especially not at any particular young man or he will think you forward and bold. Be modest and virtuous at all times as befits a Cheyenne maiden."

Owl Woman also conducted the concluding ceremony four days later. She took a coal from the fire and sprinkled it with dried sweet grass, juniper needles, and powdered white sage which burned with a sweet fragrance pleasing to Heammawihio. Little Deer was then instructed to stand over the smoke with her feet on either side of the coal. This was the rite of purification without which she would be deemed unfit to re-enter the family lodge.

The subsequent feast began and ended with prayer. Before everyone settled down to eat, a little food from each kettle was offered to the spirits by being held up to the sky. It was then placed on the ground at the fire's edge. Appalled as she was by the occasion for the festivities, Annabeth couldn't help noting Little Deer's glowing face and sparkling eyes and making comparisons with her own experience at that time of life. The girl was obviously thrilled by all the attention being lavished upon her and proud of her new status in the tribe; she was no longer a child but a marriageable maiden, with all the privileges and responsibilities it entailed. And, not for the first time, Annabeth found herself questioning the system of values in which she had been raised—and reluctantly finding them wanting.

Afterwards, she was very glad that Little Deer had had her moment of glory. For in early spring, just as the snow was beginning to melt and the buds to swell, a particularly virulent form of influenza swept through the camp and Little Deer was one of its first victims.

The Indians had no resistance. They died like flies, especially the old people and the children. Owl Woman died and so did the old chief who had accepted Annabeth into the tribe, and the infant daughter of Moon's youngest sister. The whites, Eben and Annabeth, were not affected; neither was Lance, perhaps because of his white blood. But Turtle Boy was not similarly spared. As his sister had been one of the first to die, he was almost one of the last, even as Gray Bull and Moon were consoling themselves that at least one child was left to them.

Annabeth longed to help nurse the victims and chafed under the restrictions Eben put on her activities. But he was not disposed to risk either her health or that of their unborn child, no matter how she begged and pleaded with him to allow her to do more.

"You're doing enough as it is," he scolded her, lifting a laden soup kettle to carry to a tepee where all the family members were stricken. For Annabeth kept the soup pots simmering day and night to provide for those too ill to fend for themselves. "I don't want to catch you luggin' them heavy kettles, neither," he warned her. "If I do, I'll take 'em away from you." But it was an empty threat and they both knew it.

So Annabeth chopped up whatever meat was

available and simmered it into a nourishing broth and Eben lugged kettles and built scaffolds for the dead while the death wails echoed and reechoed through the camp and the shaman's chants and drums were never silent.

But when Turtle Boy was stricken, Annabeth rebelled, insisting on going to Moon's lodge to help her nurse the child.

When the agony was over, Annabeth's weary glance fell on Lance, who was hunkered down by the fire, his stony face impassive. He showed no overt signs of grief, shed no tears for his best friend, his playmate, his almost-brother. How *could* the boy be so hardhearted, she thought, her own face contorted with tears, not realizing Lance's grief was too deep for the easement of tears. Oh, Lord, she thought in exhaustion, *why*, if one of these boys had to be taken . . . *why* . . . ? In horror she thrust the thought away from her almost as soon as it crossed her mind. But at that moment, Little Lance lifted his head and looked her full in the face and she had the eerie presentiment that he had read her mind, that he knew exactly what she had been thinking and despised her for it.

When the epidemic had run its course, Annabeth felt burned out. She fell into a deep depression brought on by overwork and worry and grief and a bout of the flu in its mildest form. It left her feeling drained and listless and so depressed that she felt life just wasn't worth living. Not here, anyway. Not in this horrible country. Oh, she was sick of the West! She wanted to go home where people died decently in their beds—usually of extreme old age—and not with their boots on! She wanted to get away from this harsh country where you died of shootings and stabbings and gunshot wounds and snakebite or from being clawed to death by a grizzly bear—as had happened to one of the women just the other day when she went to the stream for water. Or in epidemics, where people died like flies because they had no resistance or proper medical care or qualified doctors. They relied on superstition and the chants of the shaman to pull them through.

When Eben, who was concerned about her mental and physical state, tried to jolly her out of the doldrums she turned on him in a fury, dumping all of her pent-up fears and resentments on him.

He tried to reason with her. "Annie, bad things happen to people all the time. There ain't no safe place—not anywheres on earth. You just gotta learn to take it as it comes, to roll with the punches," he told her helplessly.

Her face crumpled. "You don't understand!" she wailed. "I want to go home! I want Aunt Beth and Uncle Henry and . . . and even Aunt Anna. I want to . . . to go back . . . to the farm!" Her face softened in memory. "It's so beautiful there in the spring . . . the earth freshly turned up by Uncle Henry's plow . . . the apple blossoms in the orchard—" Suddenly she launched herself into Eben's arms, burying her face in his broad chest. "Oh, Eben, I want to go *home*!" she wailed.

Over her bent head his face grew grim. "All right, Annabeth, if that's what you want, I'll take you back East," he said slowly. "Reckon that's what I shouldda done in the first place," he added heavily.

She looked up at him with tear-drenched eyes.

"You . . . you will?" she said, hopeful but not really believing what she had heard. It sounded too good to be true. Then she remembered that back in the States Eben was a wanted man. "But . . . but . . . how can you?" she fretted. "That man you killed . . . that man back in St. Louis—"

"We'll go to Independence," he decided. "It's a-bustle in the spring with pilgrims flockin' in to take the Oregon Trail. Likely I won't be noticed in all the hubbub," he reasoned. "There'll be folks going in the other direction, too. There always is. I can put you in the charge of some of them and they'll see to it that you get home all right."

"You . . . you won't come with me?" Her eyes widened in alarm.

"Be reasonable, Annie. How can I? Even if I weren't a wanted man, what in hell would I do back East? I ain't no farmer or businessman." He ran a distracted hand through his thatch of black hair. "If your aunts will look after you and the baby, well and good. I figger I could send you a little money from time to time if I went back to trappin'."

"And . . . and that's what you want for us, Eben?" she looked at him in despair. His dark face was as impassive and unreadable as any Indian's. How could he discuss their separation so calmly? Didn't he love her anymore? she thought in heartbreak. Oh, she knew she had been difficult to live with these past weeks—sunk in a lethargy and despondency so deep she was almost unreachable. But . . .

"You oughtta know it ain't!" he said roughly. "But it does seem to be what you want, don't it?"

Annabeth thought it over. It was a measure of her despair that she could even consider parting with Eben. It would be lovely to be home, she thought with a sigh. To have dear Aunt Beth and darling Uncle Henry fussing over her. And Aunt Anna would be a tower of strength when the baby was born.

But what would they think of her, coming home unwed to have a baby? By their standards she had been living in sin all these months—and maybe they would be right—maybe she had been! Even though she felt that God had blessed their union, it was undeniable that no preacher had said the words over them. Aunt Beth and Uncle Henry would forgive her just about anything, she was sure of that. But Aunt Anna? She shuddered, picturing her stern aunt's reaction to being confronted with a pregnant and unwed niece. And what's more, she thought with a sinking heart, Aunt Anna would be right—for she, Annabeth, would be bringing shame upon them in their old age. She shivered, thinking how tongues would clack in the village if she came home pregnant and unmarried. Why, Uncle Henry wouldn't be able to hold up his head amongst his cronies, nor her aunts at the sewing circle or in church or in the village general store.

But setting all that aside for the moment, how could she go back home and leave Eben behind? She swallowed a lump in her throat as big as a goose egg. Even if he didn't love her anymore—and it surely sounded like that, his voice had been so hard and cold—how could she deprive him of his child? If she went back home now, he would never even see it. Maybe he would never even know if it was a boy or a girl. That didn't seem fair. After all it was his baby too.

And, to be perfectly honest with herself, how

could she bear to say goodbye to Eben, knowing
that it would be forever? How could she live
knowing that he was somewhere in the world—in
this West that he was so much a part of—and that
she would never ever see him again? She couldn't.
It didn't even bear thinking of.

"I . . . I guess I don't want to go home all that
bad," she said in a small voice.

He looked unconvinced. "You're sure?"

"I'm sure," she said steadily.

And that, it seemed, was that. But their discussion or argument or whatever you wanted to
call it hadn't really served to clear the air, she
mused. In fact, it had given her a whole new set of
problems to mull over. Paramount among them
was her marital status—or lack of it!

It hadn't seemed all that important in the
beginning—in the first joyous rapture of loving
Eben. They after all, married in the Indian way,
she consoled herself. They were regarded as man
and wife in the society in which they were living,
and they regarded themselves as such. Theirs was
no casual liaison . . . no short-term affair but a
relationship based on love, trust, mutual affection
and respect as any good marriage should be. But
the more her mind dwelled on thoughts of home,
the more acutely she was reminded that this was
not the way the rest of the world would view it.
People whose opinions she valued, people like her
aunts, for instance, would raise their eyebrows
and say that she was living in sin. She would be
regarded as a loose woman—an immoral woman
—she was sure of it! And her baby, her precious
unborn baby, would be considered illegitimate.
A . . . she cringed at the harsh term . . . a bastard!

She put a protective hand to her gently

rounded midsection. Poor little baby, you won't even have a name! she thought in horror. Her baby wouldn't be entitled to its father's name; it wouldn't be a McDowell because she wasn't legally married to its father. What name would it go by? she wondered hysterically. Not Allan, that wouldn't be right. Allan was Asa's family name. He wouldn't want it bestowed on her . . . her bastard child.

Jamieson, then? Her maiden name? She frowned. That didn't seem right either. She hadn't thought of herself as Jamieson in a long time. She thought of herself as Eben's wife—and she was, in all but name!

Her depression deepened and intensified. She was only going through the motions of living. She felt as if she were living in a daze, her thoughts floating around in a misty never-never land, and she couldn't seem to get a grip on anything.

Eben was at his wit's end. He knew Annabéth was suffering and he didn't have the least idea how to help her. Neither did Moon, who, even in the depths of her own grief, realized that there was something very wrong with her friend. But all she could do was counsel patience. "It is her pregnancy,' Moon suggested. "She will be better when the baby comes."

But he couldn't wait that long, Eben thought frantically. The baby wasn't due for months yet. In the meantime she could waste away of this . . . this religious melancholia or whatever it was. From the disjointed words she whimpered in her sleep, he knew that her religion had some bearing on her unhealthy mental state, though he couldn't pin it down any more precisely than that. She didn't confide in him anymore; she had seemingly shut herself away from him. Oh, not physically. She never refused him or ignored his needs but something was missing. Some vital spark had gone out of her. She was so quiet and withdrawn and he couldn't seem to get through to her.

Maybe he *should* take her home, after all, he mused. He felt like it would tear the heart right out of him to lose her but the way things were it was only too likely he would lose her anyway. She couldn't go on as she was; he was sure of that.

And then, all of a sudden, on a bright and sunny spring morning, Annabeth woke up and found that the mist of fog and depression that had engulfed her had rolled away and she knew what she must do. She must presuade Eben to take her on to Oregon!

14

"*No!*" he thundered.

Annabeth sighed. She wasn't finding it easy to bring Eben around to her way of thinking. It was frustrating because she was so sure it was the only thing to do. When they got there, Dr. Whitman could perform a proper legal marriage ceremony. She and Eben wouldn't be living in sin any longer and their baby would be spared the stigma of bastardy. He could also baptize the baby when it came.

What's more, Marcus Whitman was a qualified medical man as well as a missionary. He would see her through her coming ordeal and with a qualified doctor in attendance she wouldn't dread and fear childbirth at all. Well ... not nearly so much. And, even if worse came to worst and she died in childbed, Mrs. Whitman would be there to mother her little one, just as she did the mission Indian and half-breed children and little orphaned emigrants.

It would be almost as good as going home, she thought with growing excitement. In fact, the Whitman mission would be a small slice of home for she remembered many of the people there fondly from her childhood. Remembered golden-haired, golden-voiced Narcissa Prentiss—as she had been then, before she married and went West—singing in the choir of the village church.

Maybe Eben couldn't take her back home but he *could* take her on to Oregon. If only he *would*! They had been hashing it over for what seemed like hours and she wasn't making any headway at all.

"After the baby's born, mebbe," he said, to pacify her. "It's too hard a journey for a pregnant woman. After he's born you can put him in a cradleboard and we'll go over the mountains."

"After will be too late," she cried, desperate to make him see.

"No, it won't. You're due in the moon-when-the-cherries-are-ripe. There'll still be time to cross the mountains before the cold weather sets in," he assured her.

"That's not what I mean." And then, because they had been arguing for hours and she was tired and distraught, she blurted out her most secret fear. "I'll die in childbirth if you don't get me to Dr. Whitman!" she cried hysterically.

The pipe dropped from Eben's mouth. "What kind of tomfool notion is that!" he exclaimed. It was the first he had heard of the fear she had been harboring all these months.

"It's true . . . I know it's true! My mother died in childbirth and so will I if you don't get me to Dr. Whitman!"

Eben sighed. He couldn't deny that childbirth was hazardous for a woman, just as going into battle was for a man. He didn't blame her for being scared; he was afraid for her himself. But she was letting her fear get the better of her, letting it override her usual good sense.

"Annabeth, you'll be a hell of a lot better off staying put than risking being brought to bed on the trail," he said patiently, trying to make her see reason. "I know you're scared but Moon and the midwives will know what to do for you when the time comes."

"No! I don't want to have my baby squatting over a pile of straw like an Indian squaw!" she cried, her lips trembling. "I want to have it in a bed—a real bed—with lavender-scented sheets and pillows with cases and a real doctor in attendance. I want my own people with me—white people!"

"A woman in your condition can't cross the mountains," he said firmly, as if that would put an end to the discussion.

"Plenty do!" Annabeth said stubbornly.

"In a wagon. Not on horseback!"

"Mary rode from Nazareth to Bethlehem on a donkey's back!" she retorted.

Eben was exasperated. "Annabeth I don't know how far it is from Nazareth to Bethlehem, but I'm damn sure it's a hell of a lot farther from here to Oregon!"

"Please, Eben," she looked at him imploringly. "I just know I'll die if I can't get to Oregon. And . . . and if I do die in childbed I want Mrs. Whitman to take care of our baby. I don't want it to grow up Indian!"

Eben frowned. Annabeth wasn't in any condition to bear the hardships of the trail. Any fool could see that. On the other hand, it was only too obvious she was convinced she would die in childbirth if she didn't have a proper doctor hovering over her. And while he thought this was nonsense—his ma hadn't had a doctor for any of her babies—he knew that the mind could play strange tricks on a person. He'd seen Indians—brave and courageous men—just lie down in their tracks and wait to die because they were convinced their time had come. And die they had. If Annabeth was convinced she was going to die, she just might, if only because she willed it so.

And there was another consideration she didn't even know anything about. Ever since he'd been clubbed over the head by those young Crow bucks back in the winter, he'd suffered from blinding headaches—headaches that were growing more severe and more frequent. Maybe Doc Whitman could help him. He had a heap of power in his medicine Eben knew. Why, a few years back he'd taken an arrow out of old Gabe, an arrowhead that the tough old buzzard had carried around inside him for years; so long that cartilage had grown around it and Doc had had the devil of a time getting it out. He'd cut Gabe open with a mob of drunken mountain men and Indians looking on who would have scalped him if the operation had failed. But the operation was a success and Gabe had lived.

Eben thought it over. It might not be such a bad idea to put both himself and Annabeth in Doc Whitman's capable hands. Whatever happened, it would be good for her to have hope and her own people around her. The trip would be hard on her, he knew, and there was no getting around it. But he'd make it as easy for her as he could. The wagon train migrants made a lot of their own trouble, he knew, by their insistence on hauling a lot of useless belongings along with them—everything from heavy dressers and chests to gristmills. And he wasn't any greenhorn like most of those pilgrims. He was wise in the ways of the mountains and could use that knowledge of short-cuts and water holes and hostile Indians to make the journey easier on Annabeth. And, as she had rightly observed, she wouldn't be the first pregnant woman to make the journey.

So he relented, the joy and hope in her face convincing him that he had made the right decision.

Lance refused to go with them. Eben had given him his choice, hoping that he would agree to accompany them for it would be a long time before he saw his son again—if ever! But Lance shook his head. "I belong with my people, the Tsistsistas," he insisted. "I belong with my father, Gray Bull and my mother, Silent Moon. They have no son now but me and I will not leave their lodge empty," he said with dignity. He might be cursed with white blood but he would not be faithless like the white man—like his natural father, he thought scornfully.

They traveled with the Cheyenne into the hills for at this season of the year the sap was in the pine trees, the poles were easy to peel, and it was time for the Indians' annual pilgrimage to cut new ones for their lodges. They also tapped the sap of the bark elder tree and boiled it down for sweetening, much as Uncle Henry had tapped the sap of the sugar maples back home, thought Annabeth. She helped Moon make a kind of candy of it which Lance particularly relished.

"Last year Turtle Boy made himself sick eating too much of the sweets," said Moon with a shadow in her eyes. "I am glad that Straight Arrow leaves his son with us, to fill our empty lodge and gladden our hearts."

Annabeth was glad, too. With the best will in the world she couldn't bring herself to like the boy and she was glad he brightened someone's heart. He had the opposite effect on hers.

"It's good of you and Gray Bull to have him. Oh, Moon, I'm going to miss you," she said impulsively.

"As I will miss you, Flame-Hair Woman," said Moon gravely. "You have become as dear as a sister to me. But it is good that you will be among your own people when your child is born. This I understand."

It was not, by western standards, all that far to South Pass. A gentle incline marked heights of land between the Sweetwater and the Green, the natural gateway to the West. Annabeth felt jubilant that they had gotten this far without a speck of trouble, until Eben unintentionally dampened her spirits by remarking that this was the halfway point of the Oregon Trail. Their journey had barely begun.

Still, it *was* the watershed of the continent. From here on all the streams flowed west. Spring though it was, there was still plenty of snow in the pass. Rivulets of melted snow trickled downhill and watered patches of green which, here and there, were starred with yellow flowers and clumps of wild irises. It was such a harsh unforgiving land, Ananbeth reflected, and yet it could be so heartbreakingly beautiful.

Beyond the Pass itself, which was no winding canyon as Annabeth had expected but a broad, flat, high valley, a desert barred their way to the Green River. Emigrants usually reached it in July, she knew, at which season the heat and dryness must render it well-nigh unbearable. But at this season of the year the going wasn't too bad and Eben knew of an alternate route, not followed by the wagon trains, which shortened the distance and brought them to water every twenty miles or so.

Bridger's Fort was built on Black's Fork, a tributary of the Green, in fertile wooded country with the Wasatch in sight to the west, the Uintas to the south, and similar timbered peaks almost in the dooryard.

It was the first post west of the Missouri built especially to cater to the emigrant trade.

"Old Gabe's a smart old cuss," Eben commented, when they caught sight of the palisaded fort with its strong timber gate. "He can't read or write but he could read the handwriting on the wall when it came to the fur trade. He figgers to make him a fortune shipping in supplies, horses, and provisions for the emigrants. He has a blacksmith shop for them to use to make repairs and he still does a little fur trading to keep the Indians happy."

Annabeth nodded absently, engrossed in the tricky business of negotiating the river bank. The river was high with spring runoff but Eben knew exactly the right place to ford it and led her forward confidently.

They were halfway across when Bridger himself, mounted on a piebald Indian pony, came splashing over to greet them.

"Eb, you old son-of-a-gun!" he bellowed, pumping Eben's hand enthusiastically. "Couldn't believe my ears when my scouts told me you was heading in. What you doing this far from your own stomping grounds?"

"It's a long story, Gabe, and it'll have to wait till we've rested and eaten. My wife is pretty tired."

"Wife!" Bridger shot an amazed glance at Annabeth who was bent over the saddle, rubbing her aching back. "Gawdalmighty! A white woman! Pleased to meet ya, ma'am," he added hastily. His keen eyes twinkled at Annabeth. "Ain't I told you, boy, that women and whisky would be yore downfall! Not but what this one ain't as pretty as a spotted pup!"

"Can't do without either one!" Eben retorted promptly. "Any more'n you can, you old sinner! How many Injun wives you got now, Jim?"

Old Gabe put on an injured face. "Only the one, boy, only the one. Whaddya think I am—one of them there Mormons? They come through here last summer, some of 'em pushing handcarts. Nary a one of 'em but had two, three wives and Brigham Young, their leader—why, he's got more wives than I got fingers and toes!"

Fort Bridger was built in the usual form of a stockade. A small Indian encampment had grown up around it. A strong high fence enclosed a large yard. The lodging apartments and offices opened into a hollow square protected by a strong gate.

Bridger led them inside, yelling for his Indian wife. A plump placid woman, she emerged from an inner room, clucked sympathetically when Annabeth removed her buffalo robe to reveal her pregnant condition, and led her off to one of the apartments to rest. It couldn't properly be called a bedroom, Annabeth reflected, since no such amenity could be seen. But she was too tired to be particular and flung herself down gratefully upon the stack of buffalo hides that did duty for a bed.

She was roused some time later by the savory smell of simmering stew drifting from the outer room and, scrambling awkwardly to her feet, followed her nose to the source of the mouth-watering smell. Jim's wife was dishing up the food. Jim and Eben were seated around a large plank table, seated upon *chairs*—a luxury that Annabeth had been unaccustomed to for quite some time! She moved eagerly into the room, soft-footed in her moccasins.

The men were too engrossed in their conversation to hear her approach. Eben was saying bleakly, "This is terrible news, Jim." He ran a distracted hand through his hair. "God! I don't know how I'm gonna tell Annabeth. She was real fond of Mrs. Whitman and she was counting on the doc to deliver our baby." He stood up and shoved back his chair. "I better go tell her supper's on the table. Maybe while we're eating I can think of some way to break it to her gentle-like."

"Tell me what?" Annabeth stopped in her tracks, her heart contracting with foreboding. What could be so terrible that Eben dreaded telling her of it? "Break *what* news to me?" she insisted. "Eben?" Her eyes moved from Eben's dark face to Jim Bridger's lean grizzled countenance. His keen eyes were not twinkling merrily now—there was a world of sorrow and compassion in them. "Jim?"

The tense silence seemed to stretch out interminably, though in reality it was only the space of a few heartbeats. Finally Eben said heavily, "You gotta be real brave, honey. It's real bad news—just about the worst there could be. But," he paused to lick his lips, "you gotta try to take it easy. You gotta think of the baby." He went to her and Annabeth reached out blindly, her groping fingers clutching at his arm. "Please, just *tell* me," she begged.

Eben sighed. "All right. There ain't any way to make it easier for you, I guess." He took a deep breath. "Doctor and Mrs. Whitman have been killed. Both of them."

"K-killed?" she repeated numbly, the color draining from her face. Her eyes went to Jim Bridger for confirmation of the terrible news.

He nodded sorrowfully. "That's right, ma'am. I'm sure sorry to be the bearer of bad tidings. They was killed last fall. The Whitmans and most of the people at the mission—whites, Indians, and half-breeds, alike." For a moment his face contorted with pain. "My own little daughter was among them. My little Mary Ann. It was a massacre."

"N-no!" The shrill cry echoed in Annabeth's ears but she didn't recognize it as coming from her own throat. Ripped from her own throat. "Nooooo!" As if from a great distance she saw the room and its contents—the table and chairs, the stolid Indian woman, the two men—whirling around dizzily and then she felt Eben's loving arms outstretched to catch her before she fell.

"What happened, exactly? And *why* did it happen?" asked Annabeth urgently.

She had been revived and Eben had insisted on her trying to eat a bowl of the savory stew. To please him she managed to get down a few spoon-fuls though it stuck in her throat.

"Tell me about it, please." She looked imploringly at Old Gabe.

Usually there was nothing Jim Bridger liked better than to tell a story but he hesitated, glancing at Eben who shrugged.

"I think it would help me to accept it if I could understand," Annabeth said haltingly.

"It was the measles epidemic that started it, I reckon," Jim said thoughtfully. "It was the fuse that lit the powder keg. Doc Whitman, he just about wore himself out trying to cure the sick but in spite of all he could do, the Injuns—Cayuses, they are." Annabeth nodded impatiently. "They died like flies. And then the rumor spread that Doc Whitman himself was actually causing the deaths."

"Oh, no! How could they think that?" Annabeth gasped.

"Folks don't always act too reasonable when their hearts are heavy with grief," Jim reminded her. "Even white folks. They wanted revenge and Doc was handy. I also heard tell that some educated half-breeds had been goin' around stirring up trouble—telling the Cayuses that their days as a people were numbered."

"How . . . how did they die?" she asked him, now that she understood the why of it.

"Annie—" Eben said warningly.

"No, Eben, I have to know."

He nodded slowly.

Jim cleared his throat. "Doc was caught outside . . . he was bludgeoned and tomahawked. Miz Whitman, she was giving one of her adopted young-uns a bath when she heard of it. She rushed to the door and dragged the doc inside but there wasn't nothing she could do for him. So she took the young-uns upstairs and held off the Injuns with an empty gun. But one of 'em tricked her. He'd always been friendly to 'em and he promised that if she would come out, he would take her and the children to the nearest fort. When she put down the gun he shot her down, her and fourteen others." The mountain man's eyes grew misty. "My little Mary Ann was taken captive but they treated her so bad she died of it. And Joe Meek's little gal, Helen, she was killed too. Joe was in the Willamette Valley at the time and he went back to the mission afterwards to make sure that they had a proper burial." Joe had had to remove the dead from a shallow grave when the wolves had been making free with them and then rebury them but he didn't think fit to tell *that* gruesome bit of information to the white-faced girl who sat across the table from him, tears trickling slowly down her cheeks.

"You know, Eben," the older man said thoughtfully, "if I was you, I'd steer clear of Oregon for a spell. They has gone on a killin' spree, shooting down anybody who even looks like he might have a drop of Injun blood." He got up and fumbled in a cupboard and came back to the table with a handful of what looked like pebbles, dropping them into Annabeth's hand. "Cast yer eyes on that, ma'am," he invited.

She shifted them between her fingers indifferently. They felt, for their size, amazingly heavy and she looked at Jim in wonderment. He took the largest pebble between his thumb and forefinger and held it up to the light. "Notice anything special, ma'am?" he asked.

Annabeth shook her head but Eben caught his breath in a gasp. "By God, Jim, is that what I think it is?"

"If you're thinking it's gold, boy, you'd be right! It's gold from Californy. Kit Carson, he was out there with Fremont and he brung it, riding despatch for General Kearny. There's been a big strike out there, at Sutter's Mill. 'Fore long the whole world's gonna be heading out there." Jim chuckled. "I'd go myself if I didn't know I could make my fortune right here selling flour to the greenhorns at fifty dollars the barrel! You might say I got my own gold mine right here on the Green! If I was you, Eb, I'd mosey along out there," Jim advised. "You got a good chance to make you a fortune 'fore the word spreads to the East. Next year, in '49, there'll be mad rush to the goldfields," he prophesied, "but you can get there ahead of 'em all, Eb, a whole year ahead."

Eben took the pretty pebbles from Annabeth's outstretched hand, rolling them around on his palm and then closing his fist over them. "Gold!" he mused out loud. He'd never been a man to hanker after wealth or the things that money can buy but there was no denying that a family man—a man with a wife and a child on the way—ought to think of those things. Gold would buy security and comforts for Annabeth and the baby. Would buy all the pretty things a pretty well-bred young woman ought to have. Yes, he mused, he had a better chance than most of amassing a fortune for the woman he loved; he'd be a fool to turn it down! "Gold!" he muttered, pouring the glittering nuggets from one hand to the other. "Gold in California!"

15

They lingered at Fort Bridger for several days, ostensibly to let the horses graze and get their fill of fresh green grass before tackling the desert and the mountains ahead. But Eben was more concerned about Annabeth—fearing that the shock might bring on a miscarriage and reluctant to move on till he was sure she was going to be all right.

She seemed to have weathered it pretty well, considering, he mused, though she'd cried almost all that first night through. He'd woken up in the middle of the night and, hearing her muffled sobbing, pulled her into his arms. "Don't take on so, sugar," he murmured as consolingly as he could, rubbing her back with broad sweeping strokes of his hand.

But Annabeth turned her face into his shoulder and wept and wept. She just couldn't seem to stop. She wept for Aunt Anna and Aunt Beth and Uncle Henry who were so far away—almost as good as dead for her for most likely she would never see them again. Any more than Narcissa Whitman had ever seen her own home folks—her father, Judge Prentiss and her mother and her sister, Jane, or any of the folks back home.

She wept for Asa, her earnest young husband whose life had been cut so tragically short, and their missionary friends buried back along the trail. She wept for all the Cheyenne she had known who died in the flue epidemic—tough old Owl Woman and sunny-tempered Turtle Boy and his quiet older sister, Little Deer. She wept for the grief of her friends, Silent Moon and Gray Bull.

But most of all she wept for Marcus and Narcissa, for their years of suffering and toil and privation—had it all been for nothing?—and for all their bright hopes dashed down.

Last but not least, she wept for herself. She'd hardly realized, till her own hopes were dashed, just how buoyed up she'd been at the thought of meeting old friends at journey's end. She'd been counting on Dr. Whitman performing a marriage ceremony for her and Eben and then delivering her baby when the time came. She'd been counting on the friendship of Narcissa whose brilliant sparkling eyes and clear musical voice she remembered so well. Remembering, she wept again—wept until she could weep no more and lay back in Eben's arms in exhaustion, the fountain of tears dried up at last.

"Oh, Eben, what are we going to do now?" she whimpered.

"We'll make out, Annie. You'll see," he said encouragingly. "Reckon we oughtta follow Gabe's advice and head for California. There's doctors there and preachers too. We'll make do." What he reckoned on doing, he'd already decided, was to take Annabeth to a place of safety—maybe one of those Spanish missions he'd heard about—and leave her there to await the baby's birth while he himself went up to Sutter's Fort to do a little prospecting. Likely she wouldn't cotton to the notion of being left behind so he prudently decided not mention this scheme just now. But he sure as hell couldn't take a pregnant woman to the goldfields and he had made up his mind to try his luck there—to find enough gold to support Annabeth in style; it was no more than she deserved.

She squirmed restlessly in his arms. "Why, Eben, *why*?" The age-old cry wrenched itself from her anguished heart. "Why did the Whitmans have to die? *Why* did the Indians turn on them? Why did it have to happen?"

Eben sighed. "Don't reckon anybody knows the whole answer to that, Annie." After a moment's thought, he added, "I have heard that they were a sight too civilized, too proud, too aware of their own superiority . . . I'm not saying Mrs. Whitman wasn't a fine courageous woman," he added hastily, "but she wasn't able to live among the Indians as one of them, the way you've lived among the Cheyenne. She was too busy trying to uplift them. And that goes for the doc, too. I can see how that kind of an attitude might rankle and rile 'em up. Can't you?"

Annabeth's eyes filled with tears again. "But . . . such a horrible way to die—"

"Don't none of us know how it'll be for us when our time comes," Eben reminded her gently. "I figger it's how we live that counts."

"Oh, Eben, hold me, please," she whimpered against his chest. "Never let me go!"

His arms tightened around her, his mouth tasting salt as he kissed the tears from her eyelids and her cheeks. "Ain't never going to, Annie-girl," he promised, forgetful for the moment of the exigencies of life and his own plans to go prospecting without her.

He had never, not even in their camp in the Crow country when she had so nearly been raped by that gang of ruffians, been so tender with her as he was now. His mouth claimed hers in a gently persuasive kiss, even as his hands began to rove tentatively over her body, banishing her sorrow and awakening her to passion. He used her with a soft slow delicacy, until his gentle massage sent currents of desire flaring through her body and she welcomed him with softly uttered cries of joy. As their bodies melded together, her world was filled with him and they were consumed with the wonder of it, finding comfort and consolation in each other and in the continuous reaffirmation of life and love.

They lingered at Fort Bridger much longer than they had originally planned. Eben was relieved to see Annabeth's tears turn to laughter at Jim's outrageous tall tales, relieved to see the color return to her pale cheeks and her appetite come back.

Jim fed them lavishly—with fish fresh from the river, venison, quail, even beaver tail. There was more civilized fare as well—flour, bacon, cornmeal, spices, dried fruits, coffee, and sugar that he kept in stock for the emigrants and which seemed a rare treat to Annabeth.

In the evenings he kept them royally entertained for he was a natural-born teller of tales. He spun yarns of his adventures in the Yellowstone where water came boiling out of the ground and you could, he swore, look through a glass mountain as if it were a magnifying glass. He had shot an elk through that mountain and was irked that it didn't fall dead—only to discover that

that elk had been twenty-five miles away!

He told them of the winter when it had snowed for seventy days and seventy nights without stopping and the snow was seventy feet deep. He and his fur brigade had holed up in the Great Basin where herds upon herds of buffalo had frozen solid standing up. When the thaw came, the men skinned them, rolled them into the Great Salt Lake and pickled them. "You remember, Eb, you was there," Bridger interjected. "Ain't it just as I say?"

Eben grinned. "Sure, Gabe, sure." He pulled down an eyelid to wink at Annabeth.

"Well sir," Bridger went on, magnificently ignoring this byplay. "We made meat for ourselves and the whole Shoshoni nation, enough to last ten years or more, outta them pore frozen pickled bufflers."

But the story Annabeth liked best featured Bridger all on his own. The Blackfoot tribe had run him into a box canyon. His rifle and pistol were empty and he had no spare ammunition left. He had lost his knife and there was no way out and the Blackfoot were almost upon him!

He paused deliberately, lighting his pipe, to let the tension build.

"What happened then?" demanded Annabeth, on the edge of her chair.

Bridger took a puff on his pipe, blew a plume of smoke and watched it drift away. His eyes twinkling, he finally drawled, "Why, they killed me and they scalped me and here I be!"

The two men burst into roars of laughter at the expression on her face.

That was their last evening at Fort Bridger. In the morning, with pack-horses well-laden, for Old Gabe was generous with his friends, they set out for California. Now that the Whitmans were gone, Annabeth was indifferent as to their destination. They could be married as well in California as in Oregon, she supposed. And surely, with so many Yankees settling there in recent years, there must be qualified doctors, competent doctors. There just had to be!

Since they weren't burdened and slowed down by heavy, cumbersome, overloaded wagons nor by stock to tend and herd, as the emigrants were—stock that often attracted the attention of hostile Indians—they were able to travel much faster than the wagon trains, covering territory much more easily.

From the Green River Valley, they came into the valley of the Bear, circumventing the Great Salt Lake, for Eben had no wish to tangle with the Mormons. Bridger had warned him of their hostility to gentiles—not but what they had good reason for it, having been persecuted and driven west on account of their peculiar faith.

Crossing the desert was not the ordeal it might have been for the wagon trains which struck it in mid-summer heat waves. It must be well-nigh unbearable at that season of the year, Annabeth thought, but now, in the spring it was not too bad. But perhaps that was because she was with Eben, who had an uncanny ability to find water where she could have sworn there would be none. He went his way, confident and self-assured, which greatly contributed to her ease and peace of mind. Sure that Eben could do anything, confident that she was safe in his hands, she could even relax and find beauty in the vast black basaltic masses and lava fields through which they passed. It didn't take much imagination—and Annabeth was blessed or cursed with a good bit of it—to see

the great red rock formations as castles and
fortresses standing guard against the sky. The
streaks of red, mauve, pink and green in the rocks
fascinated her.

Likewise, crossing the Sierras was not as
hazardous and harrowing as it would have been
had they been burdened with a heavy loaded
wagon. Indeed, Annabeth couldn't imagine how
wagon trains could ascend and descend those
steep precipices at all! It must require the utmost
in cooperation from everyone involved to get the
wagons through and, judging by her experience
with a wagon train last year, that, in itself, must
constitute something on the order of a miracle!

Game was plentiful and they ate well, for
Eben's aim was always true. Annabeth had lost the
aversion to wild meat that had characterized the
earlier stages of her pregnancy and there were
plenty of spring greens and wild onions to dig to
supplement their diet.

Afterwards, Annabeth couldn't decide what
she liked best about California, the flowers or the
food! Now, in late spring, the hills were abloom.
There seemed to be a riot of color everywhere she
looked. Acres and acres of bright yellow poppies,
like a mantle of cloth-of-gold. Acres of blue lupines
and pink verbena. In the Sierras there had been
delicate little alpine blooms right up to the snow
line. As they descended the slopes, the dark green
of chaparral was lit by tall white yucca candles;
and all around them was the scent of sage—a hard
spicy fragrance, sharp and pungent in one's
nostrils.

Oh, all this beauty was food for the soul all
right but at this stage of her pregnancy food for
the belly was an equally compelling need.

Jim Beckwourth's pass had brought them out of the Sierras not too far—by western standards —from the goldfields but Eben avoided the little tent-and-shanty towns that were already springing up and made for the coast, stopping at isolated rancherias to augment their food supplies with eggs and goat's milk and cheese for Annabeth. Getting her to a safe and civilized place to await the birth of their baby was highest on his list of priorities. He was distrustful of the little shantytowns with their mobs of gold-hungry riffraff and he doubted that a preacher or a medical man could be found there. Whereas, at the rancherias the tradition of Spanish hospitality was still strong and they were made welcome and plied with Mexican fare—lamb or beef stewed with peppers and onions; pinole, a kind of parched corn flavored with sugar and cinnamon; red beans and rice and tortillas. Best of all, to Annabeth's way of thinking, were thick mugfuls of rich hot chocolate, a favorite beverage among the Californios.

Eben laughed at her healthy greed. "You've got a chocolate moustache," he teased her fondly. "You're turning into a regular little pig."

"I *am* eating for two," she defended herself serenely but reached for a square of cloth to use as a napkin.

Eben forestalled her, pulling her down beside him on a carpet of flowers and licking the chocolate off her lip with a delicate flick of his tongue.

Annabeth twined her arms around his neck and lay her head on his shoulders, sighing with contentment. They had camped last night in a meadow of golden poppies. A sparkling stream of fresh water flowed down from the mountains and close by the horses grazed belly-deep in lush greenery. Above them the sky was a deep vivid blue pierced by snow-white mountain peaks. "It *is* beautiful here, isn't it, Eben? I'm glad we came. I could stay here forever, couldn't you? *Could* we? Stay here, I mean. Build us a cabin?"

It was an alluring prospect but Eben shook his head regretfully. He'd already noticed that Annabeth was developing nest-building propensities of alarming proportions. At every pleasant campsite she'd wanted to linger longer, settle down.

"I ain't no doctor, Annabeth. I don't know much about birthin' babies," he reminded her. "At the very least you'll want another woman with you when the time comes. And I'm gonna do my damndest to get you a doctor too." He hauled her gently to her feet, brushing a quick kiss across her lips. "Come on, we got a ways to travel yet," he said briskly. "We'd best be on our way."

He had it in mind to take her to Monterey but when they ran across that little whitewashed adobe mission with its red-tiled roof, Annabeth exclaimed in delight that it was a perfect place to be married.

The priest, Father Francisco, was taken aback by two Americanos, dressed in Indian garb, who appeared out of nowhere and demanded that he perform a marriage ceremony. Though upon further reflection, he decided that no one could predict what the crazy gringos would want next!

In his long lifetime the old priest had seen many changes, few of them, in his opinion, for the better. Mexico had declared its independence from Spain and annexed California which spelled the doom of the missions. They had been securalized, deprived of their wealth and power, their vast number of herds and flocks, their flocks, their acres upon acres of land.

Then, only a couple of years ago, the Americanos, led by Fremont, had proclaimed the Bear Flag Republic. But, less than a month later, other Americanos—equally mad, in the good father's opinion—had run up the American flag over the customhouse in Monterey. The native Californians had risen in revolt, a revolt that was firmly squashed by the American forces, combined under three commanders. But then the Americans had quarreled among themselves and the notorious Fremont had been hauled off to face a court-martial in faraway Washington.

The old priest shook his gray head. Who could understand these crazy gringos? And now that gold had been discovered the whole country had seemingly gone mad with gold-fever. It boded ill for the way of life he had known, the life of the missions and the lazy carefree pastoral life of the great ranchos.

But if anything was crystal clear it was this: the Americanos were firmly in the saddle and it was only wisdom to humor them.

In addition, from the looks of the woman it was well past time these two were wed!

Both Annabeth and Eben felt ill-at-ease in the dimly lit, incense-laden church with its image of the Virgin and the Stations of the Cross lining its whitewashed walls. Aunt Anna would have said that she was going over to the Scarlet Woman of Rome, thought Annabeth, stifling a hysterical giggle. But then Aunt Anna would probably think her niece had turned into a scarlet woman herself!

She was disappointed to discover that she didn't *feel* any more married than she had before and she doubted if Eben did either. But she and Eben signed the priest's register and she had her marriage lines. Her baby would not be born a bastard and that was all that counted, she consoled herself.

After the brief ceremony the padre unbent a little and with true California hospitality invited them to share his scanty meal of re-fried beans and tortillas. He proved a genial host, a soft-spoken, well-educated man who had come over from old Spain when California was still a Spanish colony. He spoke English quite well and he and Eben discussed California politics and the gold strike while Annabeth half-dozed over the wine that he had insisted on pouring them. When he asked what their plans were, Eben explained that he was taking Annabeth to Monterey to have her baby. Or, possibly San Francisco. Wherever an American doctor might be found.

The old priest looked perturbed. "Already Yerba Buena—the town the Americans call San Francisco—has become a ghost town," he told them. "Merchants have closed their warehouses and their shops. Doctors have left their patients and lawyers their practice. The mayor and the city council have shut down, as has the newspaper office. The school has closed. Sailors jump ship in the harbor and it is full of stranded vessels."

"You don't say!" Eben was startled. "The news spread that fast—!"

"A Mormon merchant-adventurer, Sam Brannan, by name, started it," Father Francisco confirmed. "I have heard that he rode throught the streets of the city, waving his hat in his hand

and shouting—Gold! There's Gold on the American River!'' The old priest shook his head, saddened but not surprised by man's greed. ''And this is happening all over, not only in San Francisco. In Monterey, it is said that the alcalde, the mayor, must grind his own coffee and peel his own onions, so empty is the town. Two-thirds of the people of Sonoma have gone also.''

''And the members of your own flock?'' Eben thought the little village that had grown up around the mission looked pretty normal.

''A few of our young men have gone,'' the priest acknowledged. ''But for the most part they have listened to reason. I have been here many years, you see. I baptized these young men and their fathers before them and, in many cases, their grandfathers. They listen when I tell them—'Gold is good to have but you cannot eat it.' Who will care for your wives and your mothers and your children while you are gone? Stay and tend your fields and your flocks and it may be that you can exchange a part of your crops for gold.''

''You are wise, padre,'' Eben commented.

''I have lived long and learned much, my son.'' He added piously, ''And, by God's grace the influence of Mother Church is still strong hereabouts.''

Eben thought this over. The padre was obviously a strong-minded individual who wielded great power in his stable little community. It was no small feat to keep every able-bodied man in the village from running off to the goldfields! Maybe this would be as good a place as any for Annabeth to wait for the baby's birth—especially in view of the mass exodus from the larger towns.

''Is there a place in the village where we could

stay?" he asked. "Dig in and wait for the baby to be born?"

The priest shook his head. "In the village, no. There is no house that is vacant. But there is a guesthouse attached to the mission. You and your wife are welcome to stay as long as you like." He sighed. "Few travelers stop here anymore. They are in too much of a hurry to get to the goldfields." His rheumy old eyes rested compassionately on Annabeth. "There is a competent midwife in the village. But a doctor—" he shook his head. "The only American doctor I know of is a Dr. John Marsh. He has a ranch on the eastern side of Mount Diablo. That is about fifty miles from Sutter's Fort."

Eben frowned. He didn't want to take Annabeth anywhere near Sutter's Fort. It sounded like everybody in the whole damn country was converging on it—gone gold-mad. But maybe he could leave Annabeth here and go bring this doctor to her. He'd get him here if he had to hogtie him and throw him over the saddle!

"What I'd like to do is leave my wife here—she needs to rest—and go hunt up this doctor," he suggested.

Annabeth, whose head had been nodding over her plate, snapped to attention. "Leave me!" she gasped in outrage. "But I don't want you to leave me here! I want to go with you!"

16

How *could* he? How could Eben propose
going off and leaving her alone when she was so
near her time? But when they were alone and she
put the question to him, he was quite unruffled.
"It ain't that near," he pointed out. "Must be six
weeks or more 'fore the baby's due."

"It's quite near enough for you not to be
thinking of going off and leaving me alone," she
told him tartly.

"You won't be alone," he reminded her. "The
padre will be close by. And the village women. And
one of them's a midwife."

"Oh, how can you?" she reproached him, her
eyes stormy with anger.

"It's you I'm doing it for—you and the baby,"
Eben defended himself. "I'll find this Doc Marsh
the padre told us about and bring him back here."

"What if he won't come?" Annabeth fretted.

"He'll come," said Eben grimly. "Whether he
wants to or not!"

Annabeth sighed, sinking down onto a chair.
The old priest had shown them around the little
guest house and then, sensing dissension, left
them alone in it to make up their minds. "I don't

271

see why you can't take me with you," she fretted. "It makes more sense for me to go to the doctor than for you to try to bring him here."

"Cause you ain't in any shape to travel now!" he said bluntly. " 'Sides, I dunno where I'll find that doctor. More'n likely he's gone off to the goldfields like everybody else in this crazy country."

"I could go to the goldfields with you—" she began hopefully.

"No, you couldn't." Eben stood firm. "I don't know what the conditions are there but it stands to reason life in them gold camps is pretty rough. Too rough for a pregnant woman!"

Annabeth pouted. Oh, this awful pregnancy that sapped her energy and made her tired all the time. And it seemed to her that Eben used her pregnancy as an excuse to keep her from doing anything that she wanted to do. Whereas, *he* was free to do exactly as he pleased! It wasn't fair! Life wasn't fair!

Her lip trembled. "You've got gold-fever just like everybody else," she accused him. "You just want an excuse to go to the goldfields and leave me behind!"

"You oughtta know it ain't like that with me, Annabeth!" he said reproachfully. "You know I want you with me." He bent and kissed her cheek tenderly. "What I don't want is for you to be brought to bed on the trail. Or in one of them hell-raisin' gold camps with no doctor and not even a woman to take care of you." He frowned. "You've been exerting yourself too much as it is—riding or walking all day every day. You oughtta be takin' it easier from now on."

"Indian women ride or walk right up to the last," she reminded him.

He wound one of her red-gold curls around his finger and then fondly watched it spring back into place. "Now just how many times have I heard you tell me that you ain't no squaw!" he teased her gently. "C'mon now, let's go tell the padre that we'll take this house for a couple of months or so. 'Till the baby's born and you're up and around again." He tugged her gently to her feet. "Maybe you can get him to teach you some Spanish to while away the time. If we're gonna stay in this country, one or the other of us oughtta 'habla espanol'," he gave the words a comic twist, "and I'm damn sure I'll never be able to twist my tongue around it!"

Annabeth grinned in spite of herself. "It can't be any worse than Cheyenne!" she retorted.

The old padre refused to take any rent for the guest house but suggested that if Eben met with good fortune in the goldfields he might care to make a small donation to the church instead, an arrangement that suited all concerned.

Eben lingered a couple of days to make sure that Annabeth was comfortably settled in and then left, promising to be back, with or without a doctor, before the baby came. Almost his last words were, "You can trust me, Annie. I'll be back before the baby's born."

"I'll hold you to that," she told him gravely, blinking back the tears she was determined not to shed.

He gave her one last hug and a lingering kiss, then mounted his horse and rode away without looking back, her misty eyes following him until he was out of sight.

Annabeth settled down to wait. She was accustomed by now to making a home under rough conditions wherever she happened to be. And, in truth, much as she had wanted to go with Eben she had to admit to herself that she was tired of always being on the move. As her pregnancy had advanced, the extra weight she was carrying had become a real burden to her tiny, small-boned frame. She felt a tremendous sense of admiration for those madonnas of the prairies who accompanied their men to Oregon or California, some jolting from coast to coast in a covered wagon or trudging mile after weary mile on foot, many with toddlers clinging to their skirts and a nursing baby in their arms. How did they do it? she wondered. It had been hard on her and she had no one but herself to look after and Eben, an experienced mountain man, to protect and care for her.

She missed him intolerably at first but she had much to fill her days. Sewing, for one thing. Above all domestic drugery she hated sewing but Aunt Anna had drilled the rudiments of that skill into her unwilling niece and now she was glad of it for the baby would need clothes—diapers and long dresses and little shirts. As she stitched, the baby began to seem much more real to her—she began to visualize him or her as a little person and she wondered what he, or she, would look like. She hoped it was a boy—a big, healthy, strapping son but if it were a girl she would name her for her mother, Rachel. It was, she thought, a pretty name for a little girl.

It occurred to her that anyone passing through to San Francisco or Monterey might post a letter for her and so she borrowed a pen and paper from Father Francisco and wrote two letters. One, a sad letter of condolence was to

Asa's family; the other, to her aunts and uncle, was a long chatty letter, telling of Asa's death and her own subsequent remarriage and pregnancy, being careful not to let on that the cart had come before the horse!

Her lack of Spanish precluded her making any real friends among the village women but Father Francisco agreed to give her language lessons in her spare time and she made rapid progress under his expert tutelage.

The nights were the worst. She had grown so accustomed to sleeping snuggled up to Eben's recumbent form that at first she couldn't sleep at all. She was used to pillowing her head on his shoulder, their bodies like spoons fitted together. She was so restless at night that she adopted the Spanish habit of the siesta, finding it easier to rest in the heat of midday, that was so much hotter than late spring had ever been back home. At night in the silent darkness she was too acutely aware that Eben had gone out of her life to rest easily. She missed his quiet even breathing when she woke in the darkness, the regular breathing that told her all was well with her world. She missed his strong arms enfolding her in a loving embrace, his caring, his gentleness, the sweetness of his kisses and his whispered love words.

She formed the habit of slipping into the church to whisper a prayer for him. With its statues of the Virgin and the saints, the stubby little candles lit before the statues, the faint odor of incense, the church was far different from the bare austere church of her childhood. But it was a church all the same—a house of God. There were, she had come to realize, many ways to worship Him and more paths to heaven than the straight and narrow one she had once been taught was the only way.

Out of curiosity—and deference to Father Francisco—she attended mass on Sundays and found the ritual beautiful, impressive and appealing. She was also impressed by the size of the congregation crowding into the little church for on Sundays devout Californios from nearby ranchos rode in to attend the service. After mass she was introduced to many of them and found herself instinctively drawn to one sweet-faced young woman about her own age, who was introduced as Maria de la Concepcion Santiago y Vallejo del Corazon.

What a mouthful! thought Annabeth. Not to be outdone, she introduced herself as Annabeth Jamieson Allan McDowell!

The sweet-faced young woman smiled. "You will be pleased to call me Maria," she invited in her slightly stilted English.

Annabeth smiled back. "And I'm just plain Annabeth."

The girl laughed, showing white even teeth. "Not 'plain' Annabeth," she protested. She cocked her head at a handsome young man who had just come up to them. "What do you say, Felipe?"

Black eyes flashed at Annabeth. "Never 'plain'!" the young man agreed gallantly. "No one with hair the color of the sunset could be called so."

"This is my brother," the girl said proudly. "Don Felipe Mario Santiago y Vallejo del Corazon!"

Don Felipe wasn't exactly plain himself, Annabeth couldn't help thinking. In fact, he was the handsomest man she had ever met!

Don Felipe was tall and dark like Eben but there all resemblance ceased. He did not have Eben's muscularity and breadth and bulk of body, being very slender and lithe with regular, almost too delicate features, enhanced by a small black moustache. Very much the aristocrat, she thought, an impression enhanced by his attire. He was dressed in a tight-fitting embroidered suit. His leather riding gloves were likewise embroidered in gold and he wore a gold and silver-trimmed sombrero. His boots were shined to perfection with bright star-shaped spurs attached.

In the loose smock she had made herself Annabeth felt suddenly unconscionably drab and even his sister, in a plain black silk gown and black lace mantilla, looked humdrum beside the resplendent figure of Don Felipe.

Maria was in mourning, Annabeth later learned from Father Francisco. Her novio, her fiancé, a young Americano, had gone on a rescue mission into the mountains 'in aid of emigrants stranded in the deep snows of the Sierras and had, himself, perished with them. It was a very great tragedy, the old priest said sorrowfully, and had, not unnaturally, turned the girl's mind to the consolations of religion. Maria was contemplating becoming a nun. "But," said the old priest severely, "the Church is not meant to be a hideaway from the heartaches and disappointments of life." He could not, in good conscience, recommend that Maria take the veil unless he was convinced that she truly had a vocation.

Annabeth nodded, without comment—a vocation must be something like a Call, she decided. She was intrigued by Maria—this very pretty potential nun—and since the girl often rode to the mission to hold consultations about her future with Father Francisco, she had ample opportunity to get better acquainted. The two girls rapidly became close friends and, before long, Maria issued an invitation for Annabeth to spend a few days with her at Rancho del Corazon.

Annabeth eagerly accepted. She was becoming bored with inactivity and she longed to see Rancho Corazon d'Oro. Father Francisco had told her it was one of the largest in these parts—immensely wealthy in land, cattle, and herds of golden palomino horses from which the ranch took its name. Moreover, the baby was not due for at least another long dreary month of waiting and Maria had promised to send a carreta for her—which Annabeth took to be some kind of wagon—so that she could travel in comfort.

The promised carreta turned out to be an ox-cart with a hooded body—not nearly as comfortable as Annabeth and Maria had supposed. Maria had not ever availed herself of its dubious comfort, having learned to ride almost as soon as she learned to walk. In addition, the road was rough, the way was long and Annabeth was beginning to question the wisdom of her trip to Rancho Corazon d'Oro long before she got there. She felt as if she were being jolted to pieces!

But when they reached their destination, she forgot all about her discomfort. Rancho Corazon d'Oro was all she had been led to believe and more.

The ranch proper was surrounded by four-foot-thick adobe walls, at the gate of which a guard was posted for these were uncertain times. The picturesque, gay and freehanded life of the Californios was passing away and the days when

any stranger at the gate was welcomed without
suspicion and with free food and a night's lodging,
was passing along with it.

Maria and Felipe welcomed her on the broad
patio that ran around all four sides of the low
rambling adobe hacienda. The front of the house
was wreathed with grapevines trained on trellises
and bright with pink Castilian roses and Annabeth
exclaimed aloud at its beauty.

Her friend led her to a sumptuous guest room
to rest, refresh herself, and wash off the dust of
travel. She was glad of the chance to lie down for a
while for the rough ride in the carreta had jolted
her miserably and her back ached almost unbearably.

But lying down didn't seem to help; she
couldn't get comfortable and when, a short time
later, Maria suggested giving her a guided tour of
the grounds, she agreed, rubbing her aching back
surreptitiously and hoping that a gentle stroll
might ease its aching.

It didn't but Annabeth was so intrigued by her
tour of inspection that, for a while, she was almost
able to forget her pain.

The outer courtyard was the hub of the
rancho and of the work constantly going on in the
dairy, the brewery, the implement-repair sheds, of
which there were several, and the weaving huts.
Even much of the kitchen work was done out-of-
doors, the women shelling beans and chopping
onions and peppers on the patio. There, too, young
men conducted flirtations with the housemaids
and old men sat on benches smoking their pipes
while the gnarled hands of their women were busy
with a bit of lacemaking. The children of the
vaqueros and household servants swarmed every-

where playing with each other and with cats, dogs, goats and a parrot that Felipe had brought back from San Francisco for Maria who preened his green and gold feathers and screamed curses in several languages when the children pulled his tail feathers. "I think he once belonged to a sailor," Maria giggled.

From the courtyard they drifted to the stables and from there to the kitchen garden and thence to the vineyard that was well-watered by a babbling brook where the housemaids knelt to do the laundry. There was a little footbridge across the brook that led to a grove of cottonwoods which looked invitingly cool but Annabeth didn't trust her footing on the slippery planks so they went back to the patio. The rancho was much like a self-sufficient little village, she thought, and it all was extremely interesting—or would be if only her back didn't ache so.

She had paused to admire a bit of lace that a toothless old crone had held up for her inspection and, when she straightened, a searing pain shot through her, making her cry out loud.

Maria was beside her in an instant, putting a supportive arm about her. "What is it, Ana?" she asked urgently. "Is it the baby—the nino?"

"It . . . it can't be!" Annabeth groaned, doubling up as another, even more severe pain tore through her. "It can't be the baby; it isn't due for another month." She clung to Maria's arm as a wave of giddiness swept over her.

"Encarnacion! Esperanza!" Maria called imperiously to two of the household women. "Help me get her into the house," she ordered, in Spanish. "Don't worry, Ana," she added reassuringly. "We have a good midwife right here on the rancho. She helped bring both Felipe and myself into the world. You'll be in good hands."

"But . . . but I *can't* have the baby *now*!" she cried, stumbling into the house with the women's assistance. "Not without a doctor! Not without Eben!"

But she did. Annabeth's tiny premature daughter was born early the next morning and lived only long enough to be baptized by Father Francisco, for Maria had sent a vaquero riding hell-for-leather to summon the priest when it seemed evident that the infant would not live.

His wise old eyes gazed with compassion upon Annabeth who was lying exhausted from her ordeal in a great four-poster bed, dwarfed by its canopy and curtains of brocade, her child in her arms.

She had wanted her baby to be born in a real bed, she remembered telling Eben. And she had been—in a bed finer than Annabeth had ever dreamed of. But at what a price! Had her trip in the jolting ox-cart precipitated the birth? She would never know for sure. Many women spent day after day jolting along in a covered wagon and gave birth to healthy full-term infants en route.

She missed Eben with an intensity that verged on desperation. If only he were with her—the child's father. He *should* be here. He had promised to be with her when the baby was born, and he was not. He would never see, touch, hold his little girl and slow tears seeped from her eyes at the thought. She was so tiny, their little daughter, so perfectly formed, with tiny delicate fingers and toes. But too weak to nurse or even to cry.

If Eben had been with her maybe this

wouldn't have happened, Annabeth thought rebelliously. Maybe their daughter wouldn't have been born too soon. If Eben had been home with her where he belonged, instead of in the gold-fields, she wouldn't have made the journey to Rancho Corazon d'Oro. It was only because she was bored and lonesome and longing for Eben that she had made the journey. If only he had stayed with her at the mission none of this would have happened. It was all his fault!

The baby made a faint mewling sound and the old priest bent over her. His voice sounded very faint and far away.

"Is it your wish that the child be baptized into the Holy Catholic Faith, my daughter?"

Annabeth's tongue came out to lick dry lips. "Yes, please, Father," she said thickly. Any baptism was better than no baptism at all, she felt sure, no matter what she had been taught about the evils of "Papists."

"And the name?" the priest prompted gently, taking the child from her arms. It was wrapped in a blanket and dressed in the Del Corazon christening robes.

"Mary Rachel," Annabeth whispered weakly. "Mary for Maria," she turned her head on the pillow to look at her friend who had stood by her all that pain-racked night, "and Rachel because it was my mother's name."

"Maria Raquel," said the old priest, turning it into Spanish for her. "Very appropriate."

"Surely Our Lady will look after the little ones in heaven since she bears her own name," whispered Maria, squeezing Annabeth's hand sympathetically, tears trembling on her black lashes. "Is it not so, Father?"

Annabeth tried to see it in that light

but . . . she would rather be looking after her own baby herself! she thought rebelliously.

In the days that followed, the loss of the child was a deep constant ache, an ache that would not be assuaged. If only Eben were with her to help her bear the pain of her loss—the terrible emptiness of the arms that ached to hold her baby. He should be with her now. He was the child's father. He should be here to share her sorrow and her grief. Oh, where *was* he? How was it, if he loved her, that he did not feel, did not sense, her grief across the miles that separated them and come hurrying back to her?

Her grief, though she wasn't aware of it, was turning to bitterness and resentment. Eben had promised to be with her when her time came. Why hadn't he come back to her in time? You could argue that the baby was premature but maybe she would not have been born too soon if . . . if Eben had stayed with her. He went away, promising to bring a doctor but he had not come back. And Mary Rachel had been born and died. If she had had a doctor, maybe that would not have happened, Annabeth thought stormily.

Maria, Father Francisco, even Don Felipe . . . all of them told her that the baby had died because it was God's will but Annabeth wasn't so sure of that. The more she thought and brooded about it, the more certain she was that Mary Rachel might not have died if only Eben had brought back a doctor as he had promised. And if he couldn't locate a doctor he should have come back to be with her in her hour of need. But he had evidently forgotten that promise too. More than a little unbalanced by grief she began storing up resentment for Eben in her heart.

Eben had not forgotten his promise. He'd gone first to Dr. John Marsh's ranch near Mount Diablo. But, as he anticipated, the medical man was long gone. "To the goldfields, senor," one of Marsh's ranch hands told him with a shrug. Eben then turned and rode the fifty-odd miles to Sutter's Fort.

John Augustus Sutter, a stocky blue-eyed Swiss emigrant, had carved out an immense empire for himself and made himself into one of the most powerful individuals in the Far West. But now he was a man facing ruin, ironically because gold had been discovered on his land. Eben found him staring morosely at the remains of his once-promising wheat crop which had been trampled down by hordes of uncaring gold-seekers.

When Eben, looking down from his horse at the devastation they had wrought, expressed his sympathy, Sutter shook his head, speaking in heavily accented English. "So what if it's been trampled into the ground." He kicked at a few stalks still standing upright. "If every stalk was still upright, I couldn't get it harvested." He shrugged. "If I could get it harvested, there would be no one to thresh it. But supposing I could have gotten it both harvested and threshed, there still would be no one to mill it." He jerked a thumb over his shoulder at a newly built flour mill. "There stands a thirty-thousand dollar flour mill idle because my workers along with my field crews have also got gold fever. I tell you, young man, people will have to eat dirt," he laughed bitterly, "and gold dust because there will be no food in all of California."

"Yore probably right," Eben admitted.

Sutter heaved a deep sigh and turned away from his devastated fields. "Well, what can I do for you, my friend? You don't look like a gold-seeker."

"I'm not. I'm lookin' for someone. Dr. John Marsh. You know him?"

"Know him? Of course I know him," Sutter boomed. "He's my neighbor, isn't he? Or was, till he caught gold fever. I hear he's panning gold on the Feather River."

So Eben went to the Feather River country. He was told that Marsh had been there, had found "color" but was disgruntled because it was too "light" had lit out for parts unknown. In these, the earliest days of the gold rush, Eben learned that this was typical behavior. Prospectors moved rapidly over the rivers and streams, skimming them and scooping up the surface gold and rather quickly moving on. The gold was always brighter in the next stream.

Eben scoured the goldfields for John Marsh and finally got word that the doctor had made a rich strike on the Yuba River. But he got there too late. Envious prospectors told him that Marsh had struck it rich on the Yuba and had gone to San Francisco to celebrate . . .

San Francisco. Eben swore softly to himself. There was just no way he could go to San Francisco, collect John Marsh and make it back to the mission before Annabeth's baby was due. And the only other doctor he'd run across in his travels was an old drunk that he wouldn't trust to treat a sick dog or a spavined horse! Eben was not a man who accepted defeat easily but not even he could conjure up a doctor out of thin air within the time limitations. And time was running out.

He wasn't a doctor but he loved her better than life itself and he wanted to be there with her in her time of travail, even if he couldn't do no more than hold her hand. With him beside her, she could draw on his strength, courage and will to live to help her through it. So he decided to head back to the mission.

Father Francisco was tending his little garden patch when Eben drew rein before the church. There was no sign of life in the adobe guest house next door—no Annabeth running out to greet him—and a feeling of alarm shot through him.

He turned a ravaged face to the old priest who had set down his watering can and abandoned his sun-scorched peppers and onions to offer a word of reassurance to the younger man.

"My wife, padre?" Eben said hoarsely. "Annabeth?"

"She is well, my son," the priest hastened to reassure him. "She is with friends."

Friends? What friends did Annabeth have in this godforsaken country? Eben's view of California would be forever tainted by the voracious gold-seekers.

"Who?" he rapped out, scarcely giving the old man time to answer. "And where? Where is she?"

"At rancho Corazon d'Oro." Father Francisco rapidly gave him directions, adding a hospitable invitation to alight, to eat and rest before going on his way. But Eben, with a bare word of thanks, turned his horse's head in the direction indicated and kicked his mount into a ground-covering lope. There'd be plenty of time for him and his horse to rest and eat, when he'd found Annabeth—seen for himself, with his own two eyes, that she was well.

SAVAGE SPLENDOR

Annabeth had not recovered quickly from the baby's birth and death—either physically or emotionally. The trials that she had undergone during the past year had taken their toll of her strength. It was, she mused, not quite a year since she had buried Asa and now she stood at the grave of her infant daughter—the child who had come and gone so quickly.

How could so much have changed? So much have happened to her within the confines of a year, she wondered? It was, when all was said, such a short span of time.

Don Felipe and Maria had been so good to her, she thought gratefully. They insisted that she stay with them for as long as she liked. Certainly until her husband returned to claim her. What was the good of her going back to the mission? they told her. Father Francisco would send her husband here when he returned.

If he returned. The doubt was uppermost in the mind of both Felipe and Maria. That Ana's husband had gone off and left her at such a time was inexcusable, they thought. Her claim that he had gone to look for a doctor they viewed with unexpressed skepticism, agreeing between themselves that it was just an excuse to go to the goldfields. Native Californians had their babies without benefit of doctors. What need had a woman for a doctor when there were experienced and capable midwives in every village? So both of them saw Annabeth as an abandoned wife, an object of pity, and hastened to reassure her that she was welcome at Rancho Corazon d'Oro, Felipe adding his persuasions to his sister's, persuasions that were often reiterated as the little yanqui recovered her strength and grew prettier day by day. The rancho was isolated, said Felipe, and Maria was often lonely. She would be doing them a favor by staying on.

At first Annabeth had little choice in the matter for she was too weak to leave her bed. Maria often kept her company in the elegantly appointed guest chamber, sympathetic and intuitively silent when Annabeth craved silence, commiserating and compassionate when she wanted to talk. Encouraged by Annabeth, she told the other girl about her betrothed, so tragically killed in the high Sierras. That both had known grief and loss created a bond between them.

"And your brother had no objection to your marrying a gringo?" Annabeth asked curiously. She couldn't imagine the elegantly aristocratic Don Felipe welcoming a yanqui trader into the family.

"Oh, no. Felipe liked Ramon," Maria gave the Spanish pronunciation to her fiance's name, Raymond. "Many Americanos marry with the girls of California." She shrugged. "In the old days, when California was still a Mexican province, all a man had to do in order to be given a grant of land and full citizenship was to convert to Catholicism and marry a local girl. Now that the treaty of Guadalupe-Hidalgo has been signed and California is part of the United States everything is upsidedown," Maria said thoughtfully. "Felipe worries that the old Spanish land grants may be invalidated by American courts. It would have been advantageous to have a yanqui in the family but—" Maria sighed, "It was not to be."

If Don Felipe was worried about anything, Annabeth reflected, he did an excellent job of concealing it. Charming and gallant, he played the role of courteous and considerate host to perfection. When she had recovered some of her strength and spirits, Felipe insisted on carrying her to and from the patio morning and night so that she might enter into the life of the rancho, kept amused and entertained by the antics of children and pets and the comings and goings of the household.

At first she felt distinctly odd, twining her arms about this handsome caballero's neck. "Don't be afraid, pobrecita," he said, his well-shaped lips curving upwards in amusement, "I shan't drop you. You are as light as a little bird in my arms."

It suggested Eben's tender care of her in the days when she had first known him but anyone less like Eben would be hard to find, she thought, as she got to know Felipe more intimately. Oh, he was every bit as kind and as gentle, and he was quite as self-assured as Eben, though in a more suavely sophisticated way.

It wasn't fair to compare them, Annabeth thought guiltily. Eben, so rough-hewn and rugged, hadn't had Felipe's advantages in life. He had been born in poverty and bred to the wilderness, which had honed his skills of self-sufficiency and survival. Felipe, on the other hand, had been born to wealth and social position, and bred to be an haciendado—"el patron" of a great rancho. No, it wasn't fair to compare them but Annabeth did anyway and, inevitably it was Eben who was found wanting.

What appealed to her most about Felipe was his quick and agile mind, a mind that matched her own. They could chat together companionably of so many things that Eben knew nothing of. Books and literature, for instance, for Felipe was well-read and educated beyond the norm of most Californios. Maria was fond of teasing him about it. "Most of our trade in cattle hides is shipped to Boston," she explained to Annabeth. "And the first item on our list of goods to be traded for is always books . . . books . . . books!" Laughingly, she teased her brother, "I do believe you would go without boots to buy books, Felipe!" Annabeth laughed with her but she enjoyed the evenings spent in the cool of the patio while Felipe read to them from his highly prized collection.

When his eyes grew tired or the light grew too dim to read by, he would send a servant for his guitar. He didn't just strum a few chords—oh, no, he was an accomplished musician, playing haunting evocative melodies of old Spain, music that was so beautiful it made your breath catch in your throat. Sometimes he played and sang the popular ballads of Mexico and Alta California, like that which celebrated the doomed love affair of Concepcion Arguello and Nicolai Rezanov, her Russian lover. All California had been brought up on it, had wept over it, and made up doleful ballads of La Favorita of the Presidio. Maria de la Concepcion Arguello had been daughter of the commandante of the Presidio when she fell in love with a foreigner, a Russian in California on a mission for his Tsar. They became betrothed but Count Rezanov needed to obtain the permission of the Tsar. He went homewards across Siberia leaving his lovely Concha or Conchita, as she was called to wait for him. More than two years passed before Concha got the word that her sweetheart was dead. After that, she put aside her pretty clothes and gaiety and quietly joined a lay order of the Franciscans, devoting the rest of her life to the poor and to good works. It had been her story, Annabeth guessed, that had influenced Maria, her namesake, to consider following her example. She also guessed that Maria had put aside the notion, at least for the time being.

It never occurred to her that Maria was preoccupied at the moment with fulfilling a more important function—that of chaperoning her brother and their pretty houseguest! Maria never left them alone together, not since the evening she had strolled onto the patio and found him serenading her. There was a world of tenderness in his eyes as he gazed at Annabeth's bright head and shadowed violet eyes.

That look had alarmed Maria. It would never do for her brother to fall in love with the pretty little American! Oh, she would love to have her dear Ana for a sister, but that couldn't be—Annabeth was already a married woman! And for the two of them to fall in love—for how could Ana be expected to resist the charm of Maria's adored, debonair, wonderful brother?—would only bring heartbreak to them both.

Maria came briskly onto the patio, her heels tapping a tattoo on its tiles. "You are tiring Ana with your nonsense, Felipe," she reproached him. "She should go back to bed. She needs her rest. And I, myself, will help her," she added swiftly, forestalling her brother's attempt to gather Annabeth into his arms. "Dios, Felipe," she said, shouldering him out of the way and giving Annabeth her arm to lean on, "how will our dear Ana ever regain her strength if you never allow her to set foot to the floor?" And chirping encouragingly, she propelled Annabeth back to her room.

That had been a week ago and today, for the first time, Annabeth felt strong enough to make her way to the family plot where the elder del Corazons, the parents and grandparents of Felipe and Maria, lay buried. The most recent grave was that of her own little daughter and Annabeth carried a bouquet of roses and carnations with which to adorn it.

Maria had offered to accompany her but Annabeth preferred going. alone. Kneeling to whisper a prayer, she laid the sheaf of flowers at the gravesite, then rose slowly to her feet to stand for a moment with burning eyes to stare down at the small grave. Finally with a sob she wrenched herself away and blundered to the gates to which she clung, trying to regain her composure.

She didn't hear the hoofbeats on the hard-packed ground nor the creak of saddle leather as the man drew rein and dismounted, tossing the reins carelessly around the spires of the wrought-iron fence. Her eyes brimming with tears, she wasn't aware of the tall man looming over her until he spoke.

"Annabeth—?" The voice was eager, yet hoarse with doubt for the woman's face was buried in her hands. "Annabeth—?"

She whirled, startled. "Eben—?" she gasped. "Eben!"

17

He'd expected to find her heavy and mishapen, swollen with child and near her time and, for a moment, he'd wondered if the slender figure in the black silk gown and rebozo actually was his Annabeth! But not even the black rebozo, a kind of thin trailing shawl which she wore over her head and which wound downwards around her arms, its folds crossing over her breast, in the Mexican fashion, could conceal the brightness of her hair.

"Eben!" she whispered again, clutching at the little cemetery's wrought-iron gates for support.

His predominant emotion was one of relief. She'd obviously gone through her ordeal and survived it. She was alive and well, though thin and pale, her pallor accentuated by her black clothing. Her eyes were deep velvet pools with dark violet shadows under them and an expression in them that he couldn't read at all. But he could sense a kind of constraint between them that had never been there before.

He couldn't understand it, any of it. Why wasn't she running into his arms, the way he'd envisioned her doing during all the days and nights of their separation? Why didn't she seem gladder to see him? What was she doing here, anyway, instead of back at the mission guesthouse where he'd left her? What was she doing wandering around out here alone outside the hacienda's walls? Why wasn't she back in the ranch house with the baby?

The baby! "I . . . I see yore lighter of your burden," he said awkwardly. "And . . . and yore alive and well, thank God!" But why was she looking at him in that strange way? It was down-right eerie! "I . . . I'm sorry I didn't get back in time. The . . . the baby musta come sooner than we figgered."

She nodded her head up and down, in a mechanical fashion.

"Is it well?"

She said nothing.

He tried again to get through to her. "Is it a boy or a girl?"

Annabeth found her voice at last. "A little girl," she said slowly.

"Well, that's fine," exclaimed Eben, a trifle too heartily. "Mighty fine!" Something was terribly wrong but he couldn't make out what it was. He moved to take her hand but she snatched it away. "Why don't we go back to the house so you can introduce me to my daughter?" he said rather desperately.

Annabeth shook her head, that strange veiled look still in her eyes. She stepped backwards, away from him. "She's not back at the house, Eben," she whispered. "She's here."

"Here?" he said blankly, not understanding.

Still clutching the iron gates, Annabeth turned to look inside the enclosure. He followed her eyes, seeing for the first time, the small grave

with its cluster of bright flowers, reading the
letters carved into the whitewashed cross. They
told him all he needed to know. "Mary Rachel
McDowell," he read aloud. "July 3, 1848-July 4,
1848."

"She lived only one short day," Annabeth told
him tearlessly and unnecessarily.

"Oh, Annie . . . I—" He reached out to take her
in his arms but she slipped away from him, saying,
"Perhaps you'd like to spend some time with her."
Her tone was cool, remote, polite. "You'll find me
back at the house. I'm sure Felipe and Maria will
be glad to give you a room for as long as you care
to stay."

He didn't like any of it. He didn't like the
spacious ranch house with its aura of wealth and
gracious living, nor its plethora of servants. He
didn't like it that Felipe and Maria were not a
married couple as he'd first assumed, but brother
and sister. Most of all he didn't like the way that
Don Felipe looked at Annabeth. There was more to
that look than there ought to be, Eben thought. It
was apparent to him that Don Felipe wanted to be
more than a gracious host to Annabeth. He looked
at her with the eyes of a lover!

Annabeth didn't seem to be aware of that but,
Eben had to admit it to himself, she did seem to fit
right in here, almost as if she were a member of
the family. Eben didn't like that either! In fact,
there wasn't one damn thing he did like about the
whole situation! He felt out of place, out of his
depth, he was hurt and bewildered by Annabeth's
cool reception. She acted like she wasn't glad to
see him, like she didn't want him here!

He was mulling over it when Don Felipe rode
in, on a magnificent palomino stallion. He rode

like one born to the saddle, Eben noted, and he accepted the attentions of the servants like one born with a silver spoon in his mouth, which, thought Eben sourly, was obviously the case. A vaquero came running up to take his horse; a maidservant appeared out of nowhere with a glass of sparkling wine on a silver salver.

Don Felipe swung out of the heavy silver-embossed Spanish saddle and, removing his embroidered riding gloves, slapped them together to rid them of dust before handing them to yet another servant. They were falling all over themselves to wait on him, Eben noted sardonically.

Annabeth introduced the two men and sent one of the maidservants off for another glass of wine for him; just like she was mistress here, Eben thought in alarm. Maria, the sister, had already been introduced and he'd liked *her* at first sight. She was sweet and pretty with a warm welcoming smile for him—warmer than Annabeth's, by God! After the introductions had been made, she had slipped away, to oversee the preparations for a gala meal, so she'd said, tactfully leaving husband and wife alone together.

Only Annabeth didn't seem to want to be alone with him and, somehow, they didn't seem to have much to say to one another. At least, Annabeth didn't seem to want to listen to anything he had to say. She'd led him quickly to one of the small bachelor guest rooms to wash away the stains of travel.

"This ain't yore room," he'd guessed, seeing the narrow bed, the room empty of small feminine clutter.

"No, mine is down the hall," she said, looking vaguely off in that direction, "beyond Maria's."

"Next to Felipe's," he guessed.

"Well, yes, as it happens, it is," she said blandly.

Eben's jaw tightened. Hell, she couldn't make it any plainer! And yet Annabeth—the Annabeth he'd known—was not the kind of woman to betray her marriage vows. And, finally, reason prevailed over jealousy. She was, after all, only recently recovered from childbirth. But why was she acting so strange? So remote? Impatiently he grasped her arm. "Annabeth, what the devil is the matter with you?" he demanded.

"Hush, here's Esperanza with a can of hot water for you," she said nervously, as if she thought he was going to hurt her or something . . . "I'll be in the Sala." And she drifted away. She just walked away, thought Eben, bemused.

And now here was this Don Felipe fellow, all decked out like he was going to a fiesta instead of a simple dinner at home. The maidservant had brought Eben a suit of clothing for him to change into but he'd clung stubbornly to his buckskins. Now he wished he'd changed into that finery— borrowed finery though it was!

Don Felipe took Annabeth in to dinner. Maria smiled up at him, Eben, expectantly and offered him her arm. Awkwardly he'd executed a small bow and escorted her to the dining room, pulling out her chair for her as he saw Don Felipe do for Annabeth.

The mahogany table was covered with a fine damask cloth with place settings of delicate bone china and crystal goblets of wine. A bowl of pink Castilian roses which Annabeth had gathered and arranged mingled their sweet scent with the aroma of wine and the richer odors of food which the maids were distributing with the soft slap of moccasined feet. It was finer food than Eben had tasted in many a day but he found that he had no appetite.

Everybody else ate and managed to carry on a conversation at the same time. Eben said nothing and picked at his food.

At this point his hostess leaned across the table and murmured. "You are not eating, Senor McDowell. Is our Californio food not to your liking? Is there something else that you would prefer?"

"It's fine, ma'am. It's just fine," he assured her. He took a large bite of some kind of beef and bean mixture on his plate and found that it was liberally laced with green chilies. Hot damn! Now he knew what the devil served up in hell! His mouth scorched, his eyes watering, he hastily reached for his goblet to wash it down, nearly knocking it over in his haste. The fringes of his buckskin sleeves dangled in the butter dish and a few drops of bright red wine sloshed onto the damask cloth. Eben felt like crawling under the table in his embarrassment. He saw Annabeth wince and lower her eyes to her plate. She was ashamed of him; Eben could see it plain as day.

Maria inconspicuously summoned a maid to soak up the drops that were so vivid on the fine white cloth. It looked, thought Eben dismally, like blood had been spilled.

He'd like to spill blood all right—the blood of that elegant young fop at the head of the table. Only his blood probably wasn't red! More than likely it was blue!

Don Felipe studiously ignored his guest's gaucherie and continued discoursing volubly on the servant problem. Every day more and more of his vaqueros ran off to the goldfields, leaving him shorthanded just when roundup was about to begin.

This gave Maria the opening she needed. She felt a good deal of sympathy for the clumsy gringo and, for the first time, out of sympathy with her dear Ana! What was the matter with her friend? she wondered with annoyance. Couldn't she see that her husband was out of his depth and suffering because of it? Why didn't she do or say something to help him? The tall muscular Americano was, perhaps, lacking in the social graces but he was mucho male, all the same. A strong brave hombre. Indignantly Maria decided to lend a helping hand.

"You have firsthand experience of the goldfields, senor. Will you not tell us about them?" she coaxed.

Thus appealed to, Eben, with a pretty woman hanging on his every word, found his feet at last as Maria skillfully drew him out to talk of his experiences. He told them of Sutter's Fort where hundreds of frame huts had sprung up overnight, though the price for cut lumber was outrageous—$500 a board foot. Maria, as the patrona of a great rancho was properly shocked at the prices that were being charged for the most basic of supplies. Eggs were a dollar and a half a dozen, Eben told her, and bacon a dollar and a half a pound. Mining utensils were almost worth their weight in gold. These high prices prevailed all over—in every gold camp where tent cities had sprung up virtually overnight.

"One hears that there is much lawlessness in these camps," Maria observed.

"That ain't so," Eben denied. "Oh, they're rowdy enough but, by and large, the men get along good. Everybody's in the same boat, you see. But," he shook his head, "I doubt this will last any longer than the easy pickings." There was no need for robbery, he pointed out, when gold nuggets lay around on top of the ground or in every stream. But when a simple pan would no longer suffice to turn up a little gold dust, the rowdier elements in the camps would prevail.

"And you, yourself, senior?" Maria asked. "Have you found your El Dorado?"

"I found a little dust," Eben admitted. "Enough to give me a grubstake."

Annabeth lifted her eyes from her plate. "You're going back?" she whispered.

"I reckon." Up to this moment Eben really hadn't thought about what he would do next. He hadn't thought beyond getting back to Annabeth.

But evidently Annabeth didn't want him anymore. She was all taken up with her new life and her new friends. He could see that she was as attracted to Don Felipe as the haciendado was to her. He was more her sort, Eben realized with a kind of despair.

And why not? Eben had to ask himself that question. Don Felipe had so much more to offer her. It wasn't just that he was rich and well-born. Eben could see that. No, it was that Don Felipe had talents and accomplishments that he, Eben, was woefully lacking.

Before Maria had turned the conversation to the gold camps—and Eben was shrewd enough to see that she'd done it for his benefit, to draw him into the conversation, they'd all been talking about books—some book that all three of them had read recently. The conversation had sparkled. Annabeth's eyes had sparkled. And he, Eben, had sat there like a bump on a log, not knowing what they were talking about and not having anything to contribute.

And now the conversation had turned to music. It appeared that Don Felipe had been teaching her to play the guitar.

It was all a far cry from Indian flutes and drums, which was all he'd been able to offer her! Just as this house was. Eben's eyes roamed around the room with its ancestral portraits lining the walls, its mahogany table and high carved Spanish chairs, its crystal goblets and fine china dishes . . .

Yes, Annabeth had fine food and fine clothes and a red-tiled roof over her head. It was a far cry from pemmican and buckskins and an Indian tepee. And it was no more than what she deserved.

But . . . a plan was coalescing in his mind. If he went back to the goldfields . . . if he could make a strike—a big one—not El Dorado, maybe, but big enough so he could buy land and cattle . . . set himself up as a rancher. Oh, it wouldn't be as grand as Corazon d'Oro, of course, but big enough, grand enough, so that she would be proud of him again. Love him again. She had to!

Because there was one thing sure—there was one thing that Don Felipe couldn't give her, for all his wealth, talents, birth and breeding—his name! She was already married to him, Eben, and by God, she was going to stay married. She was his wife and she was going to stay his wife and there wasn't a thing Don Felipe could do about that.

No, Don Felipe couldn't give her his name and he couldn't give her love either. Not the kind of love Eben had for her. Oh, he might love her a little but Eben was willing to lay odds that his ranch and social position would always come first with Don Felipe. He couldn't possibly love Annabeth in the total way that Eben did—not in a million years!

The evening got worse instead of better. After the meal, which seemed interminable to Eben, they adjourned to the patio where he had the doubtful pleasure of hearing his wife demonstrate her proficiency on the Spanish guitar. When she hit a false note, Don Felipe laughingly moved in beside her and, putting his arms around her, guided her fingers aright. "Not like that, querida—like this," he murmured, demonstrating the proper technique.

Seeing Eben's dark face draw into a scowl, Maria yawned prettily and suggested that the hour was growing late. She had to find a way to break up this uneasy quartet! Her brother, she feared, was playing a dangerous game. The buckskin-clad yanqui would as soon cut him to ribbons as look at him, she thought nervously. And in this case her adored Felipe was certainly in the wrong. He had no business coming between husband and wife!

As soon as the household settled down for the night, Eben left his narrow bachelor bed, to which he had been relegated by Annabeth, and went along to her room, his moccasined feet making no sound on the polished tile floor.

The door was unlocked. Annabeth, propped up on pillows encased in snowy linen, was sitting in bed reading a volume borrowed from Don Felipe's extensive library. She looked, Eben thought, like a little girl, with her red-gold curls spread out around her shoulders, a white cambric ribbon threaded through them, matching the bedgown lent her by Maria.

Annabeth heard the doorlatch click and glanced up from her book with a smile, thinking it was Maria, whose habit it was to join her for a late-night cup of chocolate and girlish chatter. But not tonight.

Her smile faded. "Eben!" she gasped. "You shouldn't be here!"

"Don't see why not. I'm yore husband, ain't I?" he said coolly, advancing towards the mahogany four-poster with its canopy and curtains of gold brocade.

Acutely aware of her dishabille, for the cambric nightgown was almost transparent, Annabeth laid aside her book and pulled the brocade coverlet with its gold-embrodiered family crest almost up to her chin. "You . . . you can't claim your husband's rights," she said shrilly. "I'm . . . I'm not yet recovered from childbirth," she lied, looking at him half-defiantly, half-imploringly, her eyes enormous in a pale, heart-shaped face.

His husband's rights? He'd never thought of it in just that way—as if lovemaking were a marital duty that she owed to him. He thought of it as a shared experience, a joyous experience—as pleasurable and joyous for her as for him.

"Reckon I can claim the right to talk to you," he said mildly. Sitting down on the edge of the bed, he reached for her hand but Annabeth jerked away.

The defensive little action hurt Eben intolerably. "My God, Annabeth, what ails you?" he burst out. "You act as if . . . as if I'm a stranger!" He felt like grabbing her and shaking her until her teeth rattled but he knew that wouldn't solve anything.

Annabeth had no answer for him. She, herself, didn't know what "ailed" her, as Eben put it. She just felt . . . numb . . . yes, that was it . . . numb. She hardly realized that since the baby's birth and death her emotions had frozen. That the only way she could deal with her loss was to bury her feelings in a protective shell—a little cocoon that nothing had the power to penetrate. Nothing and no one.

No one, that is, except Eben. She knew instinctively that he had the power to penetrate the emotional cocoon she had spun around herself. The knowledge disturbed her. *He* disturbed her. Profoundly. He was too offensively, disturbingly *alive!* He provoked too many powerful and disturbing emotions in her and she didn't want to feel too much or too deeply about anything or anyone—it hurt too much! No, she decided, she didn't want Eben to thaw those frozen feelings, to bring her emotions back to life. Eben was a danger to her—a threat to the peace, tranquility and security she had found at Rancho del Corazon.

"What is it you want of me, Eben?" she said wearily.

He wanted his wife back, goddammit, his vivid and vibrant little Annabeth—not this polite and frozen stranger—but he couldn't see any way to break through to her.

If only he could take her in his arms and hold her and comfort her. Their physical attraction had always been so very strong—a spark easily ignited bursting into conflagration. Maybe he could get through to her in that way. And then again, maybe he couldn't. And in any case, if he touched her, one thing would inevitably lead to another and, if what she claimed was true, she wasn't healed from childbirth yet. He took leave to doubt it—it had been weeks ago but he would have to take her word for it. He couldn't risk hurting her more than she'd been hurt already.

"Look, I'm sorry about the baby," he said desperately."Sorry I wasn't with you. Sorry you had to bear it all alone."

"That doesn't matter now," she said flatly. "Besides, I wasn't alone. Maria was with me through it all. She's been wonderful . . . she and Felipe. They've invited me to stay on here as long as I like."

"I was kinda hopin' you might wanta go back with me," Eben ventured.

Her eyes darkened ominously. "You wouldn't take me to the gold camps when I begged you to take me!" she flared.

Eben was glad to get some kind of emotional response from her, even anger.

"That was different," he defended himself. "I didn't know then what conditions were in the camps. Besides, you was carryin' and—"

"How very convenient for you that the baby died!" she said wildly. At that moment she hated him, she wanted to lash out at him and hurt him, and she had. She could see the hurt reflected in his eyes and felt a kind of vicious satisfaction in hurting him. He had hurt *her*, hadn't he? He had promised to be back with her in time for the baby's birth but he hadn't come back!

Eben reeled from the blow; he couldn't believe he had heard aright. Cruelty wasn't a part of Annabeth's nature.

"You know that ain't true, Annabeth. I'm just

as grieved at losin' our baby as you are. You know you don't mean that."

"Oh, but I do mean it," she said steadily. "A child would have a been a burden to you in the gold camps. And so would I."

"That ain't so," he denied it swiftly. "There's other women out there now. Some of 'em with families. Women that come overland in '45 and '46 and '47." *Real* women, Eben thought to himself, but had the sense not to put into words, strong women—unlike that pretty little Spanish doll Annabeth seemed so fond of. Dona Maria had been kind to him and he didn't want to offend Annabeth any further by criticizing her but she struck him as the kind of fragile flower that would shrivel up at the first hint of frost.

"When are you leaving?" She sounded downright eager to have him go.

Eben shrugged. "Sooner the better. In the morning, mebbe. Unless you want to come along and need some time to get yourself together," he added hopefully. When she said nothing, he suggested, "If you'd rather wait for me in Frisco or Monterey, I could take you to the city," he offered. "Maybe Mrs. Larkin would take you in. Her husband was consul here while California was still a Mexican province." Anything to get her away from Rancho del Corazon and Don Felipe del Corazon, he thought! "Seems to me, he added unwisely, "you'd have more in common with Rachel Larkin than with these greasers!"

Normally, Eben did not look down on members of another race or nationality but he was desperately jealous of Don Felipe and even of Annabeth's fondness for Maria. It must be her friends who had turned her against him, he reasoned.

His use of the pejorative term "greaser" was unwise, to say the least, for Annabeth reacted to it like a bull confronted with a red flag. "I have as much in common with Maria as I did with Silent Moon or Owl Woman!" she flared. "And I'll thank you to remember these 'greasers' as you call them," her tone dripped venom, "have been kind to me. They took care of me; they helped me when I needed help, when you were nowhere around!" She paused for breath. "And what's more I don't want to go to the goldfields with you—or anywhere else. I want to stay here with my friends!"

"Stay here in the lap of luxury, you mean," Eben sneered, losing patience with her at last. His eyes roamed scornfully around the sumptuous room with its carved maghoany four-poster, its brocaded bed linen and ornate hangings, over which hung a crucifix glittering with jewels.

Annabeth's eyes filled with angry tears. It wasn't that, at all, that she valued, it was the peace and security she had found at Corazon d'Oro. And he was threatening to wrest her from it. Oh, how could he begrudge her this little bit of comfort and stability?

Eben's eyes narrowed. "Or is it Don Felipe?" Some demon let loose within him—the demon of jealousy—prompted him to demand, "Is he the reason you want to stay on here?"

Annabeth looked at him in amazement. "Felipe?" she said blankly. "What has Felipe to do with it?" Her eyes widened. "Surely you don't imagine that . . . that there is anything between Felipe and me! Anything improper!"

She found her answer in Eben's grim face, his burning eyes and scornful glare.

"Oh!" she choked. "You . . . you're vile! Vile!" Her hands clenched into fists as she pounded on the coverlet and cried, "Oh, get out of here! Get out! Go away and don't come back!"

"Don't worry! I'm goin'! But first, by God, I'm gonna give you somethin' to remember me by!" Grabbing her by the shoulders he pulled her roughly into is arms, turning her face up to his. His mouth descended on hers, burning, ravishing, probing, demanding . . .

Annabeth sagged against him, beating on his chest with her tiny fists. He had never been so rough with her, so unabashedly masterful and her outraged squeals and pummeling fists availed her nothing. He merely caught them with one big hand and held them still as his mouth ravaged her lips. She fought against him wildly, sure that he was going to take her by force but he did not. His protective instincts overcame his need for complete possession and domination, though her lips were bruised and swollen when at last he raised his head.

She tasted blood and her fingers strayed to her lips which bore faint marks of Eben's teeth. "You . . . you hurt me," she whimpered, stunned. Oh, she'd always known that Eben was a man of violence, of strong passions, but never before had he let loose that violence on her.

"Good!" he panted. "I meant to. Let it be a reminder to you, while I'm gone, that it's a *man* you're married to and not that fancy boy in his popinjay clothes and his high-falutin' ways!"

"Oooh! I hate you!" Annabeth buried her face in the pillows, sobbing. "Get out of here! Get out and leave me alone!"

He went.

18

In the morning he was gone, as suddenly as he had come, even before the servants were stirring. And she was glad of it, Annabeth told herself firmly, *glad!* She was, she told herself fiercely, only sorry that she hadn't found out what a brute he was before she had bound herself to him irrevocably! She told herself these things so often that she almost came to believe them!

Everyone tactfully avoided looking at her bruised and swollen mouth but she couldn't help wondering what they were thinking and it riled her even more than the discomfort, which was, for all, only slight and superficial. Oh, it was just like Eben, that . . . that brutal and savage devil in buckskins—to make his mark on her for all to see! Unlike Felipe, she thought stormily, Eben was no gentleman!

One effect of Eben's visit was to have long-lasting repercussions. It made her look at Felipe with new eyes.

Before Eben had intruded into their quiet, pleasant lives, piercing the emotional cocoon in which she had enveloped herself, she had hardly been aware of Felipe as a man, as a sexual being. He was an entertaining companion, the brother of her dear friend, and she had taken his friendship for granted, as she had Maria's. She had been ill . . . had suffered a terrible loss . . . Maria and Felipe had, in equal measure, been kind to her, showering her with attention and gentle, undemanding affection. She felt a deep regard for them both. But, as for anything else—why, it was ludicrous! Gallantry, she was well aware, was part of Felipe's nature and she had been amused and pleasurably flattered by his mildly flirtatious manner. No more than that.

It was ridiculous! she fumed. Eben had no basis for his thoroughly unreasonable jealousy of Felipe! Didn't he trust her? Obviously not! Well, it just went to show how . . . how coarse . . . and . . . and primitive . . . and crude Eben was, deep down! Quite uncivilized, actually. Why, her friendship with Felipe was totally innocent . . . how could it be otherwise with her just recently up from childbed! She could hardly be the object of serious masculine attention, nor did she wish to be! How dare Eben accuse her of . . . of improprieties?

Eventually she simmered down and dismissed the whole unpleasant incident from her mind. It was easy to do so in the relaxed and easygoing atmosphere of the ranch. Annabeth lazed away the hot somnolent days, regaining her health and strength and beauty. Maria apologized for the dullness of life at the ranch—normally there would be fiestas and rodeos and barbecues and balls and there would be again when her year of mourning for her novio, her fiance, was up.

But Annabeth did not find it dull nor did she long for gaiety and entertainments. She found the quiet soothing; she was content to vegetate, to rest from emotional storms, to heal physically and emotionally, from the stresses and strains of the past year.

Time passed slowly like a great turgid river, without anything in particular to mark its passage—only that the pink Castilian roses had long since fallen, the apricots in the orchard had turned golden, peaches glowed yellow blushed with pink and the grapes, a luscious purple, were ready for harvesting. The grass in the pastures had turned sere and brown and the heat of late summer made one feel heavy and languid. But Annabeth and Felipe had taken to riding together in the early mornings while it was still cool enough to take pleasure in exercise.

This particular morning Felipe was riding out to inspect his manada—his herd of golden palominos. It was a ride that Annabeth especially enjoyed. She loved to see the herd of chestnut mares, their chestnut or golden colts or fillies at their sides. When questioned, Felipe explained the intricacies of breeding palominos—that only a percentage of the mares could be expected to throw the highly prized golden colts. This year's crop of foals had produced an unusually large number of palominos and he was much pleased.

Annabeth frowned. "I still don't see why you can't simply breed palominos to palominos and get—"

"Palominos?" Felipe's white teeth flashed in a grin. "It's not that simple, Ana. Only half the time will such a match produce a palomino colt. A percentage will still be chestnut, or worse yet, albino. Albinos are undesirable for a number of reasons but chiefly because of their red weak eyes," Felipe said instructively. "So you see it is better to breed chestnut mares to a palomino stallion or vice versa and eliminate the possibility of producing albinos."

After Felipe had checked to see that there was still ample pasturage in the Valley of the Golden Horses, as it was called, they trotted up to the crest of a hill for an overview of the herd.

"They are so beautiful," sighed Annabeth contentedly, gazing down at the frolicking foals, the quietly grazing mares. Standing guard over the herd was a magnificent golden stallion with a sweeping, cream-colored mane and tail.

Felipe was looking, not at his prize herd, but at her. Her convalescence was long past now, her face glowed with health, her eyes were bright, and the sun caught her hair, framing her delicate features in a red-gold nimbus.

"Not half so beautiful as you, mi alma," Felipe said huskily.

Annabeth jerked her head around in surprise, startled by the soft Spanish love words usually reserved for a sweetheart. Seeing the tender light in his eyes she felt suddenly uneasy. "We . . . we should be heading back to the hacienda," she murmured. "Maria will be wondering what has become of us."

"No, wait!" Felipe's gloved hand reached out to grip her bridle. "There is something I must say to you, querida." And, before she could stop him, Felipe was pouring out his feelings to her, feelings that went deeper than Annabeth had ever suspected.

She was appalled. Eben had been right after all. How could she have been so blind?

"Felipe—" she said desperately, trying to stem the tide and failing utterly. "You . . . you should not be speaking to me in this way! I . . . I am a married woman!"

"Married!" said Felipe scornfully. "What kind of marriage is it when your husband so neglects you, pobrecita! This husband of yours—he was not even with you when your child was born! And where is he now, I ask you?"

Annabeth bent her head, having no answer for him. If she told Felipe the truth—that she herself had driven Eben away, it would only serve to convince him that she took her marriage vows lightly.

"He is gone, lured from your side by his greed for gold!" Felipe's voice was full of scorn. "He is like all these Americanos who pour into our country looking for a way to get rich quickly, who would wrest from us our ancestral heritage, our pastoral way of life, who plunder our land and despise our people!"

Annabeth opened her mouth to leap to Eben's defense. Oh, the first white man in the country were the Spanish, all right, but they weren't peaceful rancheros. They were Spanish conquistadores. They hadn't come looking for ranch lands; they had been looking for the same thing Eben was looking for—gold, for fabulous palaces rich with golden treasure, for the famed Seven Golden Cities of Cibola. And all that time the gold was right under their noses but they didn't see—there must be a moral in there somewhere, she thought confusedly.

"Felipe . . . you're wrong. Eben isn't like that! He—"

But Felipe swept on, heedless of her protests. "I tell you, Ana, this marriage is no marriage at all!" he insisted. He had not meant to say so much, not at first, but long pent-up passion possessed him and, since he had gone so far, he might as well say it all. "In truth, Ana, it is my belief that the ceremony performed by Father Francisco was invalid and—"

"Invalid!" Annabeth gasped.

"You are neither of you Catholic," he reminded her. He hesitated, trying to put the matter as plainly, yet as kindly as he could. "I am certain Father Francisco bent the rules, consented to perform the ceremony only because the need was urgent. Because the child was so soon to be born."

"We . . . we were married in the Indian way before that," she protested, her face flaming.

Felipe's expression told her very plainly what he thought of that!

"I am certain the marriage could be annulled," he insisted. "If you wished it so."

"Anulled!" she echoed faintly.

"Even if the marriage is valid, there are ways and means—" Felipe had all the arrogance of the ruling classes. His wealth and social position were such that he had never had to do without anything he wanted; he could not conceive of a situation in which they could not continue to procure for him anything he wanted and he wanted Annabeth. "If you would but renounce your marriage, request an annulment and, of course, convert to Catholicism, I am sure that you would be free to marry whomever you wished." He smiled at her engagingly and took her hand. "Me, for instance."

Annabeth sat on her little mare in stunned silence.

"I could offer you so much, Anacita." His face hand swept out to embrace the land that spread out before them. "All of Corazon d'Oro would be yours. You would have Maria for a sister and . . . and myself as your loving and devoted husband."

Annabeth looked around her, overwhelmed. Who was it who had said Paris was worth a mass?

she wondered vaguely. She couldn't remember now and it didn't matter anyway.

To be the mistress of Corazon d'Oro was a tempting prospect, she had to admit it. To have a friend and companion in Maria. Never to know want or hardship again. To have Felipe's love and devotion lavished upon her. He would be a kind and considerate and loving husband, she was sure of that.

My God, what am I thinking of? she thought, suddenly appalled. How could she even consider such a thing? Even for a moment! It was Eben she loved—not Felipe! Oh, in the heat of emotion she'd told him she hated him but she hadn't meant it. He'd known that she didn't mean it, hadn't he? He must have!

"But . . . but I don't love you, Felipe. Not . . . not in that way—" Gently she withdrew her hand from Felipe's clasp. "I . . . I am honored by your proposal," she told him truthfully. "But I don't love you."

"You could learn to. I know that you could learn to, Ana," he said stubbornly. "Promise me that you will think over what I have said. Promise me that much, at least!"

"I . . . will think on it," Annabeth said faintly. She knew she wouldn't be able to think of anything else anyway! It would not be easy, perhaps not even possible, to dismiss such a startling proposal from her mind. She loved Corazon d'Oro, she loved her dear friend, Maria, and in some small measure, probably because he was part and parcel of it all, she loved Felipe. But would she love him if he were not the patron of Rancho del Corazon? She thought not. Oh, she valued his gallantry, his good humor, his gaiety, easy charm and sparkling wit, but there was not that vital spark between them that existed between her and Eben. There was not enough to base a marriage on. And, in any case, she wasn't free to marry.

Oh, damn all men! she thought in an agony of frustration. First Eben had come back to pierce that comfortable little shell she had built around herself and now Felipe had utterly shattered it.

Under the circumstances, she supposed she ought to leave the rancho. Go and wait for Eben somewhere else and hope that they could pick up the pieces of their lives and their marriage when he returned. But where could she go and how? The times were uncertain; it was dangerous for a lone woman to be on the roads. She didn't even have a centavo to call her own; she hadn't needed money up till now. All her needs had been amply provided for at the rancho. With no money and no means of transportation how could she go anywhere? She could not even go back to the mission for the guest house was no longer vacant; Father Francisco had lent it to a needy family. And, in any case, that would be no refuge from Felipe.

Oh, where was Eben? Why didn't he come back for her? A sudden stab of longing for him shot through her. She had pushed all thought of him away, content to exist in this cozy little cocoon she had spun around herself. It struck her now, with a sudden swift certitude, that it was and would always be Eben she loved. Such a love as comes once in a lifetime. And she had thrown it away in a fit of pique as a spoiled child might throw away a toy because it needed a little mending, because it was not quite perfection. How could she have been such a fool?

Oh, would Eben ever come back to her? Would he ever forgive her for the hateful things she had said to him? And how was she going to cope with an importunate Felipe until he did?

Eben was heading back to Rancho del Corazon after a highly profitable summer spent panning gold. Inured as he was to hardship and deprivation, he found the work exhausting. Filling a pan with sand and gravel, then lowering it into the icy mountain streams, shaking it vigorously and waiting for the heavier gold flakes to settle to the bottom was monotonous drudgery. It gave him all too much time to think and he thought constantly of Annabeth, of what she was thinking and feeling and doing. Had she gotten over the baby's death yet? he wondered. Would she be willing to pick up where they'd left off—to resume life with him again? Or had she fallen for the easy charm of Don Felipe del Corazon?

He couldn't rightly blame her if she did, he thought with a groan. Don Felipe had the wherewithal to turn any woman's head. He had good looks, wealth, birth and breeding. While he, Eben, was nothing but an almost illiterate drifter. He had nothing but love to give her and, thanks to his hard work this season, a sack of gold to lay at her feet.

He had no real lust for gold, as such. He had not succumbed to gold-fever. To him, panning for gold was not a man's work at all, arduous though it was. It required no special skill or expertise as did hunting, tracking and trapping. No honor devolved upon him who sought and found it. As far as he could see it mostly depended upon sheer luck.

No, for Eben it was only a means to an end—to give him the ability to provide well for the woman he loved. He was more than satisfied when he deemed that he had a sufficient amount of the precious yellow metal to set himself up as a rancher. It would not, of course, be as fine a ranch, as fine a home, as Corazon d'Oro. Such an establishment took generations to achieve. But he thought it would be enough to make Annabeth happy and secure. If only, he thought dismally, that small grave wouldn't always stand between them. He mostly blamed the del Corazons for setting Annabeth against him. He was puzzled by her evident bitterness towards him in regard to the baby's death. He'd done his damndest to get back to her with a doctor, hadn't he? A man couldn't do more than that.

Despite his preoccupation, Eben rode out of the foothills with more than his usual caution. In the early days of the gold strike, thievery had been almost unknown—a miner could leave a basinful of gold dust in an open tent without fear that it might be stolen. But the situation had changed with the times. Eben had heard tales of bandits on the trails picking off miners heading back home with their saddlebags stuffed with gold dust.

He saw sunlight glinting on a rifle barrel and instinctively ducked, thereby missing the first shot aimed at him. But the second, following hard on the heels of the first, grazed his forehead, just along the line of his old wound, the wound that still bothered him from time to time causing headaches so violent that more than once he had come near to blacking out. Eben largely ignored these headaches, thinking them a womanish complaint.

The second slug creased his skull and with a groan he swayed and then toppled from the saddle.

"Got 'im, Charlie!" The exultant voice came from behind a pile of rocks.

"Good shootin', Pete," a second voice rang

out.

The two bushwhackers, not bothering to reload, came out of their place of concealment and went over to inspect their victim and assess the spoils.

"A goddam Injun," grunted the first man in disgust, kicking Eben's limp form. "A Injun ain't got no place in the goldfields nohow. No more'n them damn greasers. Don't he know that this is white man's country?" he said peevishly. "Got a good mind to slit his throat for him," he grumbled.

"That's so, the only good Injun's a dead 'un," the second man agreed, busily transferring the contents of Eben's saddlebags to his own mount.

"Here now, half of that's mine!" the other protested, forgetting his bloodthirsty plans in his haste to get his share of the loot. "Oughtta be more'n half mine by rights seeing as how mine was the shot that brung him down," he grumbled.

The pair might well have come to blows over their ill-gotten gains but the clip-clop of approaching hooves and tuneless lament—"Oh, Susannah, don't you cry for me ... I've gone to Californy with a washbowl on my knee—" sent the two desperadoes scurrying for shelter.

The prospector who came in sight was heading to the goldfields, not from them, and since, aside from a few basic supplies, he had no possessions worth robbing he had no qualms about loudly and tunelessly announcing his approach.

When his eyes alighted on Eben's still form sprawled on the ground, the singer broke off in mid-course—"Oh, Susannah, don't you—" But what Susannah was not to do was lost in a soundless whistle.

The singer was a wiry little man with a ginger

moustache and a fringe of ginger whiskers. He carried no rifle but a pair of guns hung low on his thighs. He slapped the holstered pistols and both were suddenly in his hands, cocked, ready and level. The two ruffians, seeing from their hideaway that the stranger was well-armed and quite capable of looking after himself, mounted their horses and clattered off into the hills.

Shorty Gillespie heard their departure and, after a moment, sheathed his guns and dismounted. The regular rise and fall of Eben's chest told him the man was still breathing and the Good Samaritan hunkered down to loosen the thongs that bound his buckskin shirt together at the throat. "Well, whaddya know?" Shorty muttered to himself, noting the lighter skin thus exposed. "This galoot ain't no Injun, after all."

Soaking his red bandanna in water from his canteen, he wrung it out over Eben's face and neck, letting droplets trickle onto his lips. Eben's lips moved and he swallowed reflexively, the tip of his tongue protruding to lick off the moisture.

Shorty grunted with satisfaction seeing color come back into the man's face. He wrung a few final drops out of his bandanna and reached for his canteen to damp it again when Eben suddenly sat up and clutched Shorty around the neck in a death grip.

"Tryin' to rob me, are you?" Eben panted, shaking his rescuer as a terrier shakes a rat.

Shorty's eyes popped out of his head. He gasped and gagged. "Hey, leggo of me," he squawked. "I ain't tryin' to rob you, you crazy galoot. You already been robbed! Aargh!" he choked. "Leggo I say!"

Eben eased his stranglehold on the little man's neck but retained a grip on his shirt collar.

"That so?" he said, half-dazed still.

" 'Course it's so!" Shorty rubbed his throat which bore the mark of Eben's fingers. "It's a hell of a note," he croaked, tenderly exploring his Adam's apple. "Try to do a good deed and damn near get strangled in the process!" He bent and picked up the canteen he had dropped when Eben grabbed him and drained it of the little water that was left. "Dry!" he grumbled, scowling at the puddle that was rapidly soaking into the hard-packed earth.

"I can show you a stream," Eben offered, realizing that this was no enemy. "I'm sorry . . . I—" He rubbed his aching head, his fingers coming away sticky with blood.

"It warn't me, son." Shorty was anxious to make this clear. "I happened along and found you out cold. There musta been two of 'em. You can see the tracks for yourself."

Eben nodded.

"Comin' back from the goldfields with your saddlebags full, I s'pose," Shorty guessed. "How much did they get away with?"

Eben couldn't remember. "Enough," he grunted.

"Well, there's plenty more where that come from, so I hear," Shorty offered by way of consolation. "You was lucky they didn't cut your throat or at the very least, steal your horse." He offered a hand to Eben. "The name's Shorty Gillespie. What's your'n?"

Eben looked at him blankly. "I'm called . . . I am—" He shook his head, bewildered, then winced at the pain the movement produced. "My name is—" His eyes opened wider in an effort to pierce the dark mists of memory. "I don't remember," he said in alarm. "I just don't remember."

19

"Californy! That's what we'll call you," Shorty decided. "A man with no name and no past has gotta have some moniker."

Shorty had been mulling over the problem for some time, now he cocked a grizzled eyebrow at Eben as they jogged along together back towards the foothills of the Sierra Nevadas. "How does Cal suit ya?"

"As good as anything else," Eben agreed indifferently. He frowned. There was something or someone he ought to remember but . . . he groaned . . . it was as though a black veil had descended over his mind and try as he might, he just couldn't pierce it.

"Likely it'll come back to you in time, son," said the older man, correctly deducing the cause of Eben's abstraction. He chuckled. "I reckon a lotta men would envy you the chance to forget the past and make a fresh start. Yeah, there's plenty that would like to be in your shoes."

They had talked it over and agreed to form a partnership. Two or more men working together using a device called a cradle or a rocker could outproduce a loner using only a pan. With a

322

rocker, one man could shovel in the dirt while another poured water through constantly rocking the "cradle." The principle was the same as the gold pan: that gold, because of its weight—eight times as heavy as dirt—will settle to the bottom while the dirt was carried off by the water. The volume of dirt handled by this device was much greater than that of the pan so the yield was proportionately greater.

The only drawback to the rocker was that it required men to work together day after monotonous day, to get along well and be willing to share and share alike.

Eben thought that he and Shorty would get along just fine. The older man—Shorty was somewhere between 45 and 50, Eben thought—had a good-humored, weather-beaten face and a twinkle in his bright blue eyes.

He hailed from Texas, by way of Tennessee. He'd been one of Crockett's men who'd gone with him to Texas to defend the Alamo.

"Thought everybody died at the Alamo," Eben grunted.

Shorty looked injured. "Never said I made it to the Alamo, did I, son? Only that I was headed there. Got close enough to hear the guns and the Mexican trumpets playing the deguello, the 'no-quarter', and that's as close as I ever wanted to get!" he said fervently. The fact was, Shorty went on, he'd fallen ill of a fever and Crockett had left him behind in the care of a friendly Mexican family. Nobody had expected him to live but he had pulled out of the fever and followed after Crockett. "But by that time Santy Anna already had the Alamo surrounded and there wasn't no way I could slip through the lines." Not that he'd really wanted to, Shorty admitted frankly. " 'Nough good men died there—I didn't see no need to add my name to the role of honor!"

Not that he hadn't seen plenty of fighting in his day. Had fought under Houston at San Jacinto. After that, he'd joined the Texas Rangers and fought Kiowas and Comanches.

"That where you got them guns? In the Rangers?" asked Eben curiously. He'd been eye-balling Shorty's weapons for some time. Eben's rifle was like an extension of his arm but he hadn't had much experience with handguns. The way Shorty wore them, hung from belts crossing his thighs very low seemed awkward and uncomfort-able to him.

Shorty chuckled. "Them's Walker Colts, son. Down on the border I served with Sam Walker, the man that showed Colt how to improve on his original model. Six-shooters, that's what they are." He slapped the two holstered pistols and Eben blinked to see them suddenly in his hands, drawn and cocked. The Texan flipped his hands again and the guns spun and dropped into the holsters with the same effortless ease with which they had been drawn.

Eben didn't mind admitting that he was impressed.

"All it takes is practice, son," Shorty said. "Like to try 'em out?" He tossed one to Eben who hefted it, feeling the weight and the balance of it, looked down the octagon barrel and cocked the hammer.

"Got a good grip, ain't it?" Shorty said with satisfaction. "I got me a coupla spares in my saddlebags. B'longed to a friend of mine. You can try 'em out after we make camp if you've a mind to."

Eben took to the guns as a duck takes to water. In a very short time he could outdraw and outshoot his mentor. Shorty was amazed at the speed with which Eben developed proficiency with the new weapons. "You and me, boy, we could take on an army!" Shorty exulted, examining the row of tin cans Eben had set up as a target and, in the blink of an eye, had unerringly drilled.

"I don't aim to lose my gold again," Eben vowed, sheathing the smoking guns.

Eben's memory had still not returned. He could not remember *why* the gold was so important to him but he was obsessed with accumulating a respectable amount of the precious yellow metal in the shortest possible time.

As they worked, the loquacious Shorty told Eben the rest of his life story. "Had me a little spread on the Nueces," Shorty mused. "A wife, too." After the Alamo, he'd gone back to the Mexican family that had nursed him through the fever and married the eldest daughter of the house. "Rosalita was her name," Shorty reminisced. "We had us a few good years. Then she died in childbed."

A spasm crossed Eben's face.

Shorty immediately picked up on it. He knew how much his loss of memory tortured the younger man. "Maybe the same thing happened to you?" he suggested diffidently.

Eben frowned, making a mighty effort at concentration. "Not . . . not my wife . . . it was the child that died," he said finally. "My wife—" His frown deepened. He couldn't remember her name or face. There was a hazy, confused recollection of holding a small woman in his arms and of passionate lovemaking, then the black curtain descended and the dream of remembrance vanished.

"Damn!" Eben doubled up his hand into a fist and slammed it against the hollowed-out log mounted on rockers that was doing duty as their cradle. "Damn!"

"It'll come back to ya, son," Shorty said placidly. "It'll come to ya." He dumped a pail of water through the device and rocked the cradle while Eben ruefully examined his barked knuckles. "Just gotta give it time."

There wasn't much else he could do, thought Eben with resignation as he scooped up another pail of dirt and poured it through the contraption.

"Just look at it this way—when it comes back to you, you can go back to her with your pockets a-jingle," added Shorty encouragingly.

Eben nodded, not even considering the possibility that haunted him night and day—the possibility that his memory might never return. It had to!

Oh! Where *was* Eben? Annabeth asked herself over and over again with increasing despair. Wasn't he ever coming back to her? She had once thought their love strong enough to withstand anything. Had she been wrong? Had his love for her withered and died when she so foolishly sent him away? Or had something terrible happened to him? Had he been injured? Killed? Surely, surely, if that—the worst she could imagine—had happened, somehow she would know it, sense it, feel it in her heart.

Felipe, too, was waiting anxiously. His sense of honor forbade him to press his suit too strongly while Annabeth was still the wife of another man and a guest in his house to boot but his impatience grew with every passing day. The situation was untenable.

And then one day, Felipe, who was very attuned to her moods, found her weeping as if her heart would break. It was the very excuse he needed to take her in his arms, to smooth the rich red-gold hair which tumbled so entrancingly about her small heart-shaped face, and murmur soft Spanish words of love and comfort. "Hush, cara mia," he whispered into her little shell-like ear. "Do not weep so. You will spoil your lovely eyes."

For once Annabeth, in her heartache and confusion, did not turn away from him. She buried her face in his shoulder and choked out, "Oh, Felipe, I'm so afraid. So afraid that something terrible has happened to him. He would never stay away so long if . . . if . . . oh, God, he must be dead!" she wailed.

Felipe's heart leaped. It was exactly what he had been thinking himself . . . hoping for . . . for Felipe the wish was father to the thought. This uncouth yanqui of hers had been gone a long time—fall had turned into winter and winter was dragging along towards spring and still no word had come from him nor had he returned to claim his wife.

Many evils could befall a man in the gold-fields. It was not unreasonable to suppose that such a one might, indeed, be dead. And, if so, how much easier it would be for him, Felipe, to win Ana's love, he reasoned. Ah, yes, after a decent interval had passed, she was sure to turn to him, just as she was turning now, for consolation, if not for love.

He rocked her in his arms and crooned to her

in his soft Spanish tongue. When her impassioned sobbing had quieted a little, he took out a snowy linen handkerchief and dabbed tenderly at her eyes. "In the spring, after roundup, I will send men to the goldfields in search of him, mi alma," he promised her. Not only for herself but for his own peace of mind, Felipe thought grimly. If indeed, this Americano lout was dead, he would be free to woo her in earnest as he longed to do.

His heart almost broke at the look of hope that sprang into her tear-drenched eyes. "Oh, Felipe, will you?" she gasped. "But . . . but could you not do it now?" she begged, impatient to wait any longer for news of Eben.

He shook his head slowly. "Alas, no, mi alma. I cannot. The snow is still deep in the high Sierras. And I must keep every man on hand for the spring roundup—the branding of the calves." He spread his hands helplessly. "My vaqueros have been drifting off in twos and threes to hunt this accursed gold," he reminded her. "I am shorthanded as it is. And what's more, these worthless gold-seekers who roam the country feel they have a right to help themselves to any man's beef. It is too much trouble for them to hunt game in the hills," he said contemptuously. "They prefer to rustle cattle from the rancheros." Felipe had once had respect and liking for the Americanos, had even been willing to see his sister wed a yanqui trader but his experiences with the gold-seekers had been such that he was beginning to detest all Americanos—Annabeth excepted.

She nodded. She knew something of the problems that had been besetting Felipe and the other neighboring ranchers but even as she sympathized with his problems she knew that his preoccupation with ranch affairs had made her life easier this winter. He had been too absorbed to press his suit with her.

"I am sorry for your troubles, Felipe," she told him.

"De nada. It is nothing," he assured her. "And I break the code of the gentleman, bothering the head of a pretty lady with problems that are the province of a man to solve," he added gallantly.

"But you have been so good to me. I want you to share your problems with me, Felipe," she protested impulsively. She had spoken automatically, meaning it only in friendship but he took it for more.

"Do you, Ana?" His dark eyes lit up. "Do you really mean it? Because if you do, it gives me hope for us, querida!" And suddenly his arms were around her again, his lips brushing hers until they parted under his gentle insistence and he was able to drink deeply of the sweetness of her mouth. "Oh, cor de mi corazon," he groaned against her soft cheek.

Was it the Spanish love words or the tickle of his moustache, so different from Eben's clean-shaven caresses, that brought her to her senses? Whatever it was, she broke away from him, her outstretched hands shoving at his chest. "No . . . no!" she whimpered.

Always the gentleman, he let her go instantly. "Forgive me, mi alma. I . . . I forgot myself," he murmured. But she was gone, fleeing the Sala as if her life depended on getting away from him.

Reaching the safety of her bedroom, she threw herself down upon the brocaded spread and pressed her hands to her burning cheeks. Oh, God, she wondered in despair, was it possible to love two men at the same time?

When the melting snows filled the mountain streams to flood-stage, Eben and his friend abandoned their rocker and moved their operation to higher ground. Shorty, who had a positive nose for such things, located a promising vein of quartz in a towering upthrust of granite. A little preliminary work with picks revealed a vein of quartz that was literally laced with gold!

Eben drew in his breath with a gasp and Shorty tossed his hat into the air and danced a wild jig. "We've made our fortunes, Cal!" he whooped. "This here's gotta be the mother-lode!" Sobering suddenly, he added, "If only I'd thought to bring some dynamite. It'd made the work of getting it out that much easier."

"And it might just have blown us to kingdom come," Eben said dryly. The granite upthrust was weathered and worn, seamed with gigantic cracks and breaks. Even one stick of dynamite could have brought the whole crumbling mass down in a heap, Eben thought grimly. To say nothing of the possibility of causing an avalanche of snow from the higher elevations. It was not impossible that a single blow from a pick might have that same effect.

They began stripping out the quartz with exquisite care, enlarging the cracks with their picks, not so much swinging them as using them as levers to pry chunks loose. As soon as they had a sackful they carried out of the way of the leaning tower that loomed over them and broke up the quartz with blows from a flat rock in order to extract the gold. Some of it could be separated with a knife blade. The rest they panned with water from a little stream.

"Whooee!" Shorty exulted. "Gonna have me all I ever wanted outta life! No more hard work . . . no more punching longhorns! I'm gonna have me the finest stogies to smoke . . . the best likker to drink . . . handmade boots and silk shirts and—" Shorty's imagination failed him. "Whatcha gonna do with your share, Californy?"

"I dunno," said Eben indifferently. He didn't know why he was busting a gut to swing a pick on the ore-bearing rock. He only knew that something was driving him—something beyond the lust for gold. He didn't hanker for fancy clothes or fine food and drink, or even easy women, though after months of enforced celibacy the need for a woman was strong in him. But not for the kind of woman whose favors could be bought with gold.

He scowled. *Why* was he driving himself? What was the compelling urge that kept him here? Who was he? Sometimes, when he strained his mind to remember his past, he could almost recall a slender woman with flaming hair the color of the sunset but the image was shimmering, evanescent. Maybe, after all, it was only a dream.

What he wanted, he pondered, was something money could not buy. To know who he was. To have his memory return. To have a past, and a future built on the past.

With a sigh he bent his back over the pick. "C'mon, let's get busy and quit jawin'," he said gruffly.

The two men alternated the monotonous drudgery of breaking up the chunks of quartz with the less toilsome but more hazardous job of prying it out of the rock walls in which it was entombed. Since the towering crag of granite might well prove to be a tomb for either or both of them, should it topple, this latter job was the one he preferred, spiced as it was with the hint of danger. In fact, he was almost fascinated by the danger which grew proportionately greater day by day as the work undermined the foundations of the tower of rock.

He was working under this towering mass one day, or rather, almost inside it, for their work had cut a deep notch in its base—the same kind of notch a man might make in felling a tree, though wider and deeper—when he heard noises. There was a grating sound, a grinding of rock and a cold chill went down his spine. It was a warning signal, he was sure of that! But the vein he was working on was one of the richest ever—almost pure gold, he estimated, and so he kept on, heedless of the warning.

Suddenly there was a sharp crack followed by a deep groan as if the very mountains were protesting the rape of their treasure, their defiling at the hand of man.

This was a warning Eben knew better than to ignore. He lay down his pick and ran but caught his foot on an outcropping of rock and went rolling and tumbling down the slope.

Farther down the trail where Shorty was laboring at breaking up the quartz that had already been removed from the rock tower, he heard the commotion and paused to look up from his work.

"Great Gawd Almighty, Cal, get outta there!" he yelled a useless warning instinctively for he knew that the younger man could not possibly hear him over the cascade of loose rock and crumbling shale. But he screamed a warning anyway. "It's an avalanche!" and the words came echoing back to him ringing around the hills.

"Gawdalmighty, the whole goddam mountain's comin' down," Shorty groaned. He saw Eben run and fall and then his view of the younger man was lost in a shower of falling rock and debris.

When the dust settled Shorty found him, lying face up on his back, half-buried under a pile of loose dirt and rubble. Assuring himself that the man he knew as Cal was still alive, he began scrabbling through the loose dirt and stones until the body was uncovered and he could make sure that there were no bones broken.

It was a scene gruesomely reminiscent of their first encounter back last fall. Lacking water he began to slap the younger man's face in an effort to revive him. "C'mon Cal. Damn ya, wake up!" Shorty almost pleaded for he had become fond of his younger companion. "C'mon Cal!"

Black lashes fluttered, dark eyes opened. The man coughed weakly and spat dust and grit from his mouth. "Cal? Who's Cal?" he muttered weakly. "I'm Eb. Eben McDowell." He struggled and managed to prop himself up on his elbows in a half-sitting position. "And who the hell are you?" he demanded.

20

Don Felipe del Corazon was worried. That, in itself, was nothing new. He was in a perpetual state of anxiety in this spring of 1849. Times were hard. Many of his vaqueros had run off to the gold-fields. Hordes of these same gold-seekers roamed the land, helping themselves to beef and mutton from his herds and flocks. But Rancho del Corazon was well able to spare a handful of beeves or the odd sheep. No, it was a more serious problem that was carving lines of care into Don Felipe's handsome young face. He had been summoned to Monterey to prove his title in an American court to 12,000 acres of Rancho del Corazon's prime grazing land.

It was, he feared, the beginning of the end for life as he knew it. The good old days and the good old ways were passing and he had a premonition that he would never see their like again.

He frowned. He didn't like leaving the two girls, Maria and Annabeth, alone at the ranch with only a handful of vaqueros to protect them while he was away.

Still, life at the rancho was stable and secure compared to the gold camps or even the sprawling, rough tent-and-shanty city of San Francisco. Stories that came out of the camps and the city were enough to set Don Felipe's aristocratic hairs on end and he had done his best to keep them from the women. Tales of miners running amok, drinking, whoring and chasing after the Chinese who were flocking into the goldfields in order to cut off their long black pigtails for sport. Or taking potshots at Indians—again for sport. He would be the first to admit that Indians had not always fared well under the mission system—too often they were at the mercy of less than saintly priests who had overworked and underfed them. But at least they had not been used for target practice!

And his own people, the Spanish-speaking Californios, were faring little better. They had become used to being referred to slightingly as "spics" and "greasers" but a new epithet which had recently come into use made Felipe's blood boil—"Chileno." All Spanish-speaking people were referred to as Chilenos now, simply because the first boatload of whores imported into the goldfields had come from Chile. Truly, the Californios had become second-class citizens in their own country.

Americans must be the most pushy, most greedy and least tolerant people on earth, Felipe reflected. It was a wonder to him that he had fallen so deeply in love with one of them. But then Annabeth wasn't like those others. She had a sweetness all her own, the little Americana.

He had kept his promise to her and sent a man to the gold camps to get word of her loutish husband but the man had come back empty-handed. Perhaps, when he returned from

Monterey, he himself would make a trip to the camps. Something had to be done. The situation was quite untenable. He loved Annabeth; he wanted to make her his wife and give her his love and his name. They simply could not go on as they were much longer.

If only she would renounce her marriage and accept the love he was so ready to give her! But she would not. All these past months she clung faithfully to the memory of her husband—a man who had obviously deserted her. A man who let the lust for gold consume him!

Why she so mourned this loutish husband of hers was beyond his comprehension! Felipe thought angrily, tapping his riding crop against his immaculately shined boots in irritation. Oh, the man had saved her life once—well, more than once—Felipe knew all about that. He was, apparently, strong, bold and courageous, along with being—Felipe's lip curled disdainfully—ignorant, uneducated and half-savage, as savage as those Indians he had taken her to live among! Felipe had heard about that, too, and was appalled that anyone should expect a gently bred woman like Annabeth to accept such a lot in life. That she had done so with apparent cheerfulness, good humor and tolerance said much for the unusual sweetness of her nature, Felipe mused. And for her courage!

He hoped she would not have need for that courage while he was away, he thought with a frown. He had what almost amounted to a premonition of disaster about to strike. But that was nonsense—what harm could come to the girls while he was gone? There was a houseful of servants to wait on them hand and foot and he had ordered such of his vaqueros as were left to remain within an easy ride of the ranch house in case of need. That Annabeth herself was an American was an advantage—if any gringos came their way she would be able to deal with them and look after Maria who, unlike Ana, had always been sheltered and protected.

As a last precaution, he called Annabeth into his study the night before he left and presented her with a pair of antique duelling pistols.

She was startled. "Surely you don't think I'll need them?" she protested.

"One never knows," he said gravely. "It is better to be prepared for any eventuality. And you know how to use them, do you not?" he pointed out practically. "I know Maria does not."

"Oh, yes, Eben taught me how to load and shoot his rifle," Annabeth said proudly. "I imagine it's the same principle," she eyed the two matched flintlock pistols, elegantly inlaid with silver and gold, a bit dubiously.

Eben—always Eben, thought Felipe sourly. "Perhaps I'd better refresh your memory," he suggested suavely. At least it gave him an excuse to put his arm around her, he thought as he went through the motions of teaching her to load and take aim. Ever since their first and, to his regret, their only kiss back in the winter, she had shied away from any physical contact with him.

"Yes, I see," she said finally, laying the pistol used for demonstration back in its velvet-lined leather case. Clicking the lid shut, she said, "I hope I won't need to use them."

"It's only a precaution," he reminded her. "You and Maria will be well looked after while I'm gone."

"I wish you didn't have to go," she said impulsively.

There was an eager look in his eyes as he asked, rather wistfully, "Will you miss me, Ana?"

She looked at him in surprise. "Yes, of course. You are my very dear friend . . . you and Maria," she added hastily.

"You know that I want to be very much more than that." He took the hand still lying on the pistol case and raised it to his lips. Turning it over he lingeringly kissed the palm. His lips were warm and demanding, his thin black moustache caressing and tickling her soft palm and stirring her, in spite of herself.

"Feel how my heart beats for you, mi alma," he murmured, tucking her hand against his chest and drawing her into the circle of his arms.

Annabeth trembled at his touch. Felipe had been patient with her—very patient—for a long time and she sensed that his patience was wearing thin. All through that long wet winter he had restrained his desire for her, wooing her with gentle phrases and soft Spanish love words. When she, sorely beset, had reproved him for his impropriety, his warm brown eyes opened wide. "To woo you with my body, querida, yes, that would be an impropriety," he said thoughtfully. "But to woo you with words—how else am I to let you know that I love you and I want you for my wife?"

"But I am another man's wife!" she'd cried out.

"That may be remedied," he said flatly. "If you wish it so." Persuasively he added, "Just say the word, querida, and I will take steps to free you from this marriage that is no marriage."

But Annabeth had refused to say that word. And when, in the spring, the vaquero Felipe had sent to the gold camps came back with no word of

Eben and claiming that no trace of the yanqui could be found, Felipe affirmed at last that Eben must be dead.

But Annabeth had shaken her head, saying piteously, "It can't be so, Felipe. If Eben were dead I would know it here." She placed her hand to her heart. "I am sure that I would know it."

Out of pity for her distress Felipe held his peace. Time, he felt, was his ally. Sooner or later Ana would come to her senses. It would become as obvious to her as it already was to him that this worthless husband of hers was not going to come back. Dios! thought Felipe indignantly, how could a man with red blood in his veins stay away from such a woman! No man could, he decided, unless he were dead. It was Felipe's hope and Annabeth's dread.

Annabeth stood quiescent in the circle of Felipe's arm. It wasn't fair to him, she thought shamefacedly, to rely on Felipe's strength when she couldn't give him the love he longed for. Or could she? Eben had been gone for so long and who knew when, if ever, he would return? She had not had so much as a word from him in all these months. Maybe Felipe was right. Maybe Eben *was* dead and her refusal to accept it was a mere romantic notion, a way of deceiving herself.

Oh, she was in an impossible position. She loved Eben; she wanted to be faithful to him and to that love. But she wasn't being fair to Felipe, who also loved her. And, if Eben really was dead—or dead to her, if he didn't want her any longer—then she felt she could and perhaps should reward Felipe's patience. He loved her, he claimed, enough for two and she *was* attracted to him. But would never feel for him what she had felt for Eben but . . . oh, she felt so weak and confused!

Felipe held her quietly, his senses stirred by
her softly rounded curves, by the quivers that ran
through her slender frame, by the rapid rise and
fall of her bosom clad in modest black silk. His
hands, that had been at her waist, strayed
upwards to caress her breasts. "I have been
patient so very long, querida," he murmured persuasively. "Will you not give me permission to
speak to the American authorities in
Monterey . . . take steps to dissolve your
marriage?" His breath fanned her cheek. "Just say
the word," he whispered insistently before his
mouth closed over hers.

It was a slow, drugging, and very persuasive
kiss and Annabeth almost succumbed to its allure.
But not quite. Pulling out of his embrace she
hesitated yet again. "Give me a little more time,
Felipe," she begged. "Just a little more time.
When . . . when you come back from Monterey, I'll
give you my decision," she promised. "When you
come back from Monterey."

She thought of little else while Felipe was
away. At least his absence gave her a breathing
space in which to marshal her thoughts without
his physical presence, his drugging kisses, charm
and verbal persuasiveness intruding.

If there were no Eben, it would be very easy
for her to love Felipe, she was sure of that. And all
that long winter she had mourned for Eben as for
one dead. For, even if he were alive somewhere, he
was dead to her. That it was she, in her folly, who
had sent him away made it harder, not easier, to
bear. But at the time, she reminded herself, in her
grief and loss, she had needed a respite from
emotion—from loving too much.

But inevitably spring had come, following the long deadening winter, and her heart and her body had reawakened from their long hibernation. She was ready to love again. To live again.

In the privacy of her bedchamber she studied herself in the long mirror with its ornately carved wooden frame. It gave her a full-length view of her nude body—a once-too-slim body that had fully blossomed into womanhood and was riper and more curvaceous than ever before. She ran a hand up her curving flanks, past her still-narrow waist, to cup a generously rounded breast. Her whole body gleamed with health and vigor, she noted. It was more ripe and ready for a man's love than it had ever been.

Her shining hair gleamed in the candlelight, its rich red curls waving around her face. She pulled a curl back to inspect the almost faded pockmarks along her hairline. Eben had promised her that those marks would fade and then very nearly had, being barely visible now. How very long ago it seemed since he had given her that promise.

Eben! He had given her so much—her very life! He had nursed her, restored her to health, made her his beloved woman.

But Felipe had also given her much—the hospitality of his home, a refuge from the world and its troubles at a time when she sorely needed such a refuge. He had restored her to mental, if not physical, health; his companionship had restored her spirits and stimulated her mind.

Was it really possible to love two men at the same time? she wondered. For she felt that she did love them both, in quite different ways. If the choice were hers to make, which one would she choose?

Eben was in a fever to get back to Annabeth.
But, at Shorty's insistence, they detoured to
Sutter's Fort to put their gold on deposit. "Use
your horse sense, Cal . . . I mean Eb—" Shorty
said impatiently. "We can't lug all this gold all the
way down to that there ranch. It's too heavy. It'd
only slow us up. An' with all the ruffians and
roughnecks there is roaming around, we'd have to
fight our way through."

Much as he begrudged the time it would take
to make the detour to Sutter's Fort, or
Sacramento, as the shanty town that had sprung
up nearby had come to be called, he had to admit
that Shorty was right. The gold would only slow
them up. The trouble was, he thought ruefully, all
he'd been able to think of since he came back to
his right mind was getting back to Annabeth.

"That little gal of your'n has been waiting all
this time; she can wait a few days longer," Shorty
offered by way of consolation.

But was she waiting? That was the question
that gnawed away at Eben's insides so that he
could hardly eat or sleep for thinking about it.
Originally, he'd only planned to be away a month
or two at the most. Just long enough to
accumulate some gold dust—enough to ensure
their future—while at the same time giving Annabeth a chance to come to her senses. Some women
go queer after having a baby, he'd heard. He
thought that most likely that was what had
happened to Annabeth. That pregnancy and childbirth and then losing the baby had unsettled her
mind and made it easy for the del Corazons to turn
her against him.

But he hadn't figured on being away from her
all fall and winter and well into the spring. After
such a long time he couldn't be sure that Annabeth

was still at the ranch. She could be anywhere by now! She might even think that he had deserted her! Or she might have given him up for dead. His jaw tightened. That's what that smooth-talking sidewinder, that Don Felipe, would like her to believe. Eben was sure of it. He'd been mighty stuck on her back last summer. And Annabeth had liked him right well, Eben had noticed. By now, he thought glumly, it was more than likely that high-falutin' young sprig of the nobility had seduced her. Them Mexicans could sweet-talk a woman as naturally as they could fork a horse. They were bred to it, you might say, from the cradle.

Eben's full lips thinned with the anger his thoughts produced in him. By God, if that fancy-pants caballero had been toying with her affections, he would cut his heart out—not to mention a few other items!—and feed him to the buzzards.

But, on the other hand, if he had truly fallen in love with Annabeth and she with him . . . what then? Killing Don Felipe wouldn't win back Annabeth's love. It would only make her hate him.

Well, there wasn't no sense in borrowing trouble. He would just have to wait and see what the situation was when he got there and then act accordingly.

Felipe was due back any day and Annabeth was no closer to making a decision than she had ever been. If only she could be *sure* that Eben was dead. *If* he was. At times she thought he *must* be. In the West there were so many dangers that could befall a man. A fall from a horse . . . snakebite . . . infection from even a minor wound. Those were some of the most common causes of fatalities. She could think quite easily of at least a dozen others—and often did, especially in the darkest hours of night when fears were hardest to overcome and her imagination ran away with her.

And then there was illness. The chills and fever that prospectors were prone to after hour upon hour of working the icy mountain streams and which often led to pneumonia. Scurvy, too, was prevalent among the miners, she had heard, but she thought it unlikely that Eben would succumb to a disease caused by an improper and inadequate diet. He was no greenhorn! He would scour the hills for green plants and roots and tubers and nourish himself properly. She was sure of that.

But what about the gangs of bandits that were haunting the hills and preying upon unwary prospectors? Of course Eben could hardly be described as unwary but he was, after all, only one man and what chance would one man have against a gang of cutthroats? No chance at all, she feared.

Why hadn't Jose, the vaquero that Felipe had sent in search of him, been able to find him at one or another of the gold camps? He had seemingly vanished without a trace off the face of the earth. It must be, she concluded reluctantly, that he was dead.

But supposing that he *was* alive, then *why* didn't he come back to her? Or at least send her word. He had been gone the better part of a year and she had not heard a word from him—not one single word. Was he trying to punish her for her transgressions? Had she killed her love for her by her rejection of him last summer? A hundred—no, a thousand—times over she had regretted her cruelty. How could she have sent him away so harshly? She must have been out of her mind. She thought grief and loss must have rendered her temporarily insane.

She felt so alone, so vulnerable. It would be so

easy to accept Felipe's love—the closeness, caring and commitment that he offered her and which was even more appealing to her than the security and ease of living that she knew she would find with him. She was young, healthy and full of vitality again. She needed love—a man's love—she admitted to herself with ruthless honesty. She craved the kind of physical expression of affection that Eben had introduced her to. He had, she thought ruefully, ruined her forever for a life of celibacy!

And she wanted—needed—children. A new baby to hold in her arms, lessening the heartache of that small grave in the del Corazon family plot, filling the place in her heart that had been empty so long.

Oh, if only she could be sure that Eben was not ever coming back! If she just *knew*, one way or another! Anything would be better than living any longer in this awful limbo!

Maria understood and sympathized with her predicament. She herself thought that if the big yanqui were ever coming back he would have done so long before now. Oh, Annabeth's loyalty to the man was admirable, if, in Maria's opinion, a bit overdone. Maria did not like to see her adored brother kept dangling. She tapped a fingernail impatiently against white even teeth. Was there, perhaps, something *she* could do to turn her dear Ana's thoughts away from the past and towards the future—a brilliant new future as Felipe's wife?

"This has been a house of mourning too long, Ana," she declared abruptly. "It is time we set aside our black gowns and went into colors again. And I think when Felipe returns we should have a fiesta."

"A fiesta?" Annabeth was startled. "Do you think he'll be in a mood for celebrating?" she said doubtfully. Mindful of the reason for Felipe's trip to Monterey, she had grave doubts that a Spanish land grant would be upheld in an American court and feared that Felipe was doomed to disappointment.

Maria shrugged. "If he loses our case in the courts, a fiesta might cheer him up," she reasoned. "Our cousins, the Vallejos, and our neighbors, the Gutierrez and the Morenos will be able to commiserate with him since they are threatened with similar losses."

Annabeth could see the logic of this.

"On the other hand, if Felipe wins his case and retains title to the land, there will be good cause for a celebration," Maria pointed out. "And, in either case, the fiesta might be an opportune time to make a happy announcement," she suggested slyly. "To announce a betrothal, perhaps?"

Annabeth blushed and shook her head.

Maria sighed. "It must be as you wish, of course, but it would greatly please Felipe, I know, and, as for me, I would love to have you for a sister, dear Ana." But, seeing the distress on her friend's face, she obligingly changed the subject.

Had she ever thought Californios indolent? Annabeth wondered a few days later. Maria had gone through the house like a whirlwind, chivvying the maids into giving the hacienda a regular New England spring cleaning, harrying the sewing women who were making festive gowns for herself and Annabeth in the Spanish style, making out guest lists and menus and invitations, and turning the kitchens upside down. She also insisted on teaching Annabeth the Spanish dances.

Annabeth was practicing the steps of the fandango to the accompaniment of Maria's guitar the day the estranjeros came.

21

"Estranjeros" was exactly the right word for them, Annabeth reflected afterwards. You couldn't call them Americans because only a fraction of them—the Bowery contingent—were American-born. They were the scrapings of the Bowery—men who had been recruited in New York to fight in the Mexican War.

Some of them were "kanakas," native-born Hawaiians, who because of the trading ships that went back and forth between San Francisco and Hawaii, were among the first outsiders to learn of the gold strike in California.

There was a sprinkling of others—native Californians of mestizo—mixed Spanish and Indian—blood, a handful of Yankee prospectors of the more raffish sort, and a few seamen of various nationalities who had jumped ship in Frisco Bay.

But the greatest number of the estranjeros and perhaps the most dangerous element among them was a motley crew of former convicts who had escaped the Australian penal colony and taken ship for California. They were known colloquially as "Sydney ducks."

This ill-assorted gang of cutthroats had banded together in a loose confederation to prey on wealthy rancheros up and down the coast as they made their way across country to the gold-fields. Each contingent had its own nominal leader but the linchpin of the gang was a particularly brutal blackbearded Australian called simply, Sid, who enforced discipline with a belaying pin. Their greed was also a cohesive factor for there was not one among them who would not have slit his own mother's throat for a peso—or a pinch of gold dust. Taken all in all, they were quite simply the scum of the earth.

The two girls were in Annabeth's room. "Oh, I shall never get it right!" she cried, sinking breathlessly down on a divan, careless of her many-flounced skirts, her white lace camisa and fringed rebozo, for Maria had insisted that she dress the part, the better to get into the mood of the music.

"Yes, you will. Nothing could be simpler," Maria assured her. She handed the guitar to Anna-beth. "Here, you play and I'll show you again how it should be done." And she proceeded to execute a beautiful, spirited fandango for Annabeth's benefit, heels tapping and castanets clicking.

"You make it seem so simple," Annabeth groaned.

Maria stopped to catch her breath. "Maybe it's in the blood," she admitted.

"Well, it's certainly not in mine!" She put down the guitar and sank back on the cushions fanning herself, but set bolt upright in surprise when one of the housemaids burst noisily into the room, crying "Senorita! Senorita!"

Maria, who had picked up the discarded instrument and was strumming it idly, looked a little annoyed at the interruption. "You must not burst into a room so, Esperanza," she rebuked her. "Now, what is it that is so important?"

The maid's dark eyes glittered with excitement and her scoop-shouldered peasant blouse fluttered with the rapid rise and fall of her heaving bosom.

"Senorita," she panted. "Even now a party of gringos approaches from the south. The sentries that el patron posted before he left sent word to Juan Jose and he bid me run to tell you of it immediately."

"So?" Maria returned placidly, her long aristocratic fingers still flicking over the guitar strings. "Now that you have told me you can go to the kitchen and tell old Carmen to prepare more tortillas and enchiladas. There will be guests tonight and undoubtedly they will be hungry." Hospitality to strangers had always been the rule and Maria saw no reason to change it just because her brother was away. No guest at Corazon d'Oro had ever been sent away hungry or without shelter for as long as he needed it. Quite often he was also provided with a horse to ride and a few coins to jingle in his purse.

Esperanza shook her head. "You don't understand, senorita. It is not two or three men only. Juan Jose says that it is a veritable army!"

Maria's delicately penciled brows arched in disbelief. "An army? Surely you exaggerate, Esperanza." She got up and went to the window which was shuttered against the noonday heat. Opening the shutters she peered out. "Madre de Dios!" Annabeth heard her gasp. "It is an armed rabble!" She exchanged a frightened look with Annabeth who had come to join her at the window. "What shall we do, Ana?"

"Close the gates and call in the vaqueros," Annabeth said promptly, trying to put on a brave

face for Maria looked frightened half to death and
Esperanza was chattering with fright.

Maria nodded at Esperanza. "Yes, we can do
that at least. See to it, Esperanza."

But the maid who had drawn her to the
window and was peering over her mistress'
shoulder stood riveted with terror at the sight that
met her eyes. A horde of men, some on horseback,
others on foot, was spread out against the skyline
and advancing steadily on Rancho del Corazon.
They did, indeed, have the appearance of an army
marching upon a chosen objective with every
intention of taking it, Annabeth thought with
dismay.

"Go, girl, do as you are told," she said sharply
to the snivelling maid. "There is no time to be lost!
And when you have done so, come back here. It
may be that your mistress will have need of you."

Muttering a prayer, Esperanza stumbled out
of the room.

Annabeth drew Maria down on a cushioned
settee. "We must plan what is best to do and there
is little time," she said rapidly. "Listen to me,
Maria." She gave her friend a little shake, for
Maria's gentle brown eyes were dilated with
terror. "The vaqueros are all armed, are they
not?"

"Yes, yes, they are, but they are spread out all
over the ranch. The spring roundup and branding
of new calves has gone on so much longer than
usual because of our being shorthanded. There is
no telling where they can be found or how long it
will take to call them in," said Maria dully.

Ananbeth tried to keep the dismay out of her
face. "But didn't Felipe post them within an easy
ride of the house?" she protested.

Maria sighed, a guilty look on her face. "I

thought Felipe was being unnecessarily cautious, and, with him due back any day, I disbanded them. Several have been sent around to neighboring rancheros with invitations to the fiesta. I put others to rounding up steers for the barbecue." Her face brightened suddenly. "Perhaps if we offered the steers to the estranjeros they would go away and leave us alone?" she suggested hopefully.

Annabeth thought it quite probable that the horde of men she had glimpsed advancing upon the rancho would be quite capable of helping themselves to whatever they wanted without waiting for an invitation! That a handful of steers would pacify them seemed so ludicrous a suggestion that it was hardly worthy of comment.

"How many men *can* we count on to defend the hacienda and what weapons do we have in the house?" she asked practically.

Maria thought it over. "Well, there are the sentries Felipe posted," she said with a sigh. "They are all armed, of course. Most of the vaqueros who are stationed near the house are older men with families. They are armed with flintlock rifles, I believe." She looked distressed. "Most of them are not fighting men, Ana—there has never been the need for them to take up arms. Why should there be?" She looked ready to cry. "And so many of our young men have run off to the goldfields—" Her voice trailed off. "And . . . and we have my grandfather's duelling pistols for . . . for our personal defense."

Annabeth nodded somberly. A less impressive crew and arsenal to stand off what amounted to an armed invasion she couldn't imagine.

"I don't see how we can hold the house against so many, Maria," she warned her friend. "We must send the women and children across the creek. They can take shelter in the cottonwoods until . . . until the vaqueros come to our rescue." There was a line of low rolling hills beyond the cottonwood grove. If worse came to worst, the women could scatter into the hills, each one for herself. At least they wouldn't be trapped in the house once the defenses were breached, as Annabeth was almost certain they would be.

She tugged her friend by the hands. "Come, Maria, we must go with them. We mustn't be found here alone, two helpless women."

But Maria balked. "I will not run away. Felipe left me in charge in his absence and I will not betray his trust. You go with the other women, Ana. I must stay."

Annabeth did her best to persuade her that it was folly to remain but Maria, usually so gentle, would not be budged. She sent Esperanza to shoo the household women to the shelter of the cottonwoods but adamantly refused to accompany them and nothing Annabeth could say would change her mind. "In the absence of el patron, I am responsible for the rancho and its inhabitants," she insisted. "I could not face Felipe if I ran away."

Finally Annabeth gave up. She supposed that they might well be as safe in the house if they barricaded themselves in as they might be across the creek. Who could say for sure? And it might be, she thought optimistically, that the estranjeros posed no particular threat to them personally. They might be content with a little looting, helping themselves to a few pieces of portable property, a few stray beeves perhaps, and then go on their way. She had no way of knowing that these men were like a plague of locusts, descending upon the more remote ranchos up and down the valley, looting and terrorizing.

The bandidos had already accumulated a sizable amount of plunder from such forays and might have bypassed Rancho Corazon d'Oro altogether had it not been for the name, suggesting wealth and riches, carved into a board and mounted at the entrance gate.

"Eh, Jock," the blackbearded leader of the gang called to one of his particular cronies, "you 'habla spic,' don't ya? What's that mean?" he pointed to the ornately carved sign decorated with the del Corazon brand, a heart-shaped triangle.

Jock, an agile little monkey of a man, more at home on the quarterdeck of a ship than astride a horse, pulled and hauled on his mount until it came abreast of the leader's big roan. "Corazon d'Oro," he translated, "it means heart of gold."

"That's what I thought. If it don't beat all," the leader meditated. "These showy greasers just can't resist bragging on what they got. Well, we'll just relieve them of some of the excess, eh, lads?"

There was a concerted rumble of approval and enthusiasm behind him. "Yeah, Sid," one ruffian yelled out, "it's a hell of a lot easier picking up gold plate and such that's just left lying around than it is to pan gold like them dumb miners."

"You can 'ave the gold, mate," called out another man whose eyes gleamed with lechery, "just gimme one of them dark-eyed senoritas." He dug his neighbor in the ribs. "What say, Joe?"

"Gold and women. I want 'em both," the other retorted.

"Come on, then, lads! What are we waiting for?" The blackbearded leader, unaware that the wealth of the del Corazons came not from any precious ore deposits but from a herd of golden horses they had bred for generations, waved his arm high overhead as a signal. The the mob of cohorts surged behind him and flowed through the outer gates which had been left undefended through lack of manpower.

Since Maria could not be persuaded to take refuse in the cottonwood grove or, better yet, flee into the hills beyond the creek, Annabeth suggested that they barricade themselves in the sala. After securely locking and barring the door, the two girls proceeded to shove the furniture against it. They pulled and tugged at the heavy mahogany table until they had tip-tilted it and laboriously shoved it against the door. Maria then piled the chairs on top of it while Annabeth went round checking that all the shutters were closed and locked.

Then they settled down to wait. The emptiness and silence of the usually busy house was positively eerie, Annabeth thought nervously. For a time there had been the clatter of hasty footsteps within the house or in the courtyard outside, the shrill cries of women as they gathered their children together for the flight across the creek, the wails of a baby rudely awakened from its afternoon nap, the braying of a donkey being hauled away by its owner, the cackle of chickens hastily captured and thrust into a small cage.

Then . . . nothing. Everyone had gone except the two girls barricaded in the sala. Annabeth nervously reminded herself that they were not quite as alone as it seemed for Juan Jose had posted a couple of men with rifles on the red tiled roof. But she could not hear them. All that could be heard was the rapid rise and fall of their own breathing. And, presently there was the clicking together of beads as Maria settled down to tell over her rosary.

Annabeth looked at her enviously, wishing that she had thought to bring a bit of handiwork from her room with which to occupy her hands—a bit of sewing perhaps. Looking down at her idle hands, she realized that they were clammy with perspiration and wiped them nervously on her many-flounced skirt. She hadn't even taken time or thought to change into more practical attire, she realized with dismay.

In any case, it was too dim now to sew in the sala for the closed shutters closed off almost all light. The odd sunbeam dancing through the cracks would not have provided sufficient light. She watched the dust motes dancing in the light rays and tried to pray but her thoughts were too hectic, too disjointed.

She sat quietly, her hands clasped loosely in her lap and thought about her life, letting her thoughts drift where they would. Thinking about the steps that had brought her here—about how she had come to this present crisis in her life. She ought, she supposed, to be thinking about meeting her Maker, about making a good end. Instead, she thought about the men in her life—Felipe and Eben. She sat, quiet as a statue, and lived over again in memory her time with Eben. The good times and the bad. Their quarrels—how silly they seemed in retrospect! Their bright moments of happiness she treasured, counting them over as a miser his gold. How greatly they had loved and how foolish she had been to toss it so lightly away. They should have shared their grief, she realized now, as they had shared their joy in each other.

All of a sudden she knew with a sudden swift certainty what answer she would give Felipe. She knew that she could not, would not, accept that Eben was dead. Not without proof. When all this was over—if she lived through it—she would go to the goldfields herself in search of him. She would find him or she would find proof that he was dead. And without that proof she would wait for him—look for him—forever!

Suddenly the uncanny silence was broken by a fusillade of gunshots. Maria, her face white, uttered an exclamation and dropped her gold-chased rosary. It fell to the tiled floor with a clatter. She exchanged a fear-filled look with Annabeth, then, setting her lips in a thin tight line, bent and retrieved the beads. Trying to assume an air of calmness, she picked up where she had left off, "Ora pro nobis, nobis peccatoribus, nunc et in horae mortis," she prayed and Annabeth silently echoed her, translating in her mind, "Pray for us sinners, now and in the hour of our deaths."

The shots were louder now, closer to the house. Muffled shouts and curses could be heard in a mixture of Spanish and English, in between shots.

Some of the defenders had taken shelter in the various sheds and outbuildings and were now, Annabeth realized in horror, being systematically wiped out. She could hear screams and groans, a man begging in agonized Spanish to be put out of his misery, occasionally a curse, sometimes a prayer, the latter always in Spanish.

There was a series of shots, another gut-wrenching scream and then a dull thud, followed in short order by another. She guessed that the men stationed overhead had been shot down and had pitched off the roof, landing with a dull thud on the hard-packed earth of the courtyard.

Though to the two girls cowering in the sala the battle seemed to go on forever, in reality it was over in a matter of minutes. It was an easy matter for the bandidos to overcome the sentries and such vaqueros as Juan Jose, the capataz, had been able to round up on such short notice. Unlike the estranjeros, the Californios were unused to fighting . . . nor were they as well-armed as the intruders. The result was a foregone conclusion. The desperadoes shot the defenders down in cold blood or clubbed them into submission with their rifle butts.

Maria, her eyes wide with terror, clutched her rosary with one hand; the other groped for Annabeth's. Clutching each other's hands, they listened with bated breaths, waiting . . . always waiting.

They had not long to wait. The intruders made short work of breaking into the hacienda, shooting or pistol-whipping those defenders who had been posted at the house.

Presently the two terrified girls heard them roaming from room to room, breaking seldom-used locks with their rifle butts, pocketing ornaments and trinkets. The more enterprising of them dragged coverlets from the beds or cloths from the tables and filled them with loot—silver candlesticks, bejeweled crucifixes, and knick-knacks of all descriptions.

"Looks like everybody took off," they heard a harsh voice complain.

"Yeah," another voice boomed. "Well, we'll just have to hunt them up, won't we, lads! You—Bill, Archie, Simon—" a voice of authority detailed a number of men, "Scout around. See if you can find them." He licked thick lascivious lips. "Judging by the clothes in the closets, there oughtta be two ladies. I want them brought to me. You lads can take your pleasure with the maids

and cooks when you find them," he added by way
of inducement.

"To the victor, eh, Sid?" said a voice.

"Eh, what?" the harsh voice demanded.

"To the victor belong the spoils," a more
cultured voice sneered.

"Damn straight!" the harsh voice grunted.

The girls heard boots clumping in the hall and
then someone tried to open the door of the sala,
rattling the knob. Annabeth felt a wave of sickness
sweep over her and Maria clenched her hand so
tightly she was sure some of the bones would be
broken.

"Ah, Sid, c'mere," another voice sang out.
"This door is barred as well as locked. This must
be the treasure room," the voice speculated.

"Well, whaddya bastards waiting for? An
invitation? Somebody get an axe or a hatchet and
break it in," the leader ordered in tones of
irritation. The hacienda was not as rich as he had
thought. There was a disappointing lack of really
valuable plunder—and women—and he was in an
ugly mood. He put his shoulder to the door to test
it but though he was a big burly man he could not
budge it; it was indubitably barricaded on the
other side. "Some of you lads hurry up with that
hatchet," he yelled.

There was a concerted hunt for an axe and
then wild whoops of joy for the men had stumbled
across Don Felipe's wine cellar. Whooping and
hollering they broke open casks and bottles until
the cellar was awash with fine wines imported
from Spain and an even more fiery natural
product, wild grape brandy. Eventually one of the
harder-headed among them remembered the
errand they had been on and took an axe to his
leader, a half-empty bottle of wine in his other

hand.

Behind the barricaded door of the sala, Annabeth and Maria clung to each other, trembling
with terror. They had heard the calls for an axe,
heard the commotion in the wine cellar and knew
what it portended. "Oh, Ana, why did I not send
you across the creek with the other women? Why
was I so foolish? Why did I not go myself?" Maria
lamented in a whisper.

But Annabeth shook her head. It was too late,
far too late to cry over spilt milk. Besides, if the
new and horrible sounds that penetrated the
shutters were anything to go by, the women had
found no safety in the cottonwood grove. They
were little better off than she and Maria. The men
had obviously fanned out to look for them and,
judging by the screams and cries, they had found
them. The hoodlums were dragging them back
across the shallow waters of the creek or throwing
them down on the ground and raping them where
they were. Annabeth and Maria could hear cries,
some near at hand, some distant, pleas and
prayers, moans and groans, weeping and wailing
all intermingled with the hoarse shouts of the
men.

Their attention was focused on their own
predicament as an axe began hacking through the
heavy panels of the door.

Hoping fervently that at least some of the
women had managed to get away, to escape into
the hills, she detached herself from Maria and
rose to her feet, bracing one of the antique
duelling pistols on the back of the chair. She might
be degraded, raped, die of it, but she would take
one of these foul fiends with her into eternity!

"No, Ana—" Maria clutched at her wrist.
"You must not. Each pistol has only one shot.

There will not be time to reload." Her voice
faltered. "You . . . you must shoot me . . . and then
yourself. It . . . it is the only way to defend our
honor!"

Annabeth's hand wavered. As Maria had said,
the dueling pistol was a single shot weapon. She
had only one bullet. Two, if you counted the
matching pistol. One shot for Maria. One for herself. If she used it on the intruders, her gun would
be emptied for no good purpose—for a futile
gesture.

Was it courage or cowardice to shoot Maria
and then herself? Wasn't it better to live—even if
that life was one of humiliation and degradation?
While there was life, she supposed, there was
hope. Hope that somehow she would find Eben
again one day.

His voice seemed to come back to her, across
a very great distance of time and space. "Death
comes soon enough to all of us . . . most times
living is more important than dying . . . it's how
we live that counts—"

She had promised Felipe that she would take
care of Maria and she knew now the purpose for
which he had entrusted the pistols to her. But she
couldn't do it, she knew she couldn't. How, in the
name of God, could she find the necessary courage
to take her friend's life? And in the end, wasn't it
Maria's decision to make? To choose death over
dishonor or life, no matter how degraded it might
be!

Her own decision made, she dropped one of
the pistols into Maria's lap but retained her grip
on the other. "I can't," she said simply. "You must
do what you think best for yourself."

The axe was hacking away at the door panels.
Splinters of wood flew and light appeared at the

opening. Then a man's leering gargoyle face loomed up where the shattered door panels had been.

She braced herself against the chair and squeezed the trigger.

The explosion echoed and reechoed in the enclosed space. Through drifting plumes of black powder, she saw the man's face disintegrate in a splatter of blood and bone and brains.

Then the head and shoulders of another man, a burly barrel-chested individual, replaced that of the first man. "You might as well drop the gun, lydy. I knows you ain't got but one shot," he advised her. He pulled pieces of the panel out of the way until he could step through the opening thus formed. Callously kicking the fallen body of his former comrade out of the way, he squeezed into the room. "Gimme a hand with this table, lads!" he shouted.

Two or three of the Sydney ducks hastened to obey him, shoving the improvised barricade out of the way.

The big man swaggered his way into the room once the heavy table had been dispensed with. "Blimey, will ya take a good look at this lot, lads! A little Mex gal—" His eyes roamed disinterestedly over Maria and fastened greedily upon Annabeth. "And a redheaded wench the likes of which I ain't seen since I left Sydney!" His eyes latched onto the low-cut bodice of Annabeth's fiesta frock and he licked his thick flabby lips in greedy anticipation.

Seeing the direction of his gaze she pulled the fringed rebozo more tightly around her. "A white woman, all dressed up like a greaser," Blackbeard marvelled. His dirty paws reached out to fumble at Annabeth's breast, pulling the fringed rebozo away and yanking down her bodice to reveal even more of her bosom. "Dontacha go trying to hide what you got," he admonished her. "I'm gonna see it all . . . have it all 'fore I'm done with you."

Annabeth flinched away from him, appalled by the burning lust in his eyes. Then, to her surprise, Maria stepped protectively between them. "Unhand her," she said sharply.

Blackbeard blinked. "Well, well, what we got here? Two for the price of one," he chortled.

Maria was trembling but her softly rounded chin was firmly set and there was a world of courage in her voice as she proclaimed proudly, "I . . . I am Maria de la Concepcion Santiago y Vallejo del Corazon. I . . . I am la patrona of this rancho and . . . and Ana, she is my guest. Wh-what do you want with her?" In spite of herself Maria's chin began to quiver. "With . . . with us?"

So regal and imperious was Maria's tone that Blackbeard actually took a step backwards in amazement. It was rather like seeing a tiny kitten spitting at a great hulking monster, Annabeth thought hysterically. She wondered what Maria had done with the second duelling pistol and decided that she must have concealed it in a fold of her flounced fiesta skirt.

Recovering himself, Blackbeard uttered a great bellowing laugh, his dark eyes gleaming evilly. "The little greaser's got some spirit after all, ain't she, lads!" he remarked almost admiringly to his henchmen who had begun crowding into the room. Inspired by the comments of his audience, he extended a grimy paw to grope Maria, who shrank back in alarm.

"What's going on here?" A timely interruption came in the form of a tall yellow-haired man who had shouldered his way through the throng. "I thought it was supposed to be share and share alike, Sid," he snarled, eyeballing the two women.

Annabeth caught her breath. The man had the voice of authority and command and he spoke in the accents of her native New York which was more intelligible to her than that of the Sydney ducks. Was he a possible rescuer? She thought not. He certainly had a more ... more refined appearance than the burly Australian but his eyes, she noted, as they traveled insolently up and down her body, were as bleak and as hard as cold steel.

Besides, what was he doing with this band of desperadoes if he were not a part of them? No decent man would travel with this gang of cutthroats.

Regretfully, she decided that no help for herself or Maria would be forthcoming from this quarter. The newcomer was, if anything, potentially even more dangerous than Blackbeard, she decided, if only because he appeared to possess a modicum of brains as well as brawn. One look into those ice-blue eyes convinced her that he would be capable of dreaming up refinements of cruelty that the crude Australian could not even imagine.

"Now, see here, Morgan," the big man began to bluster. "Me and my men got 'ere first. It's first come, first served, see. And this 'ere wench is gonna serve me right well!" he leered, grabbing Annabeth and pulling her shrinking form close to his big body which reeked of wine, tobacco, and stale sweat. "You c'n have the Mex," he added generously, jerking a grimy thumb in Maria's direction.

The cold blue eyes flickered to Maria. "Mexican women are a dime a dozen, Sid." A casual hand reached out, yanked the gold cross from Maria's throat, and pocketed it. He then paused, scowling thoughtfully at Maria's delicately aristocratic profile. "Still . . . she's a looker." He shook his head, almost regretfully. "But she won't serve my purposes. Nope, it's the redhead I want, Sid. I've got plans for her."

A low rumbling growl issued from his opponent's throat. He let go of Annabeth so suddenly that she almost fell and lunged for the other man's throat. "You challenging me, mate?" he growled.

"Don't be a fool, Sid—any more of a fool than you can help, that is," Blue-eyes said with deceptive softness. Suddenly—so suddenly that no one had seen him draw it, a pearl-handled derringer appeared in his hand. "You ought to know by now," he said conversationally, "that I rely on Lady Luck. And this little lady, as you well know, is deadly at close range. Not army issue, of course. It won't blow quite as big a hole in your belly—but, she'll do the job. I assure you of that."

Beads of sweat stood out on Sid's forehead. He had seen Morgan use the deadly little derringer more than once. He knew that the man was utterly ruthless. He meant business, Sid was sure of that.

Sid tried a little bluster. "See 'ere. Who's boss 'ere, you or me?"

"At the moment, it would appear that I am," said the blue-eyed newcomer, half-humorously. "Have no fear, Sid," he added, with seeming generosity. "I have no intention of taking over this gang of cutthroats. I only want the redhead."

Morgan knew he had the upper hand but low-voiced grumbling and muttering among the men convinced him that he had better tread carefully. "Tell you what I'll do, Sid, to demonstrate my, er, my goodwill," he added from a sudden inspiration. "I'll gamble you for the women. Winner takes the redhead."

There was a concerted rumble of approval from the watching men, some of whom owed allegiance to Sid, while others were members of the disbanded New York Bowery regiment of which Morgan had been captain. This would be entertainment of a high order. It would add a final fillip to a day which had, for most of them, been extremely gratifying! Loot, wine, women—they had had their fill of all three. And now they had a chance to watch the two big men, their respective leaders, at a game of chance—with two beautiful women captives as the stakes!

Sid's black eyes narrowed suspiciously. His tongue came out to lick thick flabby lips. "Cards or dice?" he croaked. He had no wish to go up against Morgan whom he knew had been a professional gambler in New York before he drifted west. But he had been maneuvered into a corner. The Yank had the upper hand and he knew it. If he backed down now, he would lose face among his own men. He would be accused of having a yellow streak and they would drift out of his control.

"Name your poison," Morgan said cheerfully. He was equally proficient with either cards or dice and he was confident that he could best this lame-brained Aussie—even if he didn't cheat! He grabbed a half-bottle of wine from one of his men and raised it high. "To Lady Luck!" he made the toast and drank deep. "And to the victor—" his hard eyes glanced towards Annabeth, "To the victor belongs the spoils!"

22

Sid chose dice. He refused, however, to use Morgan's and, for a while, they were at an impasse. "You saying these dice are loaded, Sid?" demanded Morgan in a deceptively soft tone.

"Nah. Ain't saying nothing like that." The Sydney duck was quick to deny the accusation. He had achieved leadership among his own men with bravado, bluster and brutality—his way of subduing any malcontents with the heavy belaying pin he carried at his belt. But the Yankee gambler with the cold blue eyes and the handy little derringer sent chills rippling up his spine. "Stands to reason you'd just naturally have better luck with them than me," he blustered. "They know who they belong to, see," he tried to explain.

"You mean I've got them jinxed," said the gambler with a grin.

"Somep'n like that."

Eventually the impasse was solved when a bearded seaman pushed his way into the throng with an offer of dice that "has sailed the seven seas with me," and which he guaranteed to be straight. In exchange, all he asked was a front-row seat. Since he belonged neither to Sid's band of Aussie ruffians nor to the Bowery bums and there-

366

fore owed no particular allegiance to either leader, his offer was found acceptable to both parties concerned.

"Let's make it even more worthwhile," Morgan suggested, his eyes narrowing thoughtfully as he looked around the room. "I'll put up all the loot my men have accumulated against yours."

There was some grousing about this among the Sydney ducks. They had been on the spot first and had gotten a greater share of the loot but the Bowery bums were delighted at the prospect and Sid, having gotten into the spirit of the thing and determined not to be outdone, agreed. "It'll make things more interesting," he conceded. "Bring them bedspreads over here, lads." He gestured to the improvised sacks which contained the loot.

The men, those of them still sober enough to take an interest, gathered round, elbowing each other out of the way. Others, who had finished their business with the helpless women in the courtyard or the cottonwoods, drifted back to the house in twos and threes to see the fun.

They gathered round, watching every movement—each roll of the dice—with breathless interest, uttering exclamations indicative of pleasure or disappointment according to the roll of the dice and whichever band they belonged to.

At first Sid was the winner but then his luck changed and the pile of loot beside the gambler grew steadily greater.

If those dice weren't loaded, as evidently they weren't, then the New Yorker had the devil's own luck, thought Annabeth.

She and Maria had been allowed to huddle together in a corner of the room, well out of the way. She had upended one of the overturned chairs for the younger girl whose trembling legs would no longer support her. Maria's delicate face was glazed with terror and she clutched Annabeth's hands convulsively. Her other hand was concealed in the folds of her skirt and, glancing down, Annabeth saw that her friend still clenched the antique dueling pistol reflexively. Annabeth wondered, in concern, if she had forgotten it.

She squeezed Maria's free hand. "Have courage, Maria," she whispered. Then she glanced around her warily. The eyes of every man present seemed to be glued to the toss of the dice. The audience was riveted to the spectacle of the two leaders gambling for a greater share of the spoils.

Annabeth swallowed hard. She knew that she and Maria would be next. Stakes in a macabre game of chance between two evil and ruthless men.

Unobtrusively she tapped the slender artistocratic fingers that curled around the silver-chased barrel of the pistol, as if to remind the younger girl that she was still in possession of it—and hence, of the means of defense, if necessary.

"Maria!" she whispered, softly but urgently. "Maria, listen to me."

When the younger girl's face turned towards her dully, Annabeth realized she had captured her attention. "Listen," she whispered. "You must wait here. Be brave Maria. I'm going to try to slip out. Try to find help for us."

"Oh, no, Ana." Maria's face was pinched with terror. "Don't leave me alone with them," she pleaded.

"Shh—" Annabeth patted her hand encouragingly, then began to inch her way towards the door.

As luck would have it, the burly Australian turned away from the dice game to reach for a bottle of wine. He took time for a hefty swig before moving to intercept her.

Annabeth was halfway to the door when Sid barred her way with his thick, heavy but surprisingly agile body. "Where you going, my pretty?" he leered at her. "Not trying to run out on us, are you?" He caught at her arm with a huge clammy hand.

The New Yorker rose to his feet. "Let her go, Sid. She's not yours to paw." The man spoke quietly but with authority.

"Not yet, maybe. But she will be!" the bearded Australian said with bravado though, so far, the luck of the game had gone against him.

"That remains to be seen."

Annabeth turned to the gambler appealingly. "Oh, please, let me go back to my friend. I . . . I want to wait with . . . with Maria."

"You should have thought of that before." Morgan was implacable. Pulling up a chair, he ushered Annabeth into it with a mocking bow. "I prefer to keep you under my eye."

Annabeth subsided into herself, wondering wildly how this could be happening to her! To be a pawn in a game of chance between two equally cruel and ruthless men. No matter who won, she lost. And so did Maria.

As far as Annabeth could see, there wasn't anything to choose between either of the gamesters. The American was obviously *cleaner*, more fastidious, and probably more intelligent. On the other hand, the Australian, though personally more repulsive to her, might be easier to outwit. But who ever won her, she had a shrewd suspicion that she would be handed over to the men whenever the victor tired of her. And what of delicate virginal Maria . . . what would *her* fate be at the hands of such men? Annabeth shuddered.

The gold plate and coins and silver candlesticks disposed of, the men settled down to the serious business of tossing the dice for *her*!

"Best two throws out of three?" the American suggested, rolling the ivory cubes between his palms.

The big Australian shrugged. "Suits me," he grunted.

Sid won the first cast and Morgan the second. The next throw would tell the tale.

Tension mounted in the room. The men crowded round the players, jeering, kibitzing, and placing side bets. Annabeth could see sweat spring out on the Australian's forehead but the American seemed as cold as ice.

She herself felt almost breathless with anticipation. Her sweaty palms clutched the sides of her chair and her lungs and chest felt as if they would burst. There seemed to be not enough oxygen in the closely thronged room and she could only draw air into her lungs in tiny gasps. A thin mist floated before her eyes and the dots on the little ivory cubes blurred together so that she could not read her fate in them. She hoped to God she wasn't going to faint.

The big desperado slowly shook the dice in his fists and rolled them out. "Eh, look at that, lads!" he bellowed in triumph. He had achieved one of the highest scores possible.

"Top that, if you can!" Sid bragged, taking a long swig from a bottle of red wine.

Morgan calmly reached for the dice and with a casual flip of his wrist tossed out the little ivory cubes.

Annabeth was far too numb to take in the significance of the patterned dots—she was so woozy and light-headed that they blurred together. But she could clearly read her fate in the bearded face and in his violent burst of profanity. Evidently, Sid was a poor loser!

For a moment it looked as though he were going to attack his fellow player. His big hands, the backs of which were covered with thick wiry black hairs clenched, unclenched and clenched again.

A cold smile curled at Morgan's mouth. "You a sore loser, Sid?" he taunted the burly Australian.

The air was thick with tension. Annabeth held her breath, wondering if she should make a dive for safety. Sid looked angry enough to throttle Morgan with his bare hands.

A welcome diversion in the shape of a man who had been posted as lookout burst into the room and filled it with a new and different kind of tension. "Riders!" he bawled. "Coming like a bat outta hell! Judging by the cloud of dust they're raising, it must be a mob of them!"

Annabeth's heart leaped. It must be the vaqueros. Rescue was at hand! There was reason to hope again!

The news galvanized the men into action. Confident that its defenders were all dead, wounded or disarmed they had lingered longer than usual at Rancho del Corazon. It was time to move out before they met with retribution!

"We'd better split up, Sid, the better to evade pursuit," said Morgan authoritatively. "I'll take my men and head towards the goldfields, while you and your lads take a different direction—into the hills, maybe."

To split the gang suited Morgan's purposes very well. He knew if he stuck with Sid much longer, he'd have to face him down the barrel of a gun. And while he had no qualms about blowing the burly outlaw away—Sid would be no loss to anyone, thought Morgan cynically—he had no wish to take over as supreme leader of a band of ruthless desperadoes who would probably end up swinging at the end of a rope. He, Jared Morgan, had other plans for himself. Big plans. And now he had sufficient capital—the loot he had won from Sid and the red-headed wench who was gong to fit into those plans of his just fine—it was time to separate himself from this gang of hoodlums and put his Plan into operation.

The men began to scatter, some making for their horses; others scurrying around to scavenge for any loose valuables that might still be left lying about.

"Set a torch to the place, lads!" the big Australian blustered. "That'll keep the greasers busy and slow up any pursuit!"

Annabeth watched in horror as the men, bearing brands hurriedly snatched from the kitchen cook fires, set alight curtains and draperies. "Maria!" she screamed, "Maria!" as her captor dragged her from the burning building into the courtyard. Catching up a couple of horses, he threw her, willy-nilly, up onto one, where she clung desperately in a flurry of flounced skirts.

It was like a scene out of hell, Annabeth thought despairingly, from her uneasy perch on the restive mount. Flames were shooting out of the interior of the ranch house. There was a crackling, snapping sound and smell of burning wood and scorched feathers from the mattresses. The men had set fire to the sheds and outbuildings as well as to the main ranch house and the tule roofs of these buildings were soon ablaze, the flames leaping high among the reeds.

"Maria!" Annabeth screamed again, seeing her friend emerging from the burning house, half-carried, half-dragged along by the bearded Sid.

Momentarily, the burly form of the ruffian and the slender figure of her friend were silhouetted against the flame-lit hacienda.

The acrid smoke scorched her nostrils and stung her eyes and Annabeth blinked to clear them. When she looked again, she saw that Sid had leaned Maria against an ivy-twined pillar while he snatched at the bridle of a snorting, fire-crazed horse that one of his henchmen had led up to the patio.

Annabeth turned imploringly to her captor who was struggling with his own plunging, rearing mount while still holding fast to the bridle of her horse. "Oh, please, make him leave Maria behind," she begged. "Please!" She swallowed hard, trying to make her voice as soft and placating as possible. "Maria is a gently bred lady. She won't survive brutal treatment. Please!" she begged, looking at Morgan imploringly.

The gambler was callously indifferent, unmoved by Maria's plight. "She's his prize," he retorted with a shrug as he scrambled into the saddle.

Aware that her pleas were falling on deaf ears, Annabeth gave up. She craned her head to look back as Morgan led her horse through a milling, yelling mob of outlaws.

The burly ruffian, Sid, had succeeded in clubbing his horse into obedience and was advancing on Maria who clung, sobbing, to the pillar. Annabeth saw firelight gleam on the silver-chased pistol that Maria still gripped.

"Maria! The pistol! Shoot him!" she screamed. "Shoot!"

Maria looked down at the pistol wonderingly, as if only now aware that it was still in her possession. She lifted it, drawing it forth from the folds of her skirts.

Annabeth saw the barrel rise, fall, rise again, the gun wavering in Maria's grasp, as the burly Sid, heedless of the threat the firearm presented, reached out and yanked Maria from the pillar.

"No!" she cried out. "No! I am la patrona of Corazon d'Oro. Never will I leave it with such as You!"

A shot rang out.

Annabeth strained to see through a mist of smoke and tears but Jared Morgan slapped the rump of her prancing horse so that the animal jumped and then took off at a run. Annabeth, thrown off balance, clung in desperation to the high Spanish saddlehorn, her bunched-up skirts billowing about her thighs, every thought driven from her head but that of her own predicament.

Smoke hung in a heavy pall over the valley. Eben's eyes smarted from the acrid black particles hanging in the hazy air. So did Shorty's. "That's no range fire," the older man muttered. He had seen and smelled too many burned out homes on the Texas border—houses, fences, and corrals set alight by the Kiowa or the Comanche—to be deceived. He exchanged a puzzled glance with Eben. "Indians?" he said uncertainly, knowing that most of the California redskins had long since been tamed by the missionary priests.

"Like hell!" Eben retorted, digging his heels

into his horse's flanks. Shorty pounded along behind.

The ranch house was a smoldering ruin. Its sheds and outbuildings, which had gone up in flames quickly and completely, were piles of charred rubble. Women and the few men were milling haphazardly around in the courtyard, the former weeping and wailing, some of them kneeling in prayer by the bodies of their menfolk who had died defending Rancho del Corazon d'Oro.

In their midst Don Felipe del Corazon stood racked with grief and aghast at the desolation that on all sides surrounded him. He had ridden in from the south only a short time ago and had joined in helping the vaqueros to quench the blaze. The interior of the ranch house was gutted but the adobe walls and red-tiled roof was only scorched.

Don Felipe's usually immaculate clothing was streaked and smudged with soot and grime, his hands blistered and his face blackened, his eyebrows nearly singed away. His men, who were engaged in the grim task of gathering together and laying out the dead, were in similar straits.

An old woman with a wrinkled tear-stained face approached Don Felipe and plucked at his sleeve. Behind her followed a younger man bearing in his arms the broken body of a child. "El patron, el patron," the old woman whined. "Behold here the daughter of my daughter. My little Carmencita. Only eight summers did she have. The Yanquis violated her. And her mother, my daughter, Ysabel. Her, also, the Yanquis raped and, though she yet lives, she will not speak to us. She only stares at us with great empty eyes." the old woman paused and choked back a sob. "I ask vengeance, Don Felipe. The blood of my daughter's daughter cries out for vengeance against these Yanquis."

Don Felipe swallowed convulsively. "You will have it, Carmen. You and the others who have lost dear ones. On the True Cross I swear it! I . . . I will not rest until these accursed animals are brought to justice."

"Yanqui justice!" snorted the child's father, who was one of the del Corazon vaqueros.

"No! Judgement at the throne of God!" said Don Felipe fiercely. With utmost tenderness he reached out and closed the child's eyes, making the sign of the Cross over her forehead. "Lay her there, Jaime, beside . . . beside my sister. I . . . I have sent for Father Francisco. He will be here soon to say masses for the dead."

Jaime laid his sad burden down beside the still form of Dona Maria and Don Felipe knelt by his sister's body, buried his ravaged face in his hands, and wept. Never in his comfortable and basically carefree life had he seen such sights as had greeted him on his return to Corazon d'Oro. Oh, he had heard of such things happening, read of man's inhumanity to man, but, having never experienced it before, he had hardly believed in it. Never had he thought such things could happen to him or his. Were not he and his sister highly respected members of the gente de razon? Insulated from such terrors by good breeding and great wealth? How was it possible that his beloved sister lay dead before him?

A commotion in the outer courtyard caused him to raise his head. Two men—Anglos—had ridden in and the vaqueros, their blood lust aroused, had seized them and hauled them out of their saddles.

"Yanquis! Kill the Yanquis!" The cry echoed

round the courtyard. "Kill the gringos! A rope is too good for such as they!"

Some of the vaqueros were already uncoiling their reatas when Don Felipe roused himself. Raising his head from his hands, he looked—and recognized Eben McDowell.

Dios! he thought. On this day of desolation, here is one presumed dead who has come to life again! For the big broad-shouldered man in worn buckskins was clearly Ana's loutish husband. The other man he had never seen before.

"Bring them to me." Don Felipe ordered in a terrible voice.

The vaqueros hastened to obey, pinning their captives' arms behind their backs and dragging them to El Patron.

"Welcome, Yanquis, to the house of del Corazon!" said Don Felipe hoarsely.

"What in hell's gone on here?" Eben burst out. His face looked fully as ravaged as the younger man's as he surveyed the scene of desolation spread out before him. He stared aghast at the still form of Maria. "My God, what happened?" he demanded, shaking off the vaqueros, who, at Don Felipe's authoritative nod, released both him and his companion.

"The ranch was attacked by a gang of bandidos. As you see, my sister is dead." The young man's face contorted with grief. "My people tell me that she shot herself rather than be carried off into captivity."

"And Annabeth?" Eben rapped out. "What happened to her?"

"Some of the ranch women were taken away by the bandidos." Don Felipe shook his head. "I fear that Ana was among their number."

Despite his grief and desolation, Don Felipe's

inbred courtesy came to the fore. "You will pardon the rough handling by my men," he said courteously. "They have lost much this day. Their homes burned . . . their wives and sweethearts violated or carried off . . . I was not here, you understand," he went on to explain. "I have only just returned from Monterey. The raiders had already come and gone, taking the women with them."

"Who were they?" Eben demanded.

Don Felipe ran a distracted hand through his lustrous black hair. "Anglos. That is all I know. That . . . and that they will pay." His well-shaped lips drew back in a snarl. "They will pay dearly."

Eben studied the young man's ravaged face. It bore little resemblance to the handsome carefree caballero he remembered. It was a tense bloodless mask of flesh, the eyes dull and lifeless. On this day, he reckoned, the boy had become a man.

He put his hand on the young man's shoulder, his fingers biting deep into the flesh. "We will ride together, amigo."

Don Felipe stiffened. "I ride with no Yanqui—never again!" he spat out.

Eben shrugged. "Suit yourself. Me, I'm goin' after 'em." He turned on his heel.

"Wait!" Don Felipe thought it over. He knew that Ana would not give her love to a scoundrel. Moreover, his own instincts told him that Eben, despite outward appearance, was a man of integrity. Mucho hombre.

"Wait," he said again. "My men and I will ride with you." There was a pause, then he added, "Amigo."

23

The trail left by so many horses and riders was an easy one for old hands like Eben and Shorty Gillespie to follow. They led the way with Felipe and a band of his vaqueros hard on their heels. All had wanted to ride with el patron but not everyone could be spared. Some had to remain behind to bury the dead and to find shelter for the women and children. Only those who had a special reason to fight the gringos—those who had lost fathers or brothers in the defense of the rancho or whose wives or daughters had been violated—were allowed to accompany el patron.

They rode until nightfall when it became too dark to follow the trail. Eben had soon discovered that the gang had split up and scattered, some of them riding off in twos and threes in different directions. He was going on the assumption that the women had been kept together and that they were with the main band. He couldn't be sure of that, of course, but it seemed a logical assumption. In any case, he figured that the individual riders would join up with the larger group later on.

Whenever he thought of Annabeth and how she might be faring, his face set in hard grim lines.

If only he had gotten back to Rancho del Corazon twenty-four hours earlier, he would have been there to protect her or die trying to do so. Damn the accursed gold! Why hadn't he sent it to Sacramento in Shorty's charge? Well, there wasn't no use in dwelling on what might have been.

It was ironic, he thought, that Annabeth had clung to Rancho del Corazon for the security she had found there, only to be ravished and raped and carried away by a gang of cutthroats of her own nationality. For he had no illusions as to what must have happened to her. Men such as the Californios had described—men so depraved that they would rape a child, for he had heard the sorry tale and seen the little girl's body—would have no compunction about raping a full grown woman.

That was what Don Felipe thought too. Eben could see it in his haunted eyes. Eben wondered just how much of his agony was for the death of his sister and how much of it was for the fate of Annabeth. Eben had sisters, too, though he hadn't seen them for years and, though he'd loved them and felt protective towards them, he didn't think that the death of a sister was enough to put that look of torment into a young man's eyes. No, if a man looked like he was suffering all the torments of hell, it could only be for the woman he loved with that special kind of love that exists between a man and his woman. Eben knew that look well, knew that though he was a more stoic breed of man than the excitable Latin, his own face bore the marks of just such suffering. But then, Annabeth was his wife—the other half of himself.

He had to give the kid credit, though, he mused. He appeared to be holding up right well. He'd had a long ride back from Monterey, returning to the rancho to find his home a shambles, his sister dead, and his beloved friend carried off. He'd fought a fire—the blisters on Don Felipe's hands had not gone unnoticed—and rallied his men and now he was embarked on a trail that might have no end, or come to a short quick end with a bullet in the gut.

The young man in question strolled over to the fire built to heat food and coffee and ward off the night chill. He'd already made the rounds of his men, having a quiet word with each, as befitted el patron. Now he pulled a slim gold monogrammed case from his pocket and offered Eben a pre-rolled cigarito. Eben accepted it with a gruff word of thanks and bent to the fire to light it with a spill.

"I love her, too, Yanqui," he said simply.

Eben straightened slowly and applied the burning spill to the tip of his cigarette, illuminating his face and that of the young haciendado.

"I reckoned so," he said slowly, flicking the spill back into the fire, where it momentarily flared up and then died back again.

"We had given you up for dead. Everyone except Ana, that is. Oh, she mourned you as one dead, but when I pressed her to marry me, she refused. She told me that you must yet be alive—she said that she would know it in her heart if you were no longer among the living." Don Felipe threw down his own cigarette and ground it out into the dirt. "Oh, she was unhappy. She wanted love—needed love. A man's love. Yet she was true to you, always. She is good and loyal and pure in heart. And that heart will always beat for you—it will beat for you until she dies."

"Why are you telling me this?" Eben said tightly.

"I do not know," the young Californio said honestly. "Only that sometimes we do not appreciate what we have until we lose it." He looked thoughtfully at Eben. "I have had much—wealth and social position, a loving sister, and recently, until today, the hope that Ana would some day be mine—"

"If she lives I will get her back!" The vow burst from Eben's lips.

"And if she has been . . . dishonored?"

"That means nothin' to me. I . . . I would sorrow for her pain but it wouldn't affect my love for her."

"That, I think, is what I wanted to know." Felipe nodded as if satisfied. "For it would mean nothing to me either and if you were to fail her again—"

"*Again!*" Eben's face darkened.

"Well, you deserted her, did you not?" said Felipe with a certain aristocratic hauteur. "Like all yanquis with gold fever," he said scornfully, "you let your lust for riches consume you—you betrayed your love."

"Like hell!" Eben snorted. He didn't owe Don Felipe any explanations, did he? Or did he? The kid loved her too. Yet he had had respect for Annabeth's loyalty to him.

Taken all in all, Don Felipe wasn't such a bad feller, Eben figured. He had all the makings of a damn good man; the kid had done a lot of growing up that very day. He had a right, Eben supposed, to know the whole story. How he and Annabeth had parted in anger. How he'd left her—not so much to make his fortune as to give them both time to simmer down. How he had been bush-whacked and left for dead. For a time he'd not even known his own name until a subsequent blow on the head had restored his memory.

"Dios!" Don Felipe marvelled. He'd heard of

cases of amnesia but had never met anyone who'd
actually suffered from the complaint. "Then that
accounts for the scar on your forehead and also
for the fact that your friend sometimes refers to
you as 'Cal'." he said thoughtfully.

"That's right," Eben confirmed.

"And the headaches?" Do you still suffer from
them?"

"Not since I come back to my right senses."

Felipe thought it over.

"I see that you love her as she deserves to be
loved," he said with a sigh. "She will be safe with
you. If I thought she would not be, I would kill you
myself," he said frankly.

"You could try," Eben said dryly. "I take a
heap of killing!"

The young Californio glanced at him
quizzically. "First things, first, eh? First we must
get her back." And both of them, with one accord,
looked out towards the trail ahead where they
supposed Annabeth to be.

But she was not. Captain Morgan, a more
perspicacious man by far than the blackbearded
leader of the Sydney ducks, had sent his own men
scattering far and wide. "We'll meet in
Hangtown," he yelled, for he knew that some of
them might come in handy to do his dirty work.

Annabeth was relieved to see the other men
scatter. She was afraid to be alone with her captor
but on the other hand, she was even more afraid of
his henchmen, half-drunken as most of them were.
The gambler, for he was forever pigeonholed in
her mind as such, was at least cold sober.

By the time they made camp that night she
was so exhausted that she was almost beyond
caring about anything. Months of soft living at

Rancho del Corazon had not prepared her for this cross-country jaunt. Every muscle in her body was screaming for relief and her thighs and legs were chafed almost raw by the saddle leather.

When at last they halted by a little stream that wound its way along an upward-sloping rocky path strewn with boulders and scrub brush, she felt a kind of numb relief. She was so stiff and sore that when she attempted to dismount she almost fell out of the saddle, but when Morgan reached for her to help her down she flinched away from him.

His white even teeth flashed in a grin. "So you don't want me touching you, eh, little lady? Well, you might as well start getting used to it right now because I'm going to touch you plenty before I'm through with you!"

"I'd rather die than have you touch me!" she retorted, scrambling out of the saddle as best she could. Her descent was awkward and ungraceful but at least she made it under her own steam.

He shrugged. "Have it your own way. For now!"

Annabeth ignored him. She hobbled over to the thin stream of water and sinking down beside it drank thirstily. Her mouth and throat were so parched she found it difficult to swallow. At intervals during their wild ride he had offered her a sip from his canteen but she had proudly refused it. Which had been unwise if she meant to survive, she now realized.

Her captor drank and allowed the horses to have their fill.

"That's enough. They'll founder!" she said sharply, dragging her horse's head up. The horses were foam-flicked, their sides heaving; they had been ridden hard and this was the first stream they had come across in many hours.

"You know about horses, do you?" he said approvingly. "I knew you'd bring me luck, Lady Luck!"

"I simply don't relish the prospect of being afoot in this country. Nor should you!" she said tartly.

"I'm no westerner, I admit," he drawled. He unsaddled both mounts and pulled some jerky and cold tortillas from a saddlebag. "Hungry?" He broke the tortillas in half and gave her a share.

She stared at him disdainfully. She felt like throwing the food back in his face but such a display of temper, while richly gratifying, would be ultimately self-defeating, she knew. She hesitated, staring at him with hatred.

"It's not Delmonico's but it's all there is," he said gruffly. "Go ahead and eat. You need to keep up your strength."

Now where had she heard that before? Annabeth thought ironically. But she took the food he offered and began to nibble it halfheartedly. It might be hackneyed advice but that didn't make it any less true.

"I come from the East myself," she said conversationally, nibbling at the unappetizing food. "York State." There wasn't, she felt, much use in preserving a sulky silence. In fact, she had a nervous compulsion to talk, to strike up a conversation with what-was-his-name? Morgan? Ah, yes, Jared Morgan. Maybe she could establish some kind of rapport with him, she thought hopefully. He was far from being a stupid or uneducated man, she guessed. In conversation people usually revealed themselves and Jared Morgan might possibly let something slip that would give her a clue as to how to deal with him. And if he thought her a babbling bird-witted female, well, so much the better.

"I've heard of Delmonico's but I've never been there," she ventured. "It's a very exclusive restaurant, isn't it?"

"Very," he said dryly.

Annabeth sighed and took another bite of cold tortilla. She wasn't making much headway.

"I was a farm girl," she tried again. "Before I came west to . . . to be a missionary."

He stared at her for a minute. "A missionary!" he exclaimed. "You! A missionary!" He threw back his head and roared with laughter.

It was the first spontaneous emotion she had seen him exhibit and it startled her. She hadn't known quite what she expected when she'd thrown out this bit of information. To win his respect, perhaps? Certainly not laughter!

"I don't see what's so funny!" she said stiffly.

"It's rich!" he chortled. "The missionary lady and the preacher's kid! Oh, well met, Lady Luck! Somebody up there must be laughing too!"

"You . . . your father was a minister of the gospel?" she said doubtfully. Then a spark of hope began to flicker in her breast. Maybe . . . just maybe he wasn't all bad! Maybe there was still a spark of decency left in him. Maybe there was a chance . . .

He sobered suddenly, his bright blue eyes narrowing. "Don't get your hopes up, little lady," he said as if he could read her mind. "The family is never going to kill the fatted calf for this prodigal son. My father and my equally pious brother who followed him into the ministry disowned me a long time ago. After they wangled a commission for me in the New York regiment in the pious hope that I'd be killed in action, no doubt! My taste for low living was a disgrace to the family name, I'm told!"

"Oh," said Annabeth in a small voice.

"Oh!" he mocked her savagely. "Oh, yes, it's true. My respected papa found my penchant for gambling dens and houses of ill-repute too much to stomach. A son of the manse should be above reproach." His lips twisted into a reminiscent grin. "I suppose it *was* embarrassing for highly respected pillars of the church to be caught with their pants down by their pastor's son at Miss Lulubelle's or Madame Francine's exclusive establishments!"

He gave her an assessing look. "You're no raving beauty but you've got something," he muttered, half to himself. "In the right clothes, with a bit of powder and lip rouge, you'll have their eyes popping out," he said approvingly.

Annabeth recoiled. "You . . . you're not going to put me in a . . . a—?"

"Brothel?" He scowled. "You can set your mind at rest. I've done a lot of things but I'm no whoremaster. Besides, I have plans of my own for you, little Red."

"W-what plans?"

"There's easier ways to make a fortune than by standing up to your knees in icy water day in and day out," he said thoughtfully. "I aim to open a gambling house. Oh, nothing fancy at first. Just a shack in Hangtown. But it'll lead to bigger and better things. And you, little Red, will be my drawing card. A pretty girl—an American girl—is worth her weight in gold in the camps, I'm told. The poor fools who busted their butts all week to pan a few ounces of gold will flock to my establishment—just to get a glimpse of Lady Luck!'' He slapped his knee. ''By God, that's what I'll call it, The Lady Luck. Of which you, my dear, will be the personification. With you to pour drinks and deal faro, I'll make a killing. I'll clean up every last speck of gold in town.''

''But I don't know one card from another!'' Annabeth protested.

''I don't suppose you do,'' he mused. ''But you'll learn.'' He stuffed the last piece of tortilla into his mouth and delved into a pocket. Pulling out a deck of cards, he riffled them dexterously, cut the deck, and deftly fanned a portion out on the ground.

Annabeth blinked in amazement. They were all in one suit and all in sequence.

''I didn't learn that trick in the rectory, my dear. I learned; you'll learn. And I don't expect you to turn into a sharper. Your primary function will be to serve as a distraction while I—''

''Lighten their pockets,'' Annabeth suggested.

''I knew you were a fast learner,'' he said approvingly.

''And you . . . you won't expect me to . . . to—''

''Sleep with them?'' His tone held a hint of amusement. ''Only with one man, my dear, only with one.''

It was painfully plain to Annabeth who that one man would be! ''I'll sleep alone!'' she said defiantly.

''We'll see about that.'' He spoke quite pleasantly but his tone was inflexible as he got up and came toward her.

She jumped to her feet. ''No!'' she shrilled, looking around her wildly. She knew it was useless to run but assailed with a sudden desperation, she found herself speeding over the hard uneven ground, scrambling over rocks and boulders, scraping her hands and arms and ripping her skirts. She stumbled past a large boulder and came out into a wide open space where she paused momentarily, looking around her wildly, uncertain which way to turn and dismayed by the rapidly falling darkness.

He caught up with her then, his hand fastening on her shoulder as he spun her around to face him. "Where do you think you're going, you little fool? There's no hope for you out here—nothing but wild country full of wolves and bears and coyotes."

"You're a . . . a coyote yourself!" she flung at him. "Let me go!" She twisted and squirmed, trying to break his hold on her. Curling her fingers into talons she tried unsuccessfully to claw at his eyes. "Let . . . me . . . go!"

He caught at her wrists and pinioned her arms to her sides. "If I'm a coyote, you're a little wildcat!" he panted. "A little wildcat that needs taming! And I'm just the man to do it." Thrusting his knee between her legs, he threw her off balance and bore her to the ground.

"No . . . please!" Annabeth wailed, struggling to throw him off. She tried to squirm out from under him but his long legs straddled her and all of her twisting and turning only served to ignite his passion. He held her securely, his weight pressing her into the ground, one hand twisting in her tangled hair. The other worked at his clothing, loosening it.

She whimpered as his knee ruthlessly parted her thighs. "No . . . please don't. Please . . . you're hurting me," she moaned as he mounted her.

"You need to be taught who's master, woman," he grated. "Once you've learned that lesson, it'll be pleasanter for both of us, I promise you."

It was not an act of love; it was an act meant solely to demonstrate mastery and possession. There was nothing Annabeth could do in the end but submit, gritting her teeth and digging her nails into the ground and enduring it as best she could. Mercifully it was over quickly for the man's passions had been inflamed by her struggles. He emptied himself into her quickly and rolled away.

Immediately afterwards, he stood up and adjusted his clothing. "You can see there is no use in defying me, my dear," he said quite coolly. "Submit willingly and I assure you I am quite skillful enough to give you the most exquisite sensations. Defy me, as you did tonight and you will only bring quite unnecessary discomfort and even pain upon yourself." He shrugged. "It's your own choice. But either way, I *will* have my way with you. I trust you understand that now."

Annabeth lay in a state of shock, slow tears seeping beneath her lids. How what should be an act of love could be perpetrated in such a loveless—almost passionless—fashion was beyond her. She would hardly have believed it if she hadn't just experienced it. Jared Morgan was the cruelest, most ruthless, and coldest man she had ever ran across and, as he had so rightly pointed out, she was at his mercy. How would she endure it? She drew a long shuddering breath. She would endure it, endure his loveless caresses, because she must, until, somehow, with God's help, she could find a way to escape. He might possess her body, because she could not help that, but she would never let him touch her innermost soul, she vowed. And, somehow, she *would* survive.

Eben and Shorty picked up the trail easily enough the next morning for the Sydney ducks, seamen and kanakas were not frontiersmen and left a trail so easy to read that, as Eben said, "a child could follow it." They were riding fast and hard, evidently putting their faith in their ability to outdistance pursuit and heading always for the foothills of the Sierras. Their obvious destination troubled Eben for he knew that if they made it into the mountains, they might easily lose themselves in any number of wild mountain valleys.

So, he was particularly gratified when his quarry blundered into what he knew to be a box canyon. "We've got 'em now, Felipe," he said with satisfaction. "We'll string your men out along the mouth of canyon, close it off, and station a few of 'em up on the heights. They're gonna find that they've ridden into a trap."

"And the women?"

Eben frowned. It was one aspect of his plan that worried him. He didn't want any of the women mixed up in a shoot-out—least of all, Annabeth. He toyed with the notion of waiting until the desperadoes made camp for the night, then sneaking in among them to see if he could locate the women. It *might* work. He was as stealthy and light-footed as any Indian. He was reasonably sure that he could sneak in and out of camp undetected.

But to get the women out, that was another matter altogether. To sneak a passel of abused and hysterical females past the guards that were sure to be posted was not to be thought of. Regretfully, he abandoned the idea almost as soon as it crossed his mind.

Besides—his face hardened—more than likely

the women would be kept busy pleasuring the men most of the night. No, something had to be done—and fast. He didn't cotton to the idea of Annabeth spending even one more night in captivity. What was more, long before darkness fell, the renegades might discover that they had blundered into a trap. He would be a fool to let them spring it. It was a big country out here and a wild one. If one or two individuals made away with the women, there was no telling how long it might take to track them down.

He shrugged. "I can't think of any other way. We got one big advantage—surprise. They don't know how close behind we are. Way I see it, the men stationed on the canyon walls can open up on 'em first. Create a diversion. Then Shorty an' me will ride in with guns blazin'. If we're lucky, we can round up the women and make a quick get-away. You and your men stationed at the canyon mouth can open up the lines to let us through and then close them up again to cut off pursuit."

"I don't like it," said Felipe flatly.

"You got a better plan?"

"Only that there will be three of us riding in with, as you say, guns blazing. You, Shorty, and myself."

Nothing that Eben could say would dissuade him. "It is my right," Felipe insisted. "These are my people—the women, and their families before them, have served the del Corazons for generations. What is more," the younger man's face grew taut and hard, "Ana, though she belongs to you, Yanqui, is one that my heart loves."

Eben's shoulders rose and fell. "A man's gotta do what he's gotta do, I reckon." He frowned. "But yore poorly armed, compared to me and Shorty. I'll lend you one of my Colts. That way we'll each have six shots apiece."

Their plan worked better than Eben dared to hope. The motley mob of renegades were used to easy pickings—to preying on the weak and defenseless. They were utterly demoralized by the bullets raining down on them from the heights and were kept too busy trying to defend themselves and escape with whole skins to offer any organized resistance. It was every man for himself.

The women captives, some half dozen in all, were huddled together in a deep crevice within the canyon walls, well out of the range of flying bullets, and Shorty and Don Felipe, working as a team, moved in to intercept them and detach them from their captors, much as a skillful cowboy or vaquero will cut dogies out of a herd.

But, much to Don Felipe's disappointment, Annabeth's slender figure and flame-red head were not to be seen.

Eben found himself caught up in a wild melee of flailing hooves and fleeing men, desperate to escape the hail of bullets. He fought his way through and caught a glimpse of Felipe, who was catching up stray horses and mounting the screaming, half-hysterical women while Shorty guarded his back, his six-shooters spitting fire.

Eben saw a huge half-naked kanaka in the act of hurling a long spear-like weapon at Felipe and squeezed off a shot. The kanaka went down under the impact of Eben's bullet and Felipe, alerted to danger, tossed the last of the women up on a horse, sprang into the saddle himself, and rode down a second man who was threatening him with a similar weapon.

"Any sign of Annabeth?" Eben yelled, as Felipe and his entourage swept past, Shorty acting as rear guard.

"Nada." The younger man glanced back over his shoulder at Eben, his face filled with despair.

Where the *hell* was Annabeth? Eben wondered, near to despair himself. He made a wide circuit of the area, fighting his way through a mob of ruffians who were making for the canyon mouth and freedom, until he had assured himself that Annabeth was not to be found.

Had she died? he wondered. Or been killed somewhere back along the trail? But, in that case, he would have come upon her body. They wouldn't have bothered with any niceties of burial. Not this bunch.

He snapped off a shot at an unhorsed ruffian who was doing his damndest to hamstring his horse with a wicked-looking seaman's knife. It was his last bullet and Eben knew he'd better get out of there fast before the desperadoes encircled him and brought him down. He holstered his Colt revolver, which was now useless, and drew his rifle out of its sheath. It was less wieldy in close quarters than the revolver but it was still loaded. He'd save that shot until he really needed it, he decided, clubbing down a man on foot who caught at his stirrup and tried to drag him out of his saddle. His rifle reversed, using it as a club, he fought his way to the canyon mouth where the line of vaqueros stationed there parted to let him through.

The little cavalcade comprised of the women captives, Shorty Gillespie, who was nursing a blood-soaked arm, and Don Felipe, drew rein in a sheltered spot, well out of the range of flying bullets. Vaqueros whose wives or sweethearts were among their number broke ranks at the canyon mouth where they'd been stationed or came scrambling down from the heights above for a joyous, though tear-filled, reunion with their dear ones.

Eben joined them, hoping against hope that one or another of the women could give him news of Annabeth. But he was met with blank stares and shaking heads. No one knew of the whereabouts of Dona Ana.

Don Felipe was hunkered down by the side of a young woman who was stretched out on the ground, half supported by his arm. It was Esperanza, one of the housemaids.

"She has been injured." Don Felipe glanced around, to catch the eye of anyone who could give him assistance. "Summon Julio—quickly!" he said urgently. "He is her novio. Her betrothed. He should be here."

A young vaquero came running up and knelt down beside the girl whose face was paper-white. "Esperanza!" he pleaded. 'It is I, Julio. Speak to me, querida."

The girl's long-lashed eyes fluttered open. "Julio," she whispered, clutching at him with frantic fingers.

"Esperanza, hear me." Don Felipe spoke with urgency. "Do you know what happened to Dona Ana?"

Eben, who had taken time to assure himself that Shorty's wound was merely superficial, now joined the little group. Retaining his rifle, he slid down off his horse and squatted beside Felipe. "Please, senorita," he said urgently. "You must tell me. It is very important. Where is Annabeth?"

The girl's vague eyes made an effort to focus. "I . . . I was caught in the house. I had taken refuge in the wine cellar. Those men found me and dragged me upstairs. Dona Maria and . . . and

Dona Ana were in the Sala. The men . . . the leaders . . . they gambled for her, I think. The bearded man and another. He . . . he took her and—''

A rifle barked at close hand. Esperanza gasped and slumped forward, a bloody froth appearing on her lips.

"Madre de Dios!" exclaimed Felipe. "She's been shot!" The hand with which he had been supporting Esperanza's back came away sticky with blood.

Eben whirled, his rifle at the ready. His slug caught Sid's horse squarely in the chest. The blackbearded ruffian, bent on revenge for the debacle and rout of his men, had fought his way through the line of vaqueros and snapped off a shot, aimed at Eben, while everyone's attention was focused on the girl.

The injured animal gave a single spine-chilling scream as it went to it knees, Sid tumbling over its head.

By the time he had scrambled to his feet, Eben had finished reloading.

"Don't let him get away," urged Don Felipe who had relinquished his sad burden to the care of her fiance.

"He ain't goin' nowhere," said Eben grimly. He took careful aim, catching Sid in the kneecap. The big man collapsed on the ground, squealing like a stuck pig.

Together, Eben and Felipe went to where the Sydney duck lay moaning and clutching his shattered kneecap.

"Where's Annabeth?" Eben demanded coldly. "The red-headed woman?"

The big desperado drew back his lips from his teeth in a feral grin. "Dunno," he grunted.

"You know." Eben's voice was ice-cold. "And you'll talk." He drew the Bowie knife from his belt. "You'll talk."

Sid talked. It didn't take much, after all, to convince him that, when necessary, this steely-eyed man clad in faded buckskins could be quite as ruthless as himself. "The gold camps," he squealed. "One of the gold camps. He was gonna build him a gambling house in one of the camps."

"Which one?" The blade of Eben's knife dripped red.

"Hangtown, maybe. Yeah, I think it was Hangtown." His eyes swivelled to the sharp-pointed blade. "You . . . you gonna kill me now?"

"No!" The voice was Felipe's. His well-shaped lips had twisted into a smile—or rather the grotesque parody of one. "The Americano is not going to kill you, you scum," he said coolly. "I am." His smile grew broader, though it did not reach his eyes. "When I judge that you have suffered sufficiently, that is." He turned to Eben. "And when the worthless life of this pig has ended and I have seen my people safely home, I will join you in the search of Dona Ana, mi amigo," he promised. "We will scour this . . . this Hangtown." Don Felipe's aristocratic face twisted in distaste, "and all the camps of the gold-hungry gringos, if need be, until we find her!"

24

"I won't wear it!" Annabeth protested. "It's not decent! You can just take it back where it came from," she insisted, with a toss of her red head.

Jared Morgan grinned. He didn't mind the little redhead letting off a bit of steam every now and then. It showed she had spunk and added spice to their relationship. He didn't want to break her spirit. Women and horses should show a trace of spirit, he considered, as long as they were, in general, obedient to the hand that guided the rein, to the whip and spur.

He could wish, however, that the redhead would show more of that spirit in bed. Oh, she was compliant enough, she hadn't put up any real resistance since that first night. But she was indifferent to his most skillful caresses, making it plain that she found them repellent—something to be endured rather than enjoyed—and he sensed that her real self was very far away, that she was projecting her mind and her emotions elsewhere, even as he, frustrated beyond endurance by her lack of response, spread her thighs and rammed himself into her passive but essentially unwilling body. On occasion that very passivity had provoked him almost to violence.

But Jared Morgan was a man who prided himself on his self-control and he was both arrogant and self-confident enough to be convinced that his amorous skills would one day break through her wall of passive resistance and awaken the passionate self that she kept hidden from him. He didn't know the cause of her seeming frigidity; she never talked about her past. He finally put it down to her background as a mssionary. She probably believed all that guff the preachers talked about sex being sinful, he figured. Lord knew, he'd had enough of that from his own pa. With him it hadn't taken. But she had probably fallen for it, hook, line and sinker.

Well, she would come round. No woman had ever been able to resist him yet. He grinned, thinking reminiscently of past amours. His sexual adventures had not been limited to whores—by no means! One of the society ladies who attended his father's church had seduced him when he was only fifteen but from then on he had done the seducing. His mind roamed over the past in pleasurable reminiscence. There had been his prissy sister's school chum, Jenny Fairfax. Pretty Jenny hadn't been the least bit prissy, having yielded up her virginity to him in an unchaperoned buggy ride one summer afternoon. Their mutual enthusiasm had damn near made a wreck of that buggy, he chuckled.

And then there had been the winsome blonde daughter of a visiting clergyman. The last night of their visit, he had sneaked into her bedroom, knowing full well she just might scream the house down. But she had welcomed him into her bed with even more enthusiasm than Jenny had displayed.

On the whole though, he preferred older women, like the wife of the stiff-necked deacon of his father's church. His preference was for full-breasted women and generally the more mature were better endowed. And in many cases, they were pathetically grateful for the attentions of a virile young man who could pleasure them in bed in ways that their husbands either couldn't or wouldn't. The frustrated deaconess had once confided to him that her husband customarily prayed nightly to overcome his natural urges.

Jared grinned. The old coot might better have prayed for the staying power to satisfy the natural urges of his hot-blooded wife. The lady had, on occasion, taxed even his own youthful powers to the utmost!

His pleasurable reminiscences stirred his senses and he felt a tingling sensation in his groin.

"I won't wear it!" Annabeth said mulishly, bundling up the gown and handing it back to him.

"It's the color, isn't it?" he said cheerfully, stringing her along. "That old taradiddle that redheads mustn't wear pink." He shook it out and held it up against her slender frame. "You think it clashes with your hair, don't you? But I assure you, it doesn't. It's quite becoming." He felt a tightening in his groin, just from visualizing Annabeth clad in the rich pink gown with the puffed sleeves and the low-cut . . . very low-cut bodice. The decolletage would reveal pale soft mounds bisected by deep cleavage.

God! He wasn't just tightening and tingling anymore—he was rock-hard and ready!

She flounced away from him. "You know it isn't the color!" she flared. "It . . . it could be fire-engine red for all I care. It's the cut. It simply isn't decent!"

"Try it on!" His voice was harsh.

"No!"

He thrust the gown at her. "Try it on or so help me, I'll strip you and ram you into it myself."

Her chin quivering, she obeyed him wordlessly, knowing that he was more than capable of carrying out his threat. She whipped off her clothing and pulled the pink gown over her head and down her body so fast that he had barely a glimpse of pale ivory flesh, firmly pointed breasts, a narrow tapering waist, firm thighs and slender shapely legs.

"There! Are you satisfied?" she snapped, twitching the folds of the skirt down around her hips and legs.

"Satisfied?" The man's thin lips twisted into a crooked smile. "That depends on what you call satisfaction. It is, I suppose, a matter of degree." His hand reached out to trace the curve of her breast so temptingly outlined by the thin clinging material of the gown. Two firm mounds of luscious flesh swelled out of the provocative bodice, causing the man's eyes to darken with desire. He twitched at the shoulders of the gown to lower it further still and, bending his blond head, flicked his tongue out to moistly trace the cleft between her breasts.

Annabeth stiffened.

Sensing the resistance of her slight body, he growled deep in his throat, an impatient warning that he would not brook defiance. She had learned the lesson, that resistance was folly, too well to deny him now. Heeding his imperious command, she willed herself to relax, sending her mind ranging far and wide in an effort to dissociate mind and emotions from the purely physical sensations his love play inevitably evoked within her. It was, she told herself, no more than a purely physiological response to a given stimulus—just as a sprinkling of pepper up one's nose would make one sneeze, so the caresses of this not unattractive man evoked an instinctual response. There was no more to it than that. But even though her traitorous body might actually respond to Jared's skilled caresses, she had discovered that she could wander at will in the secret places of her own mind where he could not follow.

Impatiently, he slid his fingers into the bodice of her gown and lifted her breasts free, lowering his open mouth to the pink rosebud tips.

Annabeth viewed his bent head dispassionately. She had succeeded in divorcing herself from her surroundings by an act of will. Nothing he did to her could *really* touch her, her own innermost self, she assured herself. From what seemed a very great distance away she viewed his antics as a detached observer might.

Spreading his legs wide, he drew her between them. She could feel him hard against her, as rising passion gripped him, and maintained her own aloofness from the animal act she knew, with resignation, that would follow.

A hand slid under her skirt, stroking her bare hip and parting her thighs.

She trembled under the sensual assault of his probing fingers and, judging that she was ready to receive him, he carried her to the bed. Drawing the gown over her head, he renewed his assault on her senses, brushing his hands and lips over her body. She lay passive underneath his ministrations, forcing herself to relax, taking deep breaths to help herself relax and accommodate him. Was this

SAVAGE SPLENDOR

what whores did? she wondered, in order to accommodate men who were repugnant to them?

Skilled lover though Jared was, his caresses never touched the core of her inner being, as had Eben's. Jared, she decided, lacked Eben's essential tenderness—that caring and concern that he expressed through lovemaking. To Jared, the act of love was like a game of cards. It was a contest in which he had to come out the winner. Annabeth had learned that letting him win—that is, simulating a pleasure she did not feel, was the quickest way to achieve relief from his demands.

So now, as Jared's skillful fingers teased and probed, she squirmed and writhed beneath him, moaning, in an attempt to deceive him. With all the expertise of a man well-acquainted with women's bodies he worked his will on her, tantalizing her with his fingers even as he entered her.

She caught her breath with a gasp, stiffening momentarily, then willed herself to relax, to respond to his movements with movements of her own which would, hopefully, be indicative of pleasure.

Jared, who had set himself the goal of achieving a wild uninhibited response from her, knew perfectly well that there was something terribly lacking. He willed himself to break through her passive resistance, to turn the imitation of passion and pleasure into reality, but failed. His own climax came too quickly, spurred on by the tempo of her movements.

When he withdrew from her, she lay still, supine, limp with relief, slow tears seeping beneath her closed lids. Oh, Eben, she thought woefully, as she did every time Jared took her, forgive me. Forgive me! Was it really a betrayal of him? she wondered, since every time Jared took her she longed for it to be Eben.

Jared got up from the bed and dressed in silence. Occasionally he looked down at her, a baffled expression in his eyes. "Oh, stop that snivelling," he said irritably. "God! If there's anything I can't abide it's a snivelling woman!"

Annabeth listlessly wiped her eyes with the hem of the sheet she had pulled over herself.

His hand on the door, he paused before going downstairs. "Oh, Annabeth, be sure to wear that dress tonight," he said in a tone of authority.

She nodded.

Downstairs was the gambling hall Jared's cronies had erected for him. It was crude but functional. Annabeth, who had visions of a mahogany bar and walls lined with pictures of nude women in suggestive poses dancing in her head, as surprised by its starkness and severity. The Lady Luck wasn't much more than a simple barnlike structure with rough-cut board walls.

Jared was amused. "This is Hangtown, my dear, not Frisco," he'd said dryly. "We're fortunate not to be starting out in a shanty or a tent like some of the others. This is only a temporary structure for a temporary situation. When the fall rains come, we'll go to Frisco and set up a really palatial establishment in the city."

Hangtown, which had started life as "Dry Diggings" and was renamed "Placerville" for the rich placer deposits discovered in the vicinity, had since acquired a new and more ominous name for obvious reasons. Its rough and ready brand of frontier justice dealt swiftly with claim-jumpers, horse thieves, and the like. Annabeth had found herself wondering more than once if Jared might not find himself swinging from a noose one fine day. But he ran an honest game, he assured her. He had no need to cheat; you didn't when you were "the house" and you were as good a dealer as he was.

While the Lucky Lady was under construction Jared had given Annabeth a crash course on cards. He was elated to discover that she had fair card sense herself, that she was bright and quick to learn the rules of the various games and that she had an amazing ability to concentrate and remember which cards had been played.

"It comes of having to memorize the texts of Sunday sermons," she told him dryly when he complimented her upon it.

A blond eyebrow quirked. "Is that so?" he drawled. "My revered papa would have a fit of apoplexy if he thought those interminable Biblical texts and sermons that he set me to memorizing as a boy had anything to do with my subsequent success as a gambler!" He barked a laugh, then went on enthusiastically, "I tell you, Annabeth, you and I were made for each other. There's a pile of gold floating around just waiting to be picked up on the turn of a card. Between us, you and I can clean up here in Hangtown and then head out for Frisco. We'll build us the finest and the fanciest gambling house in the city. Why, I might even make an honest woman of you!" he said with the air of one conferring a great favor.

Annabeth blinked. It would hardly make an honest woman of her to become a bigamist! But then Jared did not know that she was married already. If, indeed, Eben was still alive. She had hoped that somehow, in Hangtown, she might get word of him. But her first sight of the gold camp had convinced her that hope was a vain one. It was teeming with miners of all sorts from all over the world. She had lived an isolated life for so long, first among the Indians, then on the trail and at Rancho del Corazon, that she was overwhelmed by the teeming masses of men swarming about. Finding Eben among such a throng would be like looking for a needle in a haystack.

It also speedily disillusioned her of the hope she had been nurturing regarding Jared Morgan—that she could find a way to extricate herself from his clutches. Her reception in Hangtown convinced her that she would need the protection of some strong man and Jared Morgan was probably as good as any and maybe even better than most. From the way the men had stared and swarmed around her as she rode in she decided that an American woman in a gold camp must be as great an oddity as any of Mr. P.T. Barnum's freaks and infinitely more precious! "Don't crowd us, boys," Jared had called affably, maneuvering his horse close to Annabeth's. "We'll be in town a while and you'll all get your chance to see and even talk to the little lady at the Lady Luck Saloon and gambling house."

She'd dreaded making her first appearance in the establishment—the thought of being gawked at and pawed by a horde of lecherous men revolted her. But it wasn't quite as bad as she had feared—perhaps nothing could be! She learned to turn a deaf ear to the bawdy remarks and propositions she received and, being quick-witted, she rapidly acquired the knack of fending them off with a humorous quip. What was more, she soon discovered that many of the men were not so much lecherous as just plain lonesome. They would line up at the bar for the chance of having a word with her, pouring out their gold dust as if it had no more value than specks of ordinary dirt.

Jared was delighted. Nothing could have pleased him more. But Annabeth's conscience—which had grown considerably more elastic with the passing of time—smote her. It was true that many of these men were scoundrels but a goodly proportion were honest hard-working miners starved for a woman's company and companionship. To pour drinks for them at a dollar a shot was leading them down the road to ruin—sending them reeling from the straight and narrow down the path to perdition!

But she didn't have any choice in the matter, did she? Any more than she had a choice about sharing Jared Morgan's bed. Or even a choice about the gown she was to wear tonight. She sighed. Good Lord, when she leaned over the bar to pour drinks her . . . she . . . would fall right out the front! She could only hope that Jared would have her relieve him at the faro table fairly early on before the men got too randy or the evening too rowdy.

He did. Annabeth was not as practiced or as skillful at dealing the cards as he nor as quick to figure the odds but she had assets he did not possess. Two of them! Jared chuckled to himself. A man bemused by Annabeth's breasts was not likely to pay strict attention to the cards he held in his hand. He'd be thinking of getting his hands on something else—something soft and warm and shapely. Soft white mounds of flesh that spilled invitingly out of the bodice of her gown. Jared himself had arranged that bodice so that the folds of material barely covered her nipples. A man would be kept so busy wondering how much more she was going to show—if the material would slip further down with every breath she drew—that he would hardly be able to tell an ace from a deuce! Which was exactly the effect Jared wanted. With such a tempting display of female pulchritude before his eyes, a man would linger at the faro table till he'd lost his last speck of dust. Hell, one look down that daring decolletage and a man would be willing to stake his whole poke, not knowing or even *caring* that he was getting fleeced. Such innocence and honesty shone out of those velvety eyes of hers that the possibility of getting fleeced wouldn't even cross his mind.

Jared kept a proprietary eye on the faro table and, as the evening wore on, he nodded with satisfaction. Everything was going according to plan. A pity Annabeth didn't have more of a come-hitherish air about her, he reflected, but that wasn't her style. You couldn't have everything. And by the time he was ready to make his move to Frisco she'd have found her feet, acquired a little more poise and self-assurance. What the hell, that air of artless innocence she wore was more appealing to some men than any amount of sophisticated allure. Why, a couple of men had even offered him an ounce of gold apiece simply for the privilege of sitting down at a table to chat with her for a few minutes.

The doors swung wide and a tall man, wearing well-worn moccasins and buckskins, walked in. Jared nodded to the bouncer, one of his New York contingent, who moved to intercept the Indian, saying, "We don't serve no Indians here."

"I'm not an Injun," Eben said wearily. He wanted no trouble here. He'd scoured nearly ever saloon and gambling house and tent in town—of which there were a considerable number—and was tired and dispirited. "I don't even want a drink. I'm just lookin' for someone."

The bouncer looked confused. The big man in buckskins didn't look like a miner. Where was the regulation garb of red flannel shirt, work pants and heavy waterproof boots? The bouncer decided that any man who dressed like an Injun, looked like an Injun, with dark face, high cheekbones and long hair black as a raven's wing, *was*, by God, an Injun!

He barred Eben's way. "No Injuns!" he said truculently. "Rules of the house. No chinks or niggers, either!"

Jared noticed the little confrontation and went over to where the men were standing, slipping a hand into his jacket to rest on his concealed weapon. It had come in handy more than once. "Trouble, Leroy?" he said casually.

Annabeth hadn't noticed. She was concentrating on her cards and wondering at the same time how she might discreetly pull up the front of her gown which was threatening to slip down with every move she made. "Place your bets, gentlemen, place your bets," she sang out.

Eben froze. Then slowly, slowly, he turned towards the faro table, like a man in a dream. What he saw stunned him. My God, he thought, this half-naked hussy with the painted face and reddened lips couldn't be his Annabeth! And yet . . .

Annabeth glanced up from her cards and, across the crowded room, their eyes met. The color drained from her face and her hand of cards went spilling onto the table faceup. Her mouth moved but no sound came out. Then, "Eben!" she gasped. "Eben!"

25

A hush fell over the room. The faro players stared in amazement at their lady dealer from whose white face all the blood had drained away. One of them, a callow young man who had been quietly mooning over Annabeth, cleared his throat and said nervously, "Ma'am? You been taken sick, ma'am?"

Annabeth didn't answer. She was so white and still she might have been a statue carved in marble—like one of the statues of old Pharaoh for whom the game had been named.

Jared Morgan stepped into the breach. His bright blue eyes flicking between Eben and Annabeth, he said smoothly, "Apparently you two are acquainted."

"You might say that," Eben allowed.

Jared shrugged. "Indian or not, your gold is as good as any man's," he said handsomely. "If you want to renew your acquaintance an ounce of gold will buy you a few minutes of the little lady's time."

Eben's eyes, so deep a blue that they were almost black, flickered.

"Twenty ounces of gold and she's yours for the evening." Lest the man be under any misapprehension, he hastily qualified his statement. "That's the going rate for an evening of conversation with Lady Luck. Of course, if you want a more 'personal conversation' to be conducted in privacy upstairs, it might be arranged. For a consideration. A hundred ounces of gold, shall we say?"

A ripple of voices ran around the room. Jared Morgan grinned. He had quickly summed up the stranger in the well-worn buckskins as a penniless drifter and he had no idea that his bluff would be called.

Eben stared at him coldly, taking his measure. "I'm not about to fork out a hundred ounces of gold for the pleaure of taking *my wife* upstairs!" he drawled.

"Wife!" Jared exclaimed.

Eben nodded. His hand casually brushed back his buckskin jacket to reveal the twin revolvers holstered on each hip.

The gambler quickly revised his opinion of the stranger. He had knocked around enough to know a dangerous man when he saw on. His visions of making a killing in Hangtown and then moving on with Annabeth to the city and the big time faded. "Then take her and get out!" he snarled. He jerked his chin towards Annabeth who was still standing in stupefaction at the faro table. "Go!"

"Just . . . like that—?" she whispered. She couldn't believe it. Jared Morgan was a man who liked to win. He played to win. He also had a strong sense of property and she knew that he regarded her as his possession. She just couldn't believe that he would let her go so easily or give up without a fight.

"Go on. Get out of here!" he snarled.

Annabeth didn't need a second invitation. She

slid from behind the faro table and Jared took her place. Picking up the cards she had scattered over the green cloth, he shuffled them, cut the deck and placed them in the dealing box with the top card exposed. "Sorry about the delay, gentlemen," he apologized. "Place your bets, please," he intoned. "Place your bets."

Annabeth walked slowly towards Eben, wending her way between the small tables scattered about the room. She wanted to run into his arms but she felt awkward, uncertain of her welcome. So much time had passed, so much had happened since they last parted in anger nearly a year ago.

She felt the eyes of every man in the place burning into her. The eyes of the faro players, of the men lined up at the bar or sitting at the tables, eyes blue, green, black or brown followed her progress from the room, eyes that were filled with lechery or lust or lonesomeness, or just plain curiosity.

She was even more painfully aware of Jared's eyes burning into her back with cold blue fire and, as she reached Eben who stepped aside to let her precede him, she turned for one last look back at the man who had held her body captive, though never her heart. A catlike smile was playing about his thin lips and, even as she turned, she saw his hand slip within his frock coat and knew only too well what the movement presaged.

"Eben, he's got a gun!" she cried. "A derringer!"

Jared Morgan was fast but Eben was faster. His six-gun spat fire and the gambler, derringer in hand, crumpled over onto the faro table. The spreading splotch of scarlet that decorated the front of his frilled linen shirt reminded her of a scarlet flower bursting into bloom. His hand opened and the deadly little derringer landed on the pine plank floor with a dull thud. The gambler's luck had run out!

A babble of voices sounded. "The Injun's killed Morgan," somebody shouted. Leroy, the bouncer, yelled, "Let's string him up boys!" Somebody suggested, "Let's all rush him!" There was a concerted murmur of agreement to this suggestion along with yells of "Only good Injun's a dead one!" and "Take him to the hangin' tree!"

"Hang him! Hang him!" the cry echoed round the room, making Annabeth clap her hands to her ears to shut out the horrid clamor.

Eben stepped in front of her protectively and held up his free hand for silence. The other still held the smoking six-gun. "The woman's my wife," he declared. "Morgan run off with her. He got what was coming to him. He drew first," Eben reminded them. "All of you saw it." He lowered his hand and suddenly it was filled with the second revolver. "There's six shots in this gun and five still left in the other. Any of you fellows wantta be heroes, make your play!"

A renewed clamor broke out. Eben backed slowly into the street through the door that Annabeth held open for him. "Horses at the hitching rail," he muttered. "The roan and the gray."

Scrambling up onto the one, she led the other to Eben. Before mounting, he squeezed off a shot and the flickering lantern which had lit the gambling house plunged the building into darkness. By the time the confused and angry mob had elbowed its way through the door, Eben and Annabeth were off and away!

They rode through the night, putting as much

distance as they could between themselves and
Hangtown. Thinking how close Eben had come to
swinging from the gallows tree, Annabeth gave a
convulsive shiver.

"You cold?" he said gruffly. The days had
been hot but the nights turned cold as soon as the
sun went down and he had long since shed his
buckskin jacket insisting that Annabeth drape it
round her bare arms and shoulders. He hadn't
said anything about her equally bare bosom but
Annabeth had pulled the jacket across her breasts
thankfully. The jacket was warm from his body
and smelled deliciously of his own particular body
scent—a scent that was dear to her and well-
remembered. She'd turned her head and buried
her nose in the collar, inhaling deep drafts of the
reassuringly familiar smell—a smell she
associated with all good things. Woodsmoke and
campfires and the clean fresh odor of the pines.
The warmth of his naked body pressed close to
hers and long nights filled with ecstatic lovemaking when the tepee flaps had been drawn
against intruders and they had found a blissful
consummation of desire in each other's arms and
the sweetness of its aftermath as they lay cuddled
close beneath the buffalo robes. It was the scent of
love, Eben's tender cherishing love, a scent she
had sometimes despaired of ever smelling again.

She herself reeked of the cheap perfume that
Jared Morgan had doused her in. She suspected
that he had obtained it, and probably the gown she
was wearing as well, from the whorehouse an
enterprising madam who had imported a wagon-
load of Chilean whores ran in Hangtown. She and
the madam and the madam's girls had been almost
the only women in town at the time so where else
could he have obtained such items of feminine

apparel? She hadn't dared to ask him where the perfume and the cosmetics and the gown had come from because she knew she could not have tolerated wearing them if her suspicions had been confirmed. And he would have forced her to do so.

"N-no. I'm not cold," she assured Eben.

He squinted at the sun which was beginning to paint the gray sky with streaks of pink and orange and gold. "Sun'll be high 'fore too much longer," he told her encouragingly. "We'll make camp, heat up some coffee and have a bite to eat."

"Do you think it'll be safe?" Annabeth fretted. "Those men back in Hangtown . . . won't they be on our trail?"

"They won't follow us this far," Eben said easily. "They won't want to go up against my guns. But if it'll ease your mind we can just follow the stream for a while. They won't be able to track us through the water."

He led Annabeth to a burbling stream which meandered merrily down from the mountains, and guided his horse into the water. Annabeth followed where he led.

They splashed through the icy water till they came to a place where a little hollow or dip in the ground formed a fair-sized pool before the overflow continued its mellifluous way down the valley. Annabeth exclaimed at its beauty. Tree branches overhung the water, casting dappled patterns, and wildflowers bloomed in their shade. The scent of pine was strong and birds sang in the willows, proclaiming their joy that a new day was dawning.

"We'll stop here," Eben decided, guiding his mount up the banks of the stream. Annabeth's horse clambered after it, eager, she presumed, to get out of the icy water.

She slithered out of the saddle before he could help her down. "What do you have to eat?" she said brightly. "I'm starving!"

He chuckled—that deep rumbling chuckle of his that she remembered so well. "You always did have a hearty appetite for such a little bit of a thing," he remarked. " 'Fraid there's nothing but jerky. It'll take the edge off your hunger, though, and I'll get us a fire going. Brew some coffee."

She took the proferred jerky and nibbled half-heartedly at it. She wasn't hungry at all; in fact she had never felt less like eating in her life. But she was so nervous she didn't know what to do with herself or how to act.

Oh, what *was* the matter with her? She ought to be overjoyed to be reunited with Eben again! She loved him, didn't she? Then why was there such a feeling of constraint between them?

Or was it only she who felt constraint? She peeked at him through her thick dark lashes. He was filling a battered tin coffeepot at the stream and whistling cheerfully. *He* certainly didn't seem to be suffering any discomfort she thought, watching him hunker down to fill the coffeepot at the stream and then toss in a handful of grounds from a buckskin pouch.

But in this assumption she was wrong. Eben felt quite as uneasy as Annabeth and he couldn't understand it any more than she did. Ever since he had come back to his right mind he had thought of nothing but getting back to her. And now, here they were, reunited, and he was damned if he knew what was wrong. He longed to take her in his arms and cover her with kisses, to reassure himself that she was still his Annabeth.

He couldn't even bring himself to talk to her . . . really talk. And, Lord, how he wanted to talk . . . to explain to her that he hadn't meant to stay away so long . . . that it had been unavoidable . . . that he loved her and he always would. But the words stuck in his throat.

They ate their jerky and drank their coffee in a profound silence. The silence stretched out and became so uncomfortable that they both made an effort to break it at the same time.

She said, "I think I'd like to—"

He said, at the same time, "Annabeth, I—"

They broke off in confusion, as awkwardly polite with each other as two strangers. "You go first," he suggested.

"No . . . it was a silly idea. I—" She fumbled to a stop. "What were you going to say?"

"Nothing special," he insisted. In truth, he had been only groping for words, trying to find a way to break the ice. "You go ahead," he said encouragingly.

"Oh, it's only that I'd like to have a bath."

"A bath!" He looked dubiously out over the small pond. The water ran clean enough but, "It'll be almighty cold," he said doubtfully.

"I don't care about that," she insisted. "But . . . do you suppose that some of those men from the saloon might . . . might find us? I . . . I wouldn't want anybody to see me," she faltered, a flush staining her cheeks.

He had a feeling that included him! "If you're set on having a bath," he said gruffly, "I'll stand guard. Over by the trail." He made a vague gesture indicating a path winding between a jumble of rocks and boulders. "Anybody coming from Hangtown would come from that direction," he assured her. "I'll keep watch over by them rocks." It would, he figured, give her all the privacy she craved.

She spoke a trifle breathlessly. "I'd appreciate that. I . . . I feel so soiled."

He looked at her sharply. It wasn't so much the dust of travel she wanted to wash away, he guessed, as it was the defilement she had suffered from Jared Morgan and God knew who else. Bathing in the pool fed by the icy waters of mountain streams would be, in some measure, a rite of purification, he supposed.

Remembering the price—one hundred ounces of gold—that the gambler had set for the privilege of his taking Annabeth upstairs, he said bluntly, "Did Morgan make a whore of you, Annabeth?"

Her flush deepened, staining the clear skin of her face and neck but she lifted her eyes from the ground and said bravely, "*His* whore, Eben."

He felt a violent rush of anger towards the man he had killed and at the same time, a feeling of intense relief. At least she hadn't been used and abused by every woman-hungry miner in Hangtown who could meet Morgan's price!

"It don't make no difference to me," he said gruffly, trying to reassure her.

Annabeth bit her lip. "It does to me."

"What's past is past, Annie," he said gently. "The man's dead now. Best you forget it."

She lifted velvety eyes to him. "Can *you* forget it, Eben?" she whispered. "Won't it always come between us?"

"Not if we don't let it. Whatever happened between you and him, Annie, is over and done with. Way I figger it, you done what you had to do. That's all there is to it."

Her chin quivered. "Doing what you have to do—you make it sound like some kind of virtue," she said bitterly.

"If it ain't a virtue, it's a necessity for

survival. Out here, leastways." He looked at her thoughtfully. "You don't need my forgiveness, Annabeth, but if you feel you do, I'm telling you right now you have it. What you gotta do next is forgive yourself. Put it out of your mind and forget it for both our sakes."

A tear trickled down her cheek. With infinite tenderness he reached out and brushed it away. His finger came away stained with rouge and he grinned. "You got more paint streaking your face than Gray Bull when he's painted for war. You better go have that bath. You'll feel better when you get cleaned up. We'll talk afterwards. We got a lotta catching up to do."

The water was biting cold. It numbed her body and her mind but she resolutely set about splashing the paint from her face and scrubbing ruthlessly at her body as if she could wash away the memory of the days and nights she had spent with the gambling man, trying to perform a kind of ritual cleansing.

She knew in her heart that Eben was right. What was done, was done. She couldn't let it poison the rest of their lives. To brood over it, to wallow in shame and guilt would be self-indulgent folly. If only she didn't feel so besmirched! she thought, scrubbing her breasts and belly vigorously. How could Eben ever look at her with desire again? Wouldn't he visualized her and Jared Morgan together, every time he looked at her? Every time he touched her wouldn't he wonder if the gambler had touched her in just that same way? Could he really forget that she had been Jared Morgan's whore?

Her lips were blue and her teeth were cháttering from cold when she emerged from the pond to confront another problem. What was she going to wear? She simply couldn't face the thought of putting on the low-cut whore's dress again. She just couldn't.

Remembering that Eben usually carried a spare set of buckskins in his saddlebags, she submerged herself in the icy water and called out to him.

He brought her the buckskins and a scrap of material to use as a towel and deliberately turned his back while she rubbed herself dry and shivered herself into the clothing. When he turned round again, he could not restrain a broad grin. She looked like a waif, a ragamuffin, in the outsize suit of clothes he had provided. Her hair waved round her face in damply curling tendrils reminding him forcibly of the old Anna-beth—Annabeth of the wagon train—as he had first known her. He realized with a jolt that he had been put off by her attire, by the whore's cheap scent that had clung to her, by her reddened lips and artificially blackened eyebrows and lashes. But now, with all the paint washed away she had the look of a well-scrubbed little girl and it touched his heart profoundly.

The sleeves of his shirt trailed past her finger-tips and since her hands were fully occupied clutching the waistband of his trousers around her slim waist he reached out and began rolling up the sleeves for her. Her teeth were still chattering and her hands were like ice and, one at a time, he began chafing them gently between his broad palms.

The touch of his warm flesh caressing hers sent jolts of electricity up her arms and she gasped aloud, trying to pull away but he held her fast. "Oh, God, Annie, I've missed you so!" he murmured into her hair.

She trembled at his touch, at the conviction in the deep voice telling her what she so longed to hear. "And I . . . I, you," she whispered. "Everyone said that you must be dead. You were gone so long I . . . I almost believed it myself."

"I never meant to be away all that time, Annie. You gotta believe me."

"I do . . . oh, I do," she whimpered, breathing feather-light kisses onto his face and neck.

"I'll tell you all about where I been and what I was doing later on," he promised, his lips scorching her skin with their sweet fire. He chuckled deep in his throat. "But right now I gotta show you that I'm very much alive."

She could feel his "aliveness" burning into her belly and a deep pit of fire ignited inside her, warming her throughout and making her tingle from top to toe.

All constraint had long since vanished between them. They clung together murmuring little love words. Annabeth tipped her face up to his, a gamine grin teasing at her lips. "Prove it!" she challenged him. "Prove that this isn't just a dream—that you're not just a figment of my imagination. Oh, Eben," she cried, throwing her arms about his neck, "I want you to prove it again and again!"

"I'll show you just how much of a figment I am," he growled playfully, sweeping her into his arms and carrying her to a fragrant bed of pine needles well out of sight of the trail.

Her too-loose trousers were quickly removed, she herself kicking them off with scissor-like movements of her legs while he untied the thongs that held the shirt together. Slipping it down over her bared shoulders he muttered huskily, "Lord, let me look at you, Annie, every part of you," as he feasted his long-denied eyes on her beauty.

"Every part of me belongs to you, Eben," she whispered. "I'm wholly yours, always and forever."

Doffing his own clothing, with Annabeth's eager assistance, his hands and lips worked their dearly remembered magic on her body until she was as avid as he, as eager for their merging into one flesh. The moment of his entry was so sweetly piercing that she cried out in an ecstasy of love and longing. Twining her fingers in his long black hair she met his terrible hunger with an urgency matching her own. She felt a yearning, a wanting past flesh and then a deepening of ecstasy as her world became filled with him.

He felt her body contract with ripples of pleasure and fought hard to maintain his own control for he knew it was just the beginning for her, that she was capable of much more, but it was a losing battle. He had been without her too long. "Oh, God, Annie," he groaned, his face contorting with effort, "I can't help myself. I can't hold back—"

"Then don't, my love," she crooned. "Give me yourself, all of yourself." The very force and fury of his love—so different from the too-skilled and almost mechanical caresses of Jared Morgan— was a glory to her.

He found his fulfillment in a short almost savage burst of passion and collapsed beside her. They lay breathlessly entwined in each other's arms, their bodies naked to the sun and still moist from lovemaking. She wriggled into a more comfortable position, moving her head into the hollow of his shoulder, and brushed her lips over his warm flesh murmuring endearments until she knew from his breathing that he had fallen asleep.

She dozed then and woke to find him engaged in a leisurely exploration of her body. Her lips curved into a tender smile and she arched a delicate brow at him. "What, again?" she murmured lazily, noting the hungry look in his eyes.

"Again and again and again. I can't get enough of you, Annie," he said huskily.

She raised her arms and, lacing her fingers behind his head, drew him down to her. "We do have a lot of catching up to do," she said teasingly, punctuating each word with a butterfly kiss on his face and neck, running the tip of her tongue over and between his lips. Their mouths merged in a hungry kiss.

But this time the urgency to mate was not so overpowering. They could take time to enjoy tantalizing each other's bodies, to arouse each other in a teasing fashion, to prolong the sweet delights of love play.

She flung her head back, offering her bare throat to his mouth and he trailed his lips down the slender column, nipping and nibbling, pausing to nuzzle her throbbing pulse before traveling ever lower to that which beckoned him so enticingly.

His hands had already found her breasts, his thumbs flicking the two stiff peaks of her twin spheres, circling, teasing, tantalizing, until she arched against him, whimpering for more.

His mouth replaced his hands at her breasts, moistly laving the swelling curves and taut pink nipples, the sweet suction setting her blood on fire while his hands roamed caressingly down her body, sliding down her back to cup her buttocks and pull her even closer to him so that she could feel his manhood pressed against her thighs.

Postponement became a sweet torture. Her thighs opened in invitation, urging him on with love and wanting. "Eben . . . please—!" she whimpered, writhing against him.

But he drew his body away from her and bent his head lower still. She felt his lips and tongue burn across her belly, down the insides of her thighs and cried out in sudden shock at a more intimate entry than she had expected.

"Eben . . . nooo—" she whimpered.

He raised his head. "Yes, Annie," he insisted. "I want to pleasure you in every way. I love you," he said huskily. "Every part of you."

She shook her head wildly, twisting her fingers in his hair and trying to tug him away but her hands only had the effect of pressing him closer. As he delicately probed the warm wet chasm between her thighs waves of bliss washed over her and she cried out again, not in protest but in joy of the gift he was giving her. It told her, more than mere words could ever do, of the depth and intensity of his love. She felt both proud and humbled by this new knowledge, so full of emotion she thought her heart would burst as she sobbed his name aloud.

He rose and knelt beside her, cradling her in his arms. "Annie, Annie, I didn't mean to make you cry," he crooned.

"It's . . . it's tears of joy," she sobbed into his neck. "Oh, Eben, I love you. And I love what you do to me."

"I love you. And I love what we do together," he corrected her tenderly, smoothing her hair. Grasping her hips, he pulled her down on top of him. She gasped as wild sensations of pleasure rippled through her yet again and she rode her dark lover like a great black stallion until together they were transported into a shimmering world of ecstasy.

26

"I still don't understand how you knew where to find me," Annabeth marvelled.

They were on the trail again, heading back to Rancho del Corazon. Eben felt confident enough of her love to know that he need no longer fear her affection for Don Felipe. He must have been crazy with jealousy ever to have doubted her; he knew that now. Over and over again during these past few days she had proved to him how very much she loved and needed him.

They had poured out their hearts to each other. She bitterly repented that time after the baby's death when she had sent him away. In an agony of remorse she had begun castigating herself but he had shushed her by putting a finger to her lips. "I don't want to hear no more of that, Annie. It's over and done with long ago. I reckon I wouldn't have gone off in such a huff," he said reflectively, "if I hadn't been eaten up with jealousy of Don Felipe. So envious of all the things he could give you that I couldn't."

Annabeth blushed. She hadn't been entirely guiltless in this regard, she knew. Even though she had not been physically unfaithful to Eben she knew quite well that she had let Don Felipe's

425

wealth and charm and good-breeding go to her head. She had been bedazzled by him. She admitted it now, shamefacedly, for she wanted no more misunderstandings between herself and Eben.

"But it was mostly that I . . . I felt so *secure* at Corazon d'Oro," she said thoughtfully. "It seemed like such a safe harbor, a port after a storm. I thought nothing bad could happen to me there. I . . . I wanted the settled home. I didn't know then that places and possessions don't really matter—it's *people* that matter. I didn't know that the only security there is in this world is having someone to love, someone to share your joys and sorrows with."

He reached out and clasped her hand. "Reckon I can give you that, Annie, and a little more besides. My partner and me made a big strike in the goldfields and—"

"Partner?" Annabeth wrinkled her brow in bewilderment.

He chuckled. "I forgot you don't know about Shorty Gillespie and the motherlode we found." So he backtracked, telling her all about it from the time he had left her at Corazon d'Oro to the time he returned to find her already gone. Told her how he'd been on his way back to her when he'd been waylaid by bandits and lost his memory, about how he and Shorty had panned gold all winter and made a big strike in the mountains, recovering his memory at the same time. "We're rich, Annabeth," he concluded jubilantly. "There'll be plenty to go around even after I divvy up with Shorty. Plenty for you and me. We can do whatever you want. Go down to 'Frisco and live like kings if that's what you'd like."

Annabeth felt dazed. She could hardly take it

in. She'd heard of men making big strikes in the goldfields—who had not?—but she also knew that for every man who struck it rich there were many more who barely found enough from day to day to cover their expenses. Men who were only working for their keep. It had never occurred to her that Eben might come back to her a wealthy man.

"What do *you* want to do, Eben?" she said faintly, trying to assimilate this new information.

He hesitated. What he really wanted might be more than a little unpalatable to her. "I'd like to drive a herd of beeves back to Cheyenne territory," he said finally. "Start up a ranch close by. With all the Forty-Niners pouring through, polluting the country and driving the buffalo away from their hunting grounds, the Cheyenne may be short of food this winter. I'd take a herd big enough to share the meat with them and yet keep some available as breeding stock. And I'd like to see my boy again," he added wistfully. "Make shore he don't want for nothin'."

"Then that's what we'll do," Annabeth decided.

He was startled. "You mean it, Annie? I kinda thought you might want to settle down here in California. Make a home here."

"Wherever you are, Eben, that's my home," she assured him. At first she had been alarmed. He had been so reluctant to reveal his plans to her that she feared they might be quite outlandish! But now that he had made his feelings known to her, she realized that she herself had a yearning to go back to their beginnings—to make a fresh start. She had no more desire to linger in California than he had, she reflected, and it would be good to see Silent Moon and all her old friends among the Cheyenne again.

Thinking of them reminded her of another friend—Maria. Eben had avoided mentioning her and she herself dreaded to ask the question that had been burning on the tip of her tongue. Somehow she knew the answer was not going to be one she wanted to hear. And yet it must be said.

"Eben," she said abruptly, "Do you know what happened . . . happened to Maria?"

He was silent for a long moment. Finally he sighed and said, "Best we make camp for the night, Annie. I'll tell you the rest of it after we've eaten."

They set up camp near a small stream and shared the last of their coffee and jerky. Then he picked up his tale where he had left off. She wept bitter tears over her friend's death, though he broke it to her as gently as he knew how. The news was not altogether unexpected but no less heart-rending.

He held her until the storm of tears subsided and he could kiss all trace of them away, making gentle undemanding love to her, giving her the consolation of his love to assuage her sore and aching heart.

Afterwards, lying quiet in the circle of his arms, his head pillowed on her breasts, she murmured, "We *are* going back to Corazon d'Oro before we set out for home, aren't we, Eben? I . . . I want to visit Maria's grave and that of our baby and—" she hesitated, "say goodbye to Felipe."

"We have to go back there anyway to meet up with Shorty," he reminded her. Her voice had rung clear in the night air and he shushed her suddenly, stiffening, as a faint noise alerted him to possible danger.

"What is it?" she whispered.

"Horses—heading this way." Eben sprang up and doused the fire, buckling on his pants and gun belt while Annabeth hastily scrambled into her clothes, wanting to be prepared for any eventuality.

"Amigos!" a familiar voice rang out. Then the young Californio dismounted from his horse and stepped into the faint light of the dying fire. "You will not have to go far to say farewell to Felipe, querida," he remarked.

"Felipe!" Annabeth flew to him.

With a wry glance at Eben and a half-mocking, "You permit, yanqui?" he embraced her. Then in one of the courtly gestures she remembered so well, he bent his head and put his lips where the pulse beat in her wrist.

Annabeth disengaged herself from him rather hastily, belatedly remembering Eben's former jealousy of the handsome young Californio. Unobtrusively she stepped back beside Eben and took his arm.

For a moment, tension crackled in the air—but only for a moment. Felipe's dark eyes took in the little scene—the two lovers standing with linked arms, the bed of pine boughs from which they had been roused, the indentation their bodies had imprinted on the nest of greenery telling its own tale.

"So—you are together again and all is well with you?" he smiled rather sadly, accepting defeat gracefully.

Annabeth's heart ached for him. Even in the dim light she had seen the new lines of maturity that grief had carved into his face, the tight set of his once-laughing lips. She hated to add one more drop to the cup of sorrow he had quaffed but she knew she must.

"All is well with us, Felipe," she said gently.

"So." He nodded bleakly. Turning away he caught up the reins of his horse and put his foot in the stirrup, ready to swing into the saddle when Eben spoke. "I reckon we could drain another cup outta that coffeepot, don't you, Annabeth? For a friend?" he added deliberately.

She moved to the fire and stirred it up until the coals glowed red-hot and moistened her fingertip to test the pot's warmth. "I'm sure we could, Eben," she said with a smile.

They talked much of the night away like three old and dear friends, she thought with a heartfelt sense of relief, though she became a little anxious when the men left the rest of the coffee to her and broke open a bottle of aguardiente that Felipe carried in his saddlebags. She fervently hoped the liquor wouldn't make them quarrelsome but it seemed not to have that effect and when she, exhausted by all the emotional upheaval, finally went to her pine bough bed, the men were still passing the bottle and getting on like a house afire.

"So you're goin' down to Mexico," Eben remarked. He and Annabeth had already outlined their plans for the future but Felipe, when pressed, had been deliberately vague about his own, merely remarking that he was putting Rancho del Corazon on the market before the American land commissioners could steal the rest of it away from him.

"I am resettling my people there, in Mexico, yes," he agreed. He glanced cautiously at the bed of pine boughs where Annabeth had retired for the night and said, in a low tone, too low for her to catch the import of his words, even if she were still awake. "For myself, I have made other arrangements. My sister's blood cries out for vengeance. When the matter of the rancho is settled I ride to join Joaquin Murietta."

He glanced again to where Annabeth lay peacefully slumbering. "It is better that Ana does not hear of this," he cautioned Eben. "It is for your ears alone."

Eben nodded somberly. He knew that Annabeth would be deeply disturbed if she heard that Don Felipe was contemplating joining a gang of bandidos whose specialty was preying on gringos. Joaquin Murietta, the bandit leader, was an embittered youth whose young wife had been raped and then murdered while he was away from home. Murietta had sworn vengeance on all Americans and Eben could see how this would appeal to Don Felipe. But it made his own heart sad to think of the young man throwing himself away on a life of vengeance—a life that would probably be cut short by a bullet in the back or the hangman's noose. He didn't suppose there was anything he could say that would change the kid's mind, though. So he merely said laconically, "A man's gotta do what he's gotta do. You're right about one thing, though. It's best that it don't come to Annabeth's ears."

He frowned thoughtfully. "Tell you what," he suggested. "How'd it be if I bought Rancho del Corazon from you? Left it in charge of one of your men." In the back of his mind was the thought that this would please Annabeth. There might come a time when the kid was ready to settle down again, forget the past, marry, and raise a family. In that case, his ancestral home would be preserved, for Eben would sell it back to him. Meanwhile, if the property were duly registered to an American, the greedy land commissioners would leave well enough alone.

Felipe was startled at the generous offer Eben made. "But I thought you and Ana had made other plans," he protested.

Eben shrugged. "Never can tell. We might be back this way again. I'm a wandering kind of a man. Might take a fancy to set myself up as an hidalgo. As for the stock—me and Shorty can round up what we need for the drive across country. Any that's left will seed a new herd."

Felipe thought it over. He could hardly refuse the generous offer Eben had put to him. He liked the idea of Ana's becoming mistress of Corazon d'Oro one day; he would far rather see it go to her and her husband than pass into the hands of strangers or be carved up for development by the American land commissioners.

"As you Americanos say, it is a deal, yanqui," he said with a smile. "Here is my hand on it—and the word of a del Corazon!"

The three of them rode together back to Corazon d'Oro. The hacienda itself was a smoke-blackened ruin but the vaqueros had been busy erecting temporary dwellings for their womenfolk and the courtyard was once again a beehive of activity. Donkeys brayed, chickens clucked, running hither and yon, and children yelled a welcome when el patron and his friends rode through the gates. Excited women clustered around Annabeth, exclaiming at her bedraggled appearance and embracing her in turn, for "Dona Ana" was a great favorite among them. A wrinkled crone quavered, "It is the blessing of God that you have been spared to come back to us, senora!" and the others chorused a general agreement.

The women led Annabeth away to rest and change out of the travel-stained and ill-fitting buckskins while Don Felipe made arrangements for her and Eben to be housed in one of the new dwellings for the duration of their stay.

"You look like a real Spanish senorita," Eben said approvingly when she appeared in its doorway a short time later, dressed in a scoop-necked peasant-style blouse and skirt billowing with the many layers of petticoats beneath it. Each of the younger women had insisted on lending her a petticoat and, in order to offend no one, she was wearing them all!

Eben grinned at her tenderly. "I expect to see you break into a fandango any minute," he teased as she pirouetted before him to show off her borrowed finery.

She spun to a halt, her face falling and a shadow darkening her eyes. "Maria and I were practicing the fandango the day the raiders came," she said slowly.

Oh hell, he hadn't meant to bring back bad memories! He cursed himself for his unfortunate choice of words but how could he have known? He supposed that there were many things here that would bring back memories of that terrible day—not the least of them the row of newly dug graves in the family plot. He cast around for something to take her mind off that fearful episode which was better forgotten.

"How'd you like to take a little trip to 'Frisco while them beeves are being rounded up?" he suggested diffidently. "I've got business there. Shorty and some of the men went up to Sutter's Fort to bring back our gold and I want to deposit it in a San Francisco bank." What he didn't tell her was that most of it would be transferred to Don Felipe's account for the purchase of del Corazon land and cattle.

"San Francisco!" Annabeth's eyes took on a new sparkle. It had been years since she had been in a city and by all accounts, San Francisco was booming.

But her brow creased in a purely feminine concern. "I have nothing to wear!" she wailed.

Eben chuckled. "What you got on will do just fine. When we get there we'll get you some new ready-made duds. Wouldn't you like some pretty new clothes of your own?"

"Of course I would! But," she frowned, "isn't it rather an extravagance? I won't have much use for pretty clothes where we're going. To Cheyenne territory, I mean."

"Usefulness be damned!" he roared. "I reckon a man of my means can afford a few extravagances," he reminded her more quietly. "Not the least of which is dressing his wife up in pretty clothes just for the pleasure she takes in wearing them and," his dark eyes gleamed meaningfully, "For the pleasure *he* gets in taking them off!"

His big hand reached out tentatively and tugged at the scoop-necked blouse so that it slid down over one creamy shoulder provocatively. His hand trailed over her shoulder and neck, feeling the quickened pulse that beat in her throat. Bending his head he caressed her bare shoulder with his lips. "Ain't never had no senorita," he told her with a teasing grin, his dark eyes dancing with merriment. "I don't suppose you'd be willin' to oblige me, would you, ma'am?"

She smiled up at him, her sorrow forgotten, and wound her arms around his neck. "Si, senor," she whispered huskily, as he scooped her up and carried her to the pile of hides that served as a bed. "Si, senor," she sighed, as he lay her down upon it,

"Si . . . senor."

San Francisco lived up to all of Annabeth's expectations. And then some! It was more wild and woolly than any gold camp, noisier and more crowded by far than Hangtown. In the early days of the gold strike, as she knew, the populace of San Francisco had rushed off to the goldfields. But by the fall of '48, certain leading citizens of the community had recuperated from gold fever and drifted back and by the time the winter rains set in, flooding the gold camps, ordinary miners had flowed back to the city in droves. The smarter ones quickly realized that the need for new buildings in the burgeoning metropolis was such that a laborer could command his own price, far more than a man could pan, risking rheumatism in an icy stream or breaking his back toiling at a "rocker" or a "long Tom." So they stayed on, as did young men of less physical stamina who found mining too gruelling an occupation, and lingered in the city to take jobs in the new stores and shops which were springing up everywhere to outfit the "Forty-niners" with the tools of their trade—picks, pans, shovels, camping outfits, rugged clothing and "Rockers" which sold for eighty dollars apiece. The price of food had inflated about 400 percent and grocers were among those who had returned early from the fields knowing the necessities of miners, and determined to profit from them. By mid 1849, San Francisco was a thriving, bustling metropolis with a permanent population of several thousand and a floating population of several thousand more who drifted into the city either by ship or overland, outfitted themselves and headed for the goldfields.

Annabeth was excited by the crowds, appalled by the noise and confusion, and just a little frightened. She would have been even more frightened, she decided, if Eben hadn't been there, riding stirrup to stirrup with her, as imperturbable as ever. She glanced at him rather nervously and got back a reassuring grin. Goodness, she was just a country girl and she felt green and gawky and awkward but Eben, former country boy turned mountain man, looked as self-assured as a king in his well-worn buckskins. Where *did* he get his self-confidence? she wondered a little enviously. He wore it like a second skin.

They rode slowly through the dusty pot-holed streets which must surely turn to liquid mud in the rainy season, she thought, while their plodding packhorses followed on behind. They were heading for the Parker House, the city's new and most imposing hotel which had been nearly a year in the building for lack of workmen. Eben would leave her there to rest while he deposited their funds in the bank. After that they would meet for a meal and then do some shopping. His buckskins were so worn they were almost indecent and Annabeth knew she was getting curious glances, simply because she was so obviously an American woman dressed like a Mexican.

There were very few American women visible among the crowds, she noticed. The ratio was better in the city than in the gold camps but even so, women were greatly outnumbered by men and, of these, the decent women were obviously outnumbered by prostitutes. Just as private dwellings were outnumbered by saloons and gambling houses. The city was sprawling over the hills in shacks and tents but warehouses and stores were under construction while the better gaming houses were mostly clustered around the Plaza. The largest and most dazzling of them boasted plate-glass windows and from them music and the rowdy laughter of drunken men drifted out into the street.

Annabeth shuddered. But for Eben she might be one of those garishly dressed women with their brightly painted faces, reddened cheeks and lips, and eyes exotically darkened and outlined with kohl. Two such women were going into the "El Dorado" as they rode past and she heard them exchanging ribald jokes with the men inside and a shriek of bawdy laughter. She knew well enough what the place must look like inside for Jared Morgan had often shared his plans for just such an establishment with her and she could visualize the mirrors and the chandeliers, the handsome bar, and dozens of little tables piled high with cards and bags of gold dust or piles of "slugs" worth ten or twenty dollars each. Men with red flannel shirts and hobnailed boots would be clustered around waiting for their turn at the gaming tables or watching the play and pawing the girls, just as she had been pawed and pinched by the more disreputable miners in Hangtown. She thanked God fervently that Eben had saved her from such a fate.

They took a room at the Parker House and Annabeth waited there for Eben to transact his business, for she was unwilling to venture out into the city streets unescorted. In her Mexican peasant garb she was afraid she might be accosted as a Chileno.

They found a store on the corner of Montgomery and Clay streets which sold ready-to-wear apparel. For Eben there was small choice—the inevitable flannel shirt and work pants for everyday wear and a plain dark suit for "good" which Annabeth insisted on. He grumbled a bit at having to shed the comfort of his buckskins but Annabeth, who had never seen him in anything else, was amazed at the handsome figure he cut in the dark suit and creamy linen shirt. It emphasized the darkness of his skin and the width of his broad shoulders and muscular frame. "I feel like a monkey," he grumbled, struggling with a broad heavily starched stock. "Like a monkey that's about to be hanged!" he added, inserting his fingers between the necktie and his throat, throwing back his head and tugging at the tie impatiently.

Annabeth giggled. "Well, you *look* like a gentleman," she insisted, standing on tiptoe to rearrange the stock for him. "A very handsome gentleman, I might add!"

"And *you* look like a very lovely lady," he countered. And she did. There had been a wide selection of ladies' garments and while Eben had wanted to buy out the store for her, she had chosen practical and durable calico gowns. The one exception was the garment she now wore—a jade green taffeta with a long row of tiny jet buttons down the back and a tight-fitting bodice that showed off her tiny waist to perfection. The ruffled petticoats under full skirts swished as she walked and she looked and felt every inch the lady of fashion.

They lunched at one of the new restaurants on the Bay. The Bay was a forest of masts of sailing ships which had been deserted by their crews who had jumped ship leaving their vessels to rot away and sink slowly into the mud. The more enterprising merchants had recently begun buying these abandoned vessels up cheap and converting them into floating restaurants, rooming houses, warehouses, and, of course, the inevitable saloon. The novelty of it all charmed Annabeth.

After lunch they wandered around the city which had already begun to acquire a faintly international flavor. A babel of tongues could be heard: English, of course, and Spanish, that went without saying, German and French—the French population were referred to as "Keskedees" from their habit of chattering "Qu'est que dit?"—and even Chinese.

A few of the more ambitious shops were built of brick and one even boasted a plate-glass window, like so many of the gambling palaces. Eben paused to look at the merchandise thus displayed but Annabeth's attention was riveted elsewhere.

"Look, Eben!" she hissed, tugging at his arm.

"Huh? I *am* looking." His finger tapped the glass. "How'd you like one of those—?"

"No—over there," she interrupted him. "Don't you see what I see? A church! A Protestant church!"

Eben heaved a sigh. She'd be wanting to attend divine service, he supposed. Well, tomorrow *was* Sunday and he figured he could sit through just one interminable sermon to please her. Come to think about it, he *did* have a lot to be thankful for.

But it turned out that wasn't what she wanted after all. Staring in fascination at the plain little building with a weathered board sign proclaiming "First Presbyterian Church of San Francisco," and in smaller letters, "Reverend T.D. Hunt, pastor," she exclaimed, "Oh, Eben, do you suppose Reverend Hunt would marry us?"

"Marry!" He was thunderstruck. "But we're married already," he protested.

"Ye-e-es. In a Catholic ceremony. But we're not Catholic," she reminded him.

"Don't see as that makes any difference," he grunted.

"It might. It might not be legal for a Catholic priest to marry two Protestants," she suggested, remembering the remarks Felipe made long ago about the legality of her marriage. "Those old Spanish and Mexican land grants aren't considered valid in Americans courts. Maybe the ceremony we went through at the mission isn't legal either!" She took a deep breath. "Oh, Eben, please!"

"If a marriage performed by a mission padre ain't legal there'll be an awful lot of bastards hereabouts, Annabeth," he retorted. He was, justifiably, he thought, annoyed. They'd been married in the Cheyenne way, and in the Catholic way and now she wanted to get married again. It was enough to try a man's patience! "I s'pose we could be married in the Chinese way too, while we're here," he said sarcastically, "just to make sure the knot is tied. And on the way home we could stop off in Salt Lake city and be married in a tabernacle by a Mormon elder. Damned if I don't feel as much married as a Mormon already," he complained, "and I ain't got but one wife!"

Annabeth turned away, turning her back on him, fighting tears brought on by his sarcasm. She bit her quivering lip. She wasn't going to cry right here on the street. She wasn't! "Well, if that's the way you feel about it—" she said in a stifled voice.

If that was the way he felt about it, maybe he was sorry he had ever gotten married the *first* time! she thought stormily. It didn't seem like so much to ask. It was such a *little* thing after all, but it meant so much to her!

He eyed her straight back, the stubborn tilt to her chin, for he could see her face in profile, and the funny way her red hair ruffled up when she was angry like the ruffled fur of a little spitting kitten and his heart melted. He capitulated.

It was worth it to see the way her eyes lit up when he went to her and put his hands on her shoulders and tilted her face up to his and said, "All right, Annie. You win . . . but," he warned her, his lips twisting into a grin, "this is positively the last time. I ain't gonna make a habit of it!"

"Oh, Eben!" she hugged him impulsively to the amusement of some passersby and danced off toward the church but he grabbed at her hand.

"Whoa. Hold on. Not so fast. There's a condition. We gotta go in here first or it's no deal!"

"In here?" she looked at him in a puzzled way but he linked his arm with hers and drew her into the store with the plate-glass window.

The clerk was a weedy youth who hadn't the stamina to make it in the goldfields. "Rings? Like those in our display case? A wedding ring and a betrothal ring? Yes, *sir*," and he bustled away anticipating a largish commission.

"But we were never betrothed!" Annabeth stood on tiptoe and whispered a protest into Eben's ear.

"Relax, sugar." His eyes twinkled merrily. "Since we're only getting married this afternoon, you could say we've had a rather long engagement!"

She sniffed. "Seems to me you've been taking more liberties than any engaged man would be allowed," she said tartly.

Eben grinned wickedly. "And I intend to go right on taking them!" he murmured in an undertone, just as the clerk came back with "the finest assortment of rings that had ever put to sea and doubled Cape Horn!" as he assured them.

The engagement ring was beautiful and impractical for a hard-working ranch wife—deliciously impractical, Annabeth thought—but when Eben slipped its companion band onto her finger in the little church her cup of happiness overflowed. She felt that she was truely a respectable married lady at long last. Beyond any doubt. She wished wistfully that Aunt Anna and Aunt Beth and Uncle Henry could be here to witness the event. She was sure that they would approve!

The Reverend Mr. Hunt, who was also the town chaplain and, he told them loquaciously, had had the honor of officiating at the first Protestant services to be held in San Francisco, expressed the hope that this fine upstanding young couple were planning to become permanent residents of the city. He contained his disappointment when told otherwise—that they were just passing through—but hinted that he would be gratified to see them at Sunday services the next day if they were still in town.

Annabeth glowed. She could think of nothing she would like better than to walk into Sunday services on Eben's arm! Eben felt he hadn't been so neatly trapped since he'd stumbled into a Blackfoot ambush some years ago. He'd gotten away then by the skin of his teeth but he had a feeling that Annabeth and the Reverend Mr. Hunt between them were a more lethal combination than any number of painted savages! He'd be damned glad to get back to Indian territory where a man like him belonged!

As he had long suspected, civilization just wasn't what it was cracked up to be, he thought some time later, struggling with the tiny jet buttons of Annabeth's frock. They were so small that his fingers seemed all thumbs and there seemed to be a million of the tiny slippery buttons. He thought he would never get them all undone but he did while she held her hair up out of the way of his fumbling fingers. Heaving a sigh of relief he peeled the tight-fitting garment away and bestowed several light lingering kisses on her bare neck and smooth creamy shoulders.

But there were still obstacles to be overcome, he realized with a groan. On this, their wedding night—their *third* wedding night if you wanted to keep count—she was formidable in a mass of stiff, rustling, starched petticoats, her waist encased in something that resembled armor plating. Anyway, it kind of reminded him of the suit of armor that a travelling Englishman had once bestowed on his old friend, Jim Bridger!

Eben's previous experiences with women —other than Annabeth—had been conducted almost solely with Indian women and he had never before encountered tight-laced stays. He prodded the thing with an experimental forefinger. By God, it felt like . . . it was lined with bones! "What the hell is this thing?" he grumbled.

Annabeth dimpled. "A corset. It's lined with whalebones to stiffen it," she explained. "I couldn't achieve an eighteen inch waist without it." Once upon a time she had been able to lace to seventeen inches but that had been before the baby.

Eben eyed the thing with misgiving—it looked

like an instrument of torture to him!

"It is," she admitted. "I can't take a deep breath."

Eben shook his head ruefully. "I ain't never refused a challenge yet," he said manfully, tugging on the corset strings. She had to show him how to extricate her from it though and heaved a sigh of relief when she was released from the tight lacing.

He buried his face in her soft yielding flesh, flesh that still bore the red marks of its recent confinement. "Beats me why a woman would want to do that to herself, punish herself in that way," he muttered angrily, tracing one such striation round her waist.

Annabeth had never thought about it one way or another. It was the accepted thing to do; it was what one did—"To please a man, I suppose," she murmured hazily, feeling herself quite unable to think clearly with Eben's black head burrowed between her breasts.

"Well, it don't please me!" he said angrily, rousing himself. "I've a good mind to throw it in the fire where it belongs!" He grabbed the offending garment with the express purpose of doing just that but Annabeth caught his hand in time.

"Mercy no!" she gasped. "It will make an awful stink—all those whalebones, you know. The smell would drive us right out of here! I promise I won't wear it again." She collapsed on the bed in a fit of giggles at the look of disgust on Eben's face as he held the garment at arm's length between thumb and forefinger and then pitched it into a dark corner with a muttered curse.

Weak with laughter she held out her arms to him. "Come to bed my savage lover and make wild uncivilized love to me," she murmured huskily.

He needed no second invitation. He was not about to ignore this passionate challenge to his manhood. Tearing the despised stock from around his neck with a vicious yank, he wasted no time stripping off the rest of his clothing. He saw her wide eyes focus on his magnificent maleness as he felt the swelling begin between his legs and he growled throatily, "If it's wild lovin' you want, woman, I reckon I can oblige. Gonna show you how us 'savages' handle their women." Tumbling onto the bed with her, he began to tickle her unmercifully. "First we render them helpless—" Annabeth squirmed and squealed and laughed as they rolled and tumbled together across the tangled sheets, trying to dodge his tormenting hands. "And then," he panted, "we eat 'em up alive!"

Pinning her against the bolster, he ran his mouth and tongue over her body, grazing hungrily on her lips, her throat, her breasts. Nipping and nibbling, his mouth sank possessively lower searching out the hollow of her hips, the rounded swell of her thigh, down her calf to her ankles, pressing kisses into the arch of her foot and teasing her toes with his teeth. His ravishing mouth seemed to be everywhere at once, arousing every inch of her flesh. Not even that most secret part of herself escaped his eager attentions and she felt an exquisite sense of anticipation building inside her—an anticipation that he eased temporarily and then set about rebuilding.

Their two hearts were beating in unison in an unbearable crescendo of excitement until he felt he must explode if he did not take her. Poising himself over her, he parted her willing thighs and drove himself deep inside her, wanting to fill her with pleasure until she screamed out her love for him.

He rejoiced that she was no timorous virgin but a warm and willing woman who reached out to engulf him, her moist inner self clinging to him, squeezing him, arousing him to unbearable heights of ecstasy as his big body stiffened and spurted his release.

Her own release came with his, wave upon wave of ecstasy flooding her in the most intense spasms of delight intermingled with an almost triumphant joy that he was easing himself so completely in her, that they were so supremely a part of each other and would never be separated again.

Annabeth left San Francisco with no particular regret. The trip had been fun—an experience she would not have wanted to miss—but she was not, she decided, cut out for city life. She was nearly as eager as Eben to recross the mountains, to get back to Indian territory. She must have developed a taste for the wild free life of the prairie. And yet . . .parting with Felipe and Rancho del Corazon d'Oro was heart-wrenching. So much had happened to her here. Here her child had been born and died. Here she had waited all those long months for Eben to come back to her, in despair and almost without hope that she would ever see him again. Here her dear friend, Maria, lay buried, as well as her own infant daughter. She brought flowers to scatter over the graves, reflecting that if it was meant to be, at least she could console herself with the thought that they would be here together for all eternity. The man and wife that Felipe was leaving in charge of the rancho had faithfully promised to care for the little cemetery, the whitewashed crosses and the newly dug graves.

It was hardest of all to say goodbye to Felipe

who loved her and whom she had so nearly fallen in love with. For a time he had been a very important part of her life and she knew she would always cherish the memory of him in her heart though it was unlikely that their paths would ever cross again.

He had insisted on presenting her and Eben with a very tangible reminder of his affection. For Eben, a magnificent golden stallion and for her, a gentle chestnut mare. He was planning to drive the rest of his manada to market in Mexico, the mare and stallion he intended to be the beginnings of their own manada, "so that a part of Rancho del Corazon d'Oro will always be with you."

On the last morning before their departure Annabeth leaned from her saddle to kiss him goodbye, tears glimmering on her thick dark lashes and threatening to brim over. "Vaya con Dios, Felipe," she whispered. "If only there could be two of me, one of them would go with you."

He smiled sadly. "Dear Ana. I know well that you belong with the man who holds your heart in his keeping." In one of his typical graceful gestures, he bent low over her hand and brought it to his lips, holding it there as if loath to relinquish it. "Be assured, I shall never forget you."

"Nor I you, Felipe," she whispered, brushing her fingers caressingly over his lips.

Felipe moved to where Eben was waiting, a little apart, for he knew they would want to say goodbye in privacy and he could afford to be generous.

"Goodbye, amigo." He offered Eben his hand. "Take care of her."

Eben reached down from his seat on the palomino stallion and they clasped hands in fare-well. "You know I will. His handshake was firm and hearty. "Take care of yourself, kid. And remember, if you're ever ready to buy back Corazon d'Oro—"

Felipe shook his head. "I think that day will never come. As soon as I have seen my people safely to Mexico I ride to join Joaquin." A wry smile twisted his lips. "If ever you hear of El Chico—as you say, 'The Kid'—do not believe all the evil that is rumored of him, eh, yanqui?"

"All gringos ain't like the bastards that killed your sister, Felipe," Eben reminded him.

"I will keep that in mind, my friend," Felipe returned gravely.

Eben nodded and spurred his horse, sending it off after Annabeth who had ridden off a little way fighting back tears. The cattle were milling and bawling in the holding corrals and he waved his arm as a signal to Shorty and the vaqueros who had elected to join the drive. "All right boys," he yelled, and waved again, "Move 'em out!"

Annabeth craned her head around for one last look back but already the hooves of the patient plodding cattle were stirring up thick clouds of dust, almost obscuring the figure of Felipe who was standing at the gate waving, though whether as a goodbye to her or as a signal to the vaqueros she couldn't tell.

Eben trotted up and drew rein beside her. "We gotta get going—keep ahead of the herd or we're gonna eat dust all the way to our first campsite." He reached out with a gentle finger and brushed smears of tears and dust away from her cheeks. "Dirty face!" he teased her tenderly.

Her lips curved and she gave him a watery smile. "That's my girl," he said encouragingly. "Don't look back, Annabeth. Never look back. Look forward with me—into our future."